A KINGDOM THREATENED

THE VAZULA CHRONICLES BOOK THREE

DEBORAH GRACE WHITE

LUMINANT PUBLICATIONS

A KINGDOM THREATENED

By Deborah Grace White

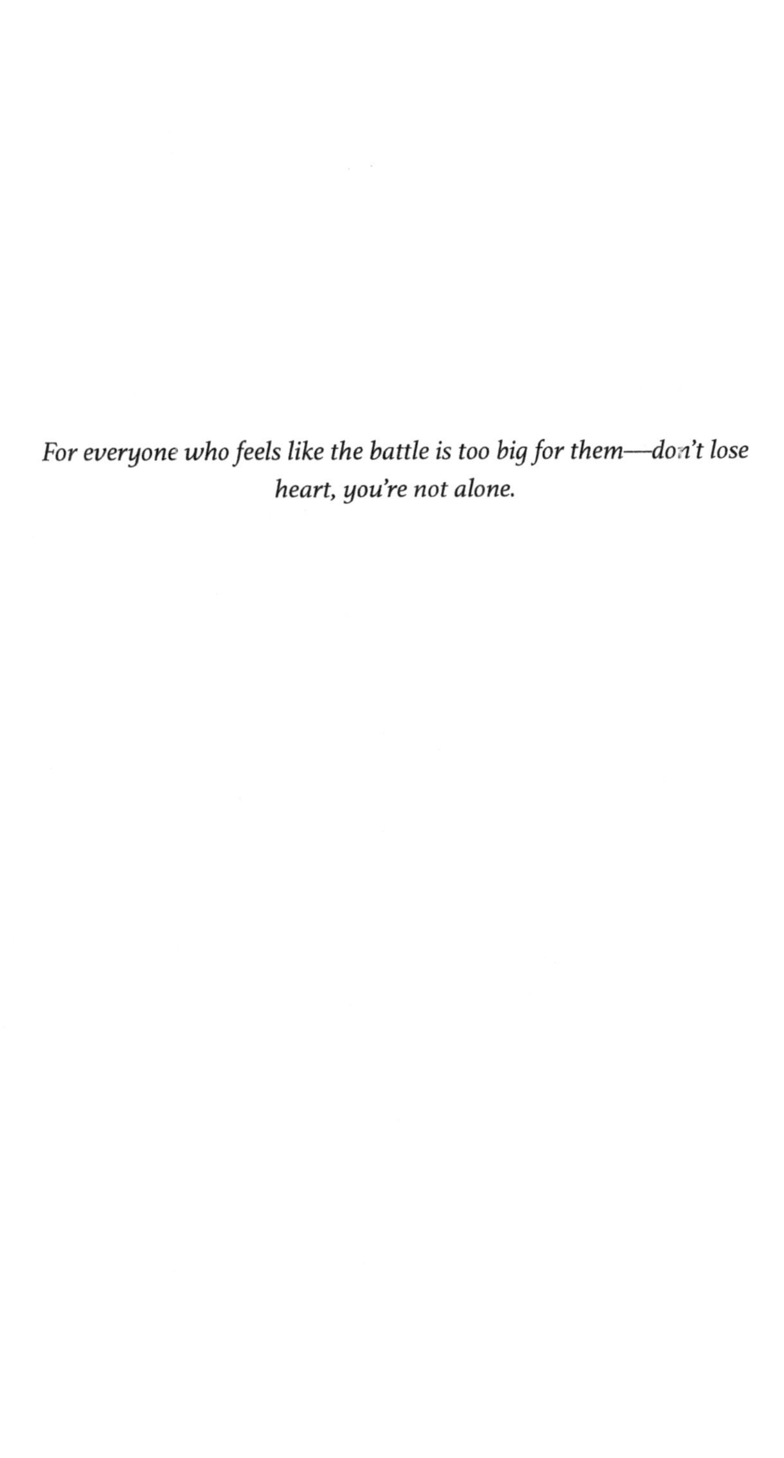

For everyone who feels like the battle is too big for them—don't lose heart, you're not alone.

KYONA
GREAT RIVER
LOCH ARINE
VALORIA
BASAL HEADLANDS
WYVERN ISLANDS
VAZULA
BRYFORD
BERLEY MANOR
TRIPLE KINGDOMS
KELP FARMS
TILSSTED
SKULSSTED
CENTER of CULTURE
HEMSSTED
OYSTER FARMS
E
S

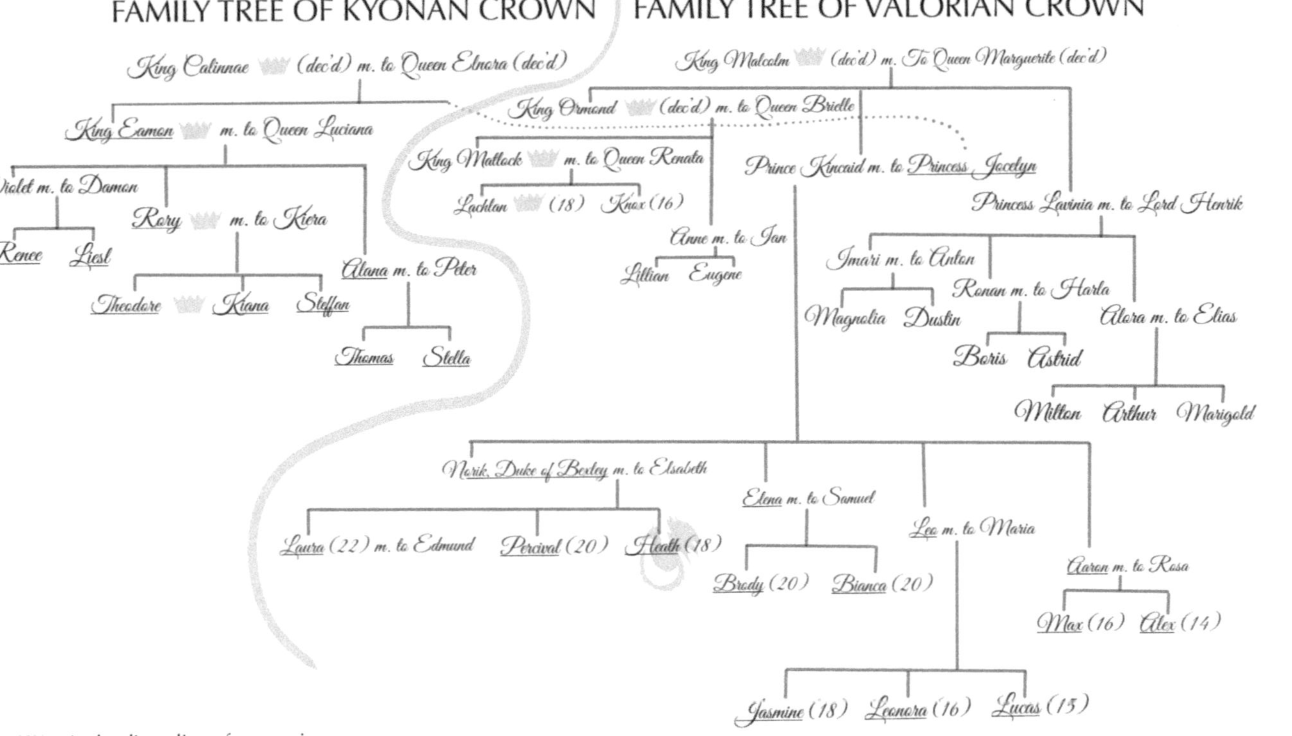

FAMILY TREE OF KYONAN CROWN

King Calinnae (dec'd) m. to Queen Elnora (dec'd)
King Eamon m. to Queen Luciana
Violet m. to Damon
Renee   Liesl
Rory m. to Kiera
Theodore   Kiana   Steffan
Alana m. to Peter
Thomas   Stella

FAMILY TREE OF VALORIAN CROWN

King Malcolm (dec'd) m. To Queen Marguerite (dec'd)
King Ormond (dec'd) m. to Queen Brielle
King Mallock m. to Queen Renata
Lachlan (18)   Knox (16)
Anne m. to Ian
Lillian   Eugene
Prince Kincaid m. to Princess Jocelyn
Princess Lavinia m. to Lord Henrik
Imari m. to Anton
Magnolia   Dustin
Ronan m. to Harla
Boris   Astrid
Alora m. to Elias
Milton   Arthur   Marigold

Norik, Duke of Bexley m. to Elsabeth
Laura (22) m. to Edmund   Percival (20)   Heath (18)
Elena m. to Samuel
Brody (20)   Bianca (20)
Lea m. to Maria
Aaron m. to Rosa
Max (16)   Alex (14)
Jasmine (18)   Leonora (16)   Lucas (15)

= in the direct line of succession
Underline = born to power-wielding line
(Brackets) = age at start of A Kingdom Submerged

CHAPTER ONE

Merletta

"That's it, nice and slow."

Merletta made her voice as encouraging as she could, noting the frustration on the guard's face. Griffin was irritated enough by his own limitations—he didn't need her impatience as well.

The guard took a shaky step across the sand, then another. Just as Merletta was thinking he'd gotten the hang of it at last, his knees gave way, and he dropped onto the sand.

"Why is it so hard?" he burst out.

Merletta tried not to smile. "Because it's an entirely new skill that your body has no experience with," she told him calmly. "I'm sure it was the same when you were learning to swim, you just don't remember."

Griffin sighed, looking up at her from his knees. "August and Paul seem to have mastered it."

Merletta looked across the beach, this time allowing her grin to break free at the wobbly gaits of the other two guards as they crossed toward the rocks. "I don't know if I'd say mastered."

"Did you find it this hard?" Griffin pressed. "When you first found out about your legs?"

"Harder," Merletta assured him promptly. "I had no one to teach me."

Griffin shook his head. "It must have been terrifying, when you first dried out."

She nodded. "It was. I was all alone, and I was certain I was dying. It took all the courage I had to get out of the water again after I finally made it back in. It was weeks before I could make the change without being afraid that this time it wouldn't work, and I'd shrivel up like the stories say."

The young guard—she guessed no more than ten years her senior—shivered slightly. "I certainly thought you were mad when you first told us we could grow legs if we just let ourselves dry out. If I hadn't seen you do it first, I would never have been willing to take the risk."

Merletta smiled secretly to herself. She didn't blame him for his skepticism. Honestly, she'd found it satisfying seeing their dramatic reaction to her performing her practiced wriggle to get from water to land, activating the change that gave her legs. Griffin had needed far more than one demonstration to be convinced. He hadn't been persuaded to try it until he'd seen August, his senior guard, successfully change back and forth three times.

Merletta chose not to remind him of that fact. The man was already collapsed on the sand, after all. It wouldn't kill her to allow him a tiny shred of dignity.

Temporarily abandoning him, she made her way across the beach to the other two with confident strides. Memories of her own early days with legs seemed distant now. She had no difficulty walking, running, even jumping. She hadn't realized how proficient she'd become until she was called upon to teach others. Compared to August and his two guards, she was a master.

"Merletta," August greeted her, without taking his eyes from his feet.

The senior guard might be a little wobbly, but his legs were strong, as his tail was when he was in the water. Merletta could see the muscles bulging in that part of his legs that emerged from the scaled shorts—all that remained of his tail once the transformation from merman to human was complete. She assumed that the men's shorts, like her own skirt, could be pulled away from the hips like snakeskin if desired. She'd never asked, of course.

"You're doing well," she told August. "When I come back, we should try to increase your speed." She grinned. "You'll like running."

"When you come back?" August repeated, with a shrewd look. "Does that mean you won't be here tomorrow?"

"It's a rest day," Merletta reminded him. "I'll probably stay in the triple kingdoms." She drew a deep breath. "Next week is my final week before my third year training commences, you know. I think it's time for me to approach your wife."

August stilled, his eyes brightening. "You've found a way to speak to her without witnesses?"

"I think so," Merletta said cautiously. "I'm going to try, anyway. And I think I should do more than speak to her. I think I should bring her out here."

Paul paused on his progress past them, raising an eyebrow. "Bring her here? To the island?"

Merletta shrugged, her eyes still on August. "I don't know your wife well enough to be sure," she told him. "But if it were me, and a near stranger told me the man I loved was alive, when I'd thought him dead for months—"

For a moment she faltered, her mind flying unbidden to Heath, and what she'd felt when she hadn't known whether he'd survived the spear wounds these very guards had inflicted on him.

"Anyway," she said, pulling herself together, "I wouldn't be content to just take their word for it. I would insist on seeing myself."

"She'll feel the same way," said August simply. "But I'm not sure it's wise."

"Neither am I," said Merletta frankly. "But I don't intend to make that decision for her."

August's face twisted into a rueful smile. "She'll like you." He sighed. "I can't deny I'm desperate to see her."

"Then it's settled." Merletta gave a decisive nod. "I'll stay in the triple kingdoms tomorrow, be seen about the place on Sage and Andre's rest day, and come back the day after. Hopefully with a passenger."

August held himself tensely as he nodded an acknowledgment. "I'd ask you to send my greetings to young Andre, but you still haven't told him I'm alive, have you?"

Merletta shook her head, guilt gnawing at her. She'd intended to tell her friends about the three guards' survival immediately after her second year test, but the reality had been a little more complicated.

"I'm going to tell him tonight," Merletta said firmly. "I'll just have to find a way to make it work."

"If you want to be back inside the triple kingdoms before sunset, you'd better get moving," Paul prompted.

Merletta sighed, glancing at the sun. He was right. Sunset was still a few hours away, but the journey from Vazula to the triple kingdoms wasn't as straightforward as it had once been.

"You'll be going in via Skulssted again?" August asked.

Merletta nodded, slinging her kelp satchel over her back in preparation for departure.

"Be careful."

Griffin's voice alerted Merletta that he'd made it across the sand. She smiled at him, trying not to show how amusing she found his stern expression when combined with his unsteady stance. He acted sometimes like he was as old and commanding as August, rather than relatively near Merletta's age. She didn't mind, really. She was grateful that the guards she'd once believed murdered for her secrets didn't appear to blame her for unintentionally ripping them away from everything they knew and loved. If anything, they'd become quite protective of her.

The thought once again drove her mind to Heath, and the sternness in his voice when he'd issued her a command of his own: *don't die.*

Those words—spoken shortly before she undertook her perilous second year test—were the last they'd shared. She had hoped he might return sooner. Her break was almost over, after all, and it would soon become considerably more difficult to sneak away to Vazula. But then again, she hadn't exactly been waiting alone for him on the island, as she usually was. She had no idea how August, Paul, and Griffin would respond to their inevitable meeting. She should probably explain to the guards the extent of her friendship with Heath. But not today.

"I'll be fine," she told Griffin cheerfully. "And I'll be back the day after tomorrow."

With the words, she waded into the shallows, relishing the cool of the water on her skin. She'd often found the depths of the ocean cold, but there was no denying that spending the entire day above the surface was hot. At least on Vazula. Heath claimed that his kingdom was cold sometimes. But it was hard to picture. Perhaps one day she'd find out for herself.

The water was up to her thighs now, and she shook off the thought as she dove forward. As she entered the water, she felt the change take place. An intense ripple passed down her scales all the way to her fins, the sensation making her realize that she once again *had* fins. The transition was so seamless now, she could barely track the moment her legs became tail once more.

Merletta swam quickly through the familiar waters between Vazula and the northern border of the triple kingdoms. But she didn't go far enough to reach the uncultivated kelp forests through which she'd snuck into the triple kingdoms so many times. On August's advice, she'd begun to vary her route into and out of the cities, in an effort to make her movements harder to track.

It took much longer to skirt around the outside of the triple kingdoms—well beyond the barrier—but it did ensure that no one watching her old waters in Tilssted would get any hint of her approach. Traveling through the area somewhere between the northwestern border and the maelstrom where she'd completed her test three weeks before, she approached Skulssted from the northwest. Since she was staying in the wealthiest of the triple kingdoms, it was at least a short swim once she entered.

She had to wait a fair while before the guard patrols left a long enough gap for her to pass through the barrier unseen, but she'd allowed enough time. The sun was only just setting in the world far above as she swam through the clean waters of Skulssted, making for Sage's family home.

She deposited her satchel in the small, detached room which Sage's parents had kindly offered her for the duration of her break between second and third years, but she kept her weapon with her. If Sage's family considered it strange, they'd well and truly gotten used to it by now. Even Sage's little sister, who could sometimes be uncomfortably blunt, didn't comment on it anymore.

Merletta had been reluctant to accept the offer of hospitality, but when Sage explained that the room in question was designed for guests, and wasn't attached to the dwelling,

Merletta had relented. It was very generous of the family to offer her the convenience of being hosted while still allowing her the independence necessary for her to spend the majority of her days on the island.

Not that Sage's parents dreamed that was where she disappeared to each day, of course.

"Merletta, there you are." Sage's mother smiled in a friendly way as Merletta swam into the room where the family ate their meals.

"Did I hold you up?" Merletta asked anxiously.

"Not at all," the older mermaid assured her. "In fact, we're still waiting for—ah, there he is."

Her husband appeared in the dwelling's doorway as she spoke, looking weary.

"Am I late for dinner?" he asked, after he'd greeted his wife and younger daughter. "We had an injury come in at the last minute, and I had to stay to oversee the report."

"What injury?" Serena, Sage's sister, piped up. "Was it a bad one?"

Her father shrugged as he lowered himself into a seat. "It'll heal. Someone burned their arm in a thermal vent when cooking."

Merletta listened in fascination as the family drifted into their seats. She'd already known that Sage's mother was a record holder at the Center, but she'd known nothing about Sage's father's job until coming to stay with the family.

They were just serving up when another voice hailed them from the doorway.

"Don't tell me I'm too late!" Sage called cheerfully. "If Serena's eaten all the squid, I'm going back to the Center."

"Sage!" Merletta half rose from her seat, delighted to see her friend. "I thought you wouldn't be here until tomorrow."

The other mermaid grinned as she embraced her parents.

"Agner let us loose from training early, so I thought I'd come straight home, get a head start on rest day."

"That's perfect," said Merletta. "Has Andre gone home for his break yet, do you know?"

"Last night, I think," said Sage, as Serena hid a snigger.

Merletta glanced at the ten-year-old, confused, but she'd fallen silent under her mother's stern gaze.

Once the meal was finished, Sage drifted back to Merletta's room with her.

"Why were you asking about Andre?" she asked, idly picking up Merletta's paua shell knife from next to the bed, and turning it over in her hand.

"I want to speak with him," Merletta said. "Tonight, if possible."

"Why?" Sage sent her a sharp look. "Did something happen today with...you know?" She widened her eyes meaningfully, and Merletta shook her head.

"No, they're all fine. But it's time to tell him."

"Are you sure?" Sage looked nervous. "I spoke to Emil at lunch yesterday, and he said—"

"It's in Emil's nature to be cautious," Merletta said firmly. "But Andre deserves our trust."

Sage fidgeted with the paua knife, still looking unsure.

"Sage." Merletta's firm tone brought her friend's eyes up to hers. "Imagine if it was you. How would you feel to be the only one who didn't know?"

Sage sighed. "You're right, of course. I'd hate it. I *did* hate it when you kept things from me last year. It's just...I do think Emil has a point. If Andre knows, it will be terribly hard to expect him not to tell his parents. His father was—I mean is— such a close friend of..." She trailed off, clearly not wanting to say August's name aloud, in spite of the fact that they were alone.

"We'll just have to trust him," said Merletta, shrugging. "He knows best whether it's safe to tell his parents."

Sage didn't say anything, but Merletta still knew what she was thinking. Emil most definitely wouldn't approve of trusting that decision to Andre. Merletta ran a hand over her face, knowing Sage was right.

It would have been so much simpler if she'd been able to just tell all her friends the moment she found out about the guards' survival, and be done with it. But that opportunity hadn't arisen straight away. She'd managed to tell Sage that night, in the brief minutes before Lorraine followed them into their sleeping area, but of course neither Andre nor Emil had been present. And when Sage had found a private moment to pass it on to Emil the next day, he'd sent back a caution against Merletta's intention to apprise all the missing guards' families of the news.

Merletta often thought Emil too cautious, but on this occasion, she'd soon realized he was right. To even discover the identity of the relevant family members would require her to ask questions which would raise suspicion. And she had no way to guess how those people would react, and whether their responses would endanger not only themselves, but all Merletta's friends.

Reluctantly, she'd held off telling Andre as well, which wasn't actually very difficult, given that she'd left the Center immediately to stay with Sage's family, and he'd been completely distracted by studying for his first year test. But he'd passed the test the day before, so that excuse could no longer stand. Even though Merletta hadn't seen much of Andre in the three weeks since her own test, she could still hardly believe she'd let it go so long without filling him in. It wasn't the action of a friend.

"Even if you're right," Sage said, "it's probably not the best time. His family is hosting his birthday celebration early, remember? To double as a celebration that he passed his test."

"I know," said Merletta eagerly. "It's tomorrow, right? That's why I want to speak to him tonight. I'm hoping he'll invite me."

"You...you want him to..." Sage hesitated, her expression hard to read as she searched Merletta's face. "Won't you be...away?"

Merletta shook her head impatiently. "It's your rest day, Sage. I was going to hang around Skulssted like I did last week. Unless..." She hesitated as a sudden thought occurred to her. "Unless you want some time with your family, without any guests. That would be completely understandable, and I really should have—"

"No, it's not that," scoffed Sage. "I see plenty of my family. It's just that I, uh...I'm actually busy tomorrow. Going to...well..." She flashed Merletta an apologetic look. "Going to Andre's celebration. My whole family is going."

"Oh." Merletta blinked, surprised and a little hurt that Sage had been keeping that information to herself. "And will Emil be there?"

Sage nodded, looking miserable. "Yes, I believe he's going, with...with his family."

Merletta turned away, tidying her small living area and trying to sound casual. "Well, that's good. It's been too long since we were all together in one place. And tomorrow could be an opportunity to get together without raising any suspicion."

Sage remained silent.

Whirling around, Merletta released her words bluntly. "It's all right to tell me, Sage. Would it be too embarrassing for Andre to have the Tilssted trainee at his celebration? Would it, I don't know, damage his reputation?"

"No!" said Sage, sounding distressed. "Honestly, it's not that. Andre's never seemed worried about that kind of thing to me."

"Then it wouldn't be inappropriate for me to ask to come?" Merletta asked, her skin burning with discomfort.

"Well..." Sage hesitated. "If I were you, I don't think I'd ask to come, Merletta."

Merletta wanted to shrink into herself, once again not meeting her friend's eye. Usually she felt very at ease with Sage, but this was quickly becoming one of the most awkward conversations of her life. If she didn't have such a specific reason for wanting to be at Andre's celebration, she would definitely have dropped the whole thing by now.

"Of course you wouldn't," Merletta said, her voice stiff. "I wouldn't *ask* for an invitation in ordinary circumstances, either. But I need to be there for a particular reason. Would it really be so bad?"

Sage hesitated, clearly searching for words. Before she could speak, however, a new figure surged into the room.

"What are you guys talking about?" Serena asked brightly.

"Go away, Serena," Sage said crisply, scowling at her little sister.

"Nope," said Serena. "Mother told me I'm allowed to be in here."

"She did not!" scoffed Sage. "This is Merletta's space."

"I don't mind her being in here," said Merletta diplomatically, as she slung her satchel over her back. "Weren't we leaving, anyway?"

Sage still looked troubled, but she made no further protest. Leaving Serena in sole possession of the territory, they swam out into the streets of Skulssted.

CHAPTER TWO

Andre's family lived in an entirely different part of Skulssted from Sage's, and the plankton lanterns were well and truly glowing by the time the two mermaids reached his dwelling.

At Sage's request, Merletta explained her reasoning for wishing to attend the celebration during the swim. When they came to a stop outside the relevant house, Sage still looked unconvinced.

But Merletta was distracted from their conversation by the sight of Andre's home. It was larger than Sage's, but less embellished. The stones were cut with precision, and there were no decorative plants poking out of windows.

"It looks like the home of a guard," noted Merletta.

Sage cast an appraising look over the dwelling. "It does, doesn't it? Andre's father came to the dining hall that one time, didn't he? He seemed fairly severe, from memory."

Merletta nodded, swimming forward to rap smartly at the door.

"Merletta, wait!" Sage said, once again sounding awkward as

she hurried after her friend. "About you coming to Andre's celebration. It's...it's a good thought. Or, it would be, if..."

"If what?" Merletta pressed, her ears catching movement within the house as someone responded to the summons.

"Perhaps I could ask my mother again," Sage muttered to herself, instead of answering.

Merletta stared at her, bewildered, but at that moment the door swung open, to reveal the very merman whom Sage had mentioned a minute before.

"Good evening, sir," Merletta said respectfully. "We've met before, but you most likely don't remember me. I'm—"

"Trainee Merletta," he interjected, his crimson tail giving a barely perceptible flick. "I remember. What brings you here, Trainee?"

"We were hoping to congratulate Andre on his successful test," Sage cut in quickly, drawing the guard's gaze to her face. "My name is Sage, of the Skulssted family Clearfoam. My mother is Rowena, and my father—"

"Ah yes." Andre's father cut her off curtly, although his posture relaxed slightly. "Skulssted Clearfoams, yes, Andre has mentioned you. And I saw your names on the list for tomorrow's celebration. Your mother is a record holder, is she not?"

"She is, sir," Sage acknowledged. She glanced at Merletta. "And Merletta is a guest of my family during her break between her second and third year studies."

"Well, well, you'd both best come in," said the guard, his voice now pleasant enough.

Sage swam forward obediently. Merletta followed more slowly, her bemused gaze on her friend's back. She'd never heard Sage introduce herself that way. Was her family high-ranking in some way Merletta didn't know about? Or was it just that her mother was a record holder?

When they entered the dwelling's main living space, it was to see a flurry of activity as the family cleared up the meal. At first Merletta was overwhelmed by a general impression of chaos as the room seemed full of brawny bodies, but a moment's observation showed that there was a rigid order to the method by which the task was being completed. A quick count showed one middle-aged mermaid—presumably Andre's mother—and six mermen.

"Merletta, Sage!" Andre's cheerful voice drew both mermaids' attention to him, as he emerged from the flurry of tails and limbs. "I wasn't expecting you."

"We wanted to congratulate you on passing your first year test," Merletta told him, borrowing Sage's excuse.

Andre beamed, but before he could respond, one of the other mermen in the room paused in passing to elbow him hard in the ribs.

"Don't congratulate him," the merman protested. "Commiserations would be more in order."

Andre rolled his eyes, not even bothering to respond to the sally. "Come on," he said to Sage and Merletta. "Let's go outside where we can breathe."

He led them through a formal living area and out a doorway to a large private coral garden.

"It's so nice to see you both," he said, his eyes bright. "You especially, Merletta. It's been ages."

"Is that your family?" Sage asked, casting a dazed look back toward the dining room.

Andre nodded, his face splitting into a grin. "Bit different from your family meals, I'm guessing. Something tells me you have servants who clear away your leftovers, right?"

"Well, uh...yes," Sage admitted, a little too obvious in her avoidance of Merletta's eye.

"So could we, if we wanted to," Andre said comfortably. "But

Father doesn't believe in luxuries. Everyone has to do their part, like one of his patrol squads."

Merletta cleared her throat, diplomatically refraining from pointing out that the fresh oysters she'd seen being removed from the table were very much a luxury where she came from.

"Why was one of them commiserating your success in your test?" she asked instead.

"Oh, ignore him," said Andre dismissively. "Didn't I ever tell you that I have four older brothers?"

Merletta stared at him. "No."

"Yep," he said, with flourish. "And all four of them are either in training or already qualified to be Skulssted guards, like my father. I'm kind of the albino dolphin of the family."

Sage snorted. "Because training to be a record holder is such a rebellious pathway."

"Do they all live here?" Merletta pressed, fascinated by these details.

"Not normally," said Andre. "But they're here for tomorrow, because of...uh..."

He trailed off, and Merletta jumped on the opening. "Your birthday and test-passing celebration," she finished for him. "That's the other reason we came to speak to you." She paused, looking around carefully to make sure they were really alone. "Will August's wife be there?"

Andre looked astonished. "Eloise? Yes, I believe she's coming."

"Excellent." Merletta gave a determined nod. "This is as good an opportunity as I'm going to get."

"Opportunity for what?" Andre asked.

Merletta drew in a mouthful of cool, salty water. "Andre, I never got the chance to properly tell you about my test a few weeks ago."

Andre cast a glance around the walled garden before dropping his voice. "You mean about the armed guards waiting to kill you afterward? Emil told me."

"Didn't you wonder how I managed to evade them?" Merletta pressed.

Andre nodded. "How?"

"I had help." Merletta watched his face carefully.

"From who?" Andre asked, growing impatient.

Merletta and Sage exchanged a glance. "You might want to sit down," Sage said.

Andre did so, his eyes riveted to Merletta's face as she told him about the guards' survival, and the truth behind their attempted murders. By the time she was finished, his face was ashen, and he seemed to be struggling for words.

"But this is..."

"Huge," Merletta supplied, nodding.

"Don't get me wrong, I'm thrilled they're alive," Andre said quickly. "But...it's confirmation of all our worst fears, isn't it? About the Center, and land sickness, and...well, everything." His eyes traveled to Merletta's face, suddenly losing their dazed look. "You've known this for three weeks. Why didn't you tell me earlier?"

"We didn't want to distract you from your test," Sage hedged.

But Merletta shook her head. "No, Sage, he deserves honesty. It wasn't just that. The truth is I was worried you would tell your father—I know he'll want to know that August is alive —and I don't know whether he can be trusted with the information. It's not a claim to be made lightly, that the guards who supposedly sacrificed themselves for the good of the triple kingdoms were actually targeted by the Center for seeing too much."

Andre was silent again, his expression troubled. Merletta didn't press him. She could see that he grasped the point, and she didn't think it would help anyone for her to drive it home.

"I've been spending most days with them," she said. "On—at the island. And today I told August that I thought I'd found a way to tell his wife about his survival without anyone being suspicious that I'd gone looking for her."

Andre's eyes traveled once again to her face, his expression telling her that his thoughts were still catching up.

"I was hoping that your celebration might be that way," Merletta prompted.

"My...what?" Andre asked vaguely.

"Your celebration tomorrow," Merletta said. "If Eloise is going to be there, and if...if I could be there, too, then I could speak to her about August. And no one would think I'd sought her out especially."

Sage fidgeted beside her, and Andre's eyes were drawn to the movement, his mind finally seeming to put the pieces together.

"You want to come to my celebration?" His voice turned hopeful as his eyes returned to Sage. "Did your family invite Merletta, as their guest?"

Sage shifted again, looking as uncomfortable as Merletta had ever seen her. "No. I did suggest the idea, but my mother... well...she didn't..."

"You did?" Merletta stared at Sage. She was grateful to know her friend had tried to include her, but a pang still went through her at the result. Sage's mother had always been perfectly pleasant toward her guest. Why didn't she want Merletta to join them at Andre's birthday event?

"I see," said Andre, sounding disappointed. "So you want... you want me to invite you, Merletta?"

Merletta's scales rustled as she wriggled on the stone seat where she'd settled. She'd never felt so pathetic, begging for an invitation.

"I know I'm not as...as refined as the rest of the guests probably will be," she said. "And the last thing I want to do is to push in where I'm not wanted. The honest truth is that I just can't think of a better way to speak with Eloise."

"No, don't be silly," said Andre quickly, looking stricken. "You're my friend, Merletta, I don't care how...how *refined* you are. It's just..."

He exchanged a glance with Sage but didn't continue.

"Just what?" Merletta asked, more uncomfortable than ever.

"Just nothing," said Andre staunchly, apparently reaching a decision. "I'd love to have you there. And you're right, it is a good opportunity to speak to her surreptitiously."

"Are...are you sure?" Merletta asked uncertainly.

"Of course I'm sure," said Andre, his voice a little more gruff than usual. "I'll tell my parents. And..." He hesitated, biting his lip. "And I'll keep the other thing to myself for now. If you're going to tell Eloise tomorrow, perhaps it's for her to decide what to do about it."

Without waiting for a response, he rose into the water and led them back through his house.

"Are you girls leaving already?" his mother asked, as they emerged into the now clear dining hall. "I didn't even get the chance to introduce myself."

"Mother, this is Sage of the Skulssted Clearfoams, and Merletta, both trainees from the program," Andre said, the words running together in his haste. "And you'll get the chance for more conversation tomorrow, if you wish. They're both coming to the celebration."

His mother stilled. "Both?" she asked delicately, her eyes flicking to Merletta, then back to her son. "Well." She pulled herself together quickly. "I'll save my greetings for then."

Sage took a quick leave of their hosts, then nudged Merletta toward the door. "Come on," she said quietly. "We should give them some space to talk."

Confused, Merletta mumbled a thanks to the family and followed Sage toward the door. She heard one of Andre's brothers mutter an audible aside as she swam through the entrance.

"But I thought she was the Tilssted orphan."

"You been holding out on us, little brother?" another piped up.

"Shut it, Ethan." Andre's voice sounded unimpressed, but Sage was tugging Merletta along, and she could hear no more.

"What was all that about?" she demanded as Sage steered her down the street.

"It's a cultural thing," said Sage shortly.

Merletta frowned. "A Skulssted versus Tilssted thing, you mean? Andre has always been so relaxed about it, I thought for sure his family wouldn't be so prejudiced against Tilssted."

"It's not that," said Sage. "It's just...oh never mind, it doesn't matter now."

She would say no more, just swam ahead with tense strokes, leaving Merletta with the sinking feeling that she was missing something.

The reaction of Sage's family the next morning to the news that Andre had invited Merletta to attend the celebration further confirmed Merletta's suspicions. Serena giggled openly, only subsiding when Sage glared at her.

Merletta followed half-heartedly when the family made their way to Andre's home at around noon. Any excitement she might have felt at the prospect of witnessing a Skulssted celebration was completely overridden by the awkward way she'd secured her invitation.

This is about August and the others, she reminded herself

firmly. *Not about inviting myself to a party.* She would speak to August's wife, and leave without further fuss.

Even with that goal in mind, she couldn't help a thrill of delight when she saw the way the space had been transformed since the evening before. The celebration was held in the very coral garden where she and Sage had told Andre about the guards' survival, but it was unrecognizable. Shells of all sizes were arranged in sculptures, live starfish adorned many surfaces, and crenellated green seaweed was festooned over everything. A stone slab had been carried out into the space, balanced on a smoothed boulder, and covered with every festive food imaginable. It was like a miniature version of the Founders' Day feast the Center hosted for its residents each year.

"Wow," said Merletta, her eyes wide as she took it all in.

"It looks beautiful, doesn't it?" Sage said, her casual tone informing Merletta that she was much more used to such displays.

"Sage." The call from Sage's mother, while calm, was clearly a command.

Coloring slightly, Sage swam to join her family, from whom she and Merletta had been separated by other arrivals. Merletta followed more slowly, meaning that she entered the gathering alone, rather than with the other four. There could be no doubt that this manner of entry had been intentionally orchestrated by Sage's mother. Merletta squirmed all over again at the memory that the older mermaid had declined to invite her along as their guest. Clearly she wanted it known that Merletta was attending on her own.

Merletta saw Andre swim forward to greet the family, addressing a respectful welcome to Sage's parents. As soon as the middle-aged couple had moved on, Sage drifted over to Merletta, Andre in her wake.

He gave the two of them a more natural smile, although

Merletta noticed he was holding himself more tightly than usual.

"Welcome," he said. "I'm so glad you're both here. Help yourself to some food. I'll be free to talk to you more later."

They chivvied him away to greet his other guests, and he was soon replaced by another familiar figure.

"Sage, Merletta. I didn't expect to see you both."

"Emil." Merletta smiled. "It's nice to see you. I heard you'd be here."

"Whereas I didn't think you would be here," said Emil bluntly.

"Merletta!" Sage's hiss cut off Emil's words. "There she is."

Merletta followed her friend's gaze, her heart racing at double speed as she saw August's wife float through the doorway.

"Is that why you're here?" Emil asked abruptly, his eyes darting between Eloise and Merletta.

"Yes, that's the only reason," said Sage, her voice a little tart. "So you can relax."

Merletta looked at her friend in confusion, but whatever Sage was talking about, Emil evidently didn't agree.

"If you expect me to be relaxed about Merletta deciding, without consulting anyone, to bring someone we've barely met into our...situation, then you don't know me well."

"You two keep squabbling," Merletta interjected over the top of Sage's protest. "I'm going to talk to Eloise."

She drifted across the room as casually as she could, hoping that Emil was wrong to be nervous about the so-called widow. During her one meeting with Eloise, she hadn't formed the impression that the mermaid was flighty, or likely to act rashly. But the news she was about to deliver would be enough to rattle even the most stoic of individuals.

Eloise had just passed out of earshot of Andre and his

family, who were still greeting new arrivals, when Merletta approached her. The older mermaid's face registered a brief look of surprise before she schooled her features into a more neutral expression.

"Merletta," she said quietly, her eyes on the room at large as she accepted food from a passing server. "I thought after our last meeting that you would be cautious about approaching me in public."

Merletta grimaced at the reminder of how Instructor Agner had followed her to Eloise's house and all but ordered her to return to the Center.

"I have been cautious," she said, her voice low and even. "That's why you haven't heard from me. But none of my instructors are here today."

"That doesn't mean no one's watching," said Eloise, her movements casual as she sucked down an oyster. "I've made some inquiries of my own since we last spoke, with interesting results. More than once I've been followed."

Merletta pursed her lips. "Then I'm glad I asked Andre to invite me today," she said. "It seems I was right that the opportunity to speak with you was too rare to pass up."

"You asked Andre to invite you?" Eloise blinked.

The older mermaid's expression once again told Merletta that she was missing something. It was on the tip of her tongue to demand why her request had been so outrageous, but she stopped herself. She didn't know how long she and Eloise would remain uninterrupted, and she had more important things to talk about.

"If I tell you something extremely shocking, can you look outwardly as if we're speaking of the currents?" Merletta asked matter-of-factly, her voice quieter than ever.

Eloise paused. "I believe so."

"Are you sure? Because this is big. As in, so big it might—"

"After that opening, please don't keep me in suspense, Merletta." There was a bite to Eloise's voice as she cut off Merletta's ramblings.

Merletta pulled in a mouthful of water, then let it out in a slow, controlled stream.

"August is alive, and I know where he is. I can take you to him tomorrow. In fact, he's expecting me to."

For a long moment, there was silence. With possibly the most impressive self-control Merletta had ever seen, Eloise raised another oyster to her mouth and shucked it down.

"Where do I meet you, and when?" she managed at last, her voice sounding unnatural.

"There's a special market day happening in the main square tomorrow," Merletta said. "It will be chaos, full of people. I'll try to hover near the central sculpture an hour after sunrise."

"I will be there," said Eloise curtly. "Now if you'll excuse me, I need a minute."

Still impressively controlled, she drifted away through the crowd. Merletta turned to find Andre's eyes on her, a question in their depths. She gave him the slightest of nods, and he drew in a long pull of water.

Another guest claimed his attention, and Merletta moved back toward her other friends. Emil's expression was hard to read, but Sage was visibly strained.

"Well?" she asked, as soon as Merletta joined them. "How did she take it?"

Merletta shook her head slowly. "Let's just say that if I was that good at controlling my emotions and reactions, my life would have been very different."

"That sounds promising in terms of her ability not to blurt it out to the wrong people," Sage said, with a hopeful glance at Emil. His expression was still inscrutable.

"She's not going to do anything foolish," Merletta said confidently. "She was cautious enough even to satisfy you, Emil. She knows people are watching."

"I hope you understand what you're doing, Merletta," said Emil seriously. "Every time you embroil others in your secrets, you put them in danger."

"She has more right to know than anyone," Merletta started, but Emil shook his head.

"I wasn't talking about Eloise. I was talking about Andre."

Merletta made an exasperated noise. "Of course we had to tell him, Emil. I should've done it from the start. It wouldn't be right to keep him in the dark when the rest of us—"

"You misunderstand," said Emil, still speaking in his usual emotionless way. "I was referring to the way you cornered him into inviting you today. It puts a much greater target on his back than the rest of us are carrying."

Merletta stared from him to Sage, who was once again fidgeting.

"Why does it do that?" Merletta asked, confused. "We're all known to be friends. Why would inviting me to his celebration change anything?"

"This is what I was trying to explain, Emil," Sage muttered. "She honestly doesn't understand."

"Enough," said Merletta darkly. "I'm clearly missing something, and it's time for someone—anyone—to explain what it is."

"Gladly," said Emil, his voice dry. "Look around you, Merletta. How many people in our generation do you see?"

Merletta frowned at the crowd. "Not as many as I'd expect," she acknowledged. "I'm surprised by how many of the guests are the age of Andre's parents, given it's his birthday celebration."

"That's because Andre's family didn't invite individuals to

this event," Emil explained. "That simply isn't how we do things in Skulssted. We invite families."

Sage nodded. "He's right. Family is everything in Skulssted. Not just in the sense that it matters which family you come from. It's almost like...like you don't exist outside your family."

Merletta's thoughts flew to the way Sage had introduced herself to Andre's father the night before, and how he'd seemed to relax when she presented herself as a representative of her family rather than a friend of Andre's from his studies.

"I see," Merletta said, subdued.

Sage shook her head. "I don't think you do, to be honest. And how could you be expected to? Last night I thought maybe you were just dismissive of the conventions. It didn't occur to me until later that you probably had no idea about them, given no one where you grew up had a family."

Merletta was silent, thinking over certain experiences during her time at the Center. Perhaps this mentality was why her presence seemed to be so offensive to the more uptight residents of the Center. Without membership of a family, she had no identity whatsoever, and no standing based on which she might enter the Center's ecosystem. Even the day she'd signed up—the mermaid on duty in the Center's receiving hall had been disdainful at the absence of any parents to formally support Merletta's application.

"What about Eloise, though?" she argued. "She's here alone."

"Because she's a widow," Sage said. "I mean..." She lowered her voice. "As far as anyone knows. She might be alone now, but she's still a representative of an honored and recognized family."

"But what about orphans?" Merletta protested.

"We don't have orphans in Skulssted," said Sage simply. "They're formally adopted into families, and take on the name and standing of the adopting parents."

"That sounds very nice," said Merletta dryly. "And like the kind of answer the Center would give to your average citizen who doesn't know enough to dig any deeper."

Sage looked taken aback, her eyes flying to Emil for support.

"She's right," Emil told her calmly. "Sometimes there isn't anyone willing to adopt the orphaned child. In which case they're sent to a charity home." He paused. "None of which are in Skulssted."

Sage's eyes widened as her gaze passed slowly from Emil back to Merletta. "You mean, like..."

"Yes, yes, like me, but I'm not from Skulssted," Merletta said impatiently.

Her irritation softened as she read the disillusionment in Sage's eyes. The other mermaid had honestly believed the pleasant picture she'd been painted of Skulssted's approach to those unfortunate enough not to possess the family required to validate existence in the wealthy city.

"You could be, for all you know," Emil pointed out.

Merletta didn't respond. She hadn't told anyone about the record she'd found in the center of the maelstrom—the one claiming her parents were named Elminia and Elric and came from Hemssted—and she didn't intend to bring it up now.

"So the point is that Andre has disgraced himself socially by inviting me to his celebration without a family to give me credibility," she said, returning to the original point. "It was heroic of him to let me push him into it, then."

"You're still missing the point," Emil informed her. "It's not about social standing. It's about the way we do things. People won't be offended that Andre invited an individual, but they will take notice."

"What do you mean?"

But even as she spoke, Merletta's eyes passed around the

garden. Emil was right that many eyes were directed toward her. Even Andre's parents kept glancing her way, their expressions a little tense.

"Inviting an individual for their own sake, rather than a family, is kind of...a statement," Sage supplied, looking uncomfortable again. "Especially when, well, when the invitation comes from a young merman toward a young mermaid."

Merletta froze in horror, finally understanding the overblown reactions of everyone who'd heard about Andre's invitation.

"So everyone will think that Andre..." She swallowed, embarrassment washing over her. Her eyes sought Sage's. "*He* didn't think that, did he? When I asked him last night to invite me, he didn't think—"

"No, no," Sage cut her off reassuringly, shaking her head. "He could see as well as I could that you had no idea what you were really asking. It's everyone else who's the problem."

Merletta groaned, resisting the urge to cover her face with her hands. Better not to show her humiliation so plainly to everyone still covertly watching the small group.

"Do you understand now what I meant about putting a target on Andre's back?" Emil asked.

Merletta flicked her tail in distress. "I do. And I wish you'd told me this before I made a fool of both myself and Andre, Sage."

"I didn't know how," Sage admitted apologetically. "I dithered so long trying to figure out how to explain it, that you blurted it out to Andre, and then it was in his hands. And he clearly didn't know how to tell you, either. Once he'd invited you, it didn't seem like there was anything to be gained from telling you why I advised against the idea initially."

"I need to leave," Merletta said curtly. "Before I do any more damage. I've done what I came to do, and clearly my presence is preventing Andre's family from enjoying the celebration."

"There's no need for that," Sage protested, but Merletta was already edging toward the door.

"It may not be safe for you to wander around alone." Emil frowned. "Perhaps I'd better swim you back to Sage's house."

Merletta shook her head emphatically. "The last thing we need is a target on your back, too. I'll be fine."

She didn't give her friends any more opportunity to argue. She was trying her best to hide it, but she'd never been so mortified in her life. She'd come to appreciate Andre's friendship a great deal, but the idea of romance with him was laughably absurd.

As she fled through the bustling streets of Skulssted, one face popped inevitably into her mind. When her thoughts strayed toward romance, there was only one direction they ever flowed.

She went straight past Sage's house, heading northward almost without thinking about it. She felt like a startled minnow fleeing toward its own school, driven by an instinctive fear of being separated from its group. Because although she'd become more comfortable with Sage and the others than she would have believed possible when she first started the program, the day's events showed the truth. They weren't her people, not really. Nor were the Tilssted dwellers she grew up with. Even Tish had made it clear Merletta was too dangerous a friend for her to have.

Even though he'd been absent for weeks, and there was no reason to think he'd come today, Merletta found herself making for Vazula from force of habit. Because when she asked herself who she felt comfortable and safe with, there was only one name that fit. It was ridiculous, because the barriers which divided them—both practical and cultural—were far greater than any between her and Andre. And yet, there was no comparison.

"Heath." The name slipped out without Merletta intending to speak aloud, just as she crossed the barrier and left the triple kingdoms behind. "I really need you right now."

CHAPTER THREE

Heath tuned out the discussion around him, his thoughts on something far from the council room in which he sat.

Reka, he thought, mentally repeating the familiar name with focused intensity.

An image flickered into his mind, of Rekavidur stretched out on the grass, looking utterly at ease, and endearingly similar to a cat basking in a patch of sunlight. Behind the dragon, a rocky shelf rose up, flashes of purple showing amidst the gray. What the color denoted, Heath had no idea. And that was encouraging in itself.

It proved that the picture was no figment of his imagination, conjured up when he thought of his friend. It was a true reflection of Reka's current situation. It was a successful use of Heath's farsight.

Heath smiled, pleased with his progress.

"Lord Heath. Do I take your amusement to mean you agree with my observation?"

The pompous voice of Lord Niel disrupted Heath's focus, and the image cut off abruptly.

Irked, Heath turned an expressionless face to the peer. "I'm flattered that you value my opinion so highly, My Lord."

"I didn't say—" Lord Niel started, but Prince Lachlan cut him off.

"Of course we would like to hear your views, Lord Heath," he said, a bite to his voice.

"You are gracious, Your Highness," said Heath blandly.

When he didn't elaborate, Lord Niel jumped back in, continuing to expound on whatever he was talking about. Heath had no idea of the details. He hadn't been listening since the insufferable nobleman began speaking. So, for the last half hour.

Heath tried again to view Reka with his farsight, but no image came into his mind. Lord Niel had broken the flow of his power, and he couldn't recapture it. He would have to ask Reka next time if that was ever a problem for dragons.

Heath gave up his efforts in disgruntlement, but his interest in Lord Niel's discussion of the practicalities of the current restrictions on power-wielders did not increase. If he was truly defiant by nature, like Percival, he would have taken a grim delight in the irony of him practicing his magic in the very room where Lord Niel was congratulating the group on the success of their regulation of power.

But all Heath felt was irritation that he was being forced to use his time so pointlessly.

When the meeting finally ended, and the small group dispersed, Heath was prevented from leaving in their wake by a quiet command from Prince Lachlan.

"A word, Lord Heath?"

Heath turned reluctantly. "Your Highness?"

Prince Lachlan waited, not speaking until the room was clear of everyone but them.

"I can't help but suspect that we did not have your full attention today, Lord Heath. It's hard to believe that you can truly have no opinion on Lord Niel's suggestions."

Heath met the prince's eyes. "To tell the truth, Your Highness, I don't see any purpose to be served by me expressing my opinions on these matters. It's been made clear to me—on each of the several occasions I've done so—that my opinion is not going to be given any weight. In light of which, it seems unnecessary for me to continue attending these meetings."

"You are the crown's liaison to the power-wielders, My Lord," said the prince curtly. "Your presence is naturally required at meetings pertaining to the regulation of power. Otherwise the power-wielders might feel they have no voice in the discussion."

Heath gave him an incredulous look, and the prince had the decency to sigh, his stiffness softening slightly.

"I had hoped this would be more of a partnership, Lord Heath," he said. "We're family, aren't we? I thought we could work together."

"So did I," Heath retorted. "But I stood in your study, Your Highness, and told you to your face that placing restrictions on power-wielders was a terrible solution to the rising tensions, and you told me that it was out of my hands, and proceeded to do it anyway."

He half expected the prince to get angry, but instead Prince Lachlan sighed again, his gaze drifting to the window, through which the afternoon sun was filtering. "I remember what I said perfectly. Do you?"

Heath frowned, trying to recall the full conversation. "You said it was out of your hands as well," he said slowly. "Are you saying you don't agree with King Matlock's policy regarding the power-wielders?"

"Of course I'm not," Prince Lachlan said shortly.

Heath considered the prince thoughtfully. No, the unfailingly loyal crown prince would certainly never say anything to question his father. But that didn't mean he wasn't thinking it.

"I take it the sentiment among the power-wielders remains negative toward these restrictions?" the prince said at last.

Heath's voice was dry. "Without exception. Not only are the restrictions insulting, but they're impractical. Power-wielders are the only ones who can even sense magic. How would the crown even know if someone was using their power in contravention of the rules?"

The prince gave him a look that was a little too shrewd, but thankfully he didn't ask the obvious question.

"Our king has a reason for every decision he makes," he said instead. "He wouldn't have taken this action lightly."

"Wouldn't have?" Heath echoed.

He studied Prince Lachlan with more interest. He'd always had the impression that the king included his oldest son in his decision-making wherever possible, presumably to prepare him for the day when he would wear the crown. But Prince Lachlan had made it sound like he didn't know his father's reasoning for imposing the ill-advised restrictions. Heath had certainly been surprised at the time by the dramatic reaction from a king who usually projected calm moderation. Was it possible Prince Lachlan had been just as taken aback?

"If your father has a reason for every decision," Heath said, when the silence stretched out uncomfortably, "I wish you would explain his reason for keeping me on in this role. The last time he spoke to me, he all but accused me of treason, if you recall. If that's what he thinks of me, and if my input is not actually desired on the situation with the power-wielders, I can't imagine why he would still wish me to act as liaison."

"I thought you said my father had been misinformed regarding the accusations against you," said Prince Lachlan, his eyes slightly narrowed as he watched Heath.

"That's right," said Heath, refusing to let himself feel any guilt for his omissions.

The king's actual words were that Heath had been keeping a potential threat secret from his king. That statement wasn't true. Merletta's people were no threat to Valoria.

Besides, even if they had been, there was nothing King Matlock could do about it. All things considered, Heath felt under no obligation to break his promise to Merletta and share the existence of her people with his king.

"Was there anything else, Your Highness?" Heath asked, when the prince made no reply.

Shaking his head, Prince Lachlan dismissed Heath, only to check him as he reached the doorway.

"Do you believe your brother's story that the men who attacked him were royal guards, Lord Heath?"

Heath hesitated, his hand on the doorknob. "I don't pretend to understand the truth about that attack," he answered. "But I believe Percival without reservation when he says that he saw guard uniforms under the cloaks of the so-called bandits."

Prince Lachlan's expression was hard to read as he once again dismissed Heath, making no move to leave the meeting room himself. A glance back showed Heath that the young prince was standing right where Heath had left him, his expression thoughtful as he gazed out the window once again.

Heath found the conversation with Prince Lachlan hard to shake. By the following morning, he was still turning it all over in his mind, very much to the detriment of his attempts to practice with his farsight.

Prior to Heath bringing it up, there had been no further mention of the king's accusation three weeks before. Heath hadn't spoken with King Matlock since, and had even gotten the impression that the king might be avoiding him. Certainly he saw no sign of approval in the sovereign's eyes when he caught sight of him from a distance.

But the question continued to burn in Heath's mind—who had ratted him out to the king? Only a very few people knew about his discovery of Merletta's civilization. He'd been foolish to let the matter sit so long. The unconfirmed suspicion was surely worse than knowing for sure.

With that thought in mind, he turned his steps toward his cousin Brody's chambers—unlike Heath, Brody's family lived in the castle when in Bryford, not having an estate of their own in the city.

"Enter!"

The cheerful call came in response to Heath's knock, and he let himself in. But it wasn't Brody who confronted him as he entered the handsomely furnished sitting room.

"Hey, little brother." Percival was lounging at his ease on an armchair, helping himself to what seemed to be leftovers from Brody's breakfast.

Heath grunted in an unenthusiastic greeting, before scanning the room to discover that both Brody and his twin Bianca were also present.

"Now this is a conundrum," said Brody, with his usual cheeky grin. "You know I'm always glad to see you, Heath. But your presence raises a ticklish question, due to the nebulous issue of your magic or lack thereof. Are you tipping us from three to four power-wielders, therefore turning this casual conversation into an illicit and criminal act? Or are you introducing a non-power-wielder into our midst, thereby making our gathering sanctioned, regardless of how many of us dangerous creatures are present?"

Percival let out a guffaw, but clearly still felt compelled to defend his little brother.

"Heath has magic, Brody. His eyesight is—"

"Yes, yes, his eyesight is excellent, we know." Brody flapped a hand at his cousin. "Much good that does anyone."

"Better than being able to control a bunch of weeds," Percival said staunchly.

But Heath waved him down as well. He'd never been bothered by Brody's jokes about his lack of magic—there was no malice in them—and he wasn't about to start now that he knew he had a powerful magic of his own after all.

"If you two are quite finished," he said.

"I never heard how that meeting yesterday went, Heath," Bianca chimed in.

"Waste of time," said Heath frankly. "As absurd as every meeting that's come before it."

"I'm glad you finally agree that the restrictions are ridiculous," said Percival, a shadow crossing his face at the mention of the rules he found so offensive.

"I always agreed they were ridiculous," said Heath tartly. "I just didn't share your view that they were entirely unprovoked."

Percival straightened in his seat, his brow darkening. "What's that supposed to mean?"

"No, don't start bickering," Brody cut in. "If you want to argue, go to your own home. Heath, you looked very purposeful when you came in here. Was there something you wanted to say particularly?"

Heath drew in a deep breath, turning away from Percival. "Yes, actually." He fixed his gaze on the twins. "Did anyone tell you what the king said to me the day Percival was attacked?"

The twins exchanged a bemused look. "No," said Bianca.

Heath searched her eyes, trying to read her reaction to his next words. "He accused me of concealing a potential threat from him."

Bianca paled slightly, and even Brody's expression was suddenly unusually serious.

"He said that? Did he...elaborate?"

Heath shook his head.

"Hang on." Percival was leaning forward now, his elbows resting on his knees as his eyes flicked between the three of them. "You two know what that was about?"

Heath ignored his brother. "I'd like to think I know the answer," he told his cousins, "but I still need to ask the question. Did either of you tell the king about our, uh, activities when you visited me at Bexley Manor?"

Brody's eyes traveled slowly to Percival and back. He said nothing, but Heath could see him processing the implication of Heath's coded words—that Percival remained unaware of Heath's secrets. Even Brody and Bianca didn't know the extent of it, of course. Only that Heath had sailed to an island where he'd met with a friend from an unspecified kingdom, one which wished to remain hidden from Valoria.

"I haven't told a soul," Brody said at last. "Honestly, I'm a little offended that you'd ask."

"I certainly didn't tell the king," Bianca said, her voice small. "But...I did tell Grandmother."

Heath nodded slowly. "Yes, she told me as much. But I just didn't want to believe she would carry tales to the crown like that. Not when I explained to her how important it was to keep it all quiet."

"So you'd rather believe we were the tattletales," Brody said dryly.

"Is it possible the king was referring to something else?" Bianca suggested.

Heath sighed. "If so, I don't know what."

"Is anyone going to explain to me what in the kingdom is going on?" Percival interjected, irate.

"No," said Heath absently. "Not today, at least."

Percival gave an outraged splutter, and Heath's eyes passed to him. His brother's angry face suddenly sparked another thought, and he abandoned the topic of the king's uncanny knowledge for the moment.

"Percival, have you had any success in trying to spot the guards who attacked you? You were going to surreptitiously check out the royal guards in the training yard, weren't you?"

"I have done," Percival said, disgruntled. "But I haven't seen anything useful. Which isn't surprising," he added quickly, his voice a touch defensive. "They were all masked when they attacked me, after all."

"Hm." Heath's mind returned yet again to Prince Lachlan's question.

"Don't tell me you're still going on your ridiculous theory that someone else dressed up as royal guards dressed up as bandits," said Percival angrily. "Isn't the fact that the crown once again called us all back to the capital proof that they're determined to keep us under their thumb? What more evidence do you need?"

"It's proof that they want to keep a close eye on us, maybe curtail our activities," Heath said unemotionally. "It's hardly proof that they want to murder us, however."

"Not all of us," grumbled Percival. "Just me."

"You'd be the worst person to murder," Heath said vaguely. "You're the most visible."

"I can see you've put a lot of thought into this," said Bianca, sounding amused.

Heath didn't answer. The truth was, the only reason he'd

thought about it at all was because he'd compared the situation to Merletta's, when advising her to become more visible so that it would be harder for those in power to kill her off without facing repercussions from the populace at large. King Matlock was surely smart enough to know that as the best known and most popular power-wielder, Percival would be the most dangerous to dispose of by brute force. That, if nothing else, made it seem unlikely that the king really had been behind the attack on Heath's brother.

"Did you really sense power on the attackers?" Bianca asked doubtfully.

Heath nodded, his thoughts still elsewhere.

"Heath, for the last time, they weren't Kyonan power-wielders," Percival said impatiently. "I didn't feel any power."

"You were a little distracted fighting for your life," Heath pointed out. "But let's not get into that again." He turned to Bianca, directing his next question at her. "About what the king said—do you think I should ask Grandmother if she knows where he got his information?"

She shrugged. "No harm in asking."

"Well, except that she might not appreciate an implication that she ratted you out," Brody interjected.

Bianca sent him a look. "Grandmother is tough enough to handle it."

Brody just grunted. "Any word at yesterday's meeting about how long we're all supposed to stay in Bryford?"

"I don't know," said Heath candidly. "I wasn't listening to a word."

His cousin chuckled appreciatively.

"What about your end of it all?" Heath asked suspiciously. "Any clandestine magic-wielding parties I should know about?" He paused. "You know what, never mind. I don't want to know."

"I like this new attitude on you, Heath," said Percival approvingly. "It might have taken me almost getting murdered to achieve it, but I'm glad you're finally figuring out which side you should be on."

Heath refrained heroically from responding. Of course in Percival's mind it was always about him. But the attack had nothing to do with Heath's change in attitude. He felt no more eager to take sides than he ever had. Sure, he thought the crown was being foolish and obstructive to a true resolution to the tension between power-wielders and everyone else. But that didn't make Percival any less foolish or obstructive.

No, the fact of the matter was that Heath's focus was elsewhere. He remembered a time when he'd longed for a stronger magic, so as to feel more fully a part of his family. But now he'd found his magic, and it was nothing like his family's. It didn't make him feel a stronger connection to the power-wielders. It drew him toward a very different type of magic-user.

Waving goodbye to the other three, Heath slipped from the room, and made his way out of the castle. He had no other responsibilities for the rest of the day. What better way to spend the time than training?

"Reka," he called quietly, as he rode out of his father's stables a short time later. "I'm here."

I know where you are. The familiar voice echoed calmly in Heath's mind as Reka's image leaped before his eyes. The dragon was flying over the ocean in a leisurely way. *I always know where you are, because you are within my sight.*

Heath couldn't help chuckling. "If one human said that to another, we'd think a murder was about to be committed."

Impossible, said Reka reassuringly. *Even if I were to kill you, it would not be a murder. There is no consequence among my kind for dragons killing humans. Only for showing aggression toward one another.*

"That is deeply comforting," said Heath solemnly.

He looked around him, struggling to take in his immediate surroundings in his preoccupation with what he was seeing through his connection with Reka. Discovering that he was nearing the edge of the city, he urged his horse forward.

"Can we train?"

CHAPTER FOUR

Heath

Reka made no reply, but in his mind's eye Heath saw the dragon put on a burst of speed, his surroundings rapidly becoming an indistinct blur. Heath grinned to himself. The dragon was on his way.

Their usual meeting place was a solid quarter of an hour's ride out of the city, requiring Heath to leave the main road and ride across fields. His meetings with the dragon had never had to be clandestine before, but given the training involved using Heath's magic, and that was now an offense, they'd had to be a little more careful. Still, it wasn't a long ride, and by the time he arrived, the dragon was already there.

"I have some more questions about farsight," Heath said, as soon as the proper greetings were complete—Reka might be casual as dragons went, but even he wasn't immune to the creatures' love of formality. "How do you keep your concentration when things in your immediate surroundings distract you?"

Reka tilted his head to one side as he considered the question. "Dragons have superior minds, I suppose. It is not difficult for me to focus on more than one thing at once."

"That doesn't help me," said Heath dryly.

"Your focus will improve with practice," said Reka, unperturbed. "What were you trying to see at the time?"

"You." Heath grinned. "You were basking in the sun like a feline."

Reka nodded sagely, showing no sign of discomfort at the information that Heath had been watching him from afar.

"That was likely accurate. I frequently spend time that way."

Heath gave a small chuckle. "What was the purple in the rocks behind you?" he asked curiously.

Reka's eyes were sharp as they considered him. "It was indeed an accurate vision," he said.

Heath waited for the dragon to elaborate, or answer the question. He did neither.

"Do you wish to practice your farsight again?" Reka asked instead. "Or would you prefer to begin working on your other sight?"

"You mean my physical eyesight?" Heath asked, baffled. "How would you help me work on that?"

Reka shook his head in an unhurried fashion. "No, I mean your ability to see things in people that others do not see. Similar to the way your father senses deception."

"Oh." Heath considered it. "I do want to develop that, I suppose. But for the moment, I'm more interested in the farsight. Maybe I can only focus on one skill at a time."

"Highly likely," Reka agreed unflatteringly. "Close your eyes."

Resisting the urge to roll them first, Heath obeyed.

"What is foremost in your thoughts?" the dragon asked.

"Uh..."

Heath's mind flew to the conversation he'd had with Brody, Bianca, and Percival. Without him speaking aloud, his brother's image flashed before his sight, still reclined in Brody's sitting room. Heath scowled. He was sick of Percival being his first concern. He didn't want responsibility for keeping his brother from disaster.

"Reka," he said, opening his eyes and looking up at the dragon. "Are you watching me all the time?"

The dragon sighed. "I see your problem with focus. It is more acute than I had realized."

"No, seriously, Reka," Heath pressed. "Do you always watch me?"

"Far from it," the dragon said. "I occasionally check in on you. But I have other things to do with my time than watch your every move."

"Then how is it that you always hear me when I call for you?" Heath asked. "If you're not watching at the time, how do you know that I'm saying your name?"

Reka's eyes narrowed in thought, apparently searching for the best way to explain the matter to his human friend.

"I follow you with my thoughts," he said eventually. "Not all the time, but regularly. A connection has been forged between us, and it is always there, even if it is not always in use. When you call my name, it is as though you send something down that connection. It pulls my attention from whatever I am doing at the time, and redirects it to you."

"But how can I use the connection to send you a message if it's not in my control—if I'm not even aware of it?" Heath asked.

Reka shook his head slowly. "It is not about what you can do. It is about what I can do. And I can hear you over the connection I have created between us through targeted use of my farsight."

Heath thought this over. "So I could set up a connection like that if I chose?"

"Theoretically," Reka agreed. "Although of course we have no idea where the limits of your human version of farsight will fall."

Heath nodded.

"With whom do you wish to set up a connection?"

"Not Percival," Heath muttered, still disgruntled.

Reka tilted his head the other way. "If we are to list everyone you do *not* wish to forge a connection with, the exercise may be time consuming."

Heath let out a reluctant laugh, although he knew Reka wasn't actually trying to be funny. It was just in a dragon's nature to respond to things literally.

"We don't need to do that," he said gravely. "I have someone specific in mind."

"Well, start by attempting to watch this someone with your farsight," Reka urged.

Heath closed his eyes to increase his dubious focus. It was Merletta, of course. It was always Merletta. The weeks since they'd seen each other had been far too long. For a moment Heath forgot his task, lost not in visions of her current activity, but in the memory of their last meeting. She'd been about to undertake her dangerous second year test, and he'd been forced to leave her in haste in order to save Percival from his mysterious attackers.

But not before he'd done what he'd fantasized about for the better part of two years, when he took her in his arms and pressed his lips to hers. The kiss had been tantalizingly short, with too much of the flavor of an interrupted goodbye.

Not goodbye, he reminded himself. Merletta had survived her test—he'd caught more than one glimpse of her since then. And although Reka hadn't yet shown any inclination to take Heath back to Vazula to meet her, there was no reason the two of them couldn't be reunited soon.

Wrenching his mind from the memory of Merletta's arms snaking around his back, Heath tried to remember what he was supposed to be doing.

"Focus," Reka said, his voice a gravelly rumble.

Farsight. Heath squeezed his eyes shut, focusing on Merletta as Reka had taught him to do—not a memory of her, not a guess about her surroundings, but just *her*.

As it usually did when he was with Reka—his abilities enhanced by the presence of the dragon's magic—Heath's vision immediately changed. At once he could see Merletta, her image slightly murky in the way that indicated she was deep underwater.

He tried to push his sight outward to reveal her surroundings, as Reka had been training him to do, but he couldn't see much beyond the girl herself. She filled his sight just as she filled his thoughts, to the exclusion of anything else.

"Do you see her?" Reka's calm voice broke through Heath's focus, but the image remained clear. "I assume it is Merletta whom you wished to see."

"It is," Heath confirmed. "And yes, I can see her. She's..." He frowned, properly taking in her expression for the first time. "I think she's upset."

Again he tried to extend his bubble of sight, desperate for a glimpse of what was around her. She was swimming pretty quickly. Was someone pursuing her? Was she in danger?

"I can't see what's happening," he told Reka, frustrated. "I can't see much beyond her face."

"Your farsight is narrow," Reka responded. "But it will broaden. Try to see something else, other than Merletta."

Heath hesitated, reluctant to pull his vision away from Merletta when he still hadn't discovered the cause of her distress. He wanted to stay with her, to keep a finger on her pulse so to speak. But Reka was his only hope of properly developing his dragon-like magic. He knew he needed to listen to his friend's instruction.

Still, he couldn't bring himself to abandon Merletta altogether. She was too important, too central to his every thought. As he turned his mind away, he found himself leaving a strand of thought with her. He didn't know how to explain it, but it felt like the mental equivalent of leaving one finger on a certain page while rifling through the rest of a book. Her image seemed to shrink but not disappear, stashed in a corner of his sight.

Reka had told him to pick a different subject. What else would he like to see? Vazula leaped into his mind, and he tried to visualize the island. Nothing happened. Heath frowned, and Reka picked up on the expression.

"You are not succeeding?"

Heath shook his head. "I'm trying to see Vazula, but nothing's happening."

The dragon nodded. "Places are more difficult than people, remember. Bring to mind our lessons about targeting your farsight. It is not a matter of trying to picture the subject by its physical appearance. Doing that simply invites your imagination to supplant the farsight. It is about dwelling on the essence of the person or object or place. That is why it is much easier to use farsight on someone you care about, or are invested in."

Heath nodded. It was an explanation Reka had given before, and it helped explain why it was easy for Heath to see someone like Percival, or Merletta. Even Reka's power wasn't strong enough to see strangers he'd never met, which meant Heath's certainly never would be, no matter how much he trained. There were ways around it, though. If you could picture a place, you could see the people who were there. Which was why it was worth attempting to master the skill of seeing locations.

It was a challenge, though. Merletta was easy to pinpoint. Her essence felt more familiar than it logically should, given she wasn't even entirely human—on some level, Heath had felt a sense of kinship with her from the moment they'd set eyes on each other. But the island wasn't as simple. How did you focus on the essence of a place? Heath paused, thinking of what Vazula meant to him.

Freedom, he thought. It meant freedom from the restrictions and the responsibilities of his normal life. And it meant Merletta. The two were inextricably linked in his mind. Unbidden, the mermaid's image flashed before his eyes again, as if the small picture in the corner of his mind had suddenly increased to full size. She was wending her way through tall fronds of some kind of seaweed. Strange thing to find within a mermaid city, he would have thought.

He focused his mind back on the island. Vazula meant freedom and peace and adventure all at once, it was true. But those things were too general. He needed to be more specific. He kept his eyes closed, imagining that the crisp coolness of the autumn day had been replaced by the sticky warmth of Vazula's air. He dwelt on small details—the cries of gulls, the smell of the salt, the sight of a coconut bobbing in the shallows. The flash of pearlescent green as Merletta's legs turned into tail.

There it was. Vazula. The image was as clear as day in his mind, brighter and more colorful than his imagination could ever paint it. A stunning jewel—an emerald in the middle of a vast sapphire ocean. He could see it from a dragon's view, but as he leaned into the image, it descended, until he was looking right at the beach he knew so well. The trees at the sand's edge rustled, and he frowned at the movement, too big to be caused by wind. Was Merletta on the island after all? But he'd just seen her underwater.

Heath felt a flash of unease at the thought that someone or something foreign was on Vazula. The island had always been a safe haven, seeming to belong completely to him and Merletta, and—to a lesser extent—Reka. With the thought, the image cut off abruptly, the unfamiliar note seeming to dilute Heath's ability to connect with the place.

He sighed, opening his eyes to see Reka watching him closely.

"You used significant power," the dragon pointed out. "That seems to have been successful."

Heath nodded. "For the most part. Places are still difficult, though."

Reka's nod was as regal as any gesture of King Matlock's. "I used to find them so as well, when I was trained in the craft as a dragonling."

Heath hid a smile at the lofty tone of the dragon who, for his kind, was more like an adolescent than an adult.

"Maybe I should try another person," Heath mused. 'Something a bit easier."

Without waiting for Reka's response, Heath turned his mind to his sister, Laura. Her essence was easy to picture. Heath had sometimes wondered if his sister's cheerful nature was the result of her magic, or the other way around. She had the ability not only to sense others' emotions, but to cheer those emotions. Many a time she had lifted the mood of the family with an effortless strand of magic. Her presence had been sorely missed in the household once she'd married and moved away. Particularly when Percival began resenting the crown's growing uncertainty about the presence of magic in the kingdom.

As Heath dwelt on Laura as a person, her image popped immediately into his mind. She was draped across a fully made bed, in spite of the hour, her feet elevated. As Heath watched, a groan escaped her lips.

Are you all right, Laura? The voice of Edmund, Laura's husband, emerged from somewhere out of Heath's sight. *The servants told me you'd gone back to bed.*

Laura waved a dismissive hand. *They needn't have worried you. I'm fine. Just ready to have this gargantuan child out of my body.*

Edmund's chuckle wafted into the picture, and the man's lithe figure appeared as he seated himself beside his wife and ran a hand over her enormous stomach. It really was the largest pregnant belly Heath had ever seen. It was hard to believe the physicians could be right when they all assured the family there was only one baby in there.

Not long now, love.

Edmund's voice was tender, and Heath pulled back from the image abruptly. He felt a trickle of guilt at his spying, although there wasn't really anything objectionable in what he'd seen.

"How do you deal with the discomfort?" Heath asked Reka.

The dragon tilted his head in apparent confusion. "Discomfort? Is it hurting you to use your farsight?"

"No, I mean the emotional discomfort," Heath clarified. "The guilt—or if that's too strong, at least the unease—of spying on people you care about, without them being able to stop you, or even knowing you're doing it."

Reka gave a rippling shrug which made his scales tinkle. "I don't have that."

Heath rolled his eyes. "Of course you don't."

It was hardly the first time he'd encountered the reality that dragons had neither tact nor sensitivity when it came to human emotions.

"Whom did you watch that prompted such emotions?" Reka asked curiously.

"My sister," said Heath. "She's pregnant—very pregnant—and she was having a private conversation with her—"

Heath.

The word was so crystal clear in his mind that Heath cut himself off abruptly. That was Merletta's voice, surely. He knew it as well as his own. Her image emerged from the corner of his mind, rushing back to full clarity. But it was much more vivid than it had ever been before. His mind was suddenly flooded with awareness of her, from the tangle of her long, dark hair to the golden tips of her fins. She was upset, and lonely. And although she couldn't possibly know that he was practicing his farsight at that moment, and that he'd unknowingly established a connection between them—for he knew with sudden certainty that was what he'd done—she'd called for *him*.

I really need you right now.

"What is it?" Reka asked curiously, studying Heath with the fascination of a scholar poring over a text. "What caused that flare of power?"

"Merletta," said Heath eagerly. "It worked, Reka. The connection thing you talked about. She was hovering in the back of my mind all this time, and when she called for me just now, it somehow activated the connection."

"Interesting," said Reka, sounding pleased. "You are truly a rapid learner, Heath. At least for your kind. I did not expect you to successfully establish such a connection so quickly."

"Thank you," said Heath distractedly. "Now let's go."

"Go?" Reka repeated, sounding perplexed. "Go where?"

"To Vazula," said Heath, impatient with the dragon's unhurried manner. "She's heading there now, and she called for me. I know you have mixed emotions about visiting the island now, Reka, but this time I'm determined. We're going to Vazula."

CHAPTER FIVE

By the time Merletta reached the shallows near Vazula, she'd had time to rethink her rash decision to flee to the island. She'd been there yesterday, and would be returning the following day. It was foolish to abandon her plan of spending the rest day being seen as much as possible in the triple kingdoms. It was important she throw off anyone who might suspect her of leaving the barrier in her free time. Of course, she reflected grimly, more than enough people had seen her at Andre's celebration, unknowingly parading herself as more than his friend.

But it was that very humiliation which had driven her to the island. She didn't really expect to see Heath, but the next best thing was to be alone, somewhere she need have no fear of interruption. The trouble was, she'd remembered too late that Vazula no longer offered that relief. There were three others living there, who would want her help and attention the moment she arrived.

Well, she was there now. Nothing would be gained by turning around. At least August would be pleased with the news that his wife was coming the following day.

When Merletta beached herself deftly on the sand, barely noticing the tingling sensation that heralded the change from tail to legs, there was no sign of anyone. She wandered over to the makeshift shelter where the three guards usually slept, and found that deserted, too. She released a long breath, pleased with her good fortune. It seemed they were out hunting, and she would be granted some solitude after all.

She decided to leave the beach, walking with sure steps to the lagoon where she'd first met Heath. It was a pleasant place to sit and think, without staring at the ocean and being reminded of all the challenges and danger and embarrassment that awaited her within it.

Merletta settled herself on one of the flat rocks near the lagoon's edge, her arms wrapped around one knee as the other leg dangled in the cool water. She closed her eyes, trying not to think but just to be. Her leg swayed with the lapping waves, and she felt the elusive peace settle over her.

She loved this place. Straddling the line of land and sea, far away from the expectations and lies of the Center, she felt like she was her full self, every part of her combined into one state of being.

The familiar rushing sound snapped her from her thoughts, and her head jerked upward, eyes searching the sky as she hardly dared to hope. Surely not. Could he really be coming, after all this time?

Her answer came in the form of a large, winged shape, which descended and deposited a windswept but beaming young man on the rocks beside her. Merletta hadn't even had the chance to greet Rekavidur before he once again took to the sky, continuing his recent habit of ignoring her.

She leaped to her feet, already dismissing the dragon from her mind as she stepped toward Heath. He beat her to it, covering the short distance between them in a few swift strides, his eyes searching her form as if checking she was unharmed and fully accounted for.

The memory of their last meeting surged into Merletta's mind, and she half expected Heath to take her in his arms and pick up right where they'd left off when Reka interrupted them weeks ago. Instead he gripped her upper arm in apparent relief, his gaze warm and intimate as it rested on her face.

"Merletta," he said, a smile curling his lips. "It seems my visions were accurate—you did survive your test."

Merletta laughed. "I didn't just survive. I passed. *And* managed to evade the armed guards waiting to murder me when I emerged."

"What?" Heath's already pale face seemed to drain of color, and his grip on her arm tightened.

"I had help with that," Merletta amended, matter-of-factly. "If August and the others hadn't intervened, I have no idea what would have happened." She saw his bafflement, and shook her head. "But of course, you don't even know about them surviving, do you?"

"Tell me everything," Heath said, his eyes intense as they searched hers. As always, he gave her the impression that she had his full attention, like nothing in all the world was more important to him than her and whatever she wanted to say.

Impulsively, Merletta tipped herself forward, her arms going around Heath's waist as she buried her face in his tunic.

"I've missed you," she whispered.

Heath froze for a moment, then his arms went around her as well, holding her in a grip that made her feel more secure than she had in weeks. Not for the first time, she knew a fleeting wish that she could stay here forever, on Vazula with no one but Heath, safe and removed from all the struggles of her underwater life.

"I've missed you as well." Heath's voice, low and throaty,

interrupted her thoughts. "More than you can imagine. I've tried to watch you, but it often doesn't work. I'm still learning to use my farsight."

"Farsight?" Merletta pulled back, her heart lighter as she looked up at him. "Is that what your extra vision is called?"

Heath shrugged. "It's what the dragons call their extra vision, and Reka seems to think mine is a version of the same thing." His eyes twinkled at her. "Albeit a much less potent version, as he likes to remind me frequently."

Merletta laughed, the sound enveloping them in the muffled stillness of the lagoon.

"I'm so glad you're here," she said softly. "It's...it's like magic. I desperately needed a friend, and I wished I could talk to you. But I didn't really think you'd be here. It's like you came in response to my call."

"I did," said Heath simply.

Merletta stared at him. "What do you mean?"

"It's a little hard to explain," Heath said, a touch evasively. "But I was using my farsight—training with Reka, actually—and I heard you call me. So I came."

Merletta was still staring, not sure how to respond.

"Thank you," she said at last. "For...for coming."

"If it's in my power, I'll always come for you, Merletta," Heath said.

When Merletta still didn't respond—too overwhelmed to put her thoughts into words—Heath cleared his throat, a hint of sternness creeping into his voice.

"But don't change the topic. You were about to tell me all about your test."

Merletta nodded, taking his hand and tugging him back to where she'd been sitting. He offered no resistance, apparently quite happy to let her drag him along and pull him down as she once again sat. She dangled her legs in the water, and Heath did the same, pausing only to remove his boots.

"Your feet are much bigger than mine," Merletta commented, her eyes passing between the two pairs.

"Well, I am two years older than you," Heath pointed out.

"I'm about to turn eighteen, Heath," Merletta laughed. "I don't think I'm going to grow much more."

Heath smiled, running a hand idly through the clear water. "Men's feet are often bigger than women's," he acknowledged. "It's like our hands, look."

He held a hand up, and Merletta pressed one of hers against it, palm to palm. He was right, of course—his fingers extended much further up than hers. For a moment she stayed pressed there, enjoying the combined warmth of their skin, so different from the cool touch of merpeople when in their underwater form. The air seemed suddenly even thicker than normal for Vazula, and her heart picked up speed. Surely Heath felt it, too, the connection between them.

All at once her mind flew to the humiliation of the morning, and her discovery that she'd accidentally announced to who knew how many strangers that she and Andre were a couple. She pulled her hand away quickly, her eyes shifting to the water before her as her cheeks heated.

"I know that, of course," she admitted. "Mermen usually have bigger hands than mermaids, too."

Understandably, Heath disregarded this uninteresting comment, his tone becoming a little businesslike.

"Tell me what's happened since I last saw you, Merletta."

Merletta let out a gusty sigh that was much too intense, the exhale carrying enough force to expel water rather than air.

"So much has happened," she said frankly. "My test was chaos, to be honest. I had to follow this trail left by trainees from the past, and like a fool, I got distracted by a pod of dolphins, then ended up running afoul of killer whales." She shuddered. "I even got stung by a jellyfish hiding from the whales. Then the trail took me down into this chasm, where I only just dodged a giant squid and made it into the tiny tunnel. But the tunnel led to the maelstrom, which was almost more deadly than all the rest!" She shook her head. "I made it to the middle, and added my name. But I was grabbed before I could take the clue left there for me."

"Grabbed?" Heath repeated, clearly alarmed by her matter-of-fact description of the sequence of disasters.

She nodded. "It wasn't actually an enemy, though. It was August and the others."

Relishing the chance to speak freely, she took her time, explaining about the surviving guards, and how they'd intervened when they saw Center guards waiting to kill her outside the maelstrom.

He was so interested, she couldn't resist going into more detail about the challenges she'd had to complete, and the dangers she'd faced. He was an attentive listener. He had no need of words to communicate that he had nowhere else he wished to be, and nothing on his mind but their conversation.

Merletta became animated as she spoke, gesturing with her hands as she described some of the test's more dramatic events. As she recounted the heart-stopping moment when she'd dived into a small hole to escape the giant squid, she shifted forward so far on her rock that her hips became submerged, triggering the change from legs to tail mid-sentence.

Unperturbed, she continued with her story, flicking her fins for emphasis, until Heath's laughter interrupted her tale.

"What?" she demanded, a little disgruntled.

"Sorry," Heath chuckled. "It just seemed like you didn't even notice that half your body just transformed."

"It's a pretty familiar sensation by now," Merletta told him.

She followed his gaze, which was fixed on her shimmering scales. "Would you prefer me to change back?"

"Of course not," said Heath comfortably. "It makes no difference to me—you're still you."

Smiling to herself, Merletta slipped the rest of the way into the water, twisting around so that her elbows rested on the rock, and the water held her weight. She continued her account, ending with the dramatic explanation of the guards' survival and timely intervention in her test.

"And now I'm a third year," she finished, letting out a sigh.

"Shouldn't that be a triumphant declaration?" Heath quizzed her. "Why do you sound depressed?"

Merletta laughed ruefully. "I'm glad I passed the test, of course. But Ibsen is the primary instructor for third year, and I'm not looking forward to more time with him. Plus, I have plenty of challenges to grapple with, even before classes start." She grimaced.

"Like what?" Heath pressed.

"Well, for one thing, the guards who survived, and who rescued me after my test..." Merletta shot him a sideways look, wondering how he'd feel about the violation of their island sanctuary. "Well, I brought them here, and showed them the truth about drying out. They sort of live here now."

"They do?" Heath started and looked around, as if expecting to see the three mermen-turned-humans standing right behind them, waiting for their introduction. "Where are they?"

"Out hunting, I assume," Merletta said. "In the ocean, that is."

Heath looked a little rattled by the revelation of the guards' presence, but he made no comment on it.

"That's not what's weighing you down," he said instead. "When I saw you earlier, back in your underwater city, you looked upset."

Merletta plucked a leaf off the surface of the lagoon and twirled it between her fingers, not meeting Heath's eyes.

"It's nothing," she said uncomfortably.

"It isn't." Heath's reply was forceful, but after a moment of silence, his voice softened. "If you can't tell me, Merletta, who can you tell?"

She let out a shaky laugh. "No one, I guess," she acknowledged, turning a rueful smile on him. "I was just thinking about my family. Or rather, my lack of family."

Heath searched her eyes, his expression sympathetic. "You've always seemed incredibly resilient about growing up without parents," he said. "But you are allowed to be upset about it, you know."

Merletta's laugh was hollow. "Being upset about it never did anyone any good at the charity home."

"But you're not at the home now," Heath said. "You're with me. I'm not looking for a way to get the upper hand over you. You're safe."

Merletta was silent for a moment. She'd forgotten just how much she'd told Heath about life at the charity home. His words meant more than he could imagine, but if she was going to get through the explanation he'd asked for, she couldn't afford to get sentimental before she even started.

"I honestly didn't think I minded about being an orphan when I started the program," she told him. "I was used to it, and I think I felt that my disadvantages made me tougher, and harder to subdue. And they did. But that was when I still saw myself as an outsider. Now I have friends at the Center, and I wish..." She swallowed, finding it hard to admit her thoughts, even to herself. "Well, I wish I *could* be part of the world they live in. I wish I could have a place there."

"You do have a place there," Heath protested. "One you've fought very hard to achieve, and should never be ashamed to claim." When she didn't answer, he frowned. "Did something happen, Merletta?"

"I just put my fins in it, that's all," Merletta said, trying to speak lightly. "Even though I've been staying with Sage's family for three weeks, I didn't understand the culture in Skulssted, and I made a rather humiliating blunder this morning." She groaned softly. "Poor Andre."

"Andre? What does he have to do with it?"

Merletta grimaced. "I sort of accidentally asked him to ask me to be his sweetheart."

"What?!" Heath started visibly, his throat bobbing as he swallowed. "I mean...how did...what does that mean?"

Merletta cringed all over again at the memory. "It means I'm an uncultured Tilssted-dweller, that's all. Andre isn't interested in me that way, any more than I am in him. I didn't realize that's what I was asking, and he was too chivalrous to explain it, or reject me outright."

"Chivalrous, is he? Which one is Andre, again?" Heath's voice was much too casual.

Merletta chuckled, her mortification softened by her amusement at Heath's obvious alarm. "You seem a little put out, Heath," she commented innocently.

He narrowed his eyes, clearly sensing that she was teasing him. But when he spoke, his voice was perfectly serious.

"I am put out. I don't like the idea of Andre asking you to be his sweetheart. I thought...well, I thought maybe...someone else had that role."

"Does someone else want it?" Merletta asked quietly, her heart picking up speed again.

Heath shifted forward, leaning down so that his elbows rested on his knees, and his face wasn't far above Merletta's.

"Do you really need me to answer that? Maybe I dreamed what happened last time we spoke?"

Merletta leaned up, straightening her arms so that she lifted further out of the water. Heath's eyes were drawn to the movement, his gaze following a droplet as it ran down her arm and into the lagoon. Then his eyes traveled slowly back to her face, and the look in their depths sent heat racing through her.

"I've sometimes wondered if it was a dream," she said, her voice not much above a whisper. "But it certainly felt real to me."

Slowly, lingeringly, Heath lifted his hand and touched a thumb to her cheek. His touch was like the searing heat of a thermal vent. It had been intoxicating when he'd held her in his arms the last time. But on that occasion, she'd been on land, walking on her legs. This time she was in her mermaid form, and the combination of Heath's warm human skin and the chill that came inevitably with her scales was electrifying. Surely it hadn't been like this every time their hands had casually brushed back when they first knew each other, before she'd discovered the truth about drying out.

But back then, Heath hadn't been to her what he was now.

Everything. He was everything.

With his eyes holding hers, and his hand still on her cheek, she lost herself completely, sure in that instant that she could—and gladly would—turn her tail on the triple kingdoms and swim away forever. Let someone else worry about the corruption, and the lies, and the danger.

She pushed herself up on her hands, and Heath responded immediately, leaning down toward her, his eyes on her lips. A thrill went over her at the knowledge that he didn't even care that she was in mermaid form. He wanted to be with her, exactly as she was. She closed her own eyes in anticipation, feeling the warmth of Heath's breath the moment before their lips brushed.

"Merletta?"

The astonished voice broke into Merletta's moment of abandon, and she pulled back, her eyes flying open. Griffin was standing near the lagoon's edge, his eyes wide and—strangely— a little angry as they darted between her and Heath.

"Griffin," she gasped. "I didn't realize you were on the island."

"Evidently." Griffin sounded disapproving, his eyes settling again on Heath.

Merletta looked at Heath as well. Although he met her eyes, his breath was a little uneven, and he didn't seem quite his usual collected self. The promise of the abortive kiss hung in the air between them, and with Griffin clearly inclined to hover, there was no hope of clearing it.

"I'm Heath." Heath rose to his feet, extending a hand toward Griffin. "I assume you're one of the guards Merletta has told me about."

"Yes, this is Griffin," said Merletta quickly. "He's one of the survivors from August's patrol."

Griffin didn't take Heath's hand, instead narrowing his eyes at the other man. "You look familiar," he informed Heath. He glanced at Merletta. "I didn't realize you were planning to bring any of your friends here as well. From the Center, is he?"

Merletta looked between them, realizing Griffin's mistake. "Oh, no, he's not from the triple kingdoms," she explained. "He's a human. He's the human—the one you know about."

"I probably seem familiar from the time you speared me," Heath interjected. He'd dropped his rejected hand, and wasn't speaking in his normal voice. "Or one of your patrol, anyway. I don't remember the details. I was a little distracted bleeding out."

"It was Larson," said Griffin, no hint of apology in his voice. "He's dead now. Along with Arlene."

There was a moment of uncomfortable silence, and then Heath's stiffness fell away like a garment.

"I'm sorry," he said quietly. "Neither of them deserved that."

"No, they didn't," said Griffin coldly. "And none of us deserve the danger you put us in by showing up here like it's nothing, least of all Merletta."

"Griffin!" Merletta protested, astonished. "That's so far out of line, it's absurd!"

"Sounds like I need to *get* in line," Heath muttered.

"What?" Merletta turned to him, confused, but he just sent her a tight smile.

"Never mind. It's probably time for me to go, anyway. I'll be back when I can."

"I wish we had more time," Merletta told him, lowering her voice and angling her body away from Griffin in a gesture of protest. "I just talked and talked, and never even asked you what's happening in your world. I assume your brother survived whatever the threat was, since you haven't mentioned his untimely death."

There wasn't much joy in Heath's smile. "Yes, he's fine. Just turning my hair gray."

Merletta chuckled, reaching up to playfully tug on a wayward tuft. "Not that I can see."

Griffin shifted pointedly, and she dropped her hand, irritated.

"We'll talk again soon," Heath promised. "Just stay safe in the meantime, all right?"

Merletta nodded, a lump in her throat at the abrupt change from near declaration to goodbye.

Heath stepped closer, pulling her into a quick embrace and dropping his voice to a whisper. "And don't doubt that you're worth more to me than every titled, over-important family in your world or mine, even if you don't know your parents' names."

Merletta couldn't help smiling up at him, her heart giving

one more erratic jump. "Actually," she told him, "I might know their names after all. I guess I didn't tell you that bit about the test."

Heath stepped back, raising his eyebrows in amazement. But Griffin was still hovering tactlessly, and Merletta shook her head.

"Later."

Heath nodded, turning his eyes to the jungle. "I'd better call Reka."

"You brought another human with you?" Griffin interjected, his frown even more pronounced. "Why not just announce the location of this island in your city's central square?"

Heath raised an eyebrow at the irate merman, looking for once like the son of a duke that he was. "Actually, Reka isn't a—"

"Isn't a very sociable individual," Merletta cut across his words hurriedly. "So he's not going to bother us." She caught Heath's eye and shook her head infinitesimally.

Heath frowned slightly, but subsided without commenting on her decision not to tell the guards about the involvement of a dragon.

"Until next time, then," he said instead.

And with nothing more than a lingering look, he plunged into the jungle and out of sight.

CHAPTER SIX

Merletta

Late the following afternoon, Merletta found herself swimming the familiar route from the island back to the triple kingdoms for the third time in as many days. Except this time she wasn't traveling alone.

Merletta glanced at the older mermaid swimming beside her. Eloise moved with a quiet grace that Merletta couldn't help but admire, even in the midst of utter turmoil in her personal life. She made no sound as she cut through the water.

"Are you all right?" Merletta asked quietly.

She knew they were nearing the uncultivated kelp forests just outside the barrier, and soon would be unable to speak freely.

Eloise turned a wan smile on her companion. "All right?" she repeated. "August is alive. I feel like I am again, too. It's just a lot to take in."

Merletta returned her smile. "You certainly took the news about drying out more calmly than any of the others did." It was true, although Eloise had opted not to make the transition herself on the occasion. Merletta didn't blame her. Eloise had enough else to focus on.

Eloise gave a faint chuckle. "I was as floored as anyone, I'm sure. I just know how to keep my emotions inside."

Merletta sighed. "Perhaps you could give me lessons."

The other mermaid gave her a shrewd look. "I don't think I should. Your strength isn't in hiding. From the little I've seen of you, I wouldn't be surprised if you're the one who actually brings the lies to light. And you won't do that by swallowing your reactions."

Merletta was silent for a moment, a little stunned by Eloise's faith in her.

"If I achieve anything of that nature," she said at last, "it won't be by myself. I wouldn't even be alive now if not for my friends, and August's patrol, let alone have all the information I do."

Eloise gave an approving nod. "Wise words. I'm glad you know you need help. None of this should be taken on lightly."

"I assume you're glad I brought you into the secret, though?" Merletta asked, confident of her answer.

"Do you need to ask?" Eloise responded, the hint of a scoff in her voice.

Merletta didn't, of course. She'd witnessed the reunion of husband and wife, and she had no doubt Eloise was willing to take whatever risks came with knowing August was alive.

"You can count me an ally, Merletta," said Eloise seriously. "I don't have much influence, and I don't know how much help I can be to you. But if you need help, come to me, and I'll try."

"Thank you," said Merletta earnestly.

She barely knew Eloise, but she still felt a weight lift from her shoulders. She was enormously grateful for the support of Sage, Emil, and Andre. But they were all similar in age to her. Having someone older—the age of a parent—whom she could trust was something she didn't take lightly.

"I don't think it's wise for us to be seen together publicly, though," Merletta added. "The last thing I want is for someone to figure out that August and the others are alive, and to go looking for them. The island really isn't that far away."

"I agree," said Eloise briskly. She flashed a sudden smile at Merletta. "And I'm grateful to you for being the one to say it. I didn't want to seem to be abandoning you, but—"

Merletta shook her head. "No, I understand completely. It's safer for both of us this way. In light of which, we need to be extra careful as we pass back through the barrier. Maybe we should go separately? Are you confident you can get past the patrols?"

Eloise gave a grim smile. "I've been married to a guard for thirty years. I know a thing or two about how they operate."

Merletta chuckled. "I'll go in at the city's northernmost point, then. Perhaps you should skirt around to the west, enter closer to home."

Eloise nodded. "Until next time, then, Merletta."

And with a powerful swish of her tail, she disappeared silently into the gloom.

Merletta turned her face southward, drawing in a deep pull of water. She was glad to have the hurdle of safely taking Eloise to Vazula and back behind her. And even more glad that Eloise had offered to take on the role of communicating the guards' survival to the families of Paul and Griffin, using her judgment as to who should be told what. They had all agreed not to share the information about drying out just yet, however. For now, the bare fact of the missing guards' survival would have to be enough.

Merletta felt a twinge of guilt as she thought of her friends. In spite of her lofty words about it being unfair to keep Andre in the dark about August's fate, she still hadn't told any of them the truth about drying out, not even Sage. She'd wondered if Emil might already know, given he was a record holder now. But she'd never confirmed it.

She would need to fill them in, but she wasn't sure how to do it without them thinking she'd lost her mind. It had been simple with the guards. She hadn't told them anything—she'd just showed them. But when she'd tentatively suggested that Sage might like to join her at the island, Sage had been hesitant enough for Merletta to drop the matter for the time being.

Focused on avoiding any nearby guard patrol, Merletta wasn't paying close attention to the landmarks. Consequently, she didn't realize until she'd crossed the barrier just how close she was to the neighborhood where she'd grown up. She felt a strange sense of nostalgia as she swam through the kelp farms. So many times she'd snuck in and out that way, back when she lived at the charity home. She'd clung to her private rebellion then, as the only way to gain a measure of control in the limited and restrictive world in which she lived.

Well, her world had expanded exponentially since then. And, perhaps inevitably, so had her rebellion.

The thought brought a grim sort of humor, and she pictured the scandalized face of the mermaid who ran the charity home if she knew that Merletta had become the head of a secret resistance operating from within the Center. Most likely she'd mainly just be offended that her own efforts had failed so dismally to subdue Merletta's rule breaking.

With nowhere to be—she still had almost a week of her break, and Sage's family wouldn't be expecting her for dinner for another hour—she directed her strokes toward her old waters. Her thoughts floated uncomfortably toward the record she'd found in the center of the maelstrom.

Elminia and Elric, Hemssted.

Merletta recalled the head at the home telling her that she had no memory of the names of Merletta's parents, when she'd challenged her during her first year at the program. Merletta had no idea whether that had been another of the head's lies, or whether she truly didn't know. But someone knew. Someone with access to Merletta's second year test. Which meant it was someone at the Center.

She was determined to search for more information about those names, but it seemed fraught with danger to try to follow the trail from her test back to whatever upper echelon of the Center's hierarchy had been behind the stunt. Perhaps she would do better to start asking questions in Hemssted.

She wrinkled her nose, still predisposed to think poorly of the city, given how unpleasant most of the Hemssted trainees seemed to be. It was unpalatable to think she might be one of them by birth.

Either way, she was unlikely to find any answers at the charity home, or elsewhere within Tilssted. She'd come within sight of the familiar building now, and she hovered for a moment, letting the current lift her. She'd been so glad to say goodbye to the place, ready to prove everyone in it wrong about her, and their sneering certainty that she would never make it in the Center's training program.

Well, they'd been right about one thing, as it turned out. She'd certainly had a lot to learn.

Putting the unwelcome memories from her mind, Merletta turned away, starting at the unexpected sight of a familiar face.

"Tish," she said, pulling up short.

"Merletta!" Tish was clearly equally surprised to see her.

For a moment they just stared at each other, the awkwardness of their last encounter disseminating through the water between them.

"Merletta?"

The somewhat abrasive voice pulled Merletta's attention to

Tish's companion. She hadn't initially even noticed the mermaid floating next to Tish.

"You're the Tilssted trainee, the one who grew up in the charity home with Letitia?"

"Uh, yes," said Merletta lamely. "I'm...that's me."

The other mermaid looked her over. "Scrawnier than I expected."

Merletta felt a flicker of amusement. She glanced at Tish, hoping to share the joke, and earned a slightly strained smile.

"I work at the same shellsmith's tower as Letitia," the other mermaid informed Merletta, extending a hand. "I've heard about you, of course. Shame I wasn't there the day you came to visit."

Merletta shook the offered hand, looking her over. Scrawny was certainly not a description that would ever be applied to this girl. Her muscled arms were twice as thick as Tish's, and she was tall, her fins almost scraping the ocean floor below them.

"I know, I don't look like a shellsmith," the other mermaid said bluntly. "My pa is still angry about the apprenticeship. He says I was built for real labor, not fussy carving and whatnot. But I didn't fancy a life on the kelp farms. Especially not now."

"Not now?" Merletta asked, frowning.

"Let's not get into politics," Tish interjected quickly. She smiled tentatively at Merletta. "It's good to see you, Mer. What brings you to these waters?"

"Sentiment," Merletta told her cheekily.

Tish gave her a look. "It may have been a while, but I think I still know you better than that."

The other mermaid let out a guffaw. "Not much sentiment hangs around charity homes, from what I've heard." She cast an expert eye over Merletta's person. "You need new shells. You've outgrown those."

Merletta glanced down at her Center-issue shells, a little

taken aback by the blunt observation. "It's all right, I can make do."

"Make do?" The other apprentice's voice had a booming quality that was attracting interest from passersby. "Aren't you a Center trainee? You shouldn't have to make do." She jerked her chin toward Merletta's chest. "Those shells are for a girl, not a full grown mermaid. How old are you?"

Merletta cleared her throat, lowering her voice partly out of self-consciousness at the candid discussion of her body's development, and partly out of deference for Tish's obvious discomfort at the attention they were gathering.

"I'll be eighteen in a few days."

"Definitely time for an upgrade," the other mermaid said. "Isn't it part of your uniform, as a trainee?"

Merletta shrugged. "I think it's supposed to be, but..."

"But what?" The apprentice gave her a shrewd look. "They're not in a rush to meet all their obligations with the trainee from Tilssted?"

"Well..."

Merletta hesitated, but why should she cover for the Center? It was perfectly true that those in charge of the program had not only failed to provide her with the education and resources she was entitled to as a trainee, but they'd often gone out of their way to make it difficult for her to succeed.

"That's it in a clamshell, yes," she said frankly. "I doubt I'll be offered a new uniform anytime soon."

"We can't have that," said the apprentice bossily. "You're one of us, and you're the *only* one of us who's one of them. It won't do for you to look like less. I can hook you up." She narrowed her eyes as she took in Merletta's form again. "I reckon I've got a pair waiting for processing right now that would fit perfectly."

"That's very kind," said Merletta quickly. "But I don't think I could wear them. They have to match the rest of the trainees' shells, and—"

The other girl cut her off with a laugh. "Bless you, love, who do you think supplies the shells for the Center, and the other fancy folk in Skulssted and Hemssted? I know what type of shells you need, don't fret."

"Again, I appreciate the offer," Merletta tried. "But I don't have any means to pay for it, to be honest."

"Don't worry about that," said the apprentice. "For you, no charge at all."

"Well...all right," said Merletta, feeling a little dazed by the force of the other girl's personality. Was this how Tish had always felt with her? "Thank you, then. When should I come back to get them?"

"I'll get started on them tonight," said the girl. "Come by the tower in three or four days."

"I'll come on rest day," Merletta said. She cast a glance at Tish, suddenly remembering that she'd expressed a desire to distance herself from her now highly visible childhood friend. "I mean, if that's all right."

"Of course it is." Tish smiled, but the expression didn't reach her eyes.

Merletta squirmed a little at the awkwardness of it all—it was so hard to believe that things had really come to such a point with *Tish*, once the only one she felt comfortable with—but she couldn't really back out now.

"Great," she said half-heartedly. "You never told me what you're doing here, by the way. Your work tower isn't around here."

"We were visiting the home, actually," Tish said.

Merletta's thoughts must have shown, because the other apprentice jumped in again.

"I can see you're surprised, and I don't blame you. If I hadn't just seen it with my own eyes, I would never have believed any place could be so cheerless! Bunch of crusty crabs. If I'd grown up there, I doubt I'd want back in anytime soon. But it makes me all the more supportive of Letitia's idea. She's trying to set up a sponsor program where apprentices like us can help some of the older beneficiaries find their way into apprenticeships. Good thought, if you ask me."

"A brilliant thought," said Merletta, both surprised and impressed as her eyes rested on Tish.

The other mermaid had always had a kind heart, but Merletta had never known her friend to show such initiative before.

"Maybe you could take part," said the other apprentice eagerly. "Come and speak about the training program, explain the pathway to get in and such like."

Merletta bit her lip. She had a strong feeling that idea would not be sanctioned by her instructors, and if she even considered it, she'd have to be very careful what she said, given that most of the training program was supposed to be highly confidential.

"I'll give it some thought," she said noncommittally.

"Good," the other girl said. "We can talk more about it when you come to get your shells. You know how to find the tower?"

Merletta nodded.

"Good, good," said the apprentice. Her voice darkened. "Assuming we're still there, and haven't been knocked down."

"What do you mean?" Merletta asked, alarmed.

"Nothing," said Tish soothingly. "She's exaggerating."

"Am I, though?" her companion said grimly. "These territorial disputes are getting out of hand. I know of at least two apprentice towers that have been leveled."

"They were closer to the barrier, though," Tish said. "And closer to the border with Hemssted. We'll be fine."

"That's what it is, of course," the other girl nodded. "The risk is being too close to one of the other cities, where they can get ideas about claiming our bedrock."

"Are they really clearing towers?" Merletta asked, aghast. "Just knocking them down?"

The apprentice nodded again. "The demolition of my friend's apprentice tower was overseen by armed Center guards, from what I heard. To make sure none of us Tilssted scum tried to intervene in the theft of our territory. They're building homes on the spot now. For rich folk from Hemssted."

"Hardly rich, if they have to live so close to Tilssted," Tish muttered.

Merletta raised an eyebrow. If even gentle Tish was making snide remarks, things must be bad.

"I knew they were building a new row of dwellings in the inner ring of the farms," she said. "But I didn't realize they were actually destroying Tilssted buildings to make way for residents from other cities. They must realize Tilssted won't put up with that."

"By farms, you mean just the kelp farms, right?" the other girl said. Her voice turned dry. "Unless they're having similar troubles at the oyster farms, and I just haven't heard about it."

Merletta's own tone was grim. "I don't think so, somehow." Her frown deepened. "This is all so ridiculous, the inward expansion. There's so much ocean out there. Why do we have to live on top of each other?"

"Who'd be willing to live out in the open ocean, though?" the apprentice said skeptically. "At the mercy of all the dangerous creatures and the currents and the risk of land sickness and all."

"I would," said Merletta dryly, her mind not really on her words.

"Would you really?"

The change in the other girl's tone made Merletta look up,

realizing what she'd carelessly said. She could see the surprise in the mermaid's eyes, but there was something else, too. Something Merletta recognized painfully well.

Hope—for the intoxicating image of a better life than the one she'd been told to resign herself to.

Tish shifted uncomfortably beside her fellow apprentice, and Merletta reminded herself that it wasn't the time or place to campaign for a change in the Center's strict prohibition on outward expansion. But still, she wasn't going to lie, and in so doing further the Center's fear-mongering.

"With the right planning and protection, I'd be willing to risk it," she said, trying to speak casually, as if her words were no big deal. "And I doubt I'm the only one. But that's a discussion that's over my head."

She didn't give the other girl a chance to question her further, instead nodding a brisk farewell.

"It was nice to meet you," she told the apprentice, her eyes traveling to Tish. "And good to see you again, Tish."

"Take care of yourself, Merletta," Tish said quietly, still looking tense.

With a nod, Merletta propelled herself through the water, heading southwest toward Skulssted.

By the time her first day of classes was finished, Merletta was heartily glad that her break had fallen such that she only had to endure one day of Ibsen's classes before Agner's two training days. She'd thought the history instructor was obstructive before, but his current attitude made his previous behavior seem almost kindly in her memory. He made no attempt to hide his displeasure that Merletta had proceeded to third year, over which he was the primary instructor.

"The role of educator," he said tartly on her first day back, his eyes as sharp as an urchin's spines, "is a position of great trust and honor. It is only awarded to the most exceptional of trainees."

His meaning was clear. It would not be awarded to Merletta if he had any say in the matter. Merletta met his gaze grimly, undaunted. He'd been actively working against her training since she began the program, and so far, he hadn't managed to prevent her from passing both first and second years. She had no intention of failing third year, either.

"Educators are responsible for the dissemination of our records to the populace of the triple kingdoms," Ibsen continued, clearly resentful of the need to waste his time on what appeared to be a set introduction to the topic, when Merletta was the only third year currently in the program. "Those duties involve the curation of records, and the distribution of information."

"The educators give records to the general population?" Merletta asked, surprised. She'd certainly never been offered anything of the kind when she lived in Tilssted.

Ibsen's tail flicked in irritation, as it always did when Merletta dared to ask a question. After a moment, he answered her, however.

"Sometimes physical records are distributed. More frequently information is shared verbally."

"So it's very important that the educators have the correct information, then, I suppose," said Merletta innocently. "And remember it accurately."

Ibsen's eyes narrowed as he studied her. "Indeed."

As soon as he turned away, Sage shot Merletta a warning look, and she subsided, raising one hand slightly in a gesture of surrender. She wasn't sure there was much point pretending to play along with Ibsen, though. It wasn't as though anything she did or said would change the hatred he had for her.

When the small group of trainees met for their combat lesson early the next morning, Andre floated up beside Merletta.

"Ibsen was really on the warpath yesterday, wasn't he?"

Merletta shrugged. "Is that any different from normal?"

"Seemed worse than last year to me," Andre commented. "You're going to need to be careful." He hesitated. "Sage told me it was your birthday a few days ago."

Merletta nodded. "That's right."

"Happy birthday," he said. "Eighteen is a big deal. I wish you'd told us."

"Why?" Merletta asked, surprised. "I don't have a home or a family to host a celebration, so there didn't seem much point."

"We could have had our own small celebration," Andre insisted.

"That's what I said," Sage chimed in. "But she didn't want to make a fuss."

"That's your job, isn't it?" The snide comment came from Lorraine as she drifted past, her eyes fixed on Andre.

"Oh, shut your clam hole, Lorraine," Andre said tartly.

He didn't seem especially bothered by his fellow second year's words, but Merletta felt her face heating at the reminder of her misstep regarding Andre's birthday celebration. Clearly the gossip had spread to Lorraine, which meant it was probably all over the Center.

"About that, Andre," she started awkwardly.

"No need to say a word," he told her firmly. "You did nothing wrong, and I didn't read anything into your request which wasn't there." His voice took on a scolding tone. "You shouldn't have swum off like that when the event had barely begun."

Merletta shrugged. "I'd done what I came to do."

"And?" Andre's eyes had become keen.

Merletta nodded curtly. "Successful communication. And…" She lowered her voice. "Successful outing the following day."

Andre looked more eager than ever, but Sage made a warning noise. Merletta looked up to see Oliver swimming past nearby, and they dropped the topic.

"Trainees!" Agner's cheerful voice carried across the square, and they all turned to see the older merman swimming toward them. "Everyone ready to fight? Merletta, welcome back. Good break?" He didn't wait for a response, rubbing his hands together as he looked at the group at large. "Excellent, excellent. We'll start you right off against Oliver, I think."

When the group broke for lunch—Merletta bruised but satisfied by her efforts, given she'd actually won a bout against Oliver for the first time—Agner signaled to Merletta to approach him. Sage and Andre cast her curious glances as they swam out of the training yard, but Oliver didn't even look back, evidently still disgruntled about his loss.

"Is everything all right, Instructor?" Merletta asked.

Agner nodded. "You did well this morning. I'm glad to see you've stayed in shape over your break." He considered her for a moment, as she waited for him to get to the point. "This year will be different for you, Merletta. Physical training isn't the focus—which means I can't help you as much as I did last year."

Merletta nodded. "I understand. Instructor Ibsen is my main instructor for third year."

Agner raised an eyebrow, and Merletta grimaced, silently acknowledging the unspoken words about the likelihood of Ibsen actually teaching her anything.

"Third year isn't an easy year to pass," Agner said. "It's not too late to change your mind, you know. You could stop here, claim a place in the guards. We'd welcome you readily."

"Thanks, Instructor," Merletta said firmly. "But I'm determined to continue."

Agner sighed. "All right," he said, his voice dropping to a mutter. "On your head be it."

Merletta frowned, debating whether to push him to explain his words. But if he had something he was willing to say, he'd say it without prompting. And she had no such expectation. Agner might not be her enemy. But that didn't mean he was her ally.

CHAPTER SEVEN

Merletta wasn't planning to go the island on her first rest day, so she slept in a little, making her leisurely way to breakfast later than usual.

Sage and Andre were both already there, snatching a bite before heading to their own homes for the day off.

"How's your tail?" Andre asked around a mouthful of mussel.

"It's fine," Merletta said dismissively, uninterested in discussing the injury Oliver had inflicted on her the day before.

He'd been a little more enthusiastic than necessary in reasserting his mastery after his loss on the first training day of the week. The most irritating part of it all had been Ileana's smirk as she paused in her training with her guard squad across the training square in order to watch Merletta get pummeled.

Merletta played with the squid in the basin before her as her friends discussed their plans with their families that day.

"Are you going to come home with me?" Sage asked her brightly.

Merletta shook her head. "Thanks for the offer, but I'm actually going to Tish's shellsmith tower." She looked up abruptly at Sage. "Does your family have a family record?"

"What do you mean?" Sage asked.

"An account of the family ancestry, written down somewhere," Merletta explained.

"Oh, that." Sage cast her a searching look. "Yes, it's on this enormous stone slab at my grandparents' house. New births and marriages are added regularly, and the older ones get re-carved as needed."

Andre nodded. "We've got one the same for each side of my family."

"Are they also at your grandparents' houses?" Merletta asked.

Andre grunted. "My mother's one is at her parents' house. My father's is actually at ours. As the oldest son, he was given care of it when he got married."

He reached across the table for some salted cod, and Merletta's eyes followed the movement absently, her thoughts on Andre's words.

"Are records like that ever displayed publicly?" she asked.

Sage frowned. "Not that I've ever seen."

"The Center doesn't keep a census?" Merletta pressed.

Andre looked blank, and Sage not much more hopeful.

"I think they have in the past," she said. "But I don't know how recently they've done it. Not in our lifetime, I don't think."

Merletta frowned, not entirely satisfied. Keeping tabs on every merperson in the triple kingdoms seemed like exactly the kind of thing the Center would do, not just in generations gone by, but now. But on the other hand, it would be an enormous undertaking. She'd never come across any evidence of it. The closest thing she'd seen was the orphan records in which her own birth was recorded. But they hadn't gone back very far, so clearly in that case only recent records were kept.

"What's all this about, Merletta?" Sage asked, her voice gentle. "Are you thinking of your own family, whoever they were?"

Merletta hesitated, her first instinct to save dignity by denying it. But she shook off the thought. These were her friends, and she had nothing to fear from being vulnerable with them. Slowly, she nodded.

"I've wondered if it might be possible to find out who they were," she said quietly. "It's probably an impossible task."

There was a moment of sympathetic silence, broken by Andre.

"If you want to see a family record, I could take you to see the one at my house today," he offered. "If your friend won't mind you getting to her shellsmith tower a little late."

Merletta's eyes shot to his, startled. "That's a kind offer, but I don't think your family would be thrilled to see me back at your house again after the birthday fiasco."

"Nonsense," said Andre stoutly. "You're very welcome."

He must have seen Merletta's skepticism, because he gave a rueful laugh. "I explained it all to my parents, and they're pretty understanding, really. My brothers probably won't be there. They all have their own homes, or else live in their training barracks, and don't usually come to my parents' for rest days."

Merletta hesitated, still unconvinced she'd be welcome, but very curious to see a family record.

"I won't take no for an answer," said Andre firmly, apparently reading her thoughts. He glanced at their companion. "We can all swim together as far as Sage's house."

Sage nodded, and the three of them rose into the water. They'd just left the dining hall when Emil swam up to them, something about his alert posture convincing Merletta that he'd been up for hours, rest day or not.

"Heading back to Skulssted?" he asked, the question directed to the group at large, but his eyes on Sage. "I thought I would have missed you."

"We had a late breakfast," Andre told the other merman cheerfully. "We're heading to Sage's house now."

"All of you?" Emil asked, faint surprise in his eyes as his gaze flicked to Andre.

"Well, Merletta and I are just passing by," Andre amended. "I'm going to take her to my house to show her the slab with our family history on it."

Emil didn't comment, but his surprise was even more palpable this time.

"Let me guess," sighed Merletta. "It's deeply offensive in some way I'm not aware of for me to look at another family's record."

"Of course not," said Emil calmly. "I just didn't realize you were so interested in Andre's family." They were swimming down the street now, and he glanced casually around them, continuing once he'd seen they were alone. "I thought the incident with Andre's celebration was a misunderstanding."

"It was." Merletta scowled, irritated with him for bringing up the awkward topic.

"No need to get angry with me," said Emil, raising his hands. "I just assumed you would want to avoid anything that might support the gossip."

"Oh, relax, Emil," said Andre, sounding put out himself. "No need to make a fanfare. I just offered to show her the record because she was interested in the concept. Anyone with nothing better to do than gossip can think what they like."

Emil looked a little surprised by the outburst from Andre, who usually spoke to the junior record holder with respect bordering on reverence.

"I didn't mean any offense," he said carefully. "I was just thinking of the safety of you both."

"Yes, you always are," said Sage, her voice almost tart. "You know, my house really isn't on the way to Andre's from here. I'll take off, let you guys get going, so Merletta can get to her friend in Tilssted sooner."

And with nothing more than a quick wave, she propelled herself forward, moving across the drop off toward Skulssted with swift strokes.

Emil frowned after her. "I think maybe I'd better swim with Sage," he said curtly.

"She did seem a little upset, didn't she?" Merletta agreed, bemused.

"What?" Emil looked confused now. "I just meant it might not be safe for any of us to wander around alone when we still have no idea what Eloise is going to do with the information you gave her."

Merletta resisted the urge to roll her eyes. Emil might be overcautious, but she certainly had no objection to him keeping a protective watch over Sage.

When Emil had left, flicking his powerful tail such that he caught up to Sage's now distant figure in no time, Merletta and Andre swam out into the drop off at a more sedate pace.

For a few minutes they traveled in silence, then Andre's voice cut into Merletta's thoughts.

"Do you think he's right to be so worried?"

Merletta didn't have to ask what he was talking about. "I often think he's too cautious," she said slowly. "But when I really stop and think about everything I've learned and done, I wonder how in the tides I'm still alive."

Andre nodded, as if her words confirmed his thoughts. "I've been meaning to speak to you about the danger," he said, his voice a little more gruff than usual.

Merletta remained silent, wondering if he was about to do what she'd half expected him to do the very first time they spoke with Eloise, and tactfully explain that he wanted out of the metaphorical maelstrom that constantly circled around her.

"I would never have thought of it if not for the...misunderstanding around my birthday celebration," Andre continued. "But I've been wondering since then whether it might be a good idea to actually encourage the gossip."

"What?" Merletta stared at him, completely thrown by the turn of the conversation. "What are you saying?"

"I'm not declaring myself or anything," Andre chuckled, looking rueful. "So there's no need to look so horrified."

"Sorry." Merletta couldn't help chuckling as well. "But I don't understand what you're suggesting."

"I'm suggesting we let everyone think we're a couple," Andre said bluntly. "Even though neither of us sees the other that way." He gave her a disarming smile. "Which I genuinely don't, just to make sure we're on the same page."

Merletta blinked at him. "Why would you want people to think it, then?" she demanded. "When you know how much danger it could put you in to be associated with me like that?"

"I'm not afraid for myself," Andre said confidently. Although the sentiment might be foolish, Merletta could tell it was sincere. "But I am concerned for you." He frowned. "Before my birthday, I hadn't thought about how very vulnerable your lack of family makes you. If you could be considered connected to me—and through me, my family—in some recognized way, it might offer a measure of protection."

Merletta was silent for a long moment, struggling with her emotions. Before Heath, she'd never thought anyone would see her romantically. One lingering look from him, one simple touch, had ignited her world like a thermal vent. And his very existence made Merletta sure she couldn't live with a deception like Andre was offering.

But she appreciated the gesture more than words could say. Heath's affection meant the world to her, but the friendship and loyalty she'd found with Sage, Andre, and Emil was no less unexpected, and no less precious. The idea that her friendship meant enough to Andre that he would risk his own safety for her temporarily robbed her of speech. If Heath's presence in her life was like the searing heat of a thermal vent, the affection of her friends was like the constant glow of the plankton lanterns which lit the darkness of the deep ocean. Different in type, but just as beautiful.

"Are you sure you don't want to be a guard, like your brothers?" she asked teasingly, unable to put her deeper emotions into words. "The protective instinct runs very deep, apparently."

Andre smiled briefly, but his face soon became serious again. "Friends protect each other, too."

"I know," Merletta acknowledged. She looked at the sandy ocean floor not far below their fins as they swam. "I can't tell you how much I appreciate the gesture, Andre. But I...just can't. There's so much I have to hide, so many secrets to navigate. I can't live that kind of lie. I don't want to."

There was a moment of silence, and Merletta forced herself to look up, worried that she'd hurt his feelings. But he didn't look offended.

"I understand," he said simply. Unless she was much mistaken, there was even a hint of relief in his voice. "Just as long as you know we've got your back."

"Thank you." There was no volume to the words—Merletta was still a little dazed by it all. A sudden thought occurred to her, and she frowned. "Were you inviting me to see the records on that basis?" she asked quickly. "Given my answer, would it be better if I didn't come?"

"No, it's fine," Andre said, sounding utterly unconcerned as he swept his dark hair out of his eyes. When he'd started the program a year before, he'd worn it short, like a guard. But he was letting it grow out, giving him a much less military look. "I really did explain it all to my parents, and they're not angry with you."

Merletta was skeptical, but their reception at Andre's house supported his light words. His father wasn't there, but his mother welcomed Merletta graciously, commenting that she was pleased to properly meet a friend of Andre's. Merletta didn't take offense at the subtle emphasis she placed on the word *friend*. She had the impression the older mermaid felt sorry for her, and although it stung a little, it was better than her being angry at her son.

When Andre announced that he was going to show Merletta the family record, his mother gave Merletta a very searching look. Merletta couldn't tell whether it was because she felt sorry for the nameless orphan, or because she was suspicious that Merletta had some design on joining the family after all. But she said nothing, merely drifting along beside the pair as they swam through the house, emerging in a sparsely furnished study.

"Whoa." Merletta raised her eyebrows. "When Sage called these slabs enormous, she wasn't kidding." One wall of the room was almost completely obscured by a huge flat expanse of stone which rested against it at a slight angle.

"Well, my husband's family record goes back a long way," said Andre's mother proudly. "As far back as anyone's I know. I suspect it's as old as it can be—well, the record that is, not the slab itself. It's been re-inscribed onto a new slab at least once, I believe. But as for the records themselves...I don't think anyone kept them earlier than this. I understand there were several generations between the founding of the triple kingdoms and the development of our written language. As far as I know, the first names on this record coincide roughly with the first written accounts. So the family started recording their members as early as possible."

She broke off, chuckling. "What am I thinking, talking about records lore with two trainees of the record holder program. You both probably know more about it than I do."

Merletta smiled politely. Neither she nor Andre answered, and they clearly weren't expected to—they weren't allowed to speak about the content of the course with anyone outside it, and Andre's mother must know that. But the older mermaid's words niggled at Merletta's mind in a way she couldn't immediately identify.

"May I?" she asked, reaching out a hand toward the massive slab.

"Of course," said Andre cheerfully. "It's pretty sturdy, as you see."

Merletta floated forward, her eyes dwelling on the family name inscribed at the top of the slab—*Seawatch*—with a crest below it. The first names were unfamiliar, clearly not in vogue anymore. She traced her fingers down row after row, noting where the names became more common.

Percival, one said. Merletta stared at it. Wasn't that the name of Heath's brother? She'd never come across it in a merman before. It certainly wasn't in fashion in her generation.

The names branched out, reminding her of the spreading shape of coral, or of the trees on Vazula, but upside down—starting small at the top, and extending wider as it went down. When she reached the bottom row, about two thirds of the way down the slab, she touched a finger to Andre's name, written in its place after all his older brothers.

"It's beautiful," she said politely. "And very impressive to go back so far."

Andre smiled warmly, and even his mother looked proud of the family history she'd married into.

"I suppose you don't have one of these," the older mermaid said as she accompanied the two of them out of the study. "Is that why you wanted to see Andre's?"

Merletta nodded, trying to sound unconcerned. "Yes, basically. I was always told that I was left at the charity home anonymously." Never mind that she knew that to be a lie now. The near-stranger beside her didn't need that information. "To have such history as that," Merletta waved a hand vaguely toward the study behind them, "is a very precious resource."

"Yes, it is," the other mermaid agreed. "And one which we perhaps take for granted sometimes." She cast a glance at her son, who looked sobered.

They'd returned to the main living area when a cheerful voice hailed them from the dwelling's doorway.

"Indigo." Andre's mother smiled warmly on the young mermaid, who looked younger than Andre. "Lovely to see you. What brings you by today?"

"Hello, Auntie," the newcomer responded, swimming forward to embrace the older mermaid. "I came looking for Andre, actually." She looked curiously from him to Merletta. "But maybe it's a bad time?"

"Not at all," said Andre. "Let me introduce you. Indigo, this is Merletta, a friend from the program. Merletta, this is my cousin, Indigo."

"Merletta?" Indigo looked Merletta over a little too casually. "We haven't met before, but I think I saw you...at Andre's birthday celebration."

Andre sighed. "She's not my girlfriend, Indigo, there's no need to be weird about it. She's a fellow trainee and a friend."

"If you say so." There was the hint of a smirk on Indigo's

face, but the look she sent Merletta was friendly enough. "So you're a trainee as well. Hopefully we'll be seeing much more of each other, then!"

"Uh, will we?" Merletta asked.

Andre shouldered his cousin with familial ease. "Indigo is about to turn sixteen. She plans to apply to the program. She's inspired by my example."

"Hardly," snorted Indigo. She flashed her cousin a grin. "It was more that I figured if you could get in, surely it can't be too hard."

Andre rolled his eyes, but he clearly didn't mind her banter. Merletta examined the two of them surreptitiously. They didn't look much alike. Indigo's skin was pale, like Andre's mother's. Clearly Andre's coloring came from his father. Her hair was almost as fair as Tish's, and her tail was a pale blue that shimmered as she swam. The whole impression made her seem insubstantial, which Merletta could already tell was an illusion.

"That's exciting," Merletta said in belated response to Andre's announcement. She smiled at Indigo. "Good luck, I hope you get in."

"Thanks," said Indigo. "Me too."

"I'll just see Merletta out, then I'll be right with you," Andre told his cousin. "But if you've come to nag me about the entry test again, nothing's changed. I'm still not allowed to tell you what's in it."

Merletta said a hasty goodbye and followed Andre into the small garden outside his front door.

"Will you be all right, going into Tilssted by yourself?" Andre asked when they were alone.

"Of course," said Merletta cheerfully. "Honestly, it's probably the safest place for me these days." She grimaced. "I don't know how they all recognize me, but there seem to be a lot of people there who would be only too ready to intervene if I ran into trouble." She chuckled as she thought of her familiar, uncultured Tilssted folk. "More aggressively than necessary, probably."

Andre grinned. "Well, I'll leave you in their capable hands, then. See you tomorrow."

CHAPTER EIGHT

Merletta

Turning away from Andre's home, Merletta hastened northward. She'd planned to pick up the promised shells from Tish's workplace—an errand to which she half-regretted committing—earlier in the day, when everyone would be busy with work and she could dart in and out. Arriving close to lunch time risked being drawn into socializing. And although she didn't object on her own behalf, Tish might not like it. It wasn't exactly consistent with Tish's expressed desire to be kept out of "whatever it is you're caught up in".

But Merletta didn't want to dwell on the discomfort of her oldest friend's decision to distance herself from their friendship. Tish was her history—the closest thing she had to a family record.

Merletta frowned as her thoughts returned to Andre's family's slab. It was impressive, no question. But something about it wasn't right. Andre's mother had claimed that it went back as far as the Center's written history, and that the first entries were made only a few generations after the triple kingdoms were founded.

But although there had been an impressive number of

names on the slab, there surely hadn't been enough to cover the triple kingdoms' whole history. It was possible Andre's mother was mistaken—she hadn't seemed especially confident in her understanding of records, and why should she be? The Center took care to keep everyone outside its circle ignorant about the finer details of such things.

Still, the explanation didn't satisfy Merletta. She'd formed the impression from her basic studies that the triple kingdoms had been around much longer than that—the instructors spoke of the three founding brothers as though they were in an ancient past that was almost lost to memory.

Plus, there was the question of their language. The Center claimed that developing a written version of the language of merpeople was one of their civilization's greatest achievements. But Heath spoke the same language as Merletta, and she had personally read written records from the island of Vazula in her own tongue. The matching language couldn't possibly be a coincidence. It pointed unarguably to some common origin between her people and Heath's. Even the appearance of names from Heath's society in past generations of merpeople supported the idea.

And there was no forgetting the shocking detail which had so thrown Merletta when she completed her second year test. The watchword in the middle of the maelstrom—that code which she would apparently require in order to access records necessary for her higher studies—was none other than *Vazula*. That alone convinced her that the history of her people was tied not only to land and humans, but to the island itself.

And the records she'd seen on the island had surely been written longer ago than the family history in Andre's house had begun. How was it possible that merpeople had been connected somehow with the inhabitants of Vazula, who had apparently left the island hundreds of years ago, when their underwater civilization supposedly hadn't yet existed then?

Something definitely didn't add up.

Merletta was distracted by the question all the way to the shellsmith tower, barely noticing the transition from Skulssted's wealthy streets to Tilssted's grimier water.

She looked up at the tower, her heart sinking at the cheerful voices and clatter of bowls. She'd arrived at lunchtime, as she'd feared.

Nothing for it now, though. The guard at the entrance waved her inside enthusiastically, his eyes dwelling first on her armband and then on her weapon. She had the fleeting thought that there wasn't much point to a guard who happily let an armed outsider enter the apprentices' tower, but there was no conviction to the thought. She had no doubt that, as she'd told Andre, the guard had recognized her, and was letting her through on the basis that she was the champion of Tilssted.

The thought made her squirm, but she pushed it aside. She was here to get her shells, nothing more. In and out. She adjusted her existing coverings absent-mindedly. They had been uncomfortably tight for some time, and there was no denying she'd be glad to have a better-fitting pair.

There was no need to ask for directions. As soon as she entered the tower, the sound of chatter and laugher drew her up three floors to a dining hall which covered an entire story. The space was full of apprentices eating lunch and talking at full volume.

Of course, that volume became instant silence when Merletta appeared.

After the first moment of appraisal, hushed whispers spread across the room. Merletta caught sight of Tish, who sent her a small and personal smile before the hubbub broke out. At the lack of reproach on her face, Merletta found herself releasing tension she hadn't even realized she was holding.

"Trainee Merletta!"

Merletta turned to see the solidly built mermaid who had offered her new shells swimming toward her.

"Here to collect your shells? They're ready for you."

"Yes," said Merletta, smiling in greeting. "And thank you again."

"No need to thank me!" the mermaid insisted, speaking too loudly. She turned an outraged face on the rest of the assembled apprentices. "Look at the state of her shells! That's what the Center provides for our trainee. You can bet the ones from the other cities have much better."

Tuts sounded from around the room, a few others calling out their disapproval.

"It's really fine," said Merletta placatingly. "These have done me well since I started."

"Sweetheart, those are a disgrace," said one mermaid sitting near Merletta's end of the long stone table.

"Thank you," said Merletta dryly, causing a few chuckles to spread throughout the room.

"You know what I mean," the apprentice insisted, her voice matter-of-fact. "They're two sizes too small, and so worn they're losing their shape."

"They do pinch a little," Merletta acknowledged. "But it's really not important."

More tutting sounded throughout the space, and the mermaid who'd offered Merletta new shells took on a scolding tone.

"Don't tell a room full of shellsmith apprentices that shells aren't important. You'll offend us. A third of the workers in this room spend most of their time on shell coverings."

"Sorry," laughed Merletta. "I didn't mean it like that."

"Come on, then," said the apprentice bossily. "I've got the new ones just here, in my room."

Merletta followed her into a tiny sleeping room, which barely had floating space once a hammock and a small work surface had been squeezed in there. A pair of scallop shells sat on the work surface, in the same uniform white as the ones worn by all the female trainees, and many of the Center's employees. They were perfectly matched with each other, and beautifully bound.

"They're perfect," Merletta said, awed.

Her benefactor snorted. "They'll do," she said prosaically. "I'll give you some privacy to change them over. Will you be all right to do it on your own?"

Merletta nodded, and the other mermaid left the room, the fronds of seaweed which formed a curtain over her doorway fluttering in her wake. Once Merletta was sure she was alone, she tried to unclip her existing shells. They were very securely fastened, and they didn't budge. Frowning, she glanced around the space and saw a small sharp tool. With its aid, she managed to get the shells off.

She exhaled a long stream of water, taking a moment to revel in the relief of being free. She hadn't even realized how tightly the undersized shells were restricting her before, but having them off was incredibly liberating. She glanced shiftily toward the window, making sure she was far enough back from it so as not to be visible to anyone swimming past down below, then rolled her shoulders a bit, letting the water swish around her.

It had been a long time since she'd been uncovered. Heath had told her once—only in response to a direct question, and flushing furiously as he spoke—that humans usually changed their coverings entirely every day. She'd been amazed. Mermen didn't wear any true coverings, of course, and mermaids only shells or similar. And they didn't tend to remove them unless they were upgrading—it wasn't unusual for an adult mermaid to go for years without taking off her shells. Heath claimed it was so humans could wash themselves. Another concept which didn't really apply to mermaids, living underwater as they did.

Merletta donned the new shells quickly, pleased with how well they fit. The band around her back was also much more comfortable than her previous one—thicker and more solid. She could breathe so freely, and yet she felt delightfully secure.

She swam back out into the main space with an extra swish to her tail, and was immediately greeted by approving murmurs.

"That's more like it," said the mermaid who'd told her that her last shells were a disgrace.

"It feels much better," Merletta acknowledged. She beamed at the apprentice who'd done the shells. "Thank you so much. I'm amazed how well you sized them."

The mermaid chuckled. "I do this for a living, you know."

"Very nicely matched pair," said one of the other apprentices, studying Merletta's new shells with a professional eye. "You did well with those."

"They were intended for the daughter of Lady Waverider, as part of her uniform for school," said the mermaid cheerfully. "I redirected them."

Merletta didn't know whether to laugh or grimace. The rest of the apprentices knew no such uncertainty—uproarious laughter met this announcement. Evidently the lady in question was known to them, and not popular.

"Well, they look great," called one voice.

"Absolutely, an excellent match for your skin tone," approved another.

Merletta couldn't help grinning. She didn't even mind the intense level of scrutiny being leveled at her form. It was so pleasant to feel part of a large and boisterous crowd. Although her friends at the program were wonderful, they were such a small and sedate group. She couldn't help wondering what it would be like to live in such a bustling community. She'd never been accepted like this in the charity home.

The comparison drew her up. She remembered what Tish had told her soon after she'd started her apprenticeship. She'd said the apprentices were depressingly similar to the beneficiaries they'd grown up with, that there was always someone willing to carry tales. She shouldn't let herself be lulled into carelessness by their approval. She was popular in Tilssted now, for reasons which she still found a little strange. But while that might make them outwardly friendly to her, it guaranteed nothing about what they might do behind her back. And any mis-stroke she made could have ramifications for Tish.

"Have you thought more about the sponsor program?" The tall apprentice eyed Merletta. "About whether you could help out?"

"Uh...not really," Merletta admitted.

The other mermaid nodded. "I suppose it's a little more complicated for you to come talk about what you do than for any of us."

Merletta nodded, grateful for the offered out. "A little, yes."

"Did you really mean it that you would live outside the barrier?"

The new voice surprised Merletta. The speaker was a stranger to her, and certainly hadn't been present when she'd made the comment.

"I told them all what you said," the other apprentice boomed, no hint of apology in her voice. "Everyone was really interested."

Merletta felt a sinking feeling in her gut, and her eyes flew involuntarily to Tish. Her friend looked nervous, one finger curling around a strand of her pale hair in the way it always did when she was anxious.

Tish dropped her eyes, and Merletta looked away, to find every other eye at the table fixed expectantly on her.

"What I said," she started carefully, "was that with the right planning and protection, I'd be willing to try."

"You're not worried about all the dangerous creatures out there?" chimed in another apprentice.

Merletta shrugged. "I'm not saying there'd be no risk. But that's where the planning comes in. There are ways to protect against predators. The guards manage it on their patrols, don't they? When's the last time we lost one of them to a shark attack?"

"But we did lose some to something, didn't we?" someone pointed out.

"Yeah, aren't you worried about land sickness?" a dark-haired mermaid asked, her eyes wide.

Merletta met her gaze, debating with herself. Part of her mind was repeating the need to proceed with care among these strangers. But on the other hand, their questions were perfectly reasonable. Why should she lie to them to protect the Center's secrets? Surely she could answer them without incriminating herself.

"No," she said simply. "I'm not."

"Or dragons?" another asked, seeming fascinated by Merletta's calm.

"I'm not worried about them, either," said Merletta.

"Brave, or stupid?" muttered a voice from the back, and a few sniggers sounded.

Merletta shrugged. "Neither, especially."

"You are brave," Tish piped up unexpectedly. "You always have been."

Merletta smiled at her friend, warmed by the display of

loyalty. That was the Tish she knew, who was so kind-hearted she would always think well of Merletta even when everyone else hated her—even when Merletta's behavior didn't entirely justify the good opinion.

"Oh, shut your clam hole," another apprentice scolded the one who'd made the disparaging remark. "You can see she's not stupid, or crazy. And I think she'd know what she's talking about —she's a *Center* trainee."

Unease snaked through Merletta once again. She wasn't speaking for the Center—surely they all understood that. She'd been asked if she personally would risk living outside the barrier, not if the Center sanctioned it. Everyone knew the answer to the second question.

She made no attempt to clarify. Her instinct told her that trying to explain the distinction between her views and the Center's would only draw attention to her own discomfort, which was the surest way to give extra intrigue to gossip and speculation.

But as she swam back toward the Center a short time later, her pleasure over the new pair of shells was tempered by an undefined foreboding as she pictured the faces of her audience. For every skeptical expression, there had been two looking at her with awe, and just as many with excitement.

Hopefully she hadn't paid too high a price for the free gift.

CHAPTER NINE

Heath shifted his weight from one leg to the other, wincing as pain shot through his muscles. Who knew crouching in one position for a few hours could be so blasted uncomfortable? And no one had done more than pass through the guardhouse in all that time. He was losing patience for his poorly thought through plan. He definitely wasn't cut out for the life of a spy.

He suddenly realized how ridiculous that thought was. Who could be better suited to being a spy than someone who had the ability to surveil others from afar, using only his mind?

This is ridiculous, he grumbled internally, as the cramp in his leg gave another painful twinge. *I shouldn't need to be physically present to see what's happening anyway. If only I was better at farsight, or if it wasn't limited to people I had some connection to.*

The thought drew him up short. Was he really complaining that he couldn't just watch anyone anywhere and at any time? He felt sobered at the reminder of just how powerful his magic had the potential to be, and how easily it could be abused. It was a weighty business, being the first human in history to possess farsight.

Chastened by his own conscience, he returned to his more primitive surveillance.

It wasn't yielding much. He knew that if he really wanted to see or hear something that would shed light on Percival's attack, he should have staked out the guardhouse immediately afterward, instead of waiting for weeks. But he'd initially returned to Bexley Manor, and even once he'd been called back to the capital, he had other things on his mind.

He had other things on his mind now, if it came to it. But the question of who had actually attacked Percival had grown larger in his thoughts in recent days. His brother had no difficulty attributing the attack to the crown, because he was convinced King Matlock wanted him out of the picture. Heath, however, was skeptical about whether the king really saw Percival as so unconquerable a threat. And, more importantly, in spite of the rising tension and the king's recent perplexing decisions regarding the power-wielders, Heath still had too much faith in King Matlock's integrity to believe he had attempted to murder Percival.

Heath had made no secret of these views, and it hadn't won him any favor with Percival. But although Heath had wondered often who was really behind the attack if not the crown, it had only recently occurred to him to ask the more troubling question of why. If Percival hadn't been attacked for the convenience of the crown, that meant there was another reason someone wanted him dead. And Heath couldn't be at ease until he knew what that reason was. Which placed a little more priority on figuring out who had been behind the attack.

And that was why he'd been crouching in a tiny unused storage cupboard inside the guardhouse of the royal guards for the last three hours.

The royal guard was made up of the elite among the guards, led by the king's most trusted knights. They didn't live in the sprawling barracks utilized by the general guard. Many of them were older and more experienced than the average guard, with homes and families of their own. And the knights certainly weren't expected to slum it in the barracks.

Their base of operations was a large and well-appointed guardhouse attached to the castle, with smaller guardhouses at each city gate. Their main focus was not on the city itself, however, but on the royal family. They were the most highly trained fighters in Valoria, and the most fiercely loyal to their sovereign.

Which obviously gave some credibility to Percival's belief that the crown was out to get him, given he swore he'd seen the uniform of the royal guard on the men who'd attacked him. It also made it all the more troubling that—assuming Heath was right, and the king wouldn't send his guards to murder someone—another party was attempting to blame the attack on this elite force.

Unfortunately for Heath, the guardhouse wasn't quite the hub of activity he'd imagined it to be. Guards occasionally passed through, but generally the two on duty simply sat at a table, one of them filling out a report of some kind while the other whittled a stick into a passing semblance of a dog. He'd heard only the occasional catches of conversation during his surveillance, none of them remotely relevant.

"You're back early."

The voice of one of the guards drew Heath's attention, and he shuffled forward slightly to peer through a crack in the wooden door of his cupboard. A third guard had appeared in the doorway of the room.

"I'm still on duty, just here on an errand for Prince Lachlan."

"What does His Highness need?" asked the whittling guard, without looking up from his work.

The newcomer shifted his feet uncomfortably. "He wants to read the record of that complaint from the head laundress."

"What?" The guard who'd been writing a report looked up, clearly exasperated. "How does he even know about that?"

"Well, uh..." The new arrival scratched his neck. "I told him."

"Why would you do that?"

"He was asking all about our uniforms. He was direct. I would have had to lie in order not to tell him," the guard said defensively.

His companion sighed. "Well, you can't do that," he acknowledged. "You'll have to ask the captain for it. The complaint was made to him, so he's likely got the report in his office. I believe he was dealing with the laundress directly, so I doubt he'll thank you for getting the crown involved."

The standing guard let out a sigh of his own. "No help for it. Do you know where he is?"

"He's in the training yard," said the whittler. "I can go ask him. You should get back to your post."

"Thanks."

The two men departed in opposite directions, leaving Heath to consider the overheard information in his cramped quarters. Prince Lachlan was asking about the uniforms of the royal guards? What kind of questions was he asking? Did that mean he believed what Percival had seen, and shared Heath's suspicions that it had been a set-up of some kind?

Hardly able to believe that he'd heard something of actual interest, Heath wanted nothing more than to go in search of his second cousin immediately. But he couldn't leave his hiding spot without detection. He'd thought himself lucky to sneak in without being seen, but he'd started to wonder long before now whether it had actually been a stupid idea. How long would he be stuck there?

While he waited for an opening to make his escape, he wondered what Prince Lachlan was up to now, and whether he'd yet received the requested report. Heath closed his eyes, trying to draw on his magic as he focused his thoughts on the crown prince. As soon as he attempted to connect in to his farsight, Merletta's image appeared, increasing from the corner of his mind as it had the day he trained with Reka. There was nothing remarkable to see. She was underwater, apparently in some kind of class. Not a very interesting one, by the expression on her face.

Heath smiled to himself, forcing his thoughts to return to Prince Lachlan. He found the full picture of the other young man a little hard to pinpoint—it always felt like the prince was holding so much inside. But they'd begun to form a friendship of sorts before things fell apart so drastically, and Heath had once felt like he knew the man behind the title, at least a little.

As he focused on who Prince Lachlan was, his sight flickered once again. This time it wasn't Merletta he saw, although he was still aware of her, continuing to live and breathe and swim and just generally *exist* on the other end of an invisible cord stretched between them. All that was a constant background hum, but the image of Prince Lachlan was clear and central. He had indeed received the report, and he was reading it as he walked, a frown creasing his forehead as he passed down what appeared to be a servants' corridor.

A shout sounded from outside the guardhouse, and Heath's concentration broke. The picture of Prince Lachlan disappeared abruptly, and the sole remaining guard heaved himself to his feet. The moment he stepped out of the room, Heath shot from the cupboard, escaping through another door into the stable yard.

He hurried toward the castle, trying to guess which part of the building the prince had been in. An inquiry of a passing servant gave no indication as to the prince's whereabouts, so Heath asked instead where he could find the laundress. Looking bemused, the servant directed him to the far side of the castle.

Heath moved as quickly as he could without actually running, but he still didn't manage to intercept the prince before he reached the laundry rooms. He tumbled into the large open chamber full of huge vats and the smell of soap just in time to hear Prince Lachlan's calm voice.

"I didn't realize it was common for uniforms to be destroyed."

"Not common, Your Highness," the laundress said fairly. "Sometimes the garments get damaged if the guards have seen active conflict, and no one blames them for that. I can even understand the occasional careless guard misplacing a uniform. But to lose them so frequently, and to tell the royal tailor they must be going astray on our end...well, that got my blood right and boiled to be frank, Your Highness. I run a tight ship here. My workers are meticulous and conscientious. I'd swear to it that we've never lost a single uniform, barring those which are damaged beyond repair, and we always burn them as instructed and make a report to the captain of the guard to that effect."

She glanced up at the end of this tirade, blinking in surprise at the sight of Heath hovering in the doorway.

"Are you lost, My Lord?" she asked.

Heath shook his head, his eyes flicking to Prince Lachlan, who was considering him shrewdly.

"Lord Heath," the prince said. "This is an unusual place to find you."

"I came in search of you, Your Highness," Heath said.

Prince Lachlan raised his eyebrows. "I wasn't aware that anyone knew of my decision to visit the laundry today. I would be interested to know who directed you here."

"By all means," sad Heath carefully. "But don't let me interrupt your discussion."

"I think my questions have all been answered," the prince said, inclining his head graciously to the head laundress. "Thank you for your time. And rest assured that your exceptional work does not go unnoticed."

"Well, thank you, I'm sure, Your Highness." The middle-aged woman's cheeks were pink with pleasure as she curtsied. "We do our best to do our bit."

With a final nod, Prince Lachlan strode from the room, Heath hurrying to keep step with him. He expected the prince to head back toward the main part of the castle, so was surprised when he instead turned down another narrow servants' corridor.

He was even more surprised when Prince Lachlan opened a random door, stuck his head into the room beyond, then gestured for Heath to precede him inside. Heath did so, to find himself in a space that was halfway between storage cupboard and repair room.

"Let's speak plainly, Lord Heath," said the prince curtly. "Who told you where I was just now?"

"No one told me," said Heath. He hesitated for a moment, then dropped the caution. "I was hiding in the guardhouse, and I overheard a guard say that you'd asked for a report from the head laundress. When a servant couldn't tell me where you were, I guessed you were heading for the laundry."

The prince stared at him, for once allowing his astonishment to show. "You were *hiding* in the guardhouse?" he repeated in ominous tones.

"Yes, I was," said Heath impatiently. "I didn't mean any harm, as I have no doubt you know. I was trying to find out what really happened when Percival was attacked. And given that's what you appear to be up to, let's not get too particular about methods. Not everyone can just command the guards to give them information.”

The prince considered him thoughtfully for a long moment. To Heath's relief, his gamble paid off. When Prince Lachlan spoke again, there was no sign of anger in his voice.

“That is what I'm trying to do,” he acknowledged. “And if you have any insights to share, I'd like to hear them.” His expression turned a little stern. “But no more hiding and eavesdropping.”

“I would prefer not to hide in cupboards, obviously,” said Heath cheerfully, carefully giving no response to the prohibition on eavesdropping. “And I'm afraid I don't have any new information. But it sounds like you do, Your Highness. Did I understand that conversation correctly? That a number of uniforms have gone missing over several loads, with the guards blaming the launderers and the launderers blaming the guards?”

“So it seems,” said the prince noncommittally. “It is of course not unusual for such disputes to arise between the various groups within a castle.”

Heath gave the prince as challenging a look as he dared. “And I suppose it's not unusual for the crown prince to personally investigate such petty disputes?”

The prince sighed, running a hand over his hair in a gesture that made him seem immeasurably more human than normal.

“You're right, of course, that usually I wouldn't get involved.” He met Heath's eyes frankly. “To be honest, Lord Heath, I placed absolutely no reliance on Lord Percival's claim that the men who attacked him wore guard uniforms. But I know you're sensible, and not given to exaggeration. If you believe him, then I place considerably more weight on that. And it didn't escape my notice that when I asked you about it, although you said you believed your brother, you didn't claim to share his opinion about what happened.”

"Which is the convoluted royal way of saying that you've reached the same conclusion I have," Heath nodded. "That someone must have been impersonating the royal guards for some undisclosed but presumably malicious reason."

The prince didn't answer, raising an eyebrow at Heath's plain speaking.

Heath shrugged. "Being polite and aloof has gotten us absolutely nowhere, Prince Lachlan. We set out to bridge the gap between the power-wielders and the court, and instead managed to turn the rift into a chasm. Not to mention I just confessed to spying on your father's guards, and unless I'm mistaken, caught you sneaking around to investigate my claims without your father knowing."

"I don't believe I could be accused of sneaking," the prince said with dignity.

Heath cast a meaningful glance around the dusty room. "Are you sure?"

The prince had the decency to look a little pained. "I can see your confusion," he said. "But I don't wish to hide anything from my king. I will of course be telling him of my discoveries today."

"Fair enough," Heath said, trying not to let his disappointment show. He had a feeling he knew what the king would say.

"I have other matters to attend to, Lord Heath." Prince Lachlan's formality had returned. "But I daresay I will speak with you again soon."

Heath nodded absently, his thoughts on the matter of the uniforms as he wandered back up the corridor, some distance behind the prince, who was walking briskly.

He suspected that the prince hadn't actually planned to tell his father about his investigations, but had felt challenged by Heath's comment, and had changed course. Heath hadn't intended it as a criticism, of course. But maybe Prince Lachlan was right. Maybe secrecy served no one.

With that in mind, he sought out his brother, who was exploring one of the city's larger markets with some friends. Heath pulled Percival aside and gave him a highly truncated version of the morning's events. He made no mention of the prince, just informed Percival that he'd been listening in on some guards, and had followed their comments to the point of discovering the missing uniforms.

"Are you serious, Heath?" Percival was predictably unimpressed. "Laundry must go missing all the time in a household as large as a castle. I'm sure our laundress has lost at least half a dozen of my garments over the years."

"But half a dozen at once?" Heath challenged.

"This is absurd," said Percival angrily. "Why are you so determined to find another explanation when the true one is so obvious? The king wanted me dead, and he sent his guards to do it."

"Percival, hush," said Heath, looking around in alarm.

They'd moved away from Percival's group, but they were still in a public market, surrounded by people on all sides.

"No, I won't hush," said Percival angrily. "Why should I cover for someone who tried to kill me?"

"If the king wanted you dead," said Heath in an exasperated undertone, "don't you think he would have managed it by now?"

"Obviously when I called him out on his failed attempt, he realized it's not so easy to knock me off without consequences," Percival said dismissively.

Heath shook his head, taking a step back from his brother. "I'm done trying to reason with you, Percival," he said shortly. "You're an arrogant fool if you truly think you're the center of all this."

Anger flashed in Percival's eyes, but before he could retort, one of his friends wandered over.

"Are you two squabbling again?" he asked lightly. "Makes me glad I only have sisters."

"You're wise," Percival said acidly. "My sister is the sweetest person I know. Brothers are nothing but trouble."

I couldn't have said it better myself. Heath held in the caustic retort. Percival might be childish enough to bicker in front of others, but Heath refused to descend to his level.

"Come on," Percival said to his friend, sounding irritated at Heath's restraint. "Let's get some skewers."

"No way," said the other young man emphatically. "I won't be eating anything from this market anytime soon."

"Why not?" Heath demanded, distracted from his frustration in spite of himself.

"Didn't you hear?" The other man was clearly pleased to be the bearer of gossip. "Two men from this market died recently, and the physicians think they ate something that poisoned their systems. They both worked in the market, but in different stalls."

Heath stared at him. "They ate something poisoned? I've never heard of that happening before. Surely that's being investigated."

"Not with actual poison in it," the man said dismissively. "Food that had gone bad, something like that."

Heath frowned. "Strange coincidence for it to happen at the same time if they worked at different stalls, though."

Percival rolled his eyes. "Of course Heath wouldn't accept the obvious explanation. He'll be searching for a complex conspiracy now."

Heath sent him an impatient look. "If you never even question what you see, Percival, you're just begging to be lied to." If there was one lesson he'd learned vicariously through Merletta, it was that.

"You're the one who isn't willing to question what the

authorities say," snapped Percival. "You're the one too blind to see what's really happening." He gestured to the market at large. "But maybe you're right, maybe we're not digging deep enough into these suspicious deaths. Were these men dissenters? Perhaps the crown picked them off, too."

He spoke flippantly, but his voice carried as it always did, and Heath saw a number of passersby looking around, their expressions shocked.

Percival's friend chuckled as if it was all a joke, but Heath felt nothing but disgust.

"You have no idea what's at stake, do you?" he said coldly.

"Don't scold, Heath," Percival said, his voice impatient.

"No more scolding," Heath said simply. "No more trying to fix every problem you cause. When your unguarded tongue lands you in *real* trouble, don't expect me to come to your rescue."

"Real trouble?" Percival raged. "In case you've forgotten, I was beaten half to death only weeks ago!"

Heath ignored him, turning on his heel and striding away. Percival was headed for danger, but it was clear that nothing Heath said or did would check him in that path.

But that didn't mean that Heath would stop searching for answers about the attack. If someone was trying to embroil the crown and the power-wielders in a web of conflict and deception, much more than Percival's safety was on the line.

CHAPTER TEN

Heath slept poorly that night, his dreams filled with visions of Merletta. Once he saw her fighting the maelstrom's thrashing waters, and another time he watched her collapse in the center of a large crowd, her body convulsing unnaturally. Other visions were more pleasant, showing her laughing with a pink-tailed mermaid, and dancing through a pod of dolphins.

These images were reminiscent of the dreams he'd had during the months he thought Merletta was dead. He'd belatedly grasped that the random visions he had of Merletta in that time had been early instances of his farsight. But that couldn't be the case for the dreams. Surely at night Merletta was sleeping, as he was, not engaging in any of the activities he'd witnessed in his dreams. And he recognized the more dramatic events from her descriptions. He could only conclude that his imagination was more vivid than he'd ever given it credit for.

Rising early, specifically to avoid running into Percival at breakfast, Heath made straight for the castle. He wanted to speak to Prince Lachlan, but it had occurred to him that there was really no need to hide in storage cupboards to do so. Little as he'd cared for it in recent weeks, he had an official role at the castle which fully legitimized private conversation between him and the prince. He knew there was a risk his cousins would think he was being disloyal if they saw him closeting himself away with the crown prince. But after the latest display of Percival's pigheadedness, he found he didn't much care what the others thought.

When he received permission to enter the prince's study, he was pleased to find the young royal alone.

"Lord Heath." Prince Lachlan considered him carefully, the consciousness of their last meeting unspoken but tangible. "Please sit."

Heath did so, getting straight to the point.

"Did you tell your father about our discovery yesterday?"

The prince cleared his throat. "I did."

Heath nodded. "I told Percival, as well," he volunteered, "hoping to convince him that he wasn't attacked on King Matlock's order."

"Is that so?" Prince Lachlan looked surprised at the unprompted disclosure. "And what did he say?"

"More or less what your father said, I'm guessing," Heath answered. "That a few missing uniforms don't prove anything, and that nothing has changed." He met the prince's heavy frown with an even expression. "Well? Am I wrong about the king's reaction?"

Prince Lachlan's jaw worked for a moment. Then he let out his breath in a long sigh. "No," he admitted. "You're not."

"Well." Heath leaned back in his chair. "It seems the only ones interested in finding out what really happened on the road that day are you and me. And I think we'll get considerably further if we work together."

Prince Lachlan hesitated. Heath could see the other man wavering, but the prince's rigid sense of duty would undoubtedly make it hard for him to investigate behind his father's back.

"Come on, Your Highness," Heath said. "We went through this yesterday in that storage cupboard—do we really need to cover it again? The way I look at it, we're conspirators now. I'm not asking you to tell me all your secrets, and I'm not promising to tell you all mine. But I think when it comes to this matter, we really do want the same thing. To find out who was behind the attack, and whether they're any further threat either to my family or the crown."

The prince considered him for a pregnant moment, then gave a curt nod. "All right," he said. "I can live with that." His face relaxed into what was almost a smile. "I always did hope we could work together, you know."

Heath returned the smile more broadly. "Good. Are we in agreement that the missing uniforms support the idea that someone wanted it to look like the attack was committed by royal guards?"

Prince Lachlan nodded again. "And the fact that they went missing over the course of several weeks suggests that the attack was orchestrated carefully, and well ahead of time."

"Not an encouraging thought," Heath said grimly. He frowned. "We know it was planned, though, because of the summons Percival received. He was only on the road alone that day because he was riding to Bryford in response to a missive from the Chief Counselor."

"Well, Lord Niel roundly denies writing any such letter. My father is of the view Lord Percival made the whole thing up," the prince said.

Heath stared. "I saw the missive myself."

"That's not what I mean," Prince Lachlan said, shaking his

head. "I saw it as well. But there was no date on it. Father believes it was a previous summons that Lord Percival unearthed in support of his allegations."

"That's definitely not the case," Heath said confidently, deciding not to waste time getting offended on his brother's behalf at the king's opinion. "I can't understand why the king would think that."

"I can," Prince Lachlan said dryly. "It's because your brother claims the letter was delivered by a royal courier, when the couriers' records show clearly that no one was dispatched to Bexley Manor that day."

Heath groaned. "What are the odds a courier's uniform has gone missing recently?"

"I wouldn't be surprised," agreed Prince Lachlan.

Heath was silent for a moment as he pondered it all. "Are you aware that my father told Percival not to respond to the summons? He could sense something was wrong with it. You know that he can detect deception. Percival is convinced Father must have been sensing that it was a trap, although without knowing that was what he could sense, of course. But what if it was actually that he could sense the lie in the signature? That it wasn't really written by Lord Niel?"

Prince Lachlan nodded slowly. "It's worth considering."

"So there's plenty to suggest the attack was staged," Heath said thoughtfully. "But none of it gives us any clue as to who staged it, and for what purpose."

For a moment there was silence, neither of them having anything more to add.

"I didn't realize your father had followed up with the couriers," Heath said thoughtfully. "Or even with Lord Niel. I had the impression that he was so furious about Percival's accusation that he refused to entertain any of it. But it sounds like an actual investigation occurred."

The prince's voice had regained a little of its stiffness as he replied. "Of course there was an investigation. My father cares about his people, Lord Heath, power-wielders included. And he's always proved himself a wise king—he understands better than anyone the importance of maintaining order and dealing swiftly with unlawful violence. He wouldn't just ignore an allegation of attempted murder."

Heath considered the prince dispassionately. Although Prince Lachlan spoke with sincerity, there was something about him...some underlying truth that Heath could sense, hiding behind false words. It wasn't just reading body language. It was his power at work, he was sure. He was seeing something others couldn't, in this case the fact that the prince wasn't being entirely honest. Was this what it felt like for Heath's father, when he used his magic? But he could not only sense deception—he could actually break its hold. Heath was sure he couldn't do that, handy as it would be.

Putting the question of his magic from his mind, Heath sifted through the prince's words, trying to find the safest way to explore what was hidden behind them.

"Has he *always* proved himself a wise king?" he challenged delicately. "It seems to me, for example, that he would have been much wiser to tell Percival—and the rest of my family—that he'd investigated the allegation."

"I believe..." Prince Lachlan sounded uncomfortable. "I believe he thought it might seem to validate the accusations your brother made—accusations which were entirely without foundation."

"Is that what *you* think?" Heath asked bluntly. When the prince didn't reply, he pushed on. "Because *I* think that by letting us all assume there had been no investigation, he communicated to Percival and the other power-wielders that he doesn't believe a word they say, and doesn't care enough about an attempt to murder them to even look into it."

The prince remained silent, and Heath narrowed his eyes. "You agree with me, don't you?" he mused. "And I know you're not going to admit it aloud, but I think you also agree with me that the restrictions on the power-wielders are a dispropor-tionate escalation of the conflict." He frowned. "Was the king really so offended by the unfortunate incident at the Winter Solstice Festival last year?"

"How could he help being angry?" Prince Lachlan burst out. "He was publicly chastised by dragons for something he wasn't even aware of! Thanks to the dishonesty of *your family*, he was reduced to discovering their illicit activities in a public scene, along with the rest of the kingdom!"

"My cousins' meetings to practice their magic weren't unlawful at the time," Heath reminded him mildly. "But of course I understand your father's feelings. I just wouldn't have expected him to be so affected by them as to take such drastic action, especially delayed as it was."

The prince scratched the back of his neck, apparently in no hurry to answer. As the silence stretched out, Heath assumed Prince Lachlan wasn't going to answer at all. He was therefore doubly surprised when his companion spoke, his voice lowered in spite of the privacy of their setting.

"I was surprised as well."

The admission was the closest Heath had heard the prince come to questioning his father in any way. He kept his mouth shut, afraid of showing his astonishment and unintentionally shaming the prince back into line. As he'd hoped, with no visible reaction, Prince Lachlan kept speaking.

"I know your family has taken a different view from the crown on the power-wielding question from the beginning, and of course I can understand why that is. We never expected everyone to agree. But I think you're reasonable enough to acknowledge that up until the Winter Solstice, every decision was made carefully, based on appropriate counsel, and applied with moderation. But in my mind, that event marked a change."

"What do you mean?" Heath pressed, when Prince Lachlan fell silent.

The prince cleared his throat. "I'm not sure how to explain it, or even if I should. I know there are some among the court who would readily claim that the restrictions indicate that my father has at last decided to be guided by their point of view."

"No need to dance around it," Heath said encouragingly. "We both know you're speaking of Lord Niel."

Prince Lachlan almost smiled, but not quite. "At any rate, I don't believe their influence has grown with my father in recent months. And it certainly isn't my influence that's led him. In fact..."

He hesitated, some part of him reluctant to admit whatever was coming next. Heath waited, amazed by the prince's sharing. He had the sense of an overfull dam—not bursting, but suffering a small breach which allowed the release of just enough pressure to prevent a break. Heath could only be glad he was the one the prince had decided to trust with this release.

"In fact," Prince Lachlan tried again, "I didn't even know he was considering it until the decision was made. He didn't include me, or explain his reasoning."

Heath frowned more deeply. "Who's in his ear then?" he asked. "If it isn't you, or the Chief Counselor?"

Prince Lachlan raised his hand helplessly. "Who's to say anyone is? I don't mean to suggest his mind has been meddled with, as once happened to his father. Perhaps he was just so distressed by the incident with the dragons that it's eaten away at him, and led him to abandon some of the caution he's always observed."

"But you don't think so," Heath said confidently.

The prince didn't answer, but he didn't need to. Heath could read it in his eyes.

He pondered the other man's words. He'd forgotten about the incident from well before his time, when the former king—then crown prince—had been magically manipulated to near-disastrous effects. The perpetrator hadn't been a power-wielder—in fact, Heath's grandmother had been the only known power-wielder in Valoria back then. A magical artifact had been used, one of the few to ever exist. Heath had always thought of that plot as involving a different type of magic entirely from that of his family, but now he thought about it, the old story might go a long way toward explaining the crown's wariness regarding magic.

The silence stretched out, the unspoken question lingering in the air: who was influencing King Matlock if not his own advisors? As strange as the mystery was, Heath almost felt encouraged. If someone else was playing on the king's understandable displeasure over the dragons' warning, it meant that King Matlock hadn't simply become unreasonable. They could probably still reach him once they had something concrete to bring him.

"Well, until we've found more information, I suppose there's nothing further to be done. I'd best get back to this report," Prince Lachlan said at last.

"More missing laundry?" Heath joked.

The prince gave a wan smile. "Not quite. Another unfounded allegation of attempted murder, actually."

"By who?" Heath asked, startled enough to overlook the somewhat unfair characterization of Percival's beating.

"It's nothing of much substance," Prince Lachlan said. "An

unexplained death in the north. A man of no known occupation collapsed in a tavern. Normally not something we would even hear about, but apparently he claimed right before he died that he'd been poisoned, and the widow demanded an investigation."

"Was there one?" Heath asked.

The prince shrugged. "A guard squad was sent out. There was nothing much to find. Other than his word, there was no reason to think he'd been poisoned. He was drinking heavily, and from all accounts it wasn't the first time. No one was especially surprised that his overindulgence reached a fatal level."

"Strange," Heath mused, his thoughts on his outing the day before. "Did you hear about the deaths in the southwest market?" he asked. "Two men, working at different stalls, who apparently both died from eating something poisonous?"

"No," said the prince offhandedly. "I hadn't heard about it. Very tragic. But if there were two cases, I daresay a health inspection has been ordered. Some of these vendors don't follow the regulations very closely, and the consequences can be serious."

Heath frowned. "Would you have access to the outcome of any such inspection?"

"If I wished to," the prince said, looking up from his report with a touch of impatience. "But I don't have any particular interest in the matter, to be honest." He searched Heath's eyes for a moment before his gaze dropped down to the report on his desk. "Are you suggesting a connection?"

"I don't know," said Heath. "It just strikes me as strange. Three deaths in a short span, all with the word 'poison' thrown around."

The prince still looked unconvinced, but he didn't dismiss the suggestion, which Heath appreciated.

"I'll look into it, see what the health inspection turned up."

Heath nodded his thanks. "And I'll see if I can find out anything more about the attack."

The prince didn't look hopeful as Heath took his leave. After all, they'd found nothing to go on. But it occurred to Heath that there was one avenue he hadn't tried yet.

CHAPTER ELEVEN

It was weeks before Heath found the opportunity to follow up on his idea. It soon became clear that Percival's inflammatory words in the market had been reported back to the castle, because the power-wielders of Heath's generation were all called to a meeting with the Chief Counselor.

The incident wasn't specifically mentioned, but Heath could almost see the thought of it simmering underneath Lord Niel's furious expression. Heath could only wonder at the tactlessness which led the king to delegate the task of meeting with the power-wielders to the Chief Counselor, who was one of the most outspoken critics of their family and was universally unpopular among the group.

There was no real substance to the meeting. It seemed to basically be an opportunity to remind them all of the rules—as if anyone was likely to forget them—and to warn them to stay in line. Percival, of course, was openly furious. Heath noted that Brody and Bianca were making little effort to hide their anger, and even the more timid of his cousins showed signs of defiance in the tilt of their chins.

If there remained any desire on the king's part to bring the two groups together amicably, he was definitely going about it the wrong way.

The result of it all was that Heath, along with the rest of them, found himself watched much more closely in the weeks that followed. Consequently, it wasn't easy for him to slip away and meet Reka. His training had to wait, and although he could have communicated with his draconic friend via farsight, he thought it best to save his questions until they could discuss them in person as well. It wasn't as though he had any great expectation that his inquiries would yield anything substantial enough to make them urgent.

For the first week or so, he thought he would be driven mad by being stuck in their city manor with an irate Percival. Percival showed no hint of remorse for his comments, even when the duke roundly took him to task for making light of treasonous talk in the marketplace. Percival held to the view that the king was at fault, and refused to acknowledge any responsibility for the increased surveillance on his brother and all his cousins.

Fortunately, before either brother could murder the other, a distraction occurred in a very unexpected form. The family was sitting down to a somewhat dreary dinner when there was a bustle in the small courtyard out the front of the manor, and a servant appeared in the doorway looking flustered.

"Lord Edmund and Lady Laura are here," he said.

"What?" The duchess stood, looking astonished. "Surely not."

But the entrance into the dining hall of a familiar, if very flushed, face soon dispelled any doubt.

"Laura, what in the kingdom were you thinking?" Heath's mother demanded, hastening to help her daughter into a chair.

"Not quite the reception I hoped for," Laura said, her voice cheerful in spite of her evident weariness.

"You know we're always glad to see you," said the duchess.

"But you shouldn't be traveling about the kingdom when you're mere weeks from delivery!"

"I tried to tell her." The long-suffering voice drew everyone's attention to the doorway, and Heath rose with the others to greet his brother-in-law.

"I got your letter, Mother," said Laura firmly, ignoring her husband's words. "And exceptions for my condition be hanged. If all the power-wielders of my generation are to be caged here like criminals—when we all know no one but Percival's done anything reprehensible—then I'll be caged here with them."

"Oi!" Percival's outrage was predictable, as was Laura's response.

"You know I love you, little brother," she said soothingly.

Heath could feel the gentle touch of her power as she sent a wave of cheer over the whole room. He felt suddenly more optimistic about life, and he leaned into the feeling, not caring in the least that it wasn't a natural response to the situation. Dragon's flame, he'd missed having his sister around!

"I love you, too, Laura," said Percival gruffly, still not quite ready to let go of his offense. "But that doesn't mean you can say anything you like and not be called up on it."

"Of course I can," Laura assured him pleasantly. "In addition to being your only sister, I've just had a grueling journey, and I'm *heavily* pregnant with the most enormous baby in Valoria's history. I can say whatever I like, and I'm sure no one will dare to criticize me."

"But I haven't done anything reprehensible!" Percival protested, ignoring her jokes. "I'm the one who was almost killed."

"Well, I'm very glad you weren't," Laura reassured him, positively coating him with her magic. "It's a very good thing Heath reached you in time. I'm sure you've been exhaustive in thanking him for racing to your rescue, but I'll take the opportunity to thank you as well, Heath, for not letting our brother die."

Heath shook his head slightly at her, amused by her audacity. If *he'd* dared to draw attention to Percival's utter lack of gratitude for Heath's intervention, Percival would have sulked for days, but he actually looked a little chastened at Laura's light words.

"It alarms me how well you've learned to weaponize your magic," muttered the duke, as he leaned down to kiss his daughter on the forehead.

She grinned up at him. "You use yours for the good of the kingdom, Father. Why shouldn't I?"

Heath chuckled, and she sent him the ghost of a wink.

But the duchess wasn't interested in these distractions.

"Stars above, Laura, if I thought it would bring you racing across the kingdom like this, I never would have written to you about the latest tension."

"Don't worry, Mother, I'm fine," Laura said, her smile more genuine. "And I still have several weeks before the physician expects the birth. Time enough to get home again, if all goes well."

She made no attempt to use her magic on their mother, which made Heath think she really was telling the truth about being all right.

"You are absolutely giant," Percival said bluntly. Apparently a trace of his ill humor remained.

"Too true, I'm afraid," Laura sighed, letting her head drop back against the high back of her chair, as her husband brought her a glass of water. "It has the physician mystified."

"It must be twins," the duchess said. "There's such a strong history of it in your father's family."

Laura shook her head. "They assure me there's only one in there."

"Hm." The duke frowned thoughtfully at Laura's bulging stomach. "I suppose we'll know for certain soon enough."

The conversation moved on, but Heath continued to watch his father's face, fascinated. He could feel the duke's power swirling subtly out from him as it probed Laura's stomach. Heath felt a flicker of his own magic, and tried to look at his father with the sight that came from his power, not his eyes. The duke was seeing something the rest of them weren't.

His interest piqued, Heath moved his attention to Laura as well, trying to see what was really happening. He leaned into his farsight, but all he could see was Laura, sitting in front of him, as his normal eyes showed. Perhaps it was the baby he needed to focus on.

Blocking out everything around him, he thought about the child—who he or she was, the family into which this baby would be born, the identity the child would have as a power-wielder, and as Laura's son or daughter. He saw nothing but darkness, but something danced across his awareness—some sense of life and wholeness and...rescue? The sensation was akin to how he'd felt when he'd learned Merletta was alive after all, or when he'd reconciled with Reka. Which made no sense. What did either of those things have to do with Laura's child?

He tried to dig deeper, but just as he thought he was getting a sense of something further, his extra sight suddenly gave out. It didn't flicker into nothing like usual, either. It felt more like it had slammed into a solid wall.

Heath blinked, sound rushing around him as he returned to his surroundings. He looked up to see his father watching him with a shrewd expression. Heath swallowed. What had the duke seen with those perceptive eyes?

As the duchess helped Laura and her husband into a guest suite, the Duke of Bexley pulled his younger son aside.

"Is all well with you, Heath?" he asked in his calm way.

"Yes, Father," Heath said a little too quickly.

The duke searched his eyes. "There's no sense beating around the bush, Heath. I felt power come out from you just now. I've sensed it growing in you for some time."

"You have?" Heath was astonished. "You never said anything. And neither has anyone else."

"If you're speaking of your brother and your cousins, then I doubt they will have noticed," the duke told him. "It takes training and finesse to recognize the subtlety of power in others. I've been living with magic for much longer than anyone in your generation."

Heath was silent, unsure how to respond.

"You needn't confide in me if you don't choose to," the duke said, no rancor in his tone. "But I just wanted you to know I've sensed it. And..." He hesitated. "It hasn't escaped my notice that you've been working more amicably with Prince Lachlan recently. And I'm glad for it. I also haven't made any secret of my disapproval of your brother's behavior, and the way it has increased friction between our family and the crown. But I hope you aren't at risk of forming the false impression that magic is harmful in itself, or in any way to be avoided."

"Of course I'm not," Heath said, suddenly understanding what his father was getting at. The duke was afraid he was hiding—or perhaps even trying to suppress—his growing magic either out of loyalty to the crown or fear of the power itself. "Our kingdom *and* our family will be best served by magic being used, and used well."

The duke searched his eyes for another long second before he nodded, apparently satisfied with what he saw.

The conversation played in Heath's mind over the following weeks, as he wondered whether he should tell his father the full extent of his growing magic. It would be useful to ask more about how the older man exercised his own gift, given the ways in which Heath's magic bore similarities.

But he couldn't quite bring himself to do it. Recent tensions notwithstanding, the duke was deeply loyal to the king, whom he served in a senior advisory position. He may well feel compelled to share the information with the crown, which Heath wasn't ready to do.

For the moment his training would have to remain between him and Reka. If he could ever get away to meet the dragon, that was.

His opportunity arose a few weeks after Laura and Edmund joined them in Bryford. They were just beginning to speak about returning to their home for the birth of the baby, and the topic dominated the conversation at breakfast.

"I think maybe you'd better stay put now," said the duchess, concerned. "What if the baby started to come while you were on the road?"

"I doubt that will happen," said Laura, as cheerful as ever. "I know I'm massive, and I won't deny I'm exhausted. But I actually feel great."

"Well, that's a mercy," said the duchess skeptically. She appealed to her son-in-law. "What do you think, Edmund?"

He looked torn. "I'd like to be home," he acknowledged. "But I'm reluctant to travel if you think there's any risk."

"Nonsense," said Laura dismissively. "There's no—ooh." Her voice changed abruptly, and Heath looked up from his porridge.

"Are you all right?" he asked.

"Of course I am," she said staunchly. "Just a big kick, that's all. Nothing to—oof."

"I don't think those are kicks," said the duchess grimly. "I think someone else has an opinion about whether it's too late to travel, and he or she is letting us know that the answer is decidedly yes."

"What do you..." Laura trailed off, her eyes widening as she took her mother's meaning. "No. The baby can't be coming yet! I should still have weeks."

"Babies don't work to physicians' schedules, love," said her mother with a smile. Her voice turned suddenly brisk. "Speaking of which, we'll call our physician. And we'll prepare the downstairs bedroom."

Everything seemed to progress rapidly after that. Every female in the manor bustled around with apparently lots to do, while Heath and Percival hovered with Edmund, at a loss for how to be helpful. Less than an hour had passed since breakfast when Heath tentatively stuck his head through the door of the downstairs bedroom.

"Is there anything you need that we can—?"

"OUT!" His normally sweet-natured sister had never spoken to him in that voice, of that he was certain. "I don't want either of my brothers in the building!"

Neither Heath nor Percival had to be told twice.

"Tough luck, Edmund," Percival told his brother-in-law sympathetically as they hurried out the front door. "No escape for you."

Edmund barely seemed to hear him, his eyes wide and his posture tense as he nodded his farewell to the two brothers. Heath and Percival walked slowly across the courtyard, temporarily allied by the family circumstances.

"Do you think she'll be all right?" Percival asked.

Heath nodded. "Surely. Mother and Father's physician treats the king himself. He's the best in Valoria."

Percival still looked troubled, but neither of them said anything further.

"Should we...go for a walk?" Heath asked vaguely.

Percival seemed to come back to reality. "I think I'll go to the training yard," he said gruffly. "Take my mind off things."

Heath was equal measures disappointed and relieved that his brother didn't want to spend the possibly long wait together. As soon as Percival disappeared, Heath struck out in a different direction altogether, already calling Reka in an undertone. This was a better opportunity than he'd had in weeks.

By the time he reached the now-familiar hillside, Reka was waiting.

"Why do you project tension?" the dragon asked curiously.

"Do I?" Heath gave a rueful smile. "I'm sorry. My sister is having her baby right now, and I'm a little worried."

"No need to apologize," said Reka comfortably. "It is not an unmanageably unpleasant taste."

Heath looked up, confused, but Reka was still speaking.

"Why are you worried about your sister having her baby? Do you fear the child will be unlikable?"

"No, it's not that, it's...let's talk about something else," Heath said firmly. "I've been meaning to ask you something, actually."

Reka waited silently, watching Heath out of unblinking yellow orbs.

"I've been trying to figure out what exactly happened the day we saved Percival," Heath pushed on. "Did you get a close look at the men who attacked him?"

"Not especially close," Reka said. "They were of no particular interest to me. I remember noting that they smelled pungent for their kind."

Heath frowned. Not what he would expect of the king's elite guard. More like the bandits they appeared at first glance to be.

"Would you recognize them again if you saw them?" he asked.

"Probably not," Reka acknowledged without regret.

"Do you remember that I thought I sensed power from them?" Heath pressed.

"Yes," said Reka slowly. "I do recall you saying that."

"Well?" Heath couldn't help being impatient at the dragon's unhurried pace. "Did you sense power?"

"I sensed yours," Reka said maddeningly. "And your brother's less potent magic."

"But from the others?" Heath insisted.

Reka's eyes narrowed in thought. "Let me recall it properly." He closed his eyes, and Heath actually felt a tendril of magic swirl out from the dragon and wrap itself around his enormous, scaled head.

"What was that?" Heath demanded. "What are you doing?"

"I'm using my magic to form a true recollection," Reka said, his eyes still narrowed, and his focus apparently undisturbed. "It is an ability of my kind, not entirely dissimilar to farsight. I can reconstruct the event so as to be accurate in every particular."

"That's amazing," said Heath. "And so handy."

"Indeed," Reka agreed gravely. He opened his eyes fully, giving off a faint hint of surprise. "You are correct," he said. "There does appear to have been some power lingering around the attackers. Not a large amount. Perhaps their magic is weak, or perhaps not all of them carry it."

"What does that mean?" Heath demanded.

"That, my recollection cannot confirm," Reka said, clearly unperturbed by the question. "It is curious, however," he added after a thoughtful pause. "I would not have expected you to identify it at the time when I did not. It suggests a level of finesse in your ability to detect power which I would not expect from a human your age."

Heath rubbed his hands over his face. "Much good it does me," he muttered.

He was confident the power he'd felt hadn't been the familiar signature of any member of his Valorian family. He could think of no course but to search for the culprits among the family tree of Kyonan power-wielders, and the thought wasn't appealing in the least.

"Did you wish only to discuss this matter?" Reka asked him. "Or did you call me here in the hope of further training?"

"Training, definitely," Heath said firmly. If Percival was using training to take his mind off Laura's situation, Heath could see no reason why he couldn't do the same.

As his thoughts flew to his sister, his power unintentionally followed. Clearly his investment in her well-being was higher than ever, because her image popped immediately into his mind, clear as day.

"Dragon's flame," he muttered, shutting it off instantly. She'd seemed to be in a great deal of pain, and that wasn't something he had any desire to witness. Plus she'd been very clear on her feelings about her brothers being present for the event.

"Let's start the training right now," he said fervently. "I've been following Merletta with my farsight since we last spoke. But not much else."

He directed his farsight down its most familiar channel, and his mind instantly gained access to Merletta's current situation. He realized with a gasp that he'd lost track of the days. She was swimming through shallow water, wearing the light expression that meant she'd temporarily left the burdens of her underwater life behind.

"Change of plan," said Heath hastily, his heart soaring at the prospect of spending the day with Merletta. "Can we go to Vazula?"

CHAPTER TWELVE

Merletta

Merletta twisted and spun as she glided through the water, eager to reach the island. It had been a long week, full of frustrating instances of Ibsen's determination to prevent her from learning enough to have a hope of passing third year. It was such a relief to be outside the triple kingdoms again, on her way to her island haven.

Not that it was quite the haven it had once been, she reflected as she beached herself a short time later to cries of greeting from Paul and Griffin. She smiled as she walked up the beach toward where they were sitting, the sand squelching pleasantly between her bare toes.

"How was your week?" she asked them. Glancing around, she added, "Where's August?"

"He's hunting," said Paul. He chuckled. "He offered to hunt for us all. He's been so cheerful since Eloise started visiting that I hardly recognize him."

"I'm glad," Merletta said with a smile. Her eyes narrowed. "But don't think you can get away with lounging around just because he's foraging for you. I want to see your progress with your running."

Paul groaned, but Griffin jumped to his feet at once. "I've got it more or less figured out, I reckon," he said, squaring his shoulders. "Let me show you."

He jogged across the beach under Merletta's critical eye, sand flying from his feet.

"Not bad," she said. "But you'll have greater success if you use your arms more. Let me show you."

An hour later, she was still so engrossed in the training session that she almost missed the rushing sound that had failed to appear the previous few rest days.

With a gasp, Merletta looked up, her heart lifting at the sight of Reka descending with Heath gripped in his talons. She had only the briefest instant to enjoy her anticipation before a cry of warning rang out, and something hit her forcefully from the side. The next thing she knew, she was pinned to the ground, trapped under the protective weight of Griffin's body.

"Hey!" Heath's familiar voice was the only way she could tell that the pair had landed. "Get off her!"

Merletta struggled out from underneath Griffin, throwing him an incredulous look. "What is wrong with you? Why did you tackle me?"

"There's a *dragon*!" Griffin shouted, as if his reaction had been the most natural thing in the world.

Movement caught Merletta's eye, and she realized that Paul had seized his weapon and was edging around behind Reka, as if attempting to surround the dragon.

"Reka isn't our enemy," said Merletta, trying to swallow her irritation at having just been slammed to the ground unnecessarily. She rubbed her hip, and saw Heath's eyes narrow as he followed the motion. "I appreciate the sentiment, but I don't need your protection, Griffin! Especially not from Reka."

"Reka?" Griffin repeated incredulously. He was half crouched with his spear gripped in his hand, and his eyes had been riveted on Rekavidur. But as he spoke, they passed accusingly to Heath. "You said that name last time. *This* is your friend who came to the island with you?"

"I should have explained properly," said Merletta. As her initial shock at Griffin's attack faded, she realized the misunderstanding was her fault more than anyone's. "Rekavidur is a friend of Heath's, and…" She looked hesitantly at the dragon. "And mine."

Reka narrowed his eyes slightly, but didn't speak. Merletta felt relieved—she'd been afraid he would deny her words outright. For a moment Merletta was distracted, wondering what his problem with her was. He'd been friendly enough when they first met, but it had been more than a year since he'd begun to behave strangely toward her.

"He's the one who flies here, bringing Heath with him. I've known him for almost two years. He won't hurt you."

"You speak for me?" Rekavidur asked, his voice a little cold.

"Reka," said Heath, sounding exasperated. "Don't be difficult."

Griffin and Paul both looked extremely taken aback at Heath's casual manner, but Merletta realized that she was once again to blame.

"I apologize, Rekavidur," she said solemnly. "I should have introduced you properly and allowed you to speak for yourself. These are others from the triple kingdoms. Griffin," she gestured to him, "and Paul. Paul, come over here. It's not polite to skulk behind them like that."

Paul, looking extremely apprehensive, moved to Griffin's side, his eyes never leaving the dragon.

"And there's another, August," Merletta went on, speaking again to Reka. "He's currently hunting underwater in his merman form. Paul, Griffin, this is Rekavidur. He comes from the dragon colony situated in Heath's kingdom."

None of the three subjects looked in the least pleased with the introduction. Reka was holding himself more tensely than Merletta had ever seen, and the two guards maintained their defensive positions.

"Merletta," Griffin managed through clenched teeth. "Can I have a word in private?"

Merletta noticed that Heath's eyes were once again narrowed as they rested on the young guard, and she sent him a silent plea for help to defuse the situation. Catching her gaze, he seemed to snap out of it, giving a swift nod.

"We haven't met," she heard him saying quietly to Paul. "I'm Heath."

He offered his hand. Paul didn't take it.

"I have no desire to fight with you, or your companion," the other guard said tensely. "But I cannot trust anyone who is allied with a dragon. My people have suffered too much loss to allow it."

Merletta groaned quietly. It wasn't a promising beginning. Heath looked confused, his eyes darting to Merletta's as he dropped his rejected hand. But before she could respond, Griffin tugged on her arm.

"Merletta? A word?"

Reluctantly, she followed him a short distance across the sand. When he stopped and pinned her with a hard stare, she met it in exasperation.

"Dragons have much better hearing than we do, you know. Reka will probably hear every word."

"Then I'll speak quietly," said Griffin, dropping his voice. "Merletta, what are you thinking? How could you lead one of his kind so close to our home?"

Merletta frowned. "First of all, I didn't lead him anywhere. I met him and Heath by chance just after I discovered this place. They were exploring themselves."

"You mean they were looking for us?" Griffin's face paled. "Is it too late, then? Are the triple kingdoms lost?"

"Don't be absurd," Merletta said, losing patience. "There's really no call to be so dramatic. They weren't looking for us. They were looking for the island. They were both as amazed to find me as I was to find them. Mermaids are considered a myth in the human world."

"It's not humans I'm worried about!" Griffin seemed to have forgotten his intention to keep his voice down. "It's dragons! They will wipe us out if they find out where our cities are. And *some* of us have families we want to protect!"

Merletta flinched slightly, her new sensitivity about her nameless status still a little raw.

"I'm sorry," said Griffin at once, seeing her reaction. "I didn't mean to hurt you, I just—"

"Really? It sounded to me like you did." Heath's voice was unimpressed as he appeared behind Merletta.

"Heath, you're not helping," said Merletta wearily. "It's natural that they're alarmed. I should have told them about Reka, but I've been putting it off, and this is the outcome."

"This isn't your fault, Merletta," said Heath. "If they won't listen to sense..."

"Sense?" Griffin scoffed. Neither man was making any attempt to speak quietly now. "Do you really think we're so easily duped?" He turned appealingly to Merletta. "Surely this is enough to show you how dangerous your friendship with this human is! He clearly doesn't care for your safety, or any of ours."

"That's not fair!" Merletta felt anger rising up in Heath's defense. "Heath almost got himself killed trying to save my life!"

"And we risked our lives to save you, as well!" Griffin shot back. "Because we thought you were the triple kingdoms' best hope, because we thought you would actually change things! Not that you'd throw it away for a pair of big seal pup eyes!"

"Hey!" Heath's voice was sharp. "Don't speak to her like that. She doesn't need anyone's encouragement to take the weight of the world on her shoulders. It's not her job to fix your civilization's problems."

"You have no voice in this conversation," growled Griffin, turning his attention to Heath. "It's bad enough that you come here like it's nothing, like our very lives aren't put at risk just by your presence. But to actually bring a *dragon*?! A vicious beast who won't hesitate to eat every one of us, then move on to the rest of our kingdoms!"

"You are rude," said Reka coldly. He still stood some distance away, but his response demonstrated the truth of Merletta's comment about his hearing. "I imagine I should enjoy annihilating you. But I would certainly never consider demeaning myself by consuming your body."

Both guards raised their spears at these words, Paul moving to join Griffin as they formed a shield in front of Merletta. Even in her frustration, the gesture softened Merletta toward the stubborn guards. In spite of believing she'd brought danger on them all, they were still determined to protect her.

"Enough!" she said, pushing past them both. "Reka, I don't know what your problem with me is, but you and I both know you're not going to *annihilate* anyone. They might be rude, but they're speaking from ignorance, not malice. It's not really their fault—they've been taught to fear dragons from earliest memory."

"With good reason," Paul said, his voice more measured than his companion's. "I have to agree with Griffin, Merletta. You should not be fraternizing with a dragon. Surely you know the history better than we do. Their kind have killed so many of ours. If given the chance, they would gladly slaughter us all."

"That's just more of the Center's lies," Merletta said impatiently. "I've known Reka for a long time. He's never shown aggression. He doesn't want to kill us all."

She looked up to find Reka's eyes fixed on her, something unreadable in the yellow orbs. For a moment her words hung in the silence, then the dragon let out a slow sigh that sounded almost sorrowful.

"No, I do not," Reka said, his gravelly voice unusually soft. "But your companions are not wrong that it is unwise—and indeed unnatural—for our kinds to interact, Merletta. If you were to take my advice, you and Heath would abandon your friendship, and each allow the other's kind to fade back into legend."

"Reka!" Heath protested. "That's ridiculous. We're not going to do that."

He shifted closer to Merletta, and she stepped forward to stand beside him, also feeling the need to reassure herself that they were united on this point.

"We can't just forget what we know, Rekavidur," she said earnestly. "Even if we wished to. My civilization has been controlled and subdued by lie upon lie for more generations than I can unravel. Pretending the lies are truth won't help anyone. We need to expose the secrets, let the truth come out."

Reka gave a rippling shrug, his voice becoming disinterested. "You will do as you choose. It is not my affair. But do not be surprised if the consequences are more than you were prepared for."

Merletta glanced at Heath, who looked just as perplexed as she felt.

"Reka," Heath asked cautiously, "what is it you're not saying?"

"Do whatever you came here to do," Reka said, ignoring the question. "I will depart for Valoria imminently. One of them was tolerable. Three is more than I am willing to countenance."

"One of *them*?" Heath repeated, Reka's tone seeming to offend him on Merletta's behalf. But Reka had already crouched, and the next moment he'd taken to the air, wheeling slowly away over the island.

"What more proof do you need that dragons hate our kind?" Griffin hissed under cover of the rush of wind created by Reka's wings. "This human isn't your friend. He's deceiving you, for some sinister purpose you don't—"

"Enough." Merletta's voice was as cold as the depths of the Center. "I acknowledge that Rekavidur's behavior was strange. But I won't hear a word against Heath." She strode over to him on the words, holding out her hand. "Come on. It sounds like you don't have long."

A pleasant shiver went over her when Heath took her hand without hesitation. Neither of them had to articulate their destination—they made for the lagoon in silence. As soon as they reached the water's edge, well out of sight of the beach, Merletta dropped Heath's hand.

"I'm sorry about that," she said, avoiding his eye.

"You're not to blame for their reactions," Heath said lightly. "I can even acknowledge that they had reason to be nervous. Reka was behaving much too dragon-ish for my liking."

"Why doesn't he like me anymore?" Merletta asked, abruptly pulling her gaze up to Heath's.

"I don't know," he said simply, and she could read his sincerity in his eyes. For a moment they held one another's gaze, then his face softened. "Don't let it trouble you. Dragons are inscrutable at the best of times. If it helps, *I* think better of you every time we meet."

Merletta returned his smile, twining her fingers through his again. "I've missed you these last few weeks," she said quietly.

"I've missed you, too," Heath told her. "What's been happening?"

"Nothing of much interest," Merletta shrugged. "I got new shells."

Heath's eyes flicked quickly to her shells then even more quickly away. "They're...very nice."

Merletta couldn't help laughing. "I forgot you humans are so private. I suppose people don't comment on coverings where you're from."

"Well, no." Heath scratched the back of his neck. "I mean, people do comment on clothing. It's just...different."

"Why?" Merletta asked curiously.

Heath made a slightly strangled noise. "It's...hard to explain."

"All right." Merletta let it go without a fight. "How about you? Have you been busy trying to make peace between your warring tribes?"

Heath made a face. "I'm starting to think that's a hopeless cause. I haven't stayed away because I was busy. I've been watched too closely, thanks to Percival's latest antics. I only got away today because there was so much kerfuffle with my sister that—"

He cut off abruptly, his eyes suddenly unfocused and his body rigid.

"Heath?" Merletta asked, alarmed. "Are you all right?"

Abruptly, his gaze snapped back to her, clear once more. "I saw her," he gasped. "Laura. She's had the babies—there were two after all! How could the physicians all have gotten it wrong?"

"Your sister?" Merletta demanded. "What do you mean two after all? She's had twins?"

Heath nodded, running a hand distractedly through his hair. "She looked pretty haggard in the image," he muttered. "Maybe that's normal, I wouldn't know, but..."

"You should go home," Merletta said firmly. "Your family needs you."

Those words seemed to pull Heath from his abstraction. His eyes were faintly distressed as they met hers. "Why is it that my family always seems to need me right when I want to be with you?"

Merletta smiled. "We'll have another chance to talk."

"Who said anything about talking?" Heath murmured, his voice suddenly a little husky.

Tentatively, he reached out, sliding a hand around the back of her neck. Merletta's pulse quickened, and she couldn't seem to remember how to swallow. She tilted her head hopefully, but in spite of his words, Heath made no move toward her. His eyes were still troubled as they rested on her face, and when he spoke his voice was strained.

"Do you think that guard is right?" he asked. "Am I too dangerous for you? If I thought my presence here really was enough to put you at risk..."

"Of course he's not right," Merletta protested. She placed her hand firmly over Heath's on her neck, trapping it in place. "Heath, you're the best thing in my life. I wouldn't trade this for anything."

Heath didn't look reassured.

"Honestly," Merletta told him, "there's no reason to think the Center knows about our meetings here. I don't know why Griffin was being so unreasonable."

Heath gave her an incredulous look. "Do you really not know?"

Merletta frowned, but before she could voice her question, the unmistakable signs of Reka's descent stirred the heavy air of the lagoon. A moment later, the dragon was alighting on the rocks beside them, his tail dangling into the water.

"Heath," he said in his gravelly voice, the word a command.

Heath made no attempt to argue this time. With a last lingering look, and a swift squeeze of the hand, he stepped back, allowing Reka to seize his shoulders.

"Goodbye, Merletta," he said. "For now."

The following fortnight passed interminably for Merletta. In spite of the softening words, Heath's farewell had felt uncomfortably final. But he would be back. She knew he would. He'd promised that he'd always come for her if it was in his power. No matter what passed, no matter the dangers, he always came back for her. If only Griffin hadn't planted such foolish concerns in Heath's already over-anxious mind.

About two weeks after the visit to the island, Merletta found herself scowling down at the writing leaf she was working on, her irritation with the youngest of the guards flaring once again. The earful she'd given him after Heath's departure hadn't made her feel better at all, perhaps because he'd shown no sign of contrition whatsoever. Even August, when he'd returned, had taken the news of the dragon's visit far more gravely than Merletta knew it deserved. The guards all knew the extent of the Center's lies from their own experience. Why did their faith in what they'd been taught about dragons run so deep?

"You're going to put a hole in the leaf if you push that hard," Sage commented from beside her.

Merletta grimaced as she followed Sage's gaze and realized she'd been pressing down so hard that the coral implement in her hand had indeed punctured the writing leaf.

"Tell me that's one of yours, not a leaf from the public records," Sage said dryly. "You don't need more reasons for Ibsen to make you do penance by assisting the scribes for the rest of the day."

Merletta made a dismissive noise in her throat at the mention of the previous day's incident. "We both know that wasn't penance. It was his latest inspiration for how to prevent me from a day of actual learning." She leaned her head to the side. "Although I did learn quite a bit. I don't think he realized Emil was overseeing the scribes that day." A grin spread over her face. "The records he had me copy out were a little above the clearance level of your average scribe."

Sage gave a light laugh, in itself an indication of how much more of a rule breaker she'd become since befriending Merletta. "I didn't know Emil was there. That was lucky."

"It was," Merletta acknowledged. "You're right that I shouldn't give Ibsen more opportunities to block me, though. You'll be glad to know this leaf is mine. Much good it does me, to have my own record of injuries suffered by workers on the oyster farms over the last six months. Something tells me that's not the kind of history that will be in the third year test."

"I doubt it," Sage agreed.

"Was it like this for you?" Merletta asked. "I wasn't paying much attention to your studies last year, but I don't remember you spending much time in the public records room like this."

Sage shook her head. "I was hardly ever in here. There are special study areas for higher level students, which you should be able to access from the start of third year."

"Yes, well, I can't," Merletta said darkly. "Ibsen says I have to earn the right to access them by passing a practice test. But he's clearly not giving me the information I need even to pass that."

Sage frowned. "You shouldn't need to spend this much time in private study, anyway. I was given most of my information in class. But when I did access the records for clarification, Ibsen had nothing to do with the process. I got in by..." She lowered her voice and looked around. "By using the watchword."

Merletta stilled, surprised. "The one from the second year test? But I know that. Where do I go?"

"It's inside the Center's central spire," Sage said softly. "At the base."

Merletta gave a decisive nod. "I'll go right now."

She'd half risen into the water already, but Sage reached out and pulled her down.

"Wait until a different day," she pleaded. "If you race straight there from talking to me, it will be obvious that I told you where to find it."

"You're right," Merletta realized, glancing over at the record holder on duty in the public records room.

Sage was still months away from her final test in the program, and she couldn't afford to antagonize the instructors just yet. Merletta glanced at the light filtering in through the room's small windows.

"I need to go, anyway! I'm supposed to be training with Freja's patrol today. I almost forgot."

"Don't keep them waiting," said Sage vaguely, returning to her own study.

Merletta swam from the records hall swiftly, dodging around the two new first years who'd started in the last fortnight. They watched her curiously as she passed. She'd heard that the Center had received a record number of applicants in recent months, including a continued stream of Tilssted hopefuls. None of them had made it through, but this pair—both from Hemssted—clearly had.

Merletta sent them a small smile, reminding herself not to be prejudiced against them simply because the other Hemssted trainees tended to be unfriendly. She still hadn't quite come to terms with the fact that she was apparently from Hemssted by birth. At least the two trainees returned her smile tentatively, which helped a little.

Freja was already in the training yard, but she didn't look impatient. As Merletta swam up, Felix appeared from one of the storage areas, a new slingshot in his hand.

"Ah, Merletta, good," Freja greeted her with a smile. "We're all here. Let's go."

Merletta caught sight of Ileana across the training yard. The look she sent Merletta was resentful. It was no surprise—she was an actual guard, unlike Merletta, and the squad she'd been assigned to wasn't nearly as senior as Freja's. But there was something more than resentment there. Merletta would almost have called it wistfulness. She shook the thought off uncomfortably. She'd suspected before now that Ileana was jealous of her, but it was still hard to fathom. At least the former trainee had so far shown no sign of approaching Merletta at all, let alone trying to hassle her as she'd once done.

As the squad swam across the drop off, heading southeast toward Hemssted, Felix came up alongside Merletta.

"You've got a lot to answer for, you know," he told her cheerfully.

"I do?" Merletta asked, narrowing her eyes in mock wariness.

Felix nodded. "I have a little sister. She was a surprise—she's much younger than me. Not to blow my own conch," he said in a tone of modesty completely belied by the accompanying wink, "but I'm kind of her hero. She's been talking for years about becoming a guard when she grows up. But now, thanks to you, she wants to be a record holder."

"Thanks to me?" Merletta repeated, astonished.

"Well, thanks to the phase you've started, anyway," Felix amended. "Every merman and his seal wants to join the program now. You've made it seem cool and exciting."

"How, by publicly heaving up her breakfast in front of half the triple kingdoms at that memorial?" chimed in one of the other guards in the patrol. He sent Merletta a roguish grin, robbing the words of any malice.

She groaned at the memory, and Felix chuckled. "No, that was just how everyone heard of her in the first place. Apparently, and these are my sister's words, not mine, Merletta has showed by being a tough outsider who can succeed against the odds that the program isn't just for snobby stuck-up academics."

"Oh, well...good for her, I guess," Merletta said blankly, trying to find herself in this heroic image.

"That was pretty half-hearted for someone whose life dream is to complete the program," laughed Felix.

Merletta acknowledged it with a rueful smile, but she didn't have it in her to fake enthusiasm. "Reality rarely reflects our dreams, does it?"

Freja made a tutting noise with her tongue. "That's very jaded for such a young mermaid, Merletta. It's not like you."

Merletta fell silent, not sure whether to be chastened or frustrated. Everyone seemed to have an idea of what she was really like, but none of it matched her own sense of self. Perhaps that was the inevitable result of her becoming so visible, through no intention of her own.

The group spent the afternoon patrolling the barrier along Hemssted's border. Merletta couldn't help examining the residents as they passed through the city on their way to the outskirts. They didn't seem disapproving and cold, as Oliver and Lorraine both were. But neither was there anything familiar about them. If this had once been her home, no trace of connection remained.

The first half of the patrol was uneventful. However, when they swapped with another group, moving up to the northern part of Hemssted's boundary, closer to Tilssted, things became more interesting. The first time they encountered a random resident attempting to cross the barrier, Merletta felt a flicker of surprise. She couldn't remember ever seeing anyone other than herself doing so, in all her years of sneaking out of the triple kingdoms.

She'd seen merpeople outside the barrier, of course. Harvesters, hunters, guards—all with legitimate reasons that took them beyond the triple kingdoms, although never far outside. But this young merman appeared to simply be exploring. His medium-length hair was a little unkempt, and he wore no adornments in it, as she would expect a merman from Hemssted to wear. They were close enough to the boundary that he could well be from Tilssted, of course.

Freja, her manner kind enough but unyielding, directed him back inside and warned him against the danger of wandering outside the barrier alone. Merletta didn't even feel uncomfortable to stay silent. She had to agree with Freja on this occasion —the merman didn't look very strong, or sufficiently prepared to wander the open ocean alone.

The second time, it was a group of three—two mermaids and one merman—and they weren't quite as young as the first one. They required a sterner approach in order to convince them to turn back, although again Merletta made no attempt to intervene in Freja's response. She was too perplexed by the unprecedented occurrence.

The third time, Felix actually had to seize one of the inquisitive mermen and drag him back across the barrier.

The disgruntled wanderer glared at them, looking ready to do battle.

"Come on," his companion muttered. "It's not worth dying over."

As he pulled his friend away, the first merman's murmured reply came wafting through the water to Merletta's ears.

"But you must have seen their weapons. They're Center

guards. Why are they turning us back when it's the Center who said it might be safe to live outside the barrier now?"

Merletta froze, gripping her spear so tightly it was painful.

"Did you hear that?" Felix asked, looking perplexed. "That's the opposite of what the Center is always reminding everyone. Why would they think the Center said anything like that?"

Merletta swallowed nervously and forced herself to move slightly in the water, knowing how suspicious her total stillness would be to any canny observer. She could only be grateful the men hadn't recognized her somehow as the Tilssted trainee, or no doubt she would be facing some very uncomfortable questions from the rest of the patrol.

Because, she reflected as the patrol headed back to the Center a short time later, she was pretty sure she knew exactly why the random Tilssted residents would think that. Just how far had the story of her conversation with the shellsmith apprentices reached?

CHAPTER THIRTEEN

"Focus, Heath."

Reka's gravelly voice betrayed a hint of impatience. Most unreasonable, Heath thought, in an immortal creature with unlimited time at his disposal.

"I am focusing," Heath said, frustrated. "I promise you, I'm thinking of nothing but Merletta right now, and I still can't see her surroundings."

"That's precisely my point," said Reka with maddening calm. "You are focused on her, yes. But the purpose of this exercise isn't to see what she's doing. It's to develop your farsight. You need to focus on your craft, not just the object of your obsession."

"It's not an obsession," said Heath, irked. "Maybe if you find your *pair*, or whatever you dragons call it, one day, then you'll understand."

"Maybe," said Reka, unconcerned. "But I hope I am not so absurdly sentimental over it as you are. Unlikely," he added after a moment of reflection, "given I am not an over-emotional human."

Happily for the progress of the training session, Heath's

reply was cut off as the dragon was suddenly hit with a new thought.

"That reminds me," he said brightly. "Today seems a good opportunity to spend some time on your other sight, the one that aids you in seeing others' emotions."

Heath opened his narrowed eyes fully, abandoning the attempt to expand his farsight beyond Merletta's features. "Really? Shouldn't we master the farsight first?"

Reka shook his head. "You are more capable with the farsight than you believe. You just need practice. It will broaden with time. Learning to use your magic in other ways as well might even be beneficial in strengthening your farsight."

"All right," said Heath amicably. "So how does the other sight work?"

"You tell me," Reka said. "What is it you see?"

Heath shrugged. "I don't really know how to explain it. I wouldn't have thought of it as seeing, but I suppose that's what it is. I can sometimes just tell things. Like that someone is hiding something, or that what they say isn't what they mean, or that they're troubled even when their features don't show it."

"But not all the time?" Reka pressed.

Heath shook his head. "Definitely not. And it's unpredictable when it will kick in."

The dragon nodded sagely. "It has so far been a random escape of your magic, not in your control. But I have no doubt you could learn to channel it."

"How?" Heath asked.

"The first step is to gain control over your magic," said Reka. "Don't misunderstand—I don't mean that your magic is somehow wild, or out of your control. On the contrary, your power, while substantial, is the most muted I've ever seen. Until recently, it felt from the outside as though it was dormant inside you, probably not even detectable to a human with only limited power, although impossible for a dragon to miss. What you need to do is wake it up, and learn how to draw it out and harness it when you wish to use it. In time, I suspect you will be able to live with your magic in a state of constant active-ness."

Heath smiled faintly. "You make it sound like a wild animal living inside me."

"Far from it," Reka contradicted. "It is not another force inside you. It is completely and inextricably you. That is a truth that the non-power-wielders—like your king—have utterly failed to grasp in attempting to impose restrictions on the use of your magic."

Heath sighed. "Yes, but let's not talk about politics today," he pleaded. "I had more than enough of it yesterday, between the meeting with Prince Lachlan and the Chief Counselor, and Percival's usual tirades over dinner."

"Nothing would please me more than to avoid discussing mundane human politics," said Reka, no acknowledgment in his lofty tone that he'd been the one to bring it up.

Heath let it go. "So how do I wake up my magic?" he asked instead.

"Well, clearly the process has already begun," Reka responded. "What we want is for you to have more control over that process. When you reach inside yourself, can you feel your magic?"

Heath frowned. "I don't really know what you mean by reach inside myself," he admitted.

Reka didn't seem daunted. For a moment he was silent, considering. Then he said, "Can you sense my magic? And that of your family?"

"Of course," said Heath. "Yours rolls off you in waves compared to theirs."

Reka nodded. "Focus on that sensation. Reach for my power with your mind, identify it, examine it."

Heath did so, noting the constant flow of the dragon's magic, and how even when Reka was resting, it reached out from him, filling the air around him.

"And now," Reka said, "look for that faint trace of similar power inside yourself."

Heath did so, using the extra indefinable sense that only power-wielders had. "Nothing floats around me like it does you," he said.

Reka nodded again. "That is partly because your power is nowhere near as strong as mine, and partly because for the most part it remains buried deep inside you. But surely you can still sense it."

Heath closed his eyes, the better to try again. After a moment of considering Reka's magic, he attempted to shut off his awareness of it, trying instead to sense the type of magic he so often felt from his father, or Percival.

He thought he could feel it, faintly. It was like theirs, and yet unlike. For a moment he pressed into the sensation, but its very foreignness was unnerving. His mind suddenly shied away from it.

"Aha," said Reka, sounding pleased. "Now we're getting somewhere. For the briefest second I felt the raw power inside you stir. Why did you pull back from it?"

"I...I don't know," Heath said, lifting one shoulder uncomfortably. "It just felt...foreign."

"It isn't foreign," said Reka patiently. "It's unfamiliar perhaps, in that it isn't quite like the magic either of a dragon or of any other human you know. But it is unquestionably part of you. It should not feel foreign."

Heath said nothing, unsure how else to explain it.

"Try again," Reka encouraged. "And this time, do not flee from it like a frightened rabbit."

Heath turned his senses again to the power he'd identified,

amazed at how quickly his mind raced back to it. Reka had talked about drawing it out and harnessing it, so he tried to encourage it to expand, to reach out from him. He thought he could feel it for a moment, stretching eagerly outward. He opened his eyes tentatively, searching Reka's face for confirmation that he was doing it right.

His mind was suddenly flooded with consciousness that had nothing to do with what his eyes could see. Reka's placid face still filled his vision, but it was meaningless, entirely unrepresentative of what was happening inside the dragon.

Reka was a flaming ball of raging conflict and divided loyalties. Heath could almost *see* his friend's former certainty as to the superior wisdom of his kind—and by extension himself—battling against other considerations. Considerations Heath could only call emotion.

"Reka," he said, astonishment making him lose his clumsy hold on his magic. He felt it retreat, but it was still present, still in his consciousness. "What's wrong? What's causing you so much turmoil?"

Reka stared at him. "What do you mean? I felt your magic at work. What did it show you?"

"I think...I think it showed me a glimpse inside your mind," Heath said, with a touch of apology. "It was...intense."

There was a long silence. "I do not like that," Reka said, the words spoken without emotion. "Perhaps I grasp in part what you meant about the discomfort of using your farsight."

"It's a little different when the boot is on the other foot, isn't it?" Heath said dryly.

"Do not be absurd." Reka's voice was once again lofty. "Dragons do not wear boots, or any other kind of covering. We have no need to hide ourselves in such a way."

Heath didn't respond, still examining his friend. It was clear that whatever he'd seen, Reka had no intention of explaining it.

But although Heath's magical vision hadn't given him any specifics as to the cause of Reka's struggle, he had an uneasy feeling that it related to the dragon's coldness toward Merletta.

"That was good progress," Reka said approvingly. "You are starting to get a feel for your magic. With practice, and patience, you will be able to encourage it to show you what you wish to see at will, not just in random spurts." He tilted his head as he looked Heath over. "But you are still so tentative. Perhaps you should speak with your grandmother. She was once afraid of her power, was she not?"

"I'm not afraid of it," Heath said quickly. "Honestly, I'm not. It just...doesn't feel like it's mine." The dragon was frowning at him, and he sighed. "I don't know how to explain it."

"Well, we're making good progress on waking it, anyway," said Reka. "No doubt it will feel more like yours once you've mastered its use."

"Yes," said Heath without conviction. "Probably.'"

"Would you like to return to your farsight training?" Reka asked. "I assume you are curious about Merletta's activities. I have been surprised that you have not asked me to take you back to Vazula since our last visit there."

Heath was silent for a moment. Reka was right—it had been weeks since he'd last seen Merletta, and he hadn't mentioned the matter to the dragon.

"I do want to see her," he said slowly. "But...well, you heard what that guard said. He claimed I put Merletta's life—all of their lives—at risk just by going there. I'd never thought I was a danger to Merletta. The island always seemed so isolated, so far from her underwater world." His voice turned rueful. "But it's not entirely isolated anymore, is it? What if they're right? What if friendship with me is a danger to Merletta's life?"

He didn't voice the rest of his thoughts. He was ashamed to put into words how thrown he'd been by the sudden addition of the guards to the island sanctuary. Vazula had always been about him and Merletta, and no one from either of their worlds had been able to claim any part of their interactions there. More than that—Merletta had given the impression that she was happiest with him, away from everyone else. It had felt like that was her true place, just as it felt like his. As if their other lives dragged them unwillingly away from where they really wanted to be.

Now...well, Merletta's world seemed to have suddenly opened up before Heath's eyes. He'd rejected her suggestions that she didn't really have a place in the Center, insisting that she'd fought hard for her place and should claim it with pride. And he'd meant what he said. But at the same time, he was uncomfortably aware that while she had the right to a place in the underwater world, he belonged outside it.

A short time ago, it had seemed like he was the only man in Merletta's world, because any others were well out of sight, and she never spoke of any enough to make him take notice. Now, she'd accidentally started some kind of confusing relationship with another trainee, and one of the guards was showing clear signs that he felt possessive over her. Even if Merletta was too oblivious to realize what Griffin's over-reactions meant.

If Heath was honest with himself, he was rattled by the competition. Half-ashamed of these thoughts, he had no intention of sharing them with Rekavidur.

He was glad of the forbearance when Reka gave a predictably maddening response to what he had shared.

"It is perhaps for the best," the dragon said, nodding wisely. "You will not endanger her by staying here, where you belong."

"I didn't mean forever," said Heath, a snap to his voice that he instantly regretted. Taking a breath, he moderated his tone. "I'm not going to end my friendship with Merletta, Reka. That's never going to happen. And if you're not willing to tell me why you disapprove of the friendship, then you can keep your scaled, fire-breathing mouth shut about it."

Reka blinked his orb-like eyes. Heath knew no other human alive would dare speak to a dragon so. But he and Reka had always been a special case, and he felt no fear, even as he saw his friend hover on the edge between offense and amusement.

"Human folly," the dragon said at last, apparently tipping toward the latter. "My mouth does not have scales."

CHAPTER FOURTEEN

Although he'd instantly refuted the dragon's suggestion that he was afraid of his magic, the comment about consulting his grandmother lingered in Heath's mind long after his training session with Reka. Heath's elderly grandparents had returned some weeks before from their annual summer trip to Kyona—the kingdom of Princess Jocelyn's birth —and Heath hadn't made time for a proper conversation with his grandmother since then.

The following day he found himself wandering toward the castle, although he wasn't expected for any formal duties. The princess wasn't hard to track down, and as always, she expressed herself delighted to have a private chat with him.

When they were settled in her receiving room, a steaming pot of tea before them, it took no time at all for a few shrewd grandmotherly questions to bring the whole tale tumbling out.

"So Reka described your magic as dormant," the princess mused, settling back into her seat with her teacup cushioned between two wrinkled hands. "That's an interesting way of putting it. I always said I could sense magic in you, but I had no explanation for why it was so...elusive." She smiled warmly at him, a hint of apology in her eyes. "I suppose I thought it might be weak—limited to slightly sharpened eyesight—and that was why it was hard to detect."

"No need to be sorry for that," Heath told her frankly. "I was never sensitive about it, even before I knew what power I had. Not that I can fully claim to know it now either," he added.

"Yes, I always admired your grace on the topic," his grandmother informed him.

He smiled in gratitude for the compliment, but the expression was half-hearted. "People always assumed I was upset or embarrassed about apparently not having magic when the rest of my family did," he told her. "But I truly wasn't. It wasn't that I thought magic was bad or anything. But it wasn't something I felt I needed. Laura's magic is wonderful, but that benefited me from *outside* the power at least as much as it benefited her from inside."

He paused, considering. "Father's magic I could see the use of, but it just seemed to create a lot of work, and high expectations from the crown. And Percival's..." Heath shrugged. "Well, he'd never believe it, probably, but I never coveted his strength. I thought it made him more arrogant, but less genuinely useful a person than if he'd just been a normal strong man."

"Hm." The elderly princess pondered his words. "I can certainly see your point there. It seems to me that something in you has been rejecting, or at least resisting, the magic since it first appeared. I accept your word for it that you're not afraid of it. The fact that you didn't embrace it because you didn't think you needed it is admirable, in one sense. I can respect that. But it's also false, ultimately. Magic was given to you. You can't just throw it away because you don't think it's necessary. It's a part of you. And it undoubtedly has a role to play in your life, and in the world around you. The truth is, the ones who least feel the need for power and influence are often those most to be trusted with it."

Heath was silent as he thought all this over. "Somehow I feel I'm being given a compliment I don't deserve," he said ruefully. He sighed. "It's become more complicated now, anyway. I might not have wanted power or influence, but I suppose I got it when the king gave me this position. A position based on the premise that I *don't* have magic, and can therefore bridge the gap."

"I see what you mean," nodded his grandmother. "But none of that is a reason for you to resist your magic."

"I know," he assured her.

He didn't tell her he was training regularly with Reka, because doing so would be admitting to a breach of the king's restrictions, and might put her in a difficult position. But surely she understood it from what he'd already said.

"Speaking of your liaison position," said his grandmother, "I'd formed the impression that you weren't engaging anymore, and I must say I've been glad to see you spending more time with Lachlan lately."

Heath broke into a genuine grin at the thought of the clandestine investigation he and his second cousin had entered into together, and the crown prince's evident inner battle. Heath didn't even need to activate his extra vision to sense that the prince was torn between enjoying the excitement and wondering if he was betraying his duty.

Heath's grandmother obviously caught the expression, because she raised a questioning eyebrow.

"Yes, we work surprisingly well together once the formality is stripped away," Heath acknowledged.

She smiled back at him, her lined face warmer and more pleasant than any Heath knew, with one significant exception.

"He's a good boy," said the princess indulgently. "Brielle and I were speaking of him just this morning. He'll be a good king one day, but probably all the better if he gives himself more of a chance to be young, and have meaningful friendships not based on his title. I think you're good for him, and Brielle agrees."

Heath blinked, taken aback at this image of his grandmother talking about him with Prince Lachlan's grandmother, also known as the dowager queen.

"Don't let him be too stiff, if you can help it," his grandmother added.

Heath nodded, half of him glad of the permission to keep prodding Prince Lachlan away from the rigid formality he'd been schooled in, and half of him dreading the idea of a further responsibility being placed on his own shoulders. He didn't want to be the one in charge of making sure the crown prince was relaxed enough to be a good future king. But looking around at the court, he didn't see any other contenders for genuine friendship with the prince. Prince Lachlan held himself too aloof.

"The truth is," Heath blurted out, "we're trying to figure out who was really behind the attack on Percival."

His grandmother lowered her tea, staring at him in astonishment. "Lachlan is investigating that with you? Even though his father has dismissed it as a robbery gone wrong?"

Heath nodded. "You won't tell the king, will you?" he asked anxiously.

"No, I certainly won't," she said. "I don't need you or anyone else to tell me that Lachlan would never do anything to hurt Valoria, or the crown. If my nephew wasn't so stubborn right now..." She trailed off, apparently deciding not to speak her frustrations with the king aloud, even to Heath. "Well, never mind that," she said briskly. "Tell me what you've found."

"Not much," Heath admitted. "Nothing that King Matlock doesn't know, little as he might accept its meaning." He told her about the guard uniforms, then hesitated. "There's an aspect of it I haven't told Lachlan. I didn't want to include him in this part of the investigation. But maybe you can help me."

"What's that?" she asked, clearly intrigued.

Heath heard a door open in the adjoining suite, which belonged to his grandfather. He hesitated for a moment, then shook off his concerns. His grandfather wasn't quite the natural confidant his grandmother was, but Heath trusted him equally. There was no harm in him hearing what was coming.

"I didn't get a good look at any of the men who attacked Percival," he said. "But I felt something. It was fleeting, because they were all fleeing as fast as their mounts could take them. But I felt it."

"What did you feel?" his grandmother pressed.

"Power," said Heath simply.

"Are you sure?" she asked, her eyes widening in alarm.

Heath nodded. "Like I said, it was only for the briefest moment. But it was familiar enough to be unmistakable." He hesitated, his voice full of meaning. "Just not so familiar that it could have been anyone in my family."

His companion stilled as she took his meaning. But before she could speak, they heard another door open through the wall. Heath assumed his grandfather was leaving his suite, but a soft knock sounded on the adjoining door a moment later.

"Enter," called the elderly princess.

The door opened, and the familiar form of Heath's grandfather appeared.

"Hello, my dear. Hello, Heath," Prince Kincaid said cheerfully. He stooped to kiss his wife's cheek. "I thought you must have company when I saw the maid hesitating at the doorway."

"Maid?" Heath asked, unspecified alarm sweeping through him.

He shifted in his chair to peer through the still-open doorway, and saw a girl walking briskly from the adjoining suite, her arms full of linen. Hastily, Heath tried to pull on his magic the way Reka had told him. He felt it there, and struggled clumsily to grasp it, to accept it as under his control. When he threw it out from him, in the direction of the retreating servant, he caught a glimpse of something that increased his unease. Divided loyalty? No, hidden loyalty.

But he could see no more. The maid had passed out of his sight, and apparently out of his range.

"Who was that?" he asked hastily. "That servant?"

"I'm not sure of her name," his grandfather admitted. "She's one of the regular servants, though. She's been part of the rotation on our suites for, I don't know, the last year at least."

Heath bit his lip, not entirely reassured.

"What just happened, Heath?" his grandmother asked, watching him closely. "I just felt power reach out from you, in a way I can't remember sensing before."

"Ah!" Heath's grandfather lowered himself into a chair, snagging a pastry from the tray in front of them all as he surveyed Heath knowingly. "Been holding out on us all, have you, Heath? Well, that's an interesting turn of events."

"I was trying to..." Heath struggled for the words to explain it. "Trying to *see* anything not visible with normal sight. And I thought I did. Although I have no idea what it means. It was only a glimpse."

His grandmother frowned. "I'll have Kincaid point out which servant it was, and keep an eye on her," she assured Heath.

"I suppose that's all we can do," said Heath anxiously. "Do you think she overheard our conversation?"

"I don't know," said Princess Jocelyn. "The servants are generally well-trained not to eavesdrop."

Heath said nothing, and his grandmother fixed him with a look.

"I haven't forgotten what you were saying, you know. Are you suggesting the men who attacked Percival were Kyonan power-wielders?"

"What?" Prince Kincaid sat up straighter. "Surely not!"

"I don't want to believe it any more than you do," Heath said. "But I felt something, and I don't know all the Kyonan power-wielders well enough to discount the possibility altogether."

His grandmother looked very troubled. "We know them all. And I'd hate to believe it of any of them. What would Kyona have to gain from such an attack? Percival was popular there."

"The fact that they were disguised as Valorian royal guards suggests that the attack wasn't so much about getting rid of Percival as about causing strife between him and the crown," Heath pointed out.

"You think they weren't actually intending to kill him?" Heath's grandfather asked incredulously. "Just to rile him up?"

"I don't know." Heath raised his hands helplessly. "I won't pretend to have the answers. It certainly looked like his life was in danger."

He cast his mind back over the event, remembering how the attackers had fled at Reka's approach. Heath had assumed that he and Reka had arrived just in time. But if the intention was always for Percival to see the uniforms and carry the tale, killing him wouldn't have achieved it. Was it possible that far from foiling the attack, Heath's arrival had actually furthered the plan? Having a dragon frighten the attackers off was a much better tale than beating Percival senseless and supposedly leaving him for dead, or whatever the attackers had planned to do.

It was a horrible thought, that he might have aided the scheme. But the idea of staying away while Percival was beaten viciously was even more horrible.

Heath pulled himself from his thoughts with a sigh, to see that both of his companions looked deeply troubled.

"I can draw up a family tree for you," Princess Jocelyn said. "One outlining all the power-wielders in both the Kyonan and Valorian branches. It won't be difficult. There are only twenty-six of us."

"Don't forget Laura's twins," Heath reminded her with a smile.

"Of course," said his grandmother, her face softening. "Twenty-eight. How could I forget little Jacqueline and Germain? It was a nice touch, using family names from both Kyona's and Valoria's royal houses." Her smile dropped away. "But I have faith in every person who'll be on this list, you know."

"I'm in no hurry to accuse anyone," Heath assured her hastily. "You know me, Grandmother. I'm not on the warpath. I'm just looking for answers."

She nodded slowly, exchanging a glance with her husband that told Heath the two of them were in need of the opportunity to discuss his revelations privately.

"Thanks for the tea," he said, standing. "I'll speak with you soon." He hesitated for a moment, his eyes resting on his grandfather with the hint of a question. "I don't know how much Grandmother has told you about all this, but—"

"Don't worry about me, I'm not going to rat you out," Prince Kincaid said, waving a dismissive hand as he repositioned to sit next to his wife. He draped an arm around her shoulder. "I was the first Valorian to fall in love with magic, and although I have great respect for my nephew, I can see clear as day he's heading down the wrong path with these restrictions. I've told him as much myself. I'm not going to stand in the way of you trying to get to the bottom of it all."

Heath nodded gratefully as he took his leave. It was encouraging to know that people as wise and experienced as his grandparents were concerned by the restrictions. But in another way, it made King Matlock's uncharacteristic harshness all the more alarming.

It was two days later that his grandmother found the opportunity to give him the family tree she'd drawn up. Her expression was unusually somber as she did so, and scanning the names, Heath could understand why. He remembered many of these individuals from his visit to Kynton with Percival the year before. They'd been a friendly bunch, welcoming the brothers with open arms, and not hesitating to claim them as family. The idea that any of them could be involved in an attack on Percival was almost as distressing as the implication that they wished to cause trouble for Valoria.

The two kingdoms hadn't always had an easy history, but they'd been at peace for a long time now. It was awful to think of anyone wanting to breach that peace, but doubly so if it was a power-wielder.

On the other hand...Heath couldn't help remembering the way magic was revered and celebrated in Kyona. It had been a shock to him and Percival to see the dramatic difference between the two kingdoms' approaches. Had someone from the Kyonan power-wielders had a similar shock when they discovered how their Valorian brethren were treated? Was it possible they'd wanted to give the Valorians enough incentive to rise up and turn on their restrictive monarch? Perhaps they'd thought temporary injuries to the magically strengthened Percival a reasonable cost to pay for that end.

But no, such warped thinking surely couldn't belong to anyone on the list in his hand. Which left him with no answers, once again.

It was with a heavy heart that Heath entered Prince Lachlan's study in response to a summons. His shoulders slumped at the anticipated question.

"Have you discovered anything useful?" Prince Lachlan didn't look especially hopeful.

Heath shook his head. "I don't know where to look," he admitted.

"Well, I've found something," the prince said.

"Really?" Heath perked up.

Prince Lachlan nodded. "It's not exactly good news, but it is something. I found the report we spoke about, regarding the deaths connected with that market."

"And?"

The prince looked troubled. "There was a health inspection, as we predicted. And they found no sign of any major health concerns at either stall, or elsewhere in the market. Which is good news in one sense, of course," he added.

"Good news for the market," Heath agreed. "But it raises questions about the men's deaths."

The prince nodded. "There's more. I've been doing some digging, and I've learned of three more deaths that fit the same details."

"What details are they?" Heath asked.

"Men, relatively young, physically strong," Prince Lachlan listed. "Either known for being unscrupulous, or known to be in need of money. Ideal candidates for mercenaries, in other words."

Heath sat up straighter, impressed by the prince's shrewd assessment. "Mercenaries?" He fitted the pieces together in his mind. "You think someone hired random men to dress up as royal guards and attack Percival, then poisoned them to ensure their silence?"

"To say I think that's what happened would be jumping considerably too far ahead," the prince corrected. "But it has occurred to me that it's a possible explanation for these deaths."

"But this is serious, Lachlan," Heath said, alarmed.

The prince raised an eyebrow, and Heath smiled in spite of the topic of discussion. "Too familiar? The title gets tedious after a while, if I'm honest."

The other man gave a sudden, unexpected laugh. "For me too. Am I to call you Heath, then?"

"If you like," Heath said absently, his mind already back on the matter at hand. "It was worrying enough that someone was willing to target Percival to create a rift between the crown and the power-wielders."

He grimaced. "Not to mention that they were savvy enough to know how to do it. If that was their intention, Percival reacted in the most perfect way possible. A way that was, I have to admit, painfully predictable for anyone who knows him."

He drew a breath. "But if whoever is behind the attack is willing to kill off their hired hands so callously in order to cover their tracks..."

Lachlan nodded. "It suggests someone particularly unscrupulous," he finished. "Exactly the type of person or group one does *not* want planning underhanded attacks against the crown."

Heath opened his mouth, then closed it. The familiar feeling of being torn by divided loyalties squirmed inside him. He felt guilty for keeping his thoughts about the attack secret from his co-conspirator. But at the same time, the idea of sharing his suspicions with the crown prince made him feel sick to his stomach.

"What is it, Heath?" Lachlan asked, leaning forward. "Is there something you're not telling me?"

Heath let out a breath. "Nothing concrete," he said. "But there is one detail I didn't mention before...about the attack."

Lachlan waited silently, doing nothing to push Heath, which he appreciated.

"I hesitate to say it," Heath continued. "For fear of it being misinterpreted."

"I'm not prone to jumping to conclusions, I believe," Lachlan said calmly.

Heath nodded in acknowledgment, then let his breath out in a long exhale. "I sensed something from the fleeing men. It felt like...magic."

Lachlan leaned back, not quite able to keep his expression impassive. "Could it have been Lord Percival's strength at work?"

Heath shook his head. "It wasn't Percival's magic. Or Reka's. They're both so familiar to me, I couldn't possibly mistake them. Every power-wielder has a signature, and I would recognize any member of my family. It wasn't any of them."

"So it was entirely unfamiliar?" Lachlan pressed.

Heath shook his head slowly. "I don't know. It was different from my family's, but..." He let out a frustrated breath. "I wish I had the time back again! It was the most fleeting of glimpses, and I just can't be sure what I sensed. It's possible I imagined the whole thing."

"If it wasn't your family," Lachlan said slowly, his sharp mind connecting the dots much too astutely, "does that mean you suspect it was a Kyonan power-wielder?"

Heath shook his head rapidly. "I don't suspect anything. I would truly find it hard to believe of any of them. But if there's even the slimmest chance, and I hid it from you..."

"I appreciate your openness," Lachlan assured him. "And I understand why you were hesitant." He drummed his fingers on the desktop, deep in thought. "I won't mention the magic to my father," he said at last.

Unbidden, Heath felt a flicker of his own magic inside him. Lachlan's face was calm, but Heath could see the depth of his discomfort over keeping such a detail from his father. He appreciated it more than he could say, but he knew the prince well enough to recognize that it would benefit no one for him to articulate the cost aloud.

"If there was any concrete evidence, it would be a different matter," Lachlan said, seeming to speak mainly to himself. "But as it stands..."

He let the words trail off, but Heath understood. In his current frame of mind, King Matlock would leap to the worst conclusions from the suggestion that magic was involved in the attack. It would make the already elusive goal of healing the rift virtually impossible.

"But I will subtly investigate whether he suspects any threat from Kyona," Lachlan finished.

Heath winced. "If I was the cause of unfounded conflict between the two kingdoms, I'd never forgive myself," he said frankly.

"I feel the same way," Lachlan assured him. "And whatever either of us thinks of my father's current policy regarding magic, I can promise you that conflict with Kyona is the last thing he wants."

Heath nodded. He would have to be satisfied with that for the present, and hope that nothing disastrous came of his decision to trust Lachlan.

CHAPTER FIFTEEN

Heath was still mulling over it all as he walked from the castle back toward the family manor. It wasn't a long walk, and the route was so familiar, he paid little attention to his surroundings.

So little attention that he failed even to notice the sound of pounding hooves until a shout of warning pulled him from his musing. He gasped at the sight of a runaway horse charging toward him at full speed. There was no sign of a rider or owner —the creature was unsaddled, and seemed to be completely out of control.

By the time Heath looked up, it was almost upon him. He threw himself to the side of the cobbled street, crying out in pain as one flailing hoof actually grazed his arm. A narrow escape indeed.

The thought had barely crossed his mind when heavy fabric fell on him, blacking out his vision completely. As he struggled with what he suddenly realized was the collapsed awning of the potter's stall next to which he'd been walking, something flickered at the edges of his awareness. Something familiar and yet foreign, its presence barely reaching his consciousness through the panicked feeling of blindness and suffocation.

Heath stilled, trying to clear his thoughts and focus. The hoofbeats had faded—he was in no further danger from the runaway horse. And although the awning was heavy, and his breath was coming in frantic bursts, it wasn't actually enough to crush him, or suffocate him. Panic was uncalled for, and would achieve nothing.

But just as his breathing started to slow, he heard another scream of warning. He made one more futile attempt to get the fabric off him, but he was too entangled. Letting go of all thought of tracking down whatever elusive sensation had piqued his interest a moment earlier, he focused his attention inward instead, trying to tease out the magic Reka assured him was strong inside.

"I need to see," Heath muttered, opening his eyes against the blackness and staring straight up.

At once, his vision flared to life. He could tell that his physical eyes were encountering nothing, but at the same time he could see with perfect clarity what was on the other side of the muffling fabric.

His eyes widened at the sight of a tall stone chimney teetering directly above him. It had been built onto the blacksmith's forge which sat beside the potter, but something had caused it to come adrift. Even as Heath watched, it began to fall outward, and he was right underneath it.

Heath didn't try again to get free of the awning—there was no time for that. With an almighty heave on the thick blanket of fabric, he instead rolled to the side, throwing his body across the ground with all his might. To his great relief, the fabric came with him. He rolled over and over until he was completely wrapped up in it, unable to get any further and with no hope of extricating himself.

But it had been enough. With a deafening crash, the chimney fell. Heath watched it happen with his other vision, and felt the pattering of stray chunks of stone as they scattered onto the top of his fabric cocoon. He was relieved to note with his extra sight that the onlookers had all been able to run out of the way of the falling stone, unhampered as they were.

As soon as the sound of crashing rock was silenced, exclamations rushed in to fill the space. After scanning the area to assure himself there was no immediate threat, Heath let his magic drop, his whole body drooping. It was still terrifying to be so enclosed, but he knew he'd escaped a gruesome death by a hairsbreadth.

Running feet approached him, and soon many hands were attempting to roll him free. Heath could only be grateful when, after a few painful tugs and drags, a commanding voice rose above the babble, bringing order to the chaos. Under the speaker's instruction, someone began to cut Heath free.

Whoever it was mercifully managed to avoid slashing him as well as the awning, and soon Heath emerged into the light with a shuddering gasp.

"Thank you," he said earnestly, turning to search for whoever had taken charge.

"Lord Heath!" The city guard was vaguely familiar to Heath. Probably a friend of Percival's. The man looked astonished at the identity of the near-victim, but Heath didn't stay to speak with him.

"I'm all right," he said quickly, in response to several inquiries. "I'm not hurt." He ran a hand over the place where the horse's hoof had got him, and held in a wince. "Not seriously hurt. I'll be fine."

"You were very lucky!" said another onlooker, with sympathy in her eyes as she glanced at the ruined building and crushed stall nearby. "The blacksmith and the potter less so."

Heath followed her gaze in alarm, but was relieved to see the men in question exclaiming in horror over the ruined workspace and smashed wares. At least she was speaking of their businesses, not their lives.

"I'm sure the king will be speaking with the blacksmith about keeping his building up to code," the guard said sternly, his eyes also on the men nearby.

"It wasn't his fault," Heath said quickly. The guard looked at him in surprise, and he faltered, "These things just happen...sometimes."

He immediately wished he hadn't spoken. The guard looked suspicious, his eyes passing thoughtfully between the slashed awning and the collapsed chimney. But Heath hated the idea of the blacksmith—who'd just suffered what could be a devastating loss—being blamed for what Heath was already afraid had been no accident.

Shaking off all suggestions that a physician be summoned immediately, Heath once again thanked his rescuers and hurried toward his home. He was shaken more than he cared to admit, but less by his near miss than by what it might mean.

He was relieved not to see Percival when he joined the rest of his family. Percival had made himself scarce since the house had been invaded by not one but two noisy infants. In fact, as soon as Heath entered the manor, he could hear one of them screaming at full volume.

Laura greeted him by way of holding the other child out at sight of him. "Heath, can you hold Jacqueline? Germain won't be satisfied with anyone but me, it seems."

Heath took his weeks-old niece carefully, lowering himself into a chair. She was so tiny and delicate, he couldn't help being nervous she would just break. But he didn't complain. He knew the strain must be wearing on Laura and Edmund. They'd never planned to have their baby—or rather, babies—in Bryford.

They were making no secret of their eagerness to return to their home, but the physician was still cautioning them that it was too soon after the birth for Laura to travel, and the babies were too young.

"Thanks, Heath." Laura let out a sigh of relief as Germain—having successfully made it into his mother's arms—stopped crying. "You're my hero—whoa." Laura swung around, studying Heath properly. "What's going on? Your emotions are...a mess."

Heath felt an involuntary shudder go over him. "I just had... an accident," he said.

Most unfortunately, his father had just walked into the room, and he gave Heath a sharp look. He must have sensed the deception in Heath's words.

"All right," Heath said quietly, his eyes now on the duke. "I'm not entirely sure it was an accident."

"What happened?"

His father's voice was calm but unyielding, and the whole incident poured out. By the end of it, Laura's eyes were wide with horror, and the duke's face was extremely grim.

"Who would dare to do such a thing?" he asked, and Heath could sense both fear and fury beneath his steady words.

"I don't know," said Heath helplessly. "It's possible that I'm overly suspicious, of course, and it was truly an accident."

No one looked convinced.

"What happened to your arm?" Laura asked suddenly, spotting the developing bruise.

"The horse's hoof nicked me," Heath told her. "But it's really nothing."

"We'll let the physician be the judge of that," said the duke, his tone still one of tightly controlled anger.

Before anyone could send for the physician, however, the door burst open, and Percival appeared.

"Heath, my friend just told me what happened! Are you all right?"

"I'm fine," Heath said soothingly, instantly switching into the usual placating role he played with Percival.

"He's not," Laura said forcefully, clutching the now-content Germain even more tightly to herself. "His arm has been trampled, and he's been scared half to death."

"You're exaggerating," Heath said. He went to raise his uninjured arm in a calming gesture, but thought better of it, given the child in his arms.

"She isn't exaggerating," interjected the duke. "This is a serious matter."

"It's more than that!" Percival raged.

His face was growing red in his anger. If Heath hadn't been able to see the real fear for him that added a frantic edge to his brother's demeanor, he would have been frustrated by Percival making such a scene about something that didn't involve him. But Percival's next words drove all other considerations from his mind.

"It's a declaration of war by the crown against power-wielders!"

"Don't be absurd," said the duke sharply.

"Absurd?" Percival repeated incredulously. "The king has tried to kill both of your sons now, Father. What will it take for you to get angry? Will he have to attack Laura, too? Or her babies?"

"Enough!" Laura's voice was unusually angry as well. "My children are off limits for using to make your point, Percival."

He raised his hands in a gesture of surrender, but his voice was no less fierce. "You know what I mean."

"I know that you're way off the mark," Heath said, exasperated. "King Matlock had nothing to do with what happened to me just now."

"Don't be a fool, Heath." Percival's eyes were bright with barely-suppressed energy. "Weren't you coming back from the castle, after a summons by Prince Lachlan? It was an ambush, just like my attack."

"I trust Lachlan completely," Heath said. "He's as much our family as any of the cousins you were so fond of in Kyona, Percival. He would never be involved in an attempt to kill me."

"You're as blinded as Father." Percival was actually quivering with tension now. "And it will get you killed."

"Calm down, Percival," Laura said.

Heath felt a wave of her power spreading out from her, but Percival clearly wasn't having a bar of it.

"Don't try to calm me down with your magic," he growled. "Just because I'm the only one in this family who can see what's happening doesn't give you permission to blind me along with the rest of them."

He stormed out, and Heath let out a humorless laugh, unable to help himself. It was Percival's suggestion that *he* was the one to see what no one else did which struck Heath as grimly amusing.

"I don't agree with Percival's interpretation of events," said the duke into the uncomfortable silence left by Percival's departure.

"Neither do I," Heath said quickly.

"But," the duke held up a hand, not finished, "I don't want you to think I'm taking this lightly." His eyes flicked from Heath to Laura, resting finally on little Germain in Laura's arms. "If someone is going after my family, I'm not going to stand idly by."

Heath nodded, a lump in his throat.

"Tell me exactly what happened again."

As his mind ran back over the events, Heath stilled. He

looked up at his father, and the duke could clearly read the hesitation in his eyes.

"Perhaps I should give you some time just to recover. We can talk later."

Heath gave him a grateful nod, although it wasn't that he needed time. It was that he had no idea how or even whether to tell his father what he'd just remembered. Because the sensation that had danced on his awareness at the time had just solidified in memory. It was the same unidentified magic he'd felt from Percival's attackers.

Which meant there was absolutely no chance what had just happened was an accident.

CHAPTER SIXTEEN

"Are you nervous?" Merletta asked Andre, noting the way his crimson tail flicked back and forth in the water.

"A little." He flashed her a grin. "Only because if Indigo gets in, I'll have to put up with her annoying questions every day instead of just on rest days."

Merletta laughed. "I don't believe you. I saw how excited you were this morning. It was kind of you to go meet your cousin at the reception hall. She would have been happy to see a friendly face when she was putting in her application."

Andre gave her a strange look. "Yes."

"He wasn't being kind," Emil said calmly, reaching across Andre to help himself to mussels from the trainees' basin. "It's an expectation. Her whole family would have been there."

"Really?" Merletta asked, equal parts fascinated and embarrassed. She'd once again displayed her ignorance of the customs of her world.

Andre nodded. "I guess...I guess they didn't do it when you applied. But there's usually a whole ceremony that happens. My aunt and uncle formally registered their approval of her chosen course, and listed the family history—anyone who'd served in the Center, their own current roles, that kind of thing."

"Wow." Merletta didn't know what else to say.

"It wasn't quite like that when you applied?" Sage asked delicately.

"Hardly." Merletta snorted. "I swam in, said I wanted to apply, the mermaid on duty looked at me like I was a sea snail, then reluctantly got the recruit-master who begrudgingly took me across the drop off and dumped me in his lobby. I waited for hours before they got to me, and then it was just me and whoever was testing me at the time."

"That's awful," said Sage indignantly. "No fanfare at all? And no encouragement, clearly. It's almost like they—"

"Wanted her to fail?" Emil's voice was dry, although quiet enough Merletta had to strain to hear. "I think we've already established that."

"Well, I didn't fail," said Merletta staunchly, not troubling to lower her own voice. "And neither will your cousin, I'm sure," she added, smiling encouragingly at Andre.

"Indigo will pass," Andre agreed. "I'm pretty confident."

"Surely we'll know soon," said Sage. "She's been sitting the entry tests for hours."

The meal was almost over when Andre glanced up, his face lighting up at something he could see over Merletta's shoulder.

She spun around in her seat to see the fair-haired young mermaid she'd met at Andre's house swimming excitedly across the dining hall, a fresh armband affixed to her arm.

"I did it, Andre!" she gushed, as she pulled up next to their table. "I passed!"

"Congratulations!" Andre rose into the water, pulling her into a hug as a grin split his face. "I knew you would."

"Am I too late to join you for dinner?" Indigo asked brightly, casting a hopeful glance at the octopus tentacles in the middle of the table.

"Not too late," Andre told her. "But you can't sit with us here. You need to sit down that end, with the other lowly first years."

Indigo glanced to the nearby slab which had been added in recent weeks to accommodate all the new trainees. There were already half a dozen merpeople sitting there—four from Hemssted, two from Skulssted. Indigo would even the numbers a little between the two wealthy cities. Tilssted, of course, was unrepresented, despite this being the highest number of first years the program had seen in decades. It seemed that, for better or worse, the program had achieved significantly higher visibility in the time Merletta had been studying there. She wondered uncomfortably if Felix was right, and she'd somehow been the cause of the program's new popularity.

"Oh," said Indigo, pulling Merletta's attention back to the present. The younger mermaid deflated visibly at her cousin's rebuff. "All right. I guess I'll see you at the ceremony tonight."

Sage rolled her eyes at Andre. "He's kidding," she told Indigo kindly. "There are no assigned seats. Of course you can sit with us."

"You can take my place," Emil said, rising from his seat. "Congratulations on passing your entry tests."

"Thank you," said Indigo politely, lowering herself into the vacated place. Her eyes followed Emil as he drifted across the room. "Is he a fourth year?" she asked Andre, clearly confused about the merman's age.

Andre shook his head, already shoving food into his mouth once more. "No, he's in his second year as a junior record holder. He'll be fully qualified in another year. He just keeps sitting with us because we're friends."

He puffed his chest out slightly as he spoke, and Indigo was visibly impressed.

Sage and Merletta exchanged a glance, then looked quickly away, valiantly swallowing their laughter. Even after all his disillusionments, Andre was still so endearingly eager. He was only just seventeen, after all. It was no surprise that he'd be proud to claim friendship with a twenty-one year old record holder like Emil.

Oliver and Lorraine were also seated at the round table which had once been sufficient for all the trainees. But shortly after Indigo joined them, they rose, making for the exit without congratulating her on successfully joining the program.

"Are they older trainees?" Indigo asked, a touch anxiously. "Do you think they were offended to have a first year sitting here?"

Andre shook his head. "Don't worry about them," he said dismissively. "They're from Hemssted, so they think they're better than everyone else."

"Oh, all right." Indigo accepted this explanation readily, reaching for some food.

Frowning, Merletta laid down the last of her salted cod. Had the trainees from different cities been so scathing about each other when she first started? She didn't think so. Perhaps they'd just seemed united against a common enemy in the form of the Tilssted interloper. But it really seemed different to her—as though the antagonism between the cities had ramped up in recent times.

"Well done on your test, that's fantastic," Sage was telling Indigo, and Merletta hastened to add her congratulations as well.

"What ceremony were you talking about earlier?" Merletta asked, as the dining hall started to empty. "Is something happening tonight?"

"Oh, just my acceptance ceremony," Indigo explained. "I

know my parents will expect Andre to come." She sent him a mock glare.

"I'll be there," he said, raising his hands defensively.

"What do you mean, acceptance ceremony?" Merletta asked, perplexed. "Aren't you just...in the program now?"

Sage shifted uncomfortably in her seat. "Well, usually there's a formal event," she explained. "Where the family of the new trainee sort of...hands them over to the Center for their education."

"Do you want to come along and see it?" Andre asked.

Indigo shot him an uncertain look, but when she caught Merletta's eyes on her, she smiled. "Of course, you're very welcome."

"Let's all go," Sage said firmly. "I'll see if I can get Emil to join as well."

Merletta allowed herself to be swept along on the current of Sage's decision, unsure whether she really wanted to witness the event. But two hours later, as she watched Indigo's parents swim her across the drop off and present her to Wivell, Ibsen, and Agner along with a satchel full of personal items, she was glad to be present.

Wivell, the chief instructor, shifted forward and spoke formal words of acceptance and welcome. Merletta could see the pride on Indigo's parents' faces, and the barely contained excitement that made Indigo's two younger siblings bounce in the water.

"We are honored by your acceptance of our daughter," Indigo's father was saying, in a tone that told Merletta the words were memorized. "And we entrust her to you until she is ready to take her place."

"We are honored by your trust," Wivell responded. He presented the family with an intricately carved coral sculpture in the shape of a sea star.

"They get to display that in her house for as long as she's a trainee," Sage whispered into Merletta's ear in explanation.

"To show off to the neighbors that their daughter made it into the program, basically," Emil added from Sage's other side.

Merletta had been surprised that he was willing to come. Sage must have found a way to persuade him. Merletta watched, fascinated, as Indigo turned and embraced her parents with what seemed to her an excess of emotion.

"Won't she be seeing them again on rest day?" she whispered to Sage.

Sage nodded. "Of course. But it's part of the tradition. They act like they won't see each other for four years—or as long as she succeeds in the program, anyway."

"Where does that tradition come from?" Merletta asked. "Was the program once at a separate location from the rest of the triple kingdoms? Or were they stricter about visiting family or something?"

Sage shrugged. "I don't think so. I mean, I've never heard anything like that." She turned to Emil. "Have you?"

He shook his head.

"When I had my ceremony," Sage added, "my mother joked that maybe someone with a difficult child introduced the gesture because they wished they could get out of the weekly visits. Trainee records are one of the areas she works in, you know, so she would have seen if there had been a wildly different way of doing the training within our recorded history."

Merletta frowned. Sage was right—given that her mother was a record holder, she should know as well as anyone where the Center's traditions came from. It seemed unlikely to Merletta that such a practice had just been invented for show.

The thought troubled her. It was like the incident with Andre's family record—the makers of the record claimed that it went back as far as the triple kingdoms' history, but it didn't seem to stretch far enough to Merletta. There was a gap of missing time before the records began.

"Does she oversee our records, then?" Merletta asked, unnerved that she hadn't known that aspect of Sage's mother's role the whole time she'd been staying with the family.

Sage nodded. "I believe so. Well," she amended, "I don't think she's allowed to have any direct involvement in mine, because of the obvious personal interest. But everyone else's, yes." She grinned at Emil. "She's not allowed to tell me the contents, of course, but I have it on good authority that your fourth year results were something I should be aspiring to."

Emil looked startled. "You and your mother talked about my results? She said that?"

"Was she wrong?" Sage asked innocently.

"Yes," said Emil. "I mean, no. That is, my results were..." He realized Merletta and Sage were both chuckling, and he scowled. "I just meant she was wrong to tell you what any other trainee got."

"She didn't tell me anything specific," Sage said, still grinning. "She just admires you, that's all."

Emil's ears had gone slightly pink, and Merletta sent Sage a look of impressed amusement. It was quite a feat to fluster Emil.

Indigo's family were starting to head back over the drop off now, their gazes still full of pride as they looked back at Indigo, now floating happily next to Andre and chatting with a cheerful Agner.

"Is the single satchel just for show as well?" Merletta asked. "Will her family bring loads of other stuff for her tomorrow or something?"

"No, that bit is real," Sage said. "Everyone is only supposed to bring what can fit in one satchel. You're supposed to leave your wealth and family behind, so that everyone enters the program as equals, with no advantage or disadvantage."

She winced slightly as she said it, but Merletta hadn't been going to take a shot at the Center's hypocrisy. Her mood was thoughtful as she reflected on the ceremony she'd just witnessed.

"They didn't do any part of this ceremony for you, did they?" Sage asked sympathetically.

"No," Merletta acknowledged. "There was no fanfare whatsoever."

Sage shook her head. "That's wrong. They should have done something at least."

"I suppose so," said Merletta without heat. The truth was that for once she was struck not by the injustice of being denied the experience of the other trainees, but by the beauty of the tradition.

"That was a very special experience," she told Indigo, when she and Sage joined the others. "Thank you for including me."

"You're welcome," said Indigo. She cast an uncertain look at Andre, who smiled encouragingly at her.

"Are you sure you're all right?" Sage asked Merletta quietly, as they led Indigo toward the female trainees' sleeping quarters, where a hammock awaited her.

"Absolutely," Merletta assured her friend.

It was true. For months now she'd been so disheartened by just how rotten the Center had become, and how impossible a task it seemed to be to expose the lies. It was encouraging to be reminded that not everything in this place was sinister. The Center had beautiful traditions and noble ideals, with plenty of well-meaning inhabitants who surely wished to live up to them.

She wanted to destroy the corruption, but not destroy the place itself, or the people. It wasn't just Tilssted that was worth saving. It was the whole triple kingdoms—even the Center.

~

Time seemed to pass more quickly in third year than it had in second. Wivell didn't contribute nearly as much to Merletta's education as he had in first year, when the test focused on the qualification to become a scribe. Merletta still spent some time each week in literacy studies, but it wasn't her main focus.

Truth be told, neither was her educator training, although it was supposed to be. Ibsen kept Merletta as busy as possible, but it was always with meaningless tasks that didn't further her education at all. Agner, of course, was both as cheerful and as merciless as ever in physical training. And Merletta usually spent one of her two physical training days each week conducting patrols with Freja's squad, a task which often went until after dinner, since guards didn't keep the same hours as the trainees.

As a result, it was some weeks before Merletta found the time to seek out the records room Sage had mentioned. It was the last day before rest day, and instead of going to training with Agner, Merletta went to meet Freja's squad as previously arranged. But when she arrived at the usual meeting point, Freja met her with an apology.

"Sorry, Merletta," she said gruffly. "It's a different type of patrol today, and we've been specifically told no trainees are to accompany us."

Merletta raised an eyebrow. "Specifically told? I thought I was the only trainee attached regularly to a squad like this."

"That's my understanding as well," Freja admitted reluctantly.

Neither of them elaborated, but surely the older mermaid must suspect, just as Merletta did, that the prohibition was targeted directly at her.

"What type of patrol is it?" she asked curiously.

Freja looked like she wasn't going to answer, but Felix chimed in.

"We're going to Tilssted to try to intervene before anyone breaks any laws which will land them in serious trouble."

Merletta looked at him in startled inquiry, and he frowned.

"You know how we keep encountering merpeople trying to wander across the barrier to explore?"

She nodded.

"Well, all the patrols are reporting the same thing. And it seems the violators are mostly from Tilssted. Apparently there's some kind of public meeting happening this morning, not sanctioned by anyone in authority, to discuss the possibility of outward expansion."

Merletta's mouth had fallen open.

"That's right," said another of the guards. "The word is they're talking about setting up a village of sorts on the other side of the kelp forests."

Merletta swallowed. "It seems like I should be there," she said hollowly.

"Merletta." Freja glanced thoughtfully at the rest of the group, then drew Merletta aside, lowering her voice. "Do you value my advice at all?"

"Of course I do," Merletta said.

Freja nodded. "Then I advise you to stay out of it."

Merletta bit her lip. "Is that your advice based on what you think is best for me, or what you think is best in the big picture?"

The squad leader looked taken aback by the blunt question, and took a moment to consider her answer. But when she spoke, it was with conviction.

"Both."

Merletta hesitated. It was impossible to tell whether Freja was just looking out for her generally, or whether she knew more than she was letting on about Merletta's role in the origin of this latest surge of interest in the ocean outside the barrier.

At her silence, Freja's tone became a little stern. "Whether you agree with me or not is neither here nor there. We're not allowed to take you along. I'm sure you have other training you could be doing."

Merletta nodded reluctantly. Freja wasn't wrong. It was as good an opportunity as she was likely to get to hunt down the records room Sage had mentioned.

As soon as the squad was out of sight, she left the training yard, making for the tall central spire of the Center. She didn't want Agner to see her hanging about and give her drills or something else to fill her unexpected free time.

Merletta had never entered the spire before, and she half expected to be stopped. But although there were guards stationed at the entrance, they gave only a cursory glance at her armband before returning their attention to the street before them. Merletta swam into the building, her eyes instantly drawn upward.

The lobby of the spire was an impressive sight, unlike any building she'd entered before. It stretched up so far that the space disappeared into gloom, and she couldn't make out the ceiling. It wasn't that it was entirely open space. The building clearly had many different levels, presumably with various offices and workspaces and who knew what else. But it wasn't like Tish's shellsmith tower, where each story had a solid floor, with only small holes to act as doorways to the next level. In this building, there were no floors—at least not in the lobby area. She could see doors opening off the central space all the way up, so knew there must be enclosed rooms at each level, but the general impression was one of a huge hollow center, with various merpeople swimming up and down inside it.

Suspecting that asking directions would bring further questions about the legitimacy of her presence, Merletta moved across the lobby with a show of purpose. Sage had said that the records room was at the base of the spire, so Merletta didn't ascend through the water. She instead moved along the wall at seabed level, and was soon rewarded by the sight of a doorway flanked by two armed guards.

She glanced up at the lintel. *Restricted Records*, it read.

Heartened, Merletta swam forward, pausing in front of the guards, both of whom were watching her closely.

The silence stretched out, and Merletta cleared her throat awkwardly. "I'm a trainee," she said. "I've come to view the records, for my studies."

Neither guard's expression changed in the slightest, but one pulled out a small writing leaf which he handed to her.

"Write the watchword here."

Merletta took the leaf, bringing her satchel around to rest it on as she retrieved her coral writing implement.

Vazula.

It was the first time she'd ever written the word, and she took a moment to admire how it looked. It was an incredibly strange sensation, handing over a physical inscription of her greatest secret to these forbidding strangers.

The guard glanced at the word for a fleeting moment, then waved her inside. She looked over her shoulder to see him destroying the leaf with emotionless efficiency.

As soon as she turned her attention forward again, all thought of the guards fled. She'd expected the restricted records room to be bigger than the public one she was used to, but in fact it was smaller. Not that it was less impressive. It was meticulously organized, with shelf upon shelf of well-maintained records stretching not outward like in the public room, but upward. The room must go up several stories, she thought.

And it was quiet! So peaceful. At present no one was in there but her—it certainly made a nice change from studying while surrounded by whispering first years.

Merletta moved slowly along the rows at the bottom level, not entirely sure what she was looking for. Where should she focus her studies if she wanted to pass her educator test? She was just reaching for a record from a section entitled *Oral History*, when a door she hadn't previously noticed opened.

A merman swam in, then pulled up short at sight of her.

"Oh." He blinked, then his eyes narrowed in suspicion. "Should you be in here?"

Merletta nodded. "I'm a third year trainee," she said, trying to sound confident. "I'm here to study."

"Ah." He studied her thoughtfully. "You'll be sitting your educator test this year, will you?"

She nodded again.

"Well, we could do with some fresh blood," he said. "Not enough are signing up for our entry level training. But I suppose you'll want to continue on to fourth year."

"Are you an educator?" Merletta asked, her interest piqued.

He grunted in acknowledgment, swimming past her and stopping in front of a section marked *Dragon Aggression*.

"You're getting a good opportunity to see our work in action," the educator said, selecting a record after careful perusal.

Two others swam into the room as he spoke.

"Did you find it?" one asked.

He nodded, handing Merletta the record. "Pass it to that mermaid, would you?" he said distractedly, already moving to the next one.

Merletta moved across the space, scanning the record as she did so. She didn't have time to properly take in its contents, but she got the gist. It was an account of dragons hunting merkind through shallow waters, actually diving into the ocean to seek them out and kill them.

It was hard to reconcile the image with Rekavidur, somehow.

"What's this for?" Merletta asked, handing the record to the impatient educator.

"There's some kind of riot happening in Tilssted," the other mermaid said distractedly. "A whole group is threatening to breach the barrier. The guards are already there, of course, but we're sending a team to try to prevent disaster with information rather than spears."

Merletta frowned. She was all for using education instead of violence, of course, but the record she'd just handled wasn't information—it was misinformation.

"Riot?" she repeated. Was this the same event Freja had described as a *public meeting*?

"You sound surprised," the mermaid said vaguely. "But it's Tilssted. What do you expect?"

Merletta narrowed her eyes. It was on the tip of her tongue to inform them that she came from Tilssted, but she thought better of it. Clearly they didn't realize she was the infamous Tilssted trainee, and if she wanted them to keep speaking freely, she would probably be wise to keep it that way.

"So you're brushing up on these records?" she asked. "So you can make sure you remember all the details?"

"No, we're going to take the records," the first educator told her, swimming over to join them. "We'll send the appropriate ones to the scribes for copies to be made, and distribute them among the rabble-rousers." He carried a stack of records in his arms, and a grim smile crossed his face as he glanced down at the top one. "This one, for example, should make them pause."

Merletta craned her neck to read it.

· · ·

Dragons have unparalleled senses—sight, hearing, smell. They can scent a mermaid from great distances, and although they cannot breathe underwater, they can survive in water for indefinite periods. Only their flame will be affected by the inability to take in air. Although our history mainly recounts dragons attacking merpeople in the shallow waters when our ancestors were foolish enough to settle near land, there are also accounts of dragons following the trail of merfolk even to the deep ocean. If once a dragon sees a mermaid, it will hunt until it finds not only the mermaid in question, but the rest of its community.

Merletta let out a shaky stream of water. That information would create terror in the mind of most merpeople. Was that the kind of panic-inducing lie to be found in this restricted records room?

"This is also a good one." The educator handed it to the mermaid, and Merletta read what she could as it passed by her.

What follows is the account of the massacre that occurred when our triple kingdoms attempted to establish a second settlement near land to the northwest, and ran afoul of a dragon colony in those parts. It is on that basis that dwellings are now allowed only within the barrier itself.

That also would surely make anyone nervous about venturing beyond the barrier.

"Not this one, I think," the merman said. "What do you think?"

The female educator took the offered record, scanning it with furrowed brow.

"Definitely not," she agreed.

Peering over her shoulder, Merletta caught a fragment.

...may be possible to coexist peacefully with both humans and dragons, but only if...

Merletta strained to see more, her mind spinning at the casual way the educators ignored information that contradicted the Center's claims about humans. But the other mermaid had already slipped the record to the bottom of the pile as she leafed through the others.

"And this one *absolutely* not." The educator gave a short, barking laugh. "Can you imagine?"

"May I see it?" Merletta asked.

The mermaid handed it to her absently, and Merletta's eyes raced across it.

"But this would be fantastic," she said, surprised. "It's so practical and useful."

The educators all paused, looking up at her incredulously.

"Basic shark defense, repelling predators, finding cover," she read. "It's instructions for how to navigate the open ocean safely. Isn't this exactly what everyone needs to see?"

The first educator plucked the record back from her with a disapproving frown. "On the contrary, it's exactly what everyone *doesn't* need," he said severely. "It would lead to chaos."

"Chaos?" Merletta repeated. "You mean, you're actively repressing any information that might actually empower them, just so you can keep them huddled in fear inside the barrier?"

"You have a great deal to learn if you think that's how the educators work," the mermaid said, her tone matching her colleague's. "We're trying to keep everyone safe. If they read something like this, it will give them a false sense of safety, and make them think they can survive out past the barrier."

"But they *can* survive out past the barrier," Merletta insisted. "If they followed these guidelines, and were sensible, and traveled in groups—"

"Enough." The educator's voice was as cold as the depths. "Who are you? You said you were a third year trainee, but a senior trainee would know better."

"I *am* a third year trainee," Merletta insisted.

"Have you learned nothing from your educator training so far?" the mermaid asked incredulously.

"I've learned more than enough today," said Merletta, her temper getting the better of her. "This isn't education."

She gestured at the records, which the third educator was sorting into two piles—presumably one for distribution, and one to remain locked in the Center's untouchable sanctum.

"Giving only the records you want them to know—records that can't be externally verified anyway—and withholding information *you* decide they don't need...that's deception, not education. And given the topic at hand, it's even worse than that. It's fear-mongering."

"Get out," snapped the merman. "I don't know who you think you are, a trainee coming in here and telling experienced educators how to do their jobs, but I will certainly be speaking to your instructors. Now *out*."

Merletta didn't wait to be told twice. She was half defiant, half regretting her burst of outraged candor. As she swam for the door, however, a section of the records room caught her eye.

Census, the inscription on the top of the shelving read.

She slowed, her heart picking up speed. This must be the older records Sage was speaking of. But she hadn't sounded confident of their contents—she would never have had reason to examine them herself. Was it possible they were more recent than she realized? Could the names of Merletta's parents be in there?

"*Out!*" roared the educators in unison.

Merletta didn't even glance backward. If she wasn't to be granted the opportunity to explore the section now, she would simply have to come back.

CHAPTER SEVENTEEN

Merletta

The whole incident in the records room played powerfully on Merletta's mind for the rest of the day. She simply couldn't shake her frustration at the approach the educators had been taught—to systematically play on the fears of the population, while withholding any information which might give them the tools to actually succeed.

And constantly niggling at the back of her mind was the census section. Were the answers she so desperately wanted within her reach after all?

Rising early after a restless night, Merletta decided to go back to the restricted records room before breakfast on her rest day. She hadn't banked on waking Sage in her preparations, but once her friend was roused, she was determined to accompany Merletta. She'd been tense herself since Merletta had told her the day before of the showdown with the educators. It hadn't helped that the Center was rife with gossip about the ongoing unrest in Tilssted. Some even started to whisper the word *uprising* in dramatic tones that made Merletta roll her eyes.

"Are we even allowed in this early?" Sage asked, her eyes

darting around her at the mostly empty streets as they swam toward the central spire.

"No idea," said Merletta. "But I guess we'll find out."

By the time they entered the spire, more merpeople were about, beginning their day's errands. As on the day before, the doorway to the records room was flanked by armed guards, although they weren't the same ones.

"We're trainees," Merletta told them, more confidently this time. "I'm in third year, and my friend is in fourth year."

"Watchword." The guard handed her another small leaf, and she scrawled *Vazula* on there hastily.

After a brief glance, the guard dropped the leaf, allowing it to float gently to the stone beneath their feet.

"Incorrect."

"What?" Merletta had already started moving forward, and had to pull up. "But..." She dove down, retrieving the leaf. She'd definitely written it correctly. "But it was correct yesterday."

"It's changed," the guard said curtly.

Merletta and Sage exchanged a glance.

"But it's been the same for years," Sage said, bewildered.

Merletta knew that, like her, Sage must be thinking of the stone slab in the middle of the maelstrom, with generations' worth of trainees' names etched onto it, and at the top, the inscription, *Watchword: Vazula*. It wasn't even in the water, so it could have been there for decades, for all they knew.

"Incorrect," the guard repeated, narrowing his eyes. In a synchronized movement, he and his fellow guard crossed their spears, blocking the entrance.

Left with no other option, Merletta and Sage drifted away, back toward the building's main exit. Neither spoke while they were still inside the spire, but it wasn't necessary. There could be no doubt in either mind that the change related to Merletta's actions the day before.

What a fool she'd been! She'd sabotaged her chance of accessing the information she needed, not only to pass her test, but possibly to find out about her family!

But then, had she been wrong? If she was never going to speak up, never going to actually try to change things, what was the point of trying to succeed in the program?

Movement above them caught Merletta's eye, and she looked up to see a silver-haired figure drifting down from a higher level. She heard Sage's quiet exclamation, and knew that her friend had also recognized the austere Record Master. Did he live up there, in the upper echelons of the Center's central spire? It would be fitting, if perhaps almost comically obvious.

He paused for the briefest moment as he passed them. None of them said a word, but Merletta didn't miss the way his storm-gray eyes lingered on her. It was all she could do not to cross her arms defensively over herself. She felt scrutinized—seen through.

They hovered, waiting for him to exit the building before coming out into the lightening water themselves at a slower pace.

"Do you think he recognized us?" Sage asked, no doubt referring to the conversation they'd had with the Record Master at the Founders' Day ceremony in Merletta's first year.

Merletta couldn't help but remember Sage's excitement on that occasion at the honor granted them. Now she sounded apprehensive—the effect of Merletta's secrets on her life.

"Yes," Merletta said shortly.

For a few minutes they swam in silence, Merletta thinking over the encounter. "You know," she said suddenly, "that's the first time I've seen him without those two guards of his. I thought they were with him at all times."

Sage shook her head. "No, I don't think so. I mean, they're often with him. But it's not unusual to see him without them. I came across him multiple times last year, when I used to come in here for the records room. He was sometimes alone."

Merletta frowned, thinking this over. From the way the guards usually hovered, she'd gotten the sense that they were excessively loyal to the Center's top figure. A theory supported by the fact that he didn't seem to have a true guard rotation— just those two. It was strange to think that they'd just leave him unattended on a regular basis.

"What are you going to do, Merletta?" Sage asked. "What are any of us going to do if we're barred from the records?"

"You'll be all right," Merletta said. "I'm sure a new watchword will be distributed to fourth years and record holders. It'll just be third years no longer allowed in, you'll see." She shrugged. "And next year, when I'm the only fourth year, there'll be some reason why fourth years aren't allowed."

"But will you be a fourth year?" Sage asked with unusual bluntness. "Without access to those records, and with no help from Ibsen in class, it won't be easy to pass the third year test. In fact, I suspect it will be near impossible."

Merletta was silent for a moment, then she stopped swimming, turning to face her friend.

"Does it even matter, Sage? What's the point of it all? If they're not going to let me learn anything, I may as well be out there campaigning for the truth instead of hiding in the Center, trying not to scratch anyone's scales the wrong way on the slim hope they'll let me inside enough for me to actually learn anything valuable."

"What are you saying?" Sage asked, sounding upset. "Are you thinking of dropping out of the program?"

"I don't know what I'm thinking of doing," Merletta said helplessly. "I just know, after yesterday, that I could never be an educator."

"But you didn't want to be a scribe either, or a guard," Sage argued. "They're all just checkpoints on the way to the end goal." She seized Merletta's arm, gripping it with surprising strength. "You have to succeed, Merletta. Beat them at their own game. Prove that it's possible, and once we're record holders together, we'll start to change things. Us, and Emil, and Andre."

Merletta didn't answer. She wasn't satisfied by the ambitions that had once driven her every move. What did it matter if she passed the program? Even in the increasingly unlikely event she succeeded, it wouldn't be for another year and a half. The residents of Tilssted were ready for change now, and willing to take risks to achieve it. And they were being lied to now. Perhaps right now, given the educators' activities.

The thought decided her on something.

"Sage, can you tell the others that we all need to talk? Before dinner tonight. Is there somewhere private we can meet?"

Sage looked apprehensive, but she nodded. "How about the room where you stayed over your break? I'll tell my family I wanted to host my friends for a social gathering outside the Center."

"Thank you," said Merletta. "And you'll tell the others?"

"Why can't you?" Sage asked suspiciously. "Where are you going?"

"There's something I need to do while I still can," Merletta answered evasively. It wasn't that she didn't trust Sage—she hoped to prove the opposite that evening. But there was no need to worry her friend. "I'll be back this afternoon."

She paused. "And just Emil and Andre, all right?"

Sage nodded, obviously understanding her point. Indigo tended to hang around them a lot, and although she was friendly enough, none of them but Andre knew her well enough to consider bringing her into their dangerous secrets.

Merletta swam quickly once she and Sage parted, heading due north. It was risky to take the most direct route past the barrier, through Tilssted. But with the patrols increasingly alert to attempts to leave the triple kingdoms, she would need the advantage of familiar waters.

Even so, it was more difficult than she could ever remember for her to get out unseen. Well before she reached the boundary, she had to be careful in traversing Tilssted's streets. The gossip hadn't been as exaggerated as she thought. There seemed to be guards everywhere, and not just Center guards, but ones from Hemssted and Skulssted, too. Every Tilssted guard she saw looked disgruntled, and who could blame them?

She saw two separate instances of Center guard squads arguing with groups of locals, and another group—whom she was fairly certain were educators—moving in the direction of the city's central square. With great effort, Merletta stopped herself from following them.

The general distraction helped her, but she still had to wait a long time before there was a sufficient gap between patrols to allow her to slip inconspicuously through the kelp forests beyond the farms.

She waited until she was well outside the barrier before speaking aloud.

"Heath." She felt foolish, speaking to open water, but pushed on anyway. "Heath, I need to speak with you. On Vazula. It...it might be the last time I can come. I hope not, but...just in case."

She said no more, trusting that he would hear her and come, as he'd told her he would.

Even if he came immediately, he wouldn't beat her to the island, so she turned her attention to August, Paul, and Griffin instead. They also deserved to know what she was planning.

When she pulled herself onto the sand on Vazula's beach, she was greeted by Paul.

"We didn't expect you today," he said, offering her a hand to pull her to her feet.

Merletta shook sand from her scaled skirt. "I made a last minute decision to come," she informed him. "Where are the others?"

"Griffin's hunting," Paul said. "But August and Eloise are close by."

"Eloise is here?" Merletta asked.

She received her answer in the form of two figures who emerged from the foliage, one clutching the other with much less than her usual dignity.

"Eloise!" Merletta called, grinning at the older woman's wobbly gait. "You've found your legs!"

"I don't like it," Eloise said. "It doesn't feel right at all."

Merletta laughed. "You'll get used to it," she promised. "It'll feel natural in no time."

"It's good to see you, Merletta," said August.

Merletta was heartened to see how much less grave his resting expression was these days.

"You too," she said. "But I'm afraid I don't exactly come with good news."

"What's wrong?" Eloise's voice was sharp, and she paused her efforts to walk, giving Merletta her full attention.

"Nothing new is wrong," Merletta told them all calmly. "But things are about to change. I'm done keeping my mouth shut. And I can't promise you and your sanctuary here won't be affected."

August and Eloise exchanged a meaningful look, and Merletta could tell they'd prepared for this moment.

"Whatever you need to do, we're behind you," August said. "We never expected you to stay silent this long. We want to see the Center's lies exposed more than anyone."

Merletta nodded, wishing his unmitigated support made her

feel more confident. If anything, it increased her nerves. The guards seemed to think she was incredibly brave, and had a clever plan. Neither belief was true.

But, she reflected, she may as well broach a more sensitive topic while she apparently had their goodwill.

"I'm expecting Heath to come any time," she said. "He deserves to know what I'm planning as well."

August frowned, but his wife put a hand on his arm. "I want to meet this human," she said firmly. "See how he compares to what we've been told."

"He's nothing like the stories," Merletta said eagerly, turning to her. "He's—"

"But he'll be bringing the dragon, won't he?" Paul interrupted her, his expression troubled.

"Well..." Merletta hesitated. "It's more the other way around, isn't it? He can't really come without—"

Her words were cut off by a sudden rush of wind, and all of them looked up at the sight of Reka descending further up the beach.

"Ten minutes." The dragon's words—clearly a warning—carried through the heavy air to the group of merpeople.

Heath emerged from the mass of wings and scales, hurrying across the sand.

"Merletta!" he cried, disregarding the others. "Are you all right? What's going on?"

"Oh, he's not at all vicious," Eloise said, sounding surprised.

"As if you can tell so quickly," August muttered.

"Of course I can tell," she responded dismissively. "Why, the boy's in love with her! He's hardly going to spear her."

Merletta didn't know whether to be embarrassed or amused, but there was no time for either. Heath had reached her, and he seized both of her hands in his.

"Why did you say it might be the last time? Talk to me, Merletta."

"I'm all right," she assured him, squeezing his hands. "I just don't know what's going to happen when I—" She cut herself off, frowning at the bandage around his arm. "What happened to you?"

"I narrowly escaped getting trampled by a runaway horse," Heath said quickly. "But that's not what we're talking about."

"It is now!" Merletta protested. "What happened?"

Heath hesitated. "I'll tell you about it...later." He glanced at the group, seeming to notice the presence of a stranger for the first time. He cast a questioning glance at Merletta, then inclined his head politely to Eloise.

"I don't believe we've met. I'm Heath."

"I'm Eloise," she said firmly, looking him up and down. "August's wife. And I'm very glad to meet you. I can see at a glance why Merletta's ready to throw her world away to defend you. Although that doesn't mean it won't get her killed, of course."

Merletta felt irritated by the older woman's words when she saw the troubled crease that appeared between Heath's eyes.

"Come on," she said, tugging on his uninjured arm. "If you only have ten minutes, let's not waste it."

She pulled him into the jungle, just far enough to be out of earshot of the others.

"Ignore her," she said, lowering herself onto a fallen log.

"You know I can't," said Heath quietly.

There was plenty of space for him to sit next to her, but he remained standing, looking down at her out of eyes that seemed much too serious for his twenty years.

"Am I a danger to you, Merletta?" he asked bluntly.

"Only to my heart," she joked.

But Heath wasn't interested in lightening the mood. She

could practically taste his intensity in the air as he suddenly dropped to his knees beside the log, staring into her eyes.

"I thought you died because of me once before, Merletta," he said, laying a hand on her knee. "And I don't think I could survive that again."

His touch was warm on the skin just below Merletta's scaled skirt, and she felt her heart leap erratically. Trying to master herself, she laid her hand over his, matching his tone.

"Heath, no part of the danger around me is your doing. And I resent the suggestion that knowing you isn't worth every bit of the risk."

Heath looked anguished. "You think I don't feel the same way? But when you're far away, deep underwater, I can't do anything to help you. I hate sending you back to people who've tried to kill you more than once, knowing there's no way I can protect you!"

Merletta hesitated. She appreciated his concern more than she could say, but it changed nothing about her reality. Limited though their time was, it didn't seem like the moment to tell him her plans.

"It seems I'm not the only one needing protecting," she pointed out. "What happened to you?"

Heath pushed himself up from his knees and lowered himself down beside her on the log. "It's a concern," he acknowledged. "It happened a couple days ago. Unless I'm completely mistaken, someone tried to kill me and make it look like an accident. The same someone who orchestrated the attack against Percival, I think."

"Heath, that's terrible!" Merletta grabbed his shoulders, scanning him more carefully.

"Not so easy when you're the powerless one, with the other in danger, is it?" Heath asked dryly. "Don't think you can distract me, Merletta. Why did you call me here?"

"Thank you for coming, by the way," said Merletta, not quite meeting his eyes. "I wasn't sure Rekavidur would bring you."

"Well, I wasn't sure, either," Heath acknowledged. "But although he didn't admit as much, I could tell that, like me, he was intrigued by the information that you thought you were going to die imminently."

"I didn't say that," Merletta corrected quickly. "I said it might be the last time I could come to Vazula. I'm hoping it won't be, but…"

She trailed off, but Heath didn't speak, clearly waiting for her to continue. She stood, suddenly unable to sit still.

"I've had enough, Heath," she said, looking toward the ocean, which was obscured by trees, rather than at him. "I wasn't made to sit quietly and keep my opinions to myself. I'm not going to pass third year. Not at the rate I'm going. I can't get near any of the information I need to pass, and I'm not even sure I want to anymore. I think some of the educators mean well, but that almost makes it worse that everything they do is a sham, designed to prop up the Center's illusions." She closed her eyes. "I thought the Center was worth saving, but I don't think I can survive inside it for long enough to do that. Not without exploding first. Which only leaves one option I can see. And that's to bring the Center down by exposing its lies to everyone outside."

Heath was silent for so long, curiosity drove her to turn so she could see his reaction.

"There's another option," he said quietly.

Merletta suddenly knew where he was going, and she turned quickly away again, unable to bear the hope in his eyes when she knew she was going to refuse him.

She heard him stand, and felt his nearness as he approached her. But still she didn't turn.

"You could come back to Valoria with me right now," he whispered, his words warm on the skin at the back of her neck.

She felt him lay a tentative hand on her shoulder, and suddenly found herself leaning back against him, without realizing she'd decided to do it. Heath's arm slipped around her waist, heat exploding along her stomach at every inch of contact as he pulled her more tightly against him.

"We could be together all the time, Merletta," he said. "Not just in snatches. You could join my world, and never have to face the dangers of the triple kingdoms again."

The picture he painted was more tempting than Merletta cared to admit. She closed her eyes, trying to commit every detail of this moment to memory. If this was the last time she saw Heath, she wanted to remember the hesitant way he touched her, as if he could hardly believe his own daring. She wanted to be able to recall precisely how it felt when he said her name.

Because these glimpses of impossible beauty were all she'd get.

She turned, stepping back from him. He released her at once, but the look in his eyes was like physical pain to her.

"I can't just swim away," she said quietly. "Not without at least trying." She reached up to fleetingly touch his cheek. "You know I can't. No matter how much I want to be with you."

Heath shifted back toward her, determination in his eyes. But the rushing that suddenly filled the air around them told them both that their time was up.

"But what are you going to do?" Heath asked desperately.

Merletta stepped back again, all thought of sentiment gone as she quickly outlined her plan.

"I don't like it," Heath said, just as Reka poked his snout through the trees. "It's not much of a plan."

"I know you don't," Merletta said, with the hint of a smile. "And I know it isn't. But it's all I've got."

Reka was pushing his way between the trunks now, and Merletta knew he wouldn't wait around. Not giving herself time to think, she darted forward, pressing a kiss to Heath's cheek before he knew what she was doing.

"Would you really have taken me back to your kingdom with you?" she asked, a little wistfully.

Heath's arm was suddenly back around her waist, holding her securely in place. "Without a moment's hesitation," he breathed, his eyes eager. "You have a sanctuary with me as long as I live. It's not too late to change your mind."

Merletta smiled sadly, even as she shook her head.

"Heath." The dragon rumbled his displeasure.

"Keep an eye out for me, won't you?" Merletta said lightly, attempting to step back from Heath's hold.

His eyes searched hers for an endless moment, then his grip slackened. Before Merletta could move back, however, he suddenly pulled her against him once more, pressing his lips to hers in a kiss that was brief and chaste, but fierce with emotion.

"Heath!" Reka's agitation was growing, and Heath released Merletta at last.

"Always," he promised, in belated response to her words.

Then, with a flash of talons and a rush of wings, they were gone.

CHAPTER EIGHTEEN

Merletta

Merletta swam back to the triple kingdoms in a daze, her thoughts as scattered as a school of minnows darting in panic from a predator. The only clear idea in her mind was her desperate hope that the moment she and Heath had just shared wouldn't be their last together.

By the time she'd made it back home, however, she suddenly remembered that she was supposed to be meeting the others at Sage's home in Skulssted, not in the Center. She swam there quickly, glad to find them all already there. She was too on edge for waiting around.

"There you are, Merletta," Andre said brightly. "We've all been dying of curiosity since Sage summoned us here. It was cruel of you to keep us waiting."

"Sorry," Merletta said. "I've been..." Her thoughts flew once again to Heath's arm around her. "Distracted." She shook her head to clear it. "Thanks for coming."

"It was a little awkward for Andre to extricate himself," Sage commented, casting him a concerned look. "Will Indigo be angry with you, do you think?"

"If she is, that's her problem," said Andre firmly. "Just because she's my cousin doesn't mean she should expect to be able to follow me everywhere."

"She seemed to feel differently," Sage pointed out.

Andre just shrugged, his eyes fixed expectantly on Merletta.

"I'm glad you didn't bring her," Merletta said frankly. "The plain truth is that I don't know her well enough to trust her, and I doubt she'd want to be part of this conversation anyway."

"Has something happened?" Emil's question—calm as it was—showed that he, too, was battling curiosity.

"What's happened is that I've realized I haven't been fair to you," Merletta said. "I've allowed myself to become too cautious."

Emil raised an eyebrow, and she couldn't help grinning.

"Cautious is a relative term, of course," she amended. She drew in a pull of water, her expression becoming serious again. "I've gotten so focused on surviving and progressing in the program, that I've lost sight of the real benefit of being in the Center."

"Which is?" Andre pressed.

"Which is using that position to benefit everyone outside, particularly those who are suffering most for the Center's lies."

"But," Emil chimed in predictably, "if you pass the program and become a record holder, you'll have greater influence to use on others' behalf."

"But I'm not going to pass, am I?" Merletta countered bluntly. "Ibsen won't teach me anything, and now I can't even access the records." She sent Sage a questioning look. "I assume you told them about what happened?"

Sage nodded, and Merletta turned back to the group at large.

"We've all heard about what's happening in Tilssted, with more and more residents trying to explore the idea of settling outside the barrier now that their homes and businesses are being overrun by the other cities. Well, I started that. Not on purpose, exactly. But when I was with Tish in Tilssted, someone asked me about whether I would be willing to live outside the barrier."

Emil groaned softly. "And of course you put your fins in it."

"No," Merletta contradicted, frowning at him. "What I did was answered without lying. That's all. I wasn't inflammatory, and I didn't volunteer information they didn't ask for. I just told the simple truth. And this is the result."

Three serious faces looked back at her.

"Don't you see?" she insisted. "That's how little it took! Which means that's how tightly the Center has been holding control over information! A few honest comments on a taboo topic, coming from someone with the loosest definition of the Center's credibility, and half the city of Tilssted is ready to take the chance and try something the Center's been telling them for generations is too dangerous! The triple kingdoms are ready for change. They're ready to be free of the Center's rigid control. And if my position as a Center trainee is enough to actually help shine some light on the truth, then I need to use it while I still have it."

"But, Merletta." Sage swallowed nervously. "There will be no going back from this."

"She's right," Emil agreed. "What you're describing is exactly what they've been afraid of since the moment you made it into the program. I think they're more afraid of you than you realize. From what I've observed, they were fearful of you too early to be logical. Even before you had the chance to show a hint of defiance."

"That's the depth of their prejudice against Tilssted," shrugged Merletta.

Emil didn't look entirely convinced. "Maybe. But if you go

out there and tell people the Center is lying to them, they're going to hit back at you. And hard."

"I'm ready," said Merletta. "I'm not afraid of what they'll do to me."

Emil met her look gravely. "But you don't know what they'll do to you."

Merletta frowned. "I've faced death before, Emil."

He shook his head. "I know someone has tried to kill you before, but you must see we've moved past that kind of blatant attack. The way the Center works..." He trailed off, shaking his head slightly. "The more I see, the more I realize how ruthless the system can be. But there isn't as much brute force involved as you might think. Whatever they do, it will be clever, and it will take you by surprise."

"Well," Merletta said, considering his words, "even if you're right, I don't see that it really changes anything. I'll just have to take whatever they send my way."

Emil's eyes were troubled as they rested not on Merletta, but on Sage. "It might not just be your way they send it, of course."

His gaze was a mixture of disapproval and concern. It tugged at Merletta's memory, until she suddenly knew where she'd seen it before. In Heath's eyes, mere hours before, when he'd told her that he didn't like her plan. Merletta sucked in a stream of water, realization cascading over her. How long had *that* been going on? And how had she been so blind as to miss it? As she cast her mind quickly back over many interactions, a further wave of understanding crashed over her, filling her with sympathy for Emil's frustratingly cautious approach.

"I don't have any desire to put anyone else in danger," Merletta said, her softened tone drawing Emil's eyes back to her. "Surely none of you are at serious risk just from being my friends. Not when you're all so well-connected, with families who would not only notice if something happened to you, but would set up an outcry. I'm not asking anything further of any of you."

"I think it's about time we did something," Andre chimed in, looking unimpressed at what he clearly thought was lack of courage from Emil. "And I want to help."

"I appreciate it, Andre," she said quickly. "But I truly didn't call you here to ask anything of you."

"Why did you call us here, then?" Sage demanded.

"To tell you everything," said Merletta. "When I saw how unashamed those educators were of their own deception, I realized where unthinking compliance leads. It was confronting, to be honest, and it made me question myself as well. I realized that although I've been telling myself that I was playing along for a purpose, I'd become casual about the truth, too. How can I criticize the Center for its deception when I've been hiding things from my own friends?"

She nodded at Andre. "Like how I delayed telling you about August for weeks, on flimsy excuses." She squared her shoulders. "But that's the least of it. I've told you all a lot of what I've discovered, but I haven't told you the biggest thing. I think even after all the unearned support you've given me, I was still afraid you wouldn't believe me. And you deserve more trust than that."

"What do you mean?" Sage sounded alarmed. "What more is there?"

Merletta met her eyes. "Remember how I told you that the name of the island where I met Heath is Vazula?"

Sage nodded, and Emil made a noise of surprise.

Merletta turned to him. "Exactly. Like from the second year test. It's no coincidence. We have some kind of history there. I can only assume it's a history that involves the humans who used to live there."

"Why do you assume that?" Emil asked.

"Because..." Merletta's eyes flicked between her three

friends, trying to assess their reactions. "There's so much more to the lies about humans than you even know. It's not just that humans are as intelligent as we are. It's that we *are* humans, or at least I think we were once."

"What in the tides are you talking about?" Andre demanded.

Merletta rolled her shoulders, trying to banish the fear that still lurked—that they'd all think she was mad.

"The day after my first year test," she said, "when I disappeared, and August's patrol saw the human, I ended up on the beach at the island, trying to pull Heath from the water and save him from his spear injuries. The only way to get him to safety was to physically pull him all the way up the sand. Which ultimately led to me drying out."

Sage's eyes were as round as pearls, but no one spoke. They were all tense, perhaps sensing that whatever was coming next would change everything.

"Which is how I found out," Merletta continued, "that drying out doesn't kill us, like we've been told." She looked at Emil, trying to read whether the young record holder already knew what she was going to say. "It causes us to transform. My tail disappeared completely, and instead I had legs. Human legs."

"Impossible," Sage breathed.

Merletta shook her head. "It's true, I promise. That's what I spent my month of leave doing after first year. I wasn't *at* the island. I was *on* the island, learning to walk, and run, and jump like a human."

No one spoke.

"And it's not just me," Merletta continued. "August, Paul, and Griffin have all found their legs. And Eloise, now," she added as an afterthought. "You can go and ask her if you don't believe me."

"We believe you," Emil assured her, looking unusually pale, even for him. "It's just...hard to take in."

Relief flooded Merletta, and she nodded. "I understand. So you truly didn't know? It's not covered in fourth year, or told to graduated record holders or something?"

"Definitely not," Emil said faintly. "I've heard very senior record holders talking about merfolk who've died by drying out."

Merletta thought this over. Was there a possibility, even the slimmest of possibilities, that *no one* actually knew? That it was information which had been lost in the murky depths of unrecorded history? That sharing that information would be hailed as a contribution rather than an attack?

She pictured the shrewd gray eyes of the Record Master as he'd studied her in the central spire that very morning.

No.

She'd come too far into the Center's maze of deception to believe anything so optimistic now. The false claims about drying out had the scent of fear-mongering all over them.

"I know it's a lot to get your head around," she told the others, all of whom were staring at her with unnatural expressions. "It changes literally everything we've been taught. I don't even know if I believe the story of how the triple kingdoms came to be anymore. If our origins are three brothers from the deepest ocean, how could it be that our bodies are designed to survive above the surface? And clearly land sickness is a blatant lie, although we all knew that already."

Andre nodded slowly, still looking dazed. "I'm glad I didn't bring Indigo," he said. "She is definitely not ready for this."

"There's no way I would have told you this if she was here," Merletta said, amused. "This isn't entry level information, shall we say." She sobered, her eyes finding Sage in particular. "I'm sorry I didn't tell you sooner."

Her friend gave her a weak smile. "I don't know whether to be angry you didn't tell me immediately, or to wish you still hadn't told me." She reached out suddenly and grabbed Merletta's arm. "No, I didn't mean that. I'm glad you told me. We don't have any need for secrets between us."

Merletta exhaled a long stream of water, a burden lifting from her shoulders. She had no idea how to put into words what Sage's assurance meant to her, so she didn't try. She just smiled back at her friend, and hoped the other mermaid would understand.

"So what's your plan?" Emil asked briskly. It was no surprise that he was the first to pull himself together. "It sounds like you want it to be visible. Are you thinking of the Founders' Day celebrations coming up?"

"*Plan* is a little generous," Merletta admitted. "And I hadn't even thought as far ahead as Founders' Day, to be honest. I know for a fact that someone has gone to the effort of specifically excluding me from joining one of the patrols responding to the Tilssted situation. So clearly that's where I need to be. And if someone asks a reasonable question to which I know a reliable answer, I'm going to give them the truth."

"As simple as that," Sage said.

"As simple as that," Merletta agreed.

"Well, we should all go," said Andre staunchly, squaring his shoulders.

Merletta shook her head. "No. You all have real futures to think about. No one's trying to block your progress. You really *can* have greater influence from inside the Center. It would just be suspicious if all four of us tried to follow a guard patrol. I doubt they'd let us. Plus it might be useful to have you all monitoring the internal reaction to whatever happens."

"I agree," Emil said. Merletta noticed that his gaze once

again flicked to Sage. "It's not wise to put all your pearls inside one oyster."

Merletta nodded approvingly. "Precisely."

The following morning, while she floated in wait outside the training yard, Merletta surprised herself by not feeling especially nervous. If anything, she felt a sense of relief. The cautious, even deceptive role she'd played for the past two and a half years had never been natural to her. It felt good to be doing something, to have the promise of some action.

When Freja appeared, Merletta swam forward confidently.

"Good morning, Freja!"

"Merletta." Freja sounded mildly surprised. "What brings you here this morning? Isn't this a day of boring classes for you?"

Merletta laughed. "That's one way to put it," she acknowledged. "But there's a change of plan today. I'm coming with you on your patrol. I assume you're being sent back to Tilssted?"

Freja nodded, looking wary. "We are, but those aren't my orders, Merletta, as you already know."

"I can follow behind if you prefer," Merletta said cheerfully. "But I'd much rather swim with the patrol."

Freja's stiffness fell from her frame, real concern lighting her eyes. "Don't you remember my advice, Merletta?"

"I do remember it," Merletta assured her. "I considered it carefully, and I know what I'm doing."

Freja studied her for a moment in silence, then gave a curt nod. "We're always glad to have you on the squad," she said gruffly.

Merletta said nothing, but she was touched—as casually as she'd spoken, she understood how big an ask it was to expect

Freja to disregard her orders. Merletta hoped no trouble would come to the older mermaid because of it.

None of the others in the group questioned Merletta's inclusion, just greeting her cheerfully. In no time at all, they were swimming toward Tilssted. For the first half an hour, Merletta hung back as the squad patrolled the streets not far from the barrier. She spared barely a thought for what Ibsen would think when she didn't show up for her class that morning. He'd probably think she'd finally had enough of his obstructive tactics and decided to quit.

Well, he'd be right, in a sense. But he'd soon find out that shutting her out was just as dangerous as letting her in.

CHAPTER NINETEEN

The patrol reached Tilssted quickly. Merletta watched silently as the guards interacted with the residents, noting that Freja's squad, at least, handled any recalcitrant locals with patience rather than aggression. It was no surprise to her—she'd worked with the patrol for a year and a half, and she knew each member quite well. But in some ways it troubled her even more. The Center had successfully created a system where even its well-meaning, good-hearted members were fully committed to furthering a cause based on lies and control.

Drifting over to where Felix was talking to a particularly belligerent merman, Merletta heard the young guard losing his patience.

"It's for your own good you're being stopped from passing the barrier. We're trying to protect you. It's dangerous out there!"

"He's right," Merletta interjected, before the local merman could respond. "It is dangerous. You shouldn't just go swimming out into the ocean alone, when you've never crossed the barrier before."

"Precisely," Felix said, sounding irritated.

Again the other merman started to speak, looking sulky, but Merletta cut him off.

"If you're going out past the barrier, you need proper planning. You should go in an organized group, and make sure someone knows where you'll be, and when you expect to be back. It would be wise to be armed against sharks—even a blunt weapon can be quite useful, if you go for the gills, or between the eyes. And you should undertake other preparations, too. Pack some provisions, but nothing that would attract predators, obviously."

The merman was staring at her open-mouthed, and she gave him a somber nod.

"There are still risks, of course. So if you're not willing to accept them, you shouldn't go at all."

He made no more attempt to speak, and Merletta turned away, to find Felix staring at her with a look almost identical to the local merman's.

"What was that?" he demanded, as soon as they'd floated out of the other merman's hearing.

Merletta shrugged. "It was all true, wasn't it?"

"Well…" Felix looked astonished. "I suppose so, but…"

"But what?" Merletta challenged.

Felix just blinked, apparently unable to find the words.

Freja had no difficulty finding them, however, when Merletta made similar comments to a trio of mermaids who threw a challenge at the guards swimming past.

"That is not our job," Freja told Merletta sharply, seizing her arm and pulling her aside. "As guards we help keep the peace. We don't try to—"

"Educate?" Merletta asked calmly. "But I'm not a guard, am I? I'm a third year trainee, which means I'm studying to be an educator."

The squad leader narrowed her eyes at Merletta. "What are

you up to, Merletta? Are you trying to be smart with me? I've worked as a Center guard for many years. Do you think I don't know how the educators work?"

"Just because they've always worked a certain way in the past doesn't mean they can't update their approach," said Merletta brightly.

"But they haven't." Freja's voice was dry.

"How do you know?" Merletta challenged.

Freja gave her a searching look. "This is how I know," she said curtly, turning and swimming swiftly south, calling to the rest of the patrol as she did so.

The group hastened through the streets of Tilssted, and Merletta soon realized they were heading for the city's central square. Well before they'd reached it, they had to slow their pace, pushing their way through the gathered crowd. The squad moved upward, although the water was still fairly crowded some way above the seabed. When they emerged into the familiar area—the site of every formal event or celebration of Merletta's childhood—she could see why. A platform had been attached halfway up the square's central stone sculpture, and several merpeople were floating atop it, addressing the gathered locals.

With a jolt, Merletta recognized the educator who was currently speaking. He was the one who'd thrown her from the restricted records room. Her curiosity turned to outrage as she caught what he was saying.

"...grieved by the danger that has been unleashed upon the residents of Tilssted, whether through malice or through careless rumor is unclear. Out of concern for the safety of everyone in the city, the Center has graciously authorized the release of restricted records relevant to the policy regarding outward expansion beyond the existing boundaries of our triple kingdoms."

He nodded to the others behind him, and they started passing out bundles of writing leaves.

"This generosity represents significant cost to the Center, both in resources and in labor from its highly qualified scribes. But such is the Center's concern for the safety of every resident of our kingdoms."

The records made their way back through the crowd, reaching those just in front of Freja's squad.

An older merman right in front of Merletta snatched a loose one out of the water with a gnarled hand, scanning it quickly.

"I'll be staying put, thanks," he said wryly, to no one in particular. "The young fools, jumping on this latest craze of outward expansion. They'd be dead out there in an hour."

He released the record into the water, turning and swimming away from the square.

Merletta retrieved it, her blood boiling as she read its contents. It was the account she'd seen in the records room, about the attempts of merfolk in generations past to settle near land to the west, ending in a so-called massacre by the dragons. There were extra details on this version of the record, though, about how vicious dragons were, and how fleeing survivors had been killed by sharks, or dragged into the depths by giant squids.

Rekavidur's image floated before Merletta's mind. Austere, dignified, mysterious...at times cold, certainly. But not vicious. Never aggressive.

The educator was still speaking, but Merletta had heard enough. This was as good an opportunity as she was ever going to get.

Disregarding Freja's startled protest, Merletta shot upward, traveling high enough that she cleared the crowd while still remaining within hailing distance of the educator on the platform. The nerves that had been missing that morning showed up as she rose, but she pushed them down.

"You said this is an account from our history?" she called, loudly enough to get everyone's attention.

The educator paused, his eyes still searching for the speaker as he answered. "That's right."

"But how can we be sure it's accurate, if no one is still alive who remembers it?" she asked.

The watchers were beginning to murmur, but Merletta kept her focus on the educator. He'd spotted her now, and she saw his eyes narrow in recognition.

"Because the events are faithfully recorded in writing, as you see," he said tartly.

"Faithfully?" Merletta paused, as if considering. "But how can we be sure? The records have to be re-copied so many times to last this long...what if a mistake was made by one of the scribes?"

"The Center doesn't make mistakes," the educator said through gritted teeth.

"Never?" Merletta asked, feigning surprise. "That's quite a feat."

"Even in the unlikely event that there was a small error in wording," the educator said, now visibly agitated, "it would hardly change the substance of the account."

"True," Merletta agreed, nodding wisely. "The substance couldn't really be changed without intentional deception."

The murmuring had stopped now, many pairs of eyes fixed on Merletta where she floated above the crowd. A glance down showed Felix, his face full of open astonishment, and an alarmed Freja beside him.

For a moment the educator seemed unsure how to respond, then he adopted a dismissive tone. "You are disrupting the education of vulnerable members of our—"

"Oh, I don't mean to disrupt," said Merletta, opening her eyes wide. "I'm a strong advocate for education. It's why I joined the program. Perhaps you don't remember meeting me the other day. I'm a third year Center trainee, currently studying to qualify as an educator."

"I remember perfectly well," the educator said, clearly holding his rage in check by the slimmest of margins. "And you are out of line."

"Yes, that's what they used to tell me at the charity home," Merletta said sorrowfully. "The one where I grew up isn't far from here."

The crowd had begun muttering again. Merletta heard a few exclamations as onlookers realized she was the infamous Tilssted trainee, and whispered the news excitedly to those beside them.

"Your background is irrelevant," snapped the educator. "As a trainee, you should know better than to make such a scene."

"But I'm just trying to assist," Merletta assured him. "As a trainee, I've studied records like these ones." She gestured to the writing leaves, floating abandoned through the water as every member of the crowd gave her their full attention. "But I've also had my own experiences outside the barrier, and I'm a little confused by the differences."

"I've had enough of this," said the educator. He nodded to a guard patrol. "Detain her."

Several of the guards swam forward, but the movement was met with general outcry.

"You're going to arrest your own just for talking?"

"Let her speak!"

"We want to hear what she means!"

Merletta looked to the educator, her eyebrow raised expectantly. He was apoplectic with anger now, but one of his fellows was whispering urgently in his ear, and he gestured to the guards to stand down.

"You are not qualified to educate anyone," said his companion, swimming forward. "You are a *trainee* only. This is an important matter, and must be left to those with the training and experience to handle it."

"Oh, I know I'm not qualified yet," Merletta assured her innocently. "I wasn't trying to comment on the official procedure of the educators. Just on my own experience."

She glanced at the eager crowd, many of whom were bobbing excitedly in the water. Merletta bit back a grin. She knew her people. Many of them were desperately curious about the topic under discussion. But *all* of them loved a good spectacle.

"What have you seen outside the barrier?" someone yelled, as if in confirmation of her thoughts.

"Lots of things," Merletta said, her eyes passing over the crowd. She gave a theatrical grimace. "I was a bit of a troublemaker at the charity home, I'm afraid. I didn't like being told what to do by a bunch of uptight old crustaceans, you know?"

There were general titters. Merletta's roving eyes passed Freja. The older mermaid's face was taut with disapproval, and Merletta looked on quickly.

"I also didn't like feeling trapped," Merletta added. "Told that there was nothing for me to expect from life but hard work and misery within the small and restrictive bubble I was born in."

The laughter had turned back to muttering, and Merletta saw nods on all sides. She was speaking straight to their hearts now—they understood perfectly the restless frustration that had made her defiant her whole childhood.

"So I used to sneak away a lot," Merletta went on. "I used to leave the triple kingdoms actually, and sneak through the barrier."

Many pairs of wide eyes rested on her, and the educator in charge once again asserted himself.

"Hearing about your misdemeanors will serve no one," he snapped. "You will stop this charade and return to the Center at once to answer to your instructors for this outrageous display."

"So, just to be clear," Merletta asked calmly, "your position is that we can learn from records written by unknown ancestors and kept hidden in the Center, but we can't learn from the actual current experience of others around us?"

The merman's jaw worked, and he seemed unable to immediately find something to say. Merletta took full advantage of his hesitation.

"I spent a lot of time outside the barrier growing up," she went on. "A *lot*. And I agree that there are dangers out there. I had some very lucky escapes early on."

"Well, there you have it." The educator tried, a bit lamely, to cut her off.

Merletta ignored him. "But by the time I was a teenager, it wasn't luck. It was experience. I learned to navigate the dangers, and I didn't take stupid risks. If I'd had anyone to help me, I certainly wouldn't have gone alone. But I didn't have the option of a group for safety."

"This. Is. Inappropriate." The educator looked to his fellows, but no one seemed to know what to do.

"I saw so many beautiful things out there," Merletta said wistfully. "So many gentle sea creatures. I was surprised the open ocean wasn't more dangerous, given what I'd always been told."

"If you'd listened to what you'd been told, you would have been safer," one of the educators snapped. "And everyone else will be safer if they listen to experienced, trained educators rather than an uneducated orphan who has no more sense than to publicly confess to her crimes."

"Crimes?" Merletta repeated, as if surprised. "I don't believe I've confessed to any crimes, have I? Sneaking off was against the charity home's rules, of course, but I'm not under their control anymore, so they can't punish me, surely. As for leaving the barrier..." She arranged her face into a look of confused innocence. "That's not a crime, is it? I thought the patrols were to keep anything dangerous out, not to keep us *in*."

The educator swelled with anger. "The guards are preventing everyone from flooding across the barrier to keep them *safe*. It is for their own good!"

"You didn't answer her question!"

The cry came from the crowd, and was taken up by many voices.

"You didn't," Merletta pointed out. "As such a highly qualified, trained educator, it's your role to know the law, isn't it? *Is* it against the law to go outside the barrier?"

The educator was silent, and Merletta saw a hint of something other than anger lancing across his face.

Fear.

"It is not," said the female educator calmly. "But that doesn't mean it's safe or wise."

"If it's not illegal, why are armed guards preventing us leaving?" someone yelled.

"Probably because they're worried you'll rush out without preparation, instead of in organized groups, with proper protections," Merletta responded. "But surely we're all smarter than that, aren't we?"

As she spoke, she saw the two main educators holding a whispered conference with a Center guard.

The mermaid swam forward. "This public meeting is finished," she announced firmly. "All Center employees *and trainees* are to return to the Center." Her gaze passed over the crowd. "With the exception of the guards, who will of course continue their patrols."

Her eyes found Merletta, narrowing with purpose.

Judging that she'd well and truly achieved her purpose, Merletta dove back down into the throng. Merpeople surrounded her at once, plying her with a dozen questions she had no opportunity to answer. Freja appeared suddenly, seizing Merletta's arm and dragging her through the crowd.

"Our patrol is done. We're going back to the Center."

"I'll swim alone," Merletta said quickly. "No need for you to travel with me."

"You came to Tilssted with us," Freja said in a voice that brooked no argument. "Which means you're my responsibility until we see you safely back to the Center."

"You don't need to do that," Merletta said in an urgent undertone. "I never meant for you and the others to get caught up in this."

Freja studied her out of hard eyes for a moment, then continued to tug her away from the crowd, apparently disregarding her words completely.

"It's a dangerous game you're playing, Merletta."

"With respect, Freja," Merletta said quietly, "I disagree. I'm well aware of the danger—perhaps more than you are—but this isn't a game. It's these merpeople's lives. It's *all* of our lives."

Freja gave her a look that was impossible to read, then turned toward the Center. With one curt command, the squad fell into formation behind her, Merletta somehow ending up at their center.

The gesture almost brought tears to Merletta's eyes, in spite of the fact that she could tell Freja was angry with her. At least she would be sure to make it back to the Center in one piece on this occasion.

She was under no illusions as to the future, though. Freja and her squad couldn't protect her any more than Sage and the others could. Merletta had crossed a line she couldn't go back from.

And she had no doubt whatsoever that there would be repercussions.

CHAPTER TWENTY

Heath hardly saw the corridor around him as he strode through the castle. His thoughts were far away and far below, as they had been almost constantly since his visit to Vazula the day before. He ran a hand distractedly through his hair, trying to focus his farsight.

He'd never wanted it to work more desperately, but he *still* couldn't see anything but Merletta's features. She was underwater, that much was clear. She seemed to be in a crowd as well, given the way she kept brushing against people. But what was the event? Was she taking her stand, as she'd declared herself ready to do?

Heath found that both hands were tangled in his hair now, and he lowered them with an effort. A passing servant threw him a startled glance, and he realized he must look like his mind was disordered. He couldn't help it. He was terrified for Merletta, even as he admired her courage in the face of overwhelming opposition.

If he was that courageous, maybe the situation for the power-wielders would be very different.

He saw Merletta moving, seeming to rise up in the water. He

was so focused on her determined face that he actually walked into a suit of armor.

"Sorry," he said hastily, his concentration broken as he stooped to help a servant straighten it.

Merletta's image receded, not disappearing altogether, but no longer occupying central place in his mind. Shaking his head to clear it, Heath looked around and realized he was only a corridor away from his destination.

He covered the short distance to Lachlan's study quickly, hoping to get the meeting over with so he could go back to watching whatever trouble Merletta was getting herself into.

The guards outside the door gestured for him to enter the study—clearly Lachlan had told them of his summons.

"Heath!" The prince stood quickly, actually coming around the desk. "I hope it wasn't too soon after your ordeal for me to call you to the castle."

"Of course not," Heath protested. "I'm fine. I was barely injured." He raised his bandaged arm in illustration.

Lachlan considered him for a moment. "From what I hear, you were extremely lucky to be barely injured."

Heath nodded, waiting for his cousin to lower himself back into his chair before taking a seat himself.

"I can't deny it," he said. "I came very close to being killed."

"I'm extremely grateful you weren't," said Lachlan mildly. He leaned slightly forward. "I understand you don't wish to take any action against the blacksmith?"

"What? No, of course I don't," said Heath. "I don't think for a moment it was his fault."

Lachlan considered him thoughtfully. "Not even if he failed to safely maintain his property?"

Heath gave his cousin a look. "I don't believe that was the case." He narrowed his eyes. "What's behind these questions? I thought we were being direct with each other now."

With a sigh, Lachlan leaned back in his chair. "We are. Which is why I called you here to tell you that I examined the site myself, and I am almost certain that the building was intentionally sabotaged."

Heath gave no reaction.

"You're not surprised?" his cousin pressed.

Heath raised his hands helplessly. "What is there to say? It was already an outrageous coincidence for a runaway horse to be set loose just as an awning fell, right under a stone chimney ready to dramatically collapse."

"And that's without even mentioning that the person passing underneath at the time is at the heart of a tense and controversial dispute between two highly influential groups within our court," the prince added heavily.

Heath couldn't help a dry chuckle. "It's generous of you to put me at the center of anything, I think."

"No, it's not," said Lachlan absently. "You're absolutely at the heart of all of this, as everyone but you can see." He sighed. "I can't tell you how sorry I am that this happened to you."

"It wasn't your fault," said Heath lightly.

Lachlan didn't respond, his eyes drifting to the window, then back to Heath's face. "I regret to say that my father wasn't persuaded by my conclusion that the chimney had been tampered with."

Heath raised an eyebrow. King Matlock was really going to pretend to believe it was an honest accident? Surely someone as sensible as the king couldn't actually want his head to be buried so far in the sand.

"There's another reason I suspect it was no accident," Heath said abruptly. "Although I don't advise you to use it to attempt to convince your father."

Lachlan inclined his head expectantly.

"I felt it again," Heath blurted out. "The...magic. Or whatever it was I sensed from the men who attacked Percival."

"What?" Lachlan was suddenly ramrod straight in his chair. "You think the same people behind that attack were responsible for trying to kill you?"

Heath shrugged. "I don't know what to think. It doesn't make sense to me. There was no way to link the incident to the crown, so no reason to think it would benefit someone trying to stir up trouble." His voice turned dry. "And from what I can tell, I haven't achieved anything in my liaison role which would make me either a risk or an asset to anyone."

"That's not true," frowned the prince. He spoke not as if he was trying to make Heath feel better, but as if he was giving genuine consideration to Heath's contribution. "But if the motivation behind the attacks relates to the conflict between power-wielders and the crown, it's hard to see how you could be considered a similar target to your brother."

"It doesn't fit with the profile of Kyonans trying to make trouble, does it?" Heath said, with a hint of relief.

"Not at all," Lachlan agreed. He hesitated. "I spoke with my father about that. I didn't mention what you said about magic. I just asked him if he thought it possible that Kyonans could have been involved in the attack on Lord Percival."

"And?" Heath asked.

Lachlan shook his head slowly. "He seemed to take the idea seriously. But when I asked him a few days later whether he'd thought more about it, he seemed very convinced that Kyona had nothing to do with it."

Heath frowned. He was relieved by the king's conclusion, but puzzled as to how he'd gotten there.

"What did he see, or who did he speak to, in those intervening days?" he mused.

"Any number of people," said the prince heavily. "I have no idea what made him so certain."

For a moment there was silence, neither of them having any answers to offer.

"The Winter Solstice Festival is approaching rapidly," Lachlan said.

Heath nodded, surprised by the change of topic. Something in the prince's demeanor gave him the sense of something more meaningful under the surface of the light comment. Reaching out with his developing magic, he encountered a confusing tangle of emotions within his cousin. A desire for answers mingled with fear of what he might learn. Suspicions undermined by the hope that they'd be proved wrong.

It wasn't enough information for him to know what was coming. Only Lachlan could reveal that. Heath waited in silence.

"I'm sure I don't need to remind you that it was a bit of a disaster last year."

"You don't," Heath agreed dryly.

"Are the dragons coming this year?" Lachlan asked. "Will they renew the peace?"

Heath looked at him in surprise. "As far as I'm aware. I haven't heard anything to the contrary."

Lachlan nodded slowly, passing a feather quill methodically through one hand.

"Heath."

Heath could tell immediately from the change in Lachlan's tone that whatever the prince was about to say had been on his mind for some time.

"I haven't asked you before because...well, I wasn't sure how to bring it up, or what I hoped to hear." The prince met his eyes calmly. "But you said we were being direct with each other. The truth is my father told me nothing about his accusation against you the day Percival was attacked. Nothing beyond what he subsequently told you—that he'd been informed you were concealing a threat against the crown. I don't know who informed him, or what the threat is supposed to be, or anything."

Heath remained silent, still waiting for a question.

"Did the accusation have anything to do with the dragons?"

Heath hesitated. "With the dragon colony? No, I don't believe so."

Lachlan considered him. "Do you know what the accusation relates to?"

There was a moment of silence as Heath debated how to respond. "I can't say for certain," he said quietly. "King Matlock didn't confide the details of the accusation in me any more than he did in you."

He paused, and Lachlan folded his hands on the desk in front of him.

"But you at least have a guess as to what he meant."

Lachlan's words weren't a question, and Heath didn't confirm or contradict them.

"What I can tell you for certain," he said instead, "is that I told the truth when I said he was misinformed. I haven't concealed any threat to Valoria. I would never do that."

Lachlan frowned at him, the expression more thoughtful than disapproving. "Does it perhaps relate to wherever you and Rekavidur go together?" he tried again.

Heath felt a familiar tension rising within him. Betraying Merletta's confidence was unthinkable. But he and Lachlan had started to develop genuine trust. Betraying that wasn't very palatable either.

Before he could decide what, if anything, to tell his cousin, a sudden shout outside the door made both of them turn.

"Is he in there? He is, isn't he?"

The familiar voice filled Heath with alarm.

"Oh no," he muttered.

"Let me in!" Percival's volume was enough to communicate his fury, even if his tone hadn't made it perfectly clear. "Let me in immediately!"

"We don't answer to—"

A dull thud cut off the guard's words, and Heath and Lachlan both shot to their feet. In two quick strides, Heath was across the room, his hand reaching for the door. It flew open so quickly he had to jump backward to avoid being hit.

"Percival, what in the kingdom are you—" He broke off abruptly, his eyes widening as he took in the two guards, both of whom were on the ground. "Perce, what have you done?" he asked, his voice hollow.

"Heath, are you all right?"

Percival's alarm was palpable, as was his continued anger. He seized his brother's shoulders, looking Heath over. Apparently satisfied that Heath was unharmed, he let his concern drop away, and anger immediately rose in its place.

"What were you thinking? You've barely set foot out of the manor since you were attacked, except to go off on the worst-timed jaunt with Rekavidur yet."

Heath heard shocked exclamations in the corridor outside—clearly someone had discovered the plight of the guards, who were already starting to come around. Percival, however, ignored everything but his own tirade.

"And then I arrive home today to discover that you've not only trotted off to the castle, but you went *willingly*, and alone, and actually in response to a summons from the royal family! Do you *want* to be murdered?"

Muttering filled the silence that followed this ringing question, and glancing behind Percival, Heath saw that a number of servants had gathered to discover the source of the commotion.

"You forget yourself, Lord Percival."

Prince Lachlan's voice was ice, and Heath felt a thrill of fear. Had Percival finally done the inevitable, and crossed a line he couldn't go back from?

Clearly Percival didn't feel the same alarm. "No, I don't," he said, turning on the prince. "I know my place, and it's protecting my family. I wasn't given strength so I could hide it in shame. I was given strength to fight for those I care about. You may not be willing to admit that your father tried to have me killed, but if you think I'm going to stand by while you lure Heath into another trap, then—"

"You go too far," snapped Lachlan. "Guards, detain him."

Heath saw Percival's defiance in his eyes, and he stepped forward pleadingly. "Percival, don't lose your head."

One of the guards seized Percival's arm, but he threw off the older man's grip easily.

"Percival!" Heath's sharp tone seemed to catch his brother's attention at last, and Percival turned to glare at him, barely seeming to notice as both guards grabbed his arms.

"I appreciate the concern," Heath told him desperately. "I know you're just worried for me. But I already told you, Lachlan would never try to harm me. He's family, isn't he?"

"Family?" Percival repeated bitingly. "You've forgotten what that means. Family is supposed to have each other's backs, no matter what the cost."

Heath felt the words twist in his heart, but he stood his ground.

"Perce, you've lost sight of the real dangers. Please, don't make this worse. We can still sort this out if you just go quietly now. But if you make things worse—"

"I guess you've chosen your side," Percival said bitterly.

And with as little fuss as if they'd been children, he threw off the guards with enough force to send them slamming into the wall, and loped off down the corridor.

The gawking onlookers—who had grown by now to a sizable crowd—parted to let him through, eyes wide as they watched the spectacle.

"Well." Lachlan's voice was surprisingly calm given what had just happened.

Heath turned pleadingly to him. "He truly believed my life was in danger," he said. "I know he's unreasonable about it, but he genuinely thinks the crown was behind what happened to him. Pigheaded as he can be, he honestly thought he was protecting his family."

Lachlan made no response to the appeal, his eyes somber as they met Heath's. "You do understand that he'll have to be arrested, don't you?"

Heath's heart was heavier than it had been in months. "I understand," he said hollowly. "But I dread the outcome."

There was still anger in Lachlan's eyes, but Heath saw sympathy as well. And the same weariness that was creeping over him.

"As do I," the prince admitted quietly.

CHAPTER TWENTY-ONE

Merletta

Merletta stared at the wall behind Wivell's head, her unseeing eyes fixed on a sea snail making its slow progress across the stone. She wasn't even attempting to listen to Wivell's lecture on etymology. She knew that focusing on the topic was beyond the current capacity of her overwrought mind.

She'd thought she was ready to speak out against the Center, and take whatever consequences came. But there was one outcome she hadn't expected, and wasn't prepared for.

Nothing.

The outcome was nothing. Beyond an increase in Ibsen's hatred—if such a thing were even possible—and Agner's uncharacteristically somber demeanor when he spoke with her in training, there had so far been absolutely no consequences for her actions in Tilssted. She couldn't tell from Wivell's usual impassive manner whether he even knew about what had happened. But surely he must.

It had been a week, and Merletta had to admit to herself that the strain was starting to tell. She knew Emil had warned her that the Center's response would surprise her, but she hadn't expected to be *this* surprised. If someone was trying to unsettle her by delaying whatever punishment was coming, it was working.

Sage shifted beside her. Merletta's friends were almost as nervous as she was. Opportunities for private discussion were rare in their shared living arrangements, but they'd managed enough whispered moments for Merletta to know that Sage shared Emil's assessment. If there was to be no official sanction within the program for Merletta stepping out of line, it probably meant a less official—and more drastic—response was being planned.

Between them, Sage and Andre didn't let Merletta go anywhere alone. When Sage was Merletta's escort, Emil often joined them, usually appearing from nowhere. Merletta wondered how she could ever have missed the way Emil quietly but unfailingly arrived anytime Sage was exposed to so much as a trickle of danger. Now she was looking for it, the habit was unmistakable.

Oliver was the only trainee in the room with them, as Wivell was only teaching the third and fourth years. Not that anyone seemed to really be hearing a word Wivell was saying. Oliver looked almost as distracted as Merletta felt, although that was presumably due to his imminent fourth year test rather than Merletta's precarious position.

Andre and Lorraine were with all the first years, undertaking some task in the scribes' hall which Merletta didn't catch. None of it mattered. Having basically decided she was willing to throw away her future as a trainee in order to start standing publicly against the Center's tactics, Merletta found she had disengaged with the program entirely. She hadn't counted on being expected to continue with classes as though everything was normal.

When Wivell released them for dinner, Merletta and Sage drifted toward the door in Oliver's wake, neither speaking.

"Third year."

Wivell's voice pulled Merletta up short. She glanced at Sage, who was watching her nervously, then swam back toward the middle-aged merman.

"Yes, Instructor Wivell?" she asked, her calm voice belied by the way her heart was pounding. Was the reaction she'd been waiting for coming at last? The thought was almost a relief.

"I understand from Instructor Ibsen that you were absent from his class last week without explanation."

Merletta hesitated, unsure whether an answer was expected from her.

"I wanted to remind you," Wivell went on in his usual emotionless way, "that trainees are only allowed a very limited number of absent days before they are considered to have failed to meet the requirements of their course."

Merletta blinked. That was it?

"Thank you for informing me, Instructor," she said blankly.

Wivell waited, perhaps expecting her to apologize, or give some kind of assurance that she would miss no more classes. But Merletta didn't intend to make any such promises.

When she didn't speak, Wivell dismissed her again with a curt nod, and swam toward the door himself.

"That's all?" Sage asked incredulously, as soon as they were alone.

"There's no way that's all," Merletta said grimly. "I can only assume he's laying the foundation to force me from the program through the rules if other means fail."

"Honestly, I'm encouraged that he feels the need for a non-violent backup plan," Sage said frankly.

Merletta nodded thoughtfully. She could see the logic in

Sage's words, but they did nothing to change the sense of impending doom that still hung over her.

"Sage, have you been given a new watchword for the records room?"

Sage shook her head. "Not so far."

A flash of guilt went over Merletta. "I'm sorry, Sage," she said. "I never meant to jeopardize your studies."

"Don't be ridiculous," said her loyal friend firmly. "You're not the one who changed a password that's stood for generations, for less than honorable reasons. Besides," she shrugged, "it really hasn't impacted me so far. Both Ibsen and Wivell are drilling Oliver hard in preparation for his final test, and as a fellow fourth year I'm sitting in on every lesson. I'm learning as much as my head can hold."

Relief buoyed Merletta for a moment. She still felt neither regret nor excessive fear over the gamble she'd taken with her own life, but she had no desire to destroy her friends' futures.

"I need to speak to Emil," she mused. "As soon as possible."

"He'll be at dinner tonight, I assume," Sage said. "You can speak to him then."

Merletta shook her head. "I need to speak with him privately. There's something I need his help with, while I still have time."

When Sage gave no response, Merletta looked up. Her friend's face was hard to read.

"I think he said at lunch that he was fulfilling his weekly training requirement with the guards this afternoon," she said at last. "You could try to catch him as he's leaving."

"Thanks," said Merletta. She expected Sage to offer to accompany her, but she didn't.

Deciding not to press, Merletta sped off toward the training yard alone. Her path took her past the scribes' hall just as the first and second years were pouring out.

"Merletta!"

Andre's voice held a hint of concern, and Merletta turned reluctantly. She didn't want to miss her chance to catch Emil alone.

"Hi, Andre." Her gaze passed to the pale-haired mermaid swimming quickly to catch up with her cousin. "Hi, Indigo."

"Where are you going?" Andre asked. He dropped his voice slightly. "Why are you alone?"

"Sage went to dinner," Merletta told him, with a warning glance at Indigo, who was now within hearing. "I'm just going to the training yard briefly before I join her."

"I'll go with you," Andre said.

"Yes, we'd love to come."

Indigo's voice was bright, and Merletta glanced at her in confusion. The first year had seemed a little wary of Merletta when she'd started the program, but in the weeks since she'd become excessively friendly. She almost always joined Andre when he played unofficial bodyguard, and was very chatty and cheerful on those occasions, evidently eager to get to know her cousin's friend.

Merletta would be flattered, if only she could stop herself from being suspicious.

"Thank you both, but there's no need," she said firmly. "I'll meet you at dinner shortly."

"But—" Andre started to protest, but Merletta cut him off.

"Honestly, it's fine," she insisted.

Andre still looked concerned, but Merletta gave him no chance to argue.

"See you at dinner," she told him, swimming on toward the training yard.

Several guards were leaving the area, obviously on their way to the evening meal, and Merletta hung back to allow them to pass. Hoping she hadn't already missed Emil, she swam inside the training square. To her relief, she spotted him returning a borrowed weapon to one of the open storage areas around the edges of the space. His long pale hair flowed around him, partially braided in an attempt to keep it from his face while he trained. There was a reason most guards—unlike the rest of the triple kingdoms' mermen—tended to wear their hair short.

"Emil," she greeted him quietly, swimming up behind him.

He turned, scanning the empty water around her with creased brows. Obviously he was as concerned by her solitary state as Andre had been, although he made no comment.

"Merletta. What brings you to the training yard?"

"You, actually," Merletta told him. "I was hoping to speak to you alone."

Emil glanced around them, at the various guards still training. "Let's swim," he said. "Less conspicuous than floating around talking."

Merletta nodded her agreement, and they began to move slowly toward the street outside.

"Has something happened at last?" Emil prompted her quietly.

Merletta didn't ask what he meant. "Still nothing," she said. "Beyond a half-hearted comment from Wivell that if I miss too many classes I'll fail by default." She drew in a calming mouthful of water. "But the blow is coming. I can tell."

"It was inevitable the moment you opened your mouth and accused the Center publicly," Emil said. He wasn't entirely able to keep his voice free of the disapproval Merletta knew he still felt regarding her decision.

Merletta was silent for a moment as they passed within hearing range of a trio of guards doing warm-up exercises. When they emerged into the mostly deserted street, she spoke.

"I didn't actually accuse anyone of anything." She gave him a wry smile. "I think you must have rubbed off on me, because I was more careful than you realize."

"Careful?" Emil repeated incredulously.

"No, it's true," Merletta insisted. "I didn't accuse the Center of lying. I just suggested—without actually even saying it—that their records aren't as reliable as we might hope because they can't be verified against mistakes."

Emil was silent for a moment, considering this. "That was restrained of you," he admitted. "But you will still face punishment for revealing information you learned as part of the program. You took a vow of confidentiality when you signed up."

"But I didn't reveal anything I'd learned in the program," Merletta told him. "Or anything I've seen in official records. I intentionally didn't. I only talked about my own firsthand experiences, outside the barrier. And commented that they didn't tally with the record the educators had just made public. I think that's why they haven't moved against me officially. I didn't do anything that would earn more than a slap on the wrist according to their public stance. I even got the educators to admit in front of everyone that I didn't break the law when I snuck outside the barrier."

Emil sent her a calculating look.

"That was wise," he said, sounding insultingly surprised. "It seems I owe you an apology. I've been thinking you were more reckless than you actually were."

"I do sometimes think before I speak," Merletta said mildly. "Particularly when I'm about to publicly take aim at the most powerful institution in the ocean, knowing it contains at least some people who want me dead."

Emil gave a grim chuckle. "Apparently you've learned something in the program, after all."

"Lots of things," Merletta agreed. "But one thing I still don't know." Her voice turned brisk. "Which brings me to the reason I sought you out. I don't know how long I have before I'm thrown out, or killed, or whatever they have planned for me. And I don't want to waste what might be my last chance to find out about my parents."

"Your parents?" Emil repeated. "I thought you were left anonymously at the home."

Merletta shook her head. "They told me that, but it was a lie. There was a record of my parents' names, but the public copy was damaged. And what appears to be an accurate version of it was left in the center of the maelstrom. It was the stolen item I was supposed to retrieve during my second year test."

Emil had come to a stop now, staring openly at her. "Are you serious?"

"Completely," she told him. "I think the aim was to rattle me so much that I'd be an easy target for the guards waiting to finish me off once I got out of the maelstrom." She glanced around, making sure they weren't in hearing distance of anyone. "But August and the others intervened, so it didn't work."

Emil folded his hands behind his back, gripping them together so tightly the muscles in his lean arms bulged.

"What did the record say?" he asked.

Merletta swallowed. She'd never actually said the names aloud before. "It said their names were Elminia and Elric, and they were from Hemssted."

One of Emil's fair eyebrows went up at the name of the city, and Merletta rolled her eyes.

"Can you overcome your prejudice, or is our friendship over?"

The genuine amusement in Emil's smile seemed to break through his shock over the whole revelation. "If I can deal with having a friend from Tilssted, I suppose I can tolerate one from Hemssted."

"Hemssted might be in my blood, but I am, and always will be, from Tilssted," Merletta said bluntly. "But that's not the point."

"What is the point?" Emil asked.

"I saw a section marked *census* in the restricted records room," Merletta said, speaking quickly. They'd almost reached the dining hall now, and their window for private speech was rapidly closing. "But the educators threw me out before I could look at it. Do you think there's any chance they're in there?"

Emil frowned thoughtfully. "It's possible," he said. "Who knows? Elminia is not a common name, is it? Why are you asking me?"

"Do you still have access to the records?" Merletta asked. "As a record holder?"

Emil nodded slowly. "They've changed the process recently." He gave her a look. "For some reason. Now, instead of a watch-word, we need to prove our position as record holders to be allowed in."

"Do you think..." Merletta trailed off hopefully. When Emil didn't immediately speak, she added, "It could be my dying wish."

Emil let out a laugh in spite of himself at her wheedling tone. "You're incorrigible," he told her, as they swam into the dining hall. "Whatever they taught you at that charity home, it wasn't how to take things seriously, was it?"

Merletta grinned. "I wouldn't know. I wasn't listening in classes there, either."

Emil shook his head, still smiling. "I'll try," he promised. He lowered his voice. "I'll do it on Founders' Day. There won't be many lingering around the records room to ask questions."

"But you'll miss the celebrations," Merletta protested.

"I don't care about that." His tone left Merletta in no doubt as to the truth of his words.

"Thank you." Merletta hoped he could see the sincerity in her eyes. "It means more than I can say. I know helping me isn't without risk."

Emil shook his head, his own expression back to its habitual seriousness. "I've never been afraid for myself," he told her.

Merletta was struck with a vivid memory of Andre making a similar declaration, back when he suggested they fake a relationship. She'd thought the sentiment foolish, but sincere. Emil's was no less sincere, and if anything, more meaningful. Because Emil wasn't foolish. He didn't say anything he didn't mean, and he didn't do anything he hadn't carefully thought through first.

"Thank you," she said again.

Her eyes shifted to the nearby trainees' table, and she was surprised to see Sage and Andre watching their conversation attentively. Merletta sent her friends a smile, noting that Sage's responding smile was a little strained.

Emil was approached by another junior record holder, and drifted off to sit with his fellows, as he'd been doing more often since the trainees' table got flooded with first years. Merletta lowered herself into a seat beside Sage.

"Did you sort out...whatever it was?" Sage asked, her voice a little too casual.

Merletta nodded, gratitude softening her voice. "He agreed to help me."

"I'm glad," said Sage, although she didn't sound entirely glad.

"What's wrong?" Merletta asked. She lowered her voice. "I'm sorry I didn't explain what I was going to ask him about...I didn't want to miss the opportunity. I'll tell you about it when we next—"

"No need," Sage said, shaking her head vigorously. "I wasn't trying to pry." She took a bite of her cod, then laid it down again. "He's always admired you a great deal, you know. Ever since you started the program. And he's taken more of an interest in you than you know. He asks me about you all the time. And he's been really worried ever since he found out you're in danger. He doesn't say it, but I can tell it weighs on his mind."

Merletta stared at her friend, understanding washing over her. She'd already discovered her obliviousness about Emil's feelings. It seemed she'd been doubly blind where it came to Sage.

"Sage, I think you're very much under the wrong impression," she said carefully.

Sage's face was a little pinker than usual, but she didn't look up from her food. Before Merletta could say another word, however, an unexpected voice broke into the conversation.

"Is it true that you often used to sneak outside the barrier as a child?"

Merletta turned, astonished that Oliver was speaking to her, and with only a mild version of his usual sneer.

"Yes," she said. "Almost daily."

He raised an eyebrow. "You expect us to believe that you survived out there alone, not just once, but lots of times?"

Merletta shrugged. "I don't expect you to believe anything." She paused. "Well, that's not true," she amended. "I expect you'll probably believe whatever you're told, like a good unquestioning trainee. But I don't have high expectations that you'll believe what *I* tell you. It's true, though, whether you believe it or not."

Impolite as her words were, she spoke without malice. And, somewhat to her surprise, Oliver didn't seem to take offense.

"I see why they idolize you in Tilssted," he said unemotionally. "They seem to value guts over sense in that city."

Merletta stared at him. "Did you just call me brave?"

His sneer became a little more pronounced, but it seemed more reflex than actual emotion. "I don't believe I said that."

Merletta looked him over curiously, wondering what went on behind that unexpressive face.

"What do they value in Hemssted?" she asked, almost wistfully. Verbalizing her supposed origins for the first time to Emil had re-ignited the powerful curiosity about her history that had plagued her since her second year test.

"Influence," said Oliver simply, surprising Merletta again by engaging with the question. "And a good family name, I suppose."

"You suppose?" Lorraine sounded amused. "Says a mighty member of the Ol line."

Oliver couldn't quite hide his satisfied smile, and Merletta looked at the second year mermaid curiously. "The Ol line?"

Lorraine's smile fell away, and Merletta could tell that she regretted entering the conversation. But she didn't seem willing to openly snub Merletta when Oliver was speaking to the hated Tilssted trainee so civilly.

"Oliver's family is very well respected," she said, clearly not inclined to elaborate.

Andre was looking at Oliver skeptically. "Your name is Oliver Ol?"

"Of course not," Oliver said scornfully. "We're not like Skulssted. We don't need two names just to figure out who we are."

"You don't have family names in Hemssted?" Sage asked.

Oliver made an impatient noise. "Of course we do. My family name is Ol. My father is Olbert. My mother is Olisha. Formally, that is. Before she married my father, her name was Arisha, and that's still what most people call her. As a boy, I was named according to my father's family line. My sister, Arlette, is named according to my mother's."

Merletta stared at him, fascinated. "Is that common practice in Hemssted?" she asked.

Oliver nodded, his lip curling slightly. "I thought everyone would know that."

"The rest of the triple kingdoms aren't as obsessed with Hemssted's so-called influence as you are," Andre said tartly.

But Merletta didn't care about Oliver's arrogance. She was too engrossed in thinking through the implications of his words. It seemed like confirmation that her parents really did come from Hemssted, if the names on the record had been accurate. Was that why their names both started with El? And applying the logic about the way naming worked, did that mean her mother's name had first been Merminia?

Merletta was unprepared for the sudden rush of emotion that came over her. It was foolish, perhaps, to react so strongly to a simple explanation of naming customs. But it conjured up an image of two merpeople trying to decide what to name their baby, a baby who they might have wanted, and been excited to meet.

"I need to speak to Emil," she muttered, pushing herself up from her seat. If Emil was going to search the census records on her behalf, this information would be useful.

Sage sent her an inscrutable look as she rose, but there was no privacy for Merletta to explain herself. It wasn't until she was halfway across the room that she remembered the interrupted conversation she'd been having with Sage.

A glance back over her shoulder showed the other mermaid already leaving the dining hall, not even glancing back.

CHAPTER TWENTY-TWO

Merletta

Founders' Day arrived with the usual fanfare, but Merletta couldn't bring herself to care about any of it. Not only was she still living under a shadow as she waited for the repercussions of her display in Tilssted, but she was filled with nervous excitement over Emil's planned investigations.

Would he find out who she was? Who she'd been born, at least. And did she want to know? She'd heard how it worked in Skulssted, and she knew Hemssted would be no different. If she'd been abandoned to an impoverished charity home, it meant no one in her parents' circle had wanted her after their death. No one had even come looking for her, or tried to tell her about her parents. Did she want to learn the identity of a community that had rejected her so brutally?

A less logical, but no less pervasive, thought lingered behind all of that. What if her parents hadn't abandoned her unwillingly by death? What if they'd given her up because they didn't want her? Because something had been wrong with her from the very start, just like they'd always told her at the charity home?

Merletta tried to shake these morbid thoughts, but she was certainly far from any festive mood. Her stomach was too unsettled to even look forward to the feast, which would undoubtedly be extravagant and delicious.

Andre took part in the games with his usual enthusiasm—nothing seemed to dim his natural optimism for long—but Sage hovered close to Merletta, apparently perfectly content just to watch. Emil, of course, wasn't present.

The drop off was so full of merpeople, it was hard to believe they could all really be affiliated with the Center. It seemed half the triple kingdoms was there, eager to enjoy a day of relaxation and celebration after the various uncertainties and conflicts of the preceding months.

When Andre emerged victorious from his category of the combat competition, Sage and Merletta coaxed him into taking a break. The afternoon was dwindling. It was almost time for the feast.

"Where's Indigo?" he asked cheerfully. "Didn't she see me win?"

"I don't know." Sage frowned as she cast an eye over the crowd. "I haven't seen her for a while, actually. Wait, is that her there?"

"Yes!" Andre brightened, then his face creased in confusion. "Who's that she's talking to? I've seen him around...isn't he extremely senior amongst the guards? Why would Indigo be speaking with him?"

Merletta looked up, her attention caught. The merman in conversation with Indigo did look familiar, now Andre mentioned it. He was tall and weedy, with a nondescript silvery tail and pale hair and skin. Her eyes narrowed in suspicion. Was he one of the Record Master's personal guards? She thought so, but it was hard to be sure from such a distance.

"Come on," she said, grabbing Sage's arm and swimming around a throng of revelers. Andre trailed behind them.

There was a temporary stand set up on the edge of the drop off, on which equipment was stored for the combat trials. Merletta swam behind it, ducking low to the reef so as to be out of sight.

"Yes, I'm sure." Indigo's voice was low, but Merletta had no trouble catching the words. "She's been here the whole time. I've been watching, as instructed. I don't think she's going anywhere. I heard her and my cousin talking about the feast earlier."

Merletta's stomach lurched unpleasantly. There was surely no one but her Indigo could be talking about. The guard responded in a voice too quiet for Merletta to make out. Then silence fell.

Easing out from her hiding place slightly, Merletta saw the guard swimming abruptly away and Indigo bobbing alone.

Merletta turned to Andre, a shiver running over her.

"Stay here," he told her in an undertone.

His voice was more grim than she'd ever heard it. With a flick of his tail, he swam out to where Indigo still floated.

"What was that, Indigo?"

"Andre!" She sounded surprised to see him, but there was no sign of the guilt Merletta had expected. "Where did you come from?"

"Tell me I didn't just hear what I thought I did, Indigo," Andre said. "Because it sounded like you'd been spying on Merletta for that senior guard."

Indigo's voice communicated nothing but confusion. "But... haven't you been doing the same thing all this time?"

"What?" Andre protested. "Of course not!"

"Andre..." Indigo still sounded more perplexed than anything. "I've known since before I even entered the program that she was disrespectful of the Center, and highly unpre-dictable. Surely your friendship with her can't be real."

"It's absolutely real," Andre spluttered.

Merletta dared another glance out, to see Andre studying his cousin's face. Even from her limited vantage point, Merletta could see the genuine distress on his features.

"Indigo, there's so much you don't know. Merletta is...she's trustworthy. She's not the one who..." He ran a hand through his shoulder-length hair, clearly torn about what to reveal.

"So is your romantic relationship with her real as well, then?" Indigo asked dryly.

Andre sent her an exasperated look. "That was only ever a misunderstanding, Indigo. I told you that already."

The young mermaid shook her head, still looking completely lost. "Andre, you don't have to pretend for me," she insisted. "I know what you're doing. I was approached almost as soon as I started classes and instructed to befriend her so as to keep an eye on her. It made sense of your friendship with her, which had previously confused me. I realized you'd been asked the same thing, and I've been at a loss as to why you haven't told me as much. But you don't have to keep it a secret from me."

"You have it all wrong, Indigo," said Andre, visibly upset. "Who asked you to spy on her?"

"Let's not be dramatic," said Indigo dryly.

Before Andre could respond, another first year swam up to the pair, his eyes wide with excitement.

"Did you hear, Indigo? They've made an arrest. Apparently someone's been stealing records from the Center and falsifying them."

"Oh have they?" Merletta emerged from her hiding place, done with cowering behind a shield.

Indigo started visibly, her eyes flying between Merletta and

Andre. The other first year, however, turned to her eagerly, apparently not connecting the news to her.

"That's what I just heard," he confirmed. "I think it's just happened. Everyone's talking about it."

Merletta looked out across the drop off, realizing that he was right. The competitions had been suspended, and most of the attendees were in small clumps, gossiping animatedly.

"Wait." Merletta froze as the first year's words sank in. She'd assumed the accusation was about her, but that didn't make sense. "Did you say they're *going* to make an arrest?"

"No, it's just happened," he repeated. "But apparently they got away."

"Who?" Sage's voice was sharp beside Merletta, clearly sharing the same fear that had suddenly gripped her friend. "Did they say who he was?"

Surely not, was all Merletta could think. Emil was a qualified record holder, respected and well known within the Center. He came from a wealthy family in Skulssted, who would vigorously resist any efforts to label him a traitor. Why would they target him instead of Merletta, who was a much more logical target? She'd been so sure her well-connected friends were safe.

"I don't remember the name, but I think it was a mermaid, not a merman," the trainee said. "They found the evidence in her room."

Merletta and Sage exchanged confused looks. Was it possible they'd read this completely wrongly, and this incident actually had nothing to do with Merletta? Sage was her only female friend in the Center.

In the Center.

The realization hit Merletta a moment before the booming voice rang out.

"Trainee Merletta?"

Feeling suddenly trapped in a nightmare, she turned

slowly to see an unfamiliar guard. He was wearing the armbands of a senior Center guard. She nodded numbly, too terrified by her suspicions to be defiant. It was all for show, of course. There could be no doubt he knew exactly who she was.

"I have some questions to ask you," he said. "With regards to an offense committed by a shellsmith apprentice."

Merletta could hardly draw in water, her heartbeat spiraling out of control.

"I don't...I don't know what you're talking about," she managed.

Pull yourself together! shouted a voice in her head. Could she seem any more guilty?

"Are you connected with a shellsmith apprentice named Letitia?" the guard asked, his voice still much louder than necessary. Everyone within range had fallen silent, all of them watching, rapt, as the drama unfolded. "Our information is that you grew up in the same charity home in Tilssted."

"That's right," said Merletta, proud to hear that her voice was now steady.

"And you consider her a friend?" the guard pressed.

Merletta swallowed. Tish had wanted to be separated from her, but clearly it was too late for that. In which case, Merletta would never disown her.

"I certainly do," Merletta said.

"Are you aware that this Letitia has been found in possession of confidential Center records?" the guard challenged. "Records which had been copied to appear official, but with contents substantially changed?"

"That's a lie," said Merletta furiously. "She would never do any of that. She doesn't want anything to do with the Center."

"So you admit that she is hostile toward the Center?"

"No!" Merletta cried. She looked around for aid, but Sage

and Andre were both as helplessly horrified as she was, and there was no one else to turn to.

"Surely this matter can be handled more privately."

The mild voice belonged to Agner. The combat instructor swam up alongside the guard, looking exasperated more than anything.

"It's not Center policy to conduct matters in secrecy," the guard informed him. "We conduct our affairs in the open, for transparency."

Merletta didn't know whether to laugh or cry.

The guard turned to her again. "Do you have any idea of how this Letitia would have gotten her hands on the original records?"

Muttering was spreading around Merletta on all sides, but she ignored it. She didn't care what these people thought of her. She cared about Tish.

"Information to report."

The voice made Merletta turn in confusion. Sage's mother had swum forward, and was floating to attention before the guard.

"Speak," he invited the record holder.

"At my superiors' request, I provided Trainee Merletta with houseroom during her most recent break from classes. I can report that she traveled to Tilssted more than once during that time to visit a friend from her childhood. She always took a satchel with her."

Merletta heard a strangled noise from Sage behind her, but she was too terrified for Tish to dwell on the twisting pain in her gut at this betrayal by her former hostess. Still, it was a heavy weight to swim under—first Indigo, now Rowena. Both mermaids who'd been kind to her—both close family of friends she trusted. It shouldn't be a surprise that if a new trainee like

Indigo had been asked to spy on her, a fully qualified record holder had been given the same instructions.

The muttering had escalated to shocked whispers, which Merletta continued to ignore.

"Where is she?" she demanded of the guard. "What have you done to her?"

The merman raised an eyebrow in dignified surprise. "As a matter of fact, she's gone. When guards attempted to apprehend her, she fled across the barrier. She was pursued, but not located. Our view is that she is unlikely to return to the triple kingdoms, where she must know severe sanctions await her."

"No."

Merletta's voice was little more than a whisper. She had a horrible feeling she knew what that meant. But surely not. Surely they wouldn't kill sweet, gentle Tish, who'd always kept her head down and never scratched anyone's scales the wrong way. Surely they wouldn't be so vicious.

Unbidden, Merletta's thoughts flew to the two murdered members of August's patrol, and the story of betrayal and violence the three survivors had to tell.

Yes, they would. They wouldn't even hesitate.

"No!" The word came out more loudly now. "If she's gone, it's because you killed her! Tish would never cross the barrier! She's terrified of the open ocean."

"The ocean which you claim is so safe?"

Ibsen's sneering face appeared alongside the head guard, full of vicious satisfaction. How long he'd waited for this moment!

With an effort, Merletta tuned him out as well.

"Where is she?" she repeated in increasing desperation.

"I already told you," the guard said coldly.

Merletta met his eyes for a long moment, then turned to her friends.

"If there's any chance I'm not too late…" she whispered.

"Go." Andre's voice was as hard as stone, his back turned pointedly on his cousin. "We'll delay them in any way we can."

Sage's face was devoid of all color, but she nodded her agreement. For a moment Merletta held her friend's eyes, fully aware this might be the last time she ever saw Sage. But there was no time for sentiment.

Ignoring the guard completely, she plunged forward, working her tail powerfully as she fled across the drop off. There were guards everywhere, and she expected to be seized, but no one laid a hand on her.

"Do not pursue her." The senior guard's voice rang out over the crowded drop off. "If you cross out of the safety of the barrier at this hour, your chances of survival are almost nonexistent."

Merletta didn't check her pace, even as she suddenly understood why none of the guards were publicly arresting her. She realized that she'd just given them an excellent explanation for her imminent death, one which would cast no blame on them. She had to admit they'd been clever in finding a way to avoid turning her into a martyr. As far as the triple kingdoms were concerned, she'd been publicly accused of a crime which would cast uncertainty on all her previous words, then had fled arrest to perish in the ocean with her accomplice.

There could be no doubt whatsoever that guards would follow at a distance, to finish the job properly once there were no witnesses.

But even knowing all that, Merletta didn't hesitate as she raced out into Skulssted and turned toward Tilssted. She was playing into their hands and swimming into their trap, but she didn't see what other choice she had. Not with Tish's life on the line.

Please, please still be alive, she begged her friend silently.

As she swam through the darkening streets, she cursed her own idiocy. She'd told herself she was ready to face whatever consequences were directed at her, even if they killed her. Emil had tried to warn her that it wouldn't be anything so blatant, but she'd still failed to grasp the subtlety of the Center's attacks. She'd been so sure her friends were safe from repercussions due their positions of privilege and influence. She should have realized that her enemies—their hands tied from targeting her openly—would take aim at her only friend who had nothing and no one to protect her.

Merletta could tell she was being followed, no doubt by the anticipated guards, but she was skilled at evasive swimming. By the time she reached Tilssted, she knew she'd put some distance between herself and her pursuers. It made little difference— they knew exactly where she was going—but it might buy her a precious few minutes.

Disregarding polite conventions, she swam straight up the side of the shellsmith tower, sticking her head through the small window on Tish's floor. A group of apprentices were eating dinner together, and Merletta's eyes latched eagerly on to the bossy mermaid who'd made her shells.

"Where's Tish?" she cried.

Everyone jumped, their eyes flying in shock to the window.

"Merletta?" The apprentice looked astonished. Muttering ran throughout the room, indicating to Merletta that they'd all heard the allegations against her.

"Where is she?" Merletta demanded.

"She was taken away by some Center guards only a short while ago," the girl said. "They accused her of stealing something, and took her away for questioning."

"Tish has never stolen anything in her life," Merletta cried, an edge of desperation to her voice. "And they didn't take her away to question her—they took her away to murder her! They want to be rid of me, so they've concocted a bunch of lies to implicate Tish so that I—never mind the details! Where exactly did they go?"

Most of the mermaids around the table were staring at her with mouths open, but Tish's friend sprang into action.

"I watched them leave through the window. Come on!"

After a minute which felt like an eternity, she emerged at the bottom of the building, swimming straight toward the boundary. Merletta streaked after her, her heart in her throat as she watched the nearest kelp farm appear up ahead.

"They went through right there," the apprentice said, pointing to a passageway through the undulating fronds of kelp.

"Thank you." Merletta darted forward, not pausing to look back at her guide, spurred on by fear and the desperate hope that she wasn't too late.

The guards on her tail would have no trouble tracking her this far, but maybe she could get Tish away somewhere safe first.

The farms were silent, empty of laborers now the sun had set far above. Merletta pushed blindly through the fronds, barely noticing when the ripple of the barrier went over her. Trusting in the shellsmith apprentice's assurance that the guards had taken Tish straight through in the indicated direction, she stuck to the path between the fronds, following its trajectory straight through the forests beyond with frantic strokes.

When she emerged into open water, there was no patrol visible, which in itself struck her as suspicious. Her eyes scanned the dark water in panic, but it was her ears which alerted her to someone in the area. A cry of anger emanated from a jagged trench nearby—Merletta knew the spot well.

She sped toward it, her ever-present spear gripped tightly in her hand. When she rounded a rocky pile, she struggled for a moment to make sense of the scene before her. She saw more than one pair of flailing arms, the flash of a weapon, and the shimmer of scales. Then her eyes found Tish, huddled against a rock in obvious terror, but still alive.

It was all Merletta could do not to cry out in relief, but she retained enough sense not to give away her position. Her eyes flew back to the other merpeople present. With a shock, she saw another familiar face, and everything clicked into place. It seemed only two guards had been sent to deal with Tish—a generous assessment of her threat level, if anything. But they hadn't banked on another player. Specifically, a middle-aged mermaid with decades of close experience with guards, and a raging fury against the Center's murderous ways.

Where Eloise had come from, Merletta didn't know. But she was holding her own impressively against the two guards, given she wielded only a crude weapon. Even as Merletta watched, however, she took a blow to her arm which caused her to fall back, her face twisting in pain.

Merletta had observed long enough. Moving silently, she surged forward and struck out at the nearest guard, cracking the blunt end of her spear over his head. With a shout, he gripped his head with both hands, listing crazily in the water. The other guard turned to Merletta, his eyes widening in shock, then narrowing in recognition. Merletta flipped her spear around, baring her teeth in a snarl as she advanced with the sharpened end of her weapon forward.

It was a dangerous time of evening to shed blood into the water, but she would rather go down fighting with everything she had than being cautious.

She never had to strike the guard. Eloise propelled herself forward, plunging her own weapon into the guard's tail.

The guard screamed in pain, and everyone present tensed instinctively as blood leaked from the wound. The guard looked to his fellow for support, but the other merman was still dazed from the blow to his head.

Eloise gave Merletta a meaningful look, and Merletta didn't waste another moment. Seizing Tish's arm, she hauled her friend through the water, swimming away from the triple kingdoms in Eloise's wake.

The guard shouted in anger, but he didn't pursue them. With the speed at which blood was now pouring from his tail, he would be desperate to get himself and his companion back across the barrier to safety before predators came in response to the trail.

"Merletta," Tish gasped. "Merletta, I...I don't...I was just... and then..."

"I know," Merletta grunted, still dragging her friend along. "I'm so sorry, Tish. I'm so, so sorry." She looked desperately at Eloise. "What do I do? Where can I take her? They'll kill us all if we go back there."

"There's only one place we can go now," Eloise said grimly. "And I don't know how safe we'll be even there."

Merletta was silent, seeing the truth of Eloise's words. She could only hope they were able to outstrip any pursuers. They had the advantage of knowing the way well.

"Thank the tides I left it a little late to return tonight," Eloise said. "I was lingering in the trench, waiting for it to be clear for me to cross the barrier, when I heard those guards sending the patrol off without explanation. Well, that told me something was up, before I even got a proper look at how they were dragging her through the kelp." She cast a calculating glance at Tish. "If you want to live, I suggest you start swimming, and swimming hard," she informed the terrified mermaid. "We'll never outswim them with Merletta having to tug you all the way there."

"All the way where?" Tish gasped. "We...we shouldn't be out here. It's dark, and we're way past the barrier, and—"

"There aren't as many things trying to kill you out here as you think, Tish," Merletta told her, as gently as she could. She jerked a thumb back toward the barrier. "And we now know for a fact someone's trying to kill you in there."

Tish said no more. Her obvious terror tugged at Merletta's heart, but as Eloise had predicted, they made much better time once Tish was swimming properly for herself.

When they reached the island, Tish hung back, her eyes wide as they rested on the land, silver under the moonlight.

"I'll stay with her," Merletta said. "You get the others. None of them can stay here now. If no one else, Ileana definitely knows about the island. I suspect she told someone high up in the guards long ago."

Eloise was already half out of the water, and Merletta heard Tish cry out in terror as the older mermaid flicked her tail fully clear.

"It's all right, Tish," Merletta told her friend desperately. "I know it's a lot to take in, but it's going to be all right."

"But..." Tish's voice was a squeak. "But she'll dry out."

"It won't kill her," Merletta assured her friend. "Watch."

Looking like she could hardly bear to witness it, Tish complied, her face going from fear to shock so rapidly, Merletta was afraid she'd suffer heart failure.

"I know," Merletta told her friend. "I'm sorry there was no time to explain it all first, tell you more gently. I've been sitting on this for a long time now, but I know how terrifying it all is at first."

Tish said nothing, either then or in the agonizingly slow half an hour it took for Eloise to reappear with the others. August came last, walking backward and obscuring their footprints in the sand with a large palm frond.

"I don't know if it will be enough," he said grimly. "But I've done my best to hide the evidence of our time here."

Merletta bit her lip. It might be enough to hide it from anyone studying the place from the water. It was unlikely to fool someone properly exploring the island, however. The question was whether anyone searching for them would know about drying out, and would ascend onto shore in their search.

"Eloise tells me time is critical," August said, as soon as he'd entered the water. Paul and Griffin followed behind him, their expressions determined as their legs transformed seamlessly to tails. "It's not ideal to travel at night, but we need to shelter somewhere far enough away that a haphazard search won't find us. We know some places. By the time they can do a methodical search in the daylight, we'll have moved on."

Merletta shook her head. "This isn't like last time, where they thought you were dead. They know Tish, Eloise, and I are out here, and they'll be determined to find us, and make sure we don't survive to tell our tale. If we hide anywhere in the vicinity of the triple kingdoms, they will find us."

"But where else can we go?" Griffin demanded. "This is a sheltered part of the ocean, Merletta. The deep ocean is no joke. I don't think we can afford to risk it, not when we have nowhere specific to go."

"Actually..." Merletta swallowed. "I might have somewhere to go. Somewhere I've been offered safe haven before. But it's a long journey."

"You want to travel across the open ocean?" Tish repeated, aghast. "We'd all die for certain."

"No we wouldn't," August said confidently. "We survived out in the depths for almost a year before we came to this island. If we travel during the daylight, and take appropriate precautions, there's no reason we can't traverse the ocean safely."

"I'm glad to hear you say that," Merletta told him. "Because the place I'm thinking of will take days to get there. Possibly a whole week, if I've understood the distances correctly."

"Where?" Griffin and August spoke at the same time.

Knowing how the younger guard would feel about her answer, Merletta focused her eyes on August. She drew in a deep pull of water, her emotions a more tangled mess than she could ever remember them being before.

"Heath's kingdom."

CHAPTER TWENTY-THREE

"If you think I'm sharing a carriage with that traitor, you don't know me at all."

Percival was clearly trying for dignified outrage, but it came across more sulky than anything. Heath didn't know whether he wanted to roll his eyes or punch his brother in the face.

"That's enough, Percival." The Duke of Bexley's voice was frigid.

Unprompted, Heath's magic stirred inside him, reaching out curious tendrils. His father's anger he could perceive with his ordinary senses. But the fear—almost all-consuming in its intensity—was deeper below the surface. It was pervasive, however, muddying all his father's thoughts and reactions. It made trying to read the older man's state of mind like peering through murky water.

At the thought, his extra sight instantly threw another image in front of his awareness. Merletta, swimming rapidly through the water, her expression tight. What was distressing her? Was she in danger? Heath tried to cast his sight wider, and he thought he caught a glimpse of another mermaid swimming behind Merletta. A fair-haired girl he didn't recognize. They appeared to be swimming over a canyon, no hand-crafted structures in sight. Were they on the way to the island?

Heath's father threw him a sharp look, reminding Heath how skilled the duke was at sensing the use of power.

He drew back from the magic inside him, Merletta's image fading back into a tug on the edge of his consciousness. It was a great effort to pull his thoughts away from her without knowing what was happening, but his own surroundings required his full attention. Even if Merletta was going to Vazula, he wouldn't be at liberty to join her there that day.

"I don't care how angry you are, Father," Percival said, his voice as steely as the duke's. "The only way I'm getting into a carriage with Heath is if you physically force me in. And we both know you can't do that. I'll ride."

"Percival, please." Their mother's voice was strained. Heath could sense her embarrassment that the servants were witnessing the display. "You know the terms of your release. Your father went to great lengths to convince King Matlock to let you return to Bexley Manor. And one of the conditions is that you travel there in a vehicle driven by a royal coachman."

"It's outrageous," Percival muttered, and Heath's patience finally snapped.

"What's outrageous is the fact that you're complaining! If it wasn't for Father's intervention, you'd still be in the dungeons!"

"I was only in the dungeons because I was fool enough to believe Father when he told me that if I went with the guards willingly, the king would be reasonable," Percival retorted hotly.

"Get in, Percival." Their father's voice was calm, but unyielding.

"I told you, I'm not spending hours shut up with—"

"I'll ride," said Heath curtly, turning his back on his brother.

It wasn't as though he was itching to sit with Percival, either.

The two of them had barely spoken since Percival ran from the guards outside Prince Lachlan's study. Heath knew that his brother blamed him bitterly for not taking his side when he'd only acted out of a belief that Heath's life was in real danger. But what did Percival really expect him to do? The fact that Percival had made it out of the dungeons and was allowed to return to Bexley Manor—effectively under house arrest—was testament to their father's diplomacy. And perhaps to the fact that enough moderation remained in King Matlock to wish to avoid open hostilities between the crown and the power-wielders. Not to mention the king must be ready to have Percival and his polarizing influence away from the throngs of the capital.

Percival recognized neither the diplomacy nor the moderation, of course. His sense of being unjustly oppressed had only grown more intense through the experience. He seemed incapable of comprehending that regardless of his intentions or motivations, what he'd actually done was attack two of Prince Lachlan's personal guards in order to force his way into the crown prince's study, then fled when they attempted to apprehend him.

The journey was slow and tedious, but not nearly as much as it would have been if Heath had been in the carriage with Percival and his mother. The duke rode beside Heath, but they hardly spoke. Every now and then the older man threw Heath a calculating glance, clearly feeling the magic Heath was using as he tried to see Merletta.

The ride took half the day, and Heath wasn't sure what to make of the fact that Merletta continued to swim swiftly, with only occasional breaks, for its entire duration. Surely the trip from her kingdom to Vazula was nowhere near that long...but where else would she be going? He wished he could get her attention by calling her name, the way she could his. But she wasn't Reka—the connection only went one way.

When they arrived at the manor, Heath lost no time in escaping to the cliffs. He wasn't under house arrest, after all. He could come and go as he pleased. He'd only joined the family out of solidarity.

For his parents, not Percival.

He was just about ready to wash his hands of his impossible brother. Happily for her, Laura and her family had finally been cleared to return to their home in a different part of the kingdom.

Sitting on his favorite spot on the cliffs, Heath closed his eyes and tried to call to mind every lesson Reka had taught him about using his magic. He focused on Merletta, and her image saturated his mind, crystal clear. She was still swimming, speaking quietly with someone alongside her. With a great effort, Heath coaxed his vision outward, expecting to see the pale-haired mermaid again.

But it was a merman swimming alongside Merletta, a spear clutched in his hand. It was Griffin—the guard who'd taken such offense at Heath's presence on the island, or more accurately, in Merletta's life.

Well, that was unsettling.

Where were they going? The question remained unanswerable, and Heath let the vision fall with a sigh. Whatever her troubles, Merletta had no need of him at that moment. She was far away, and he couldn't reach her. His family, on the other hand, were getting deeper into trouble with every passing day.

Pushing himself to his feet with a groan, he trudged back toward the manor.

The week after their arrival at Bexley Manor passed interminably. Percival was avoiding Heath, which suited him just fine. Heath spent much of his time practicing his farsight or poring over the family tree his grandmother had given him. Neither pastime provided him with any new information.

"What's that?"

His father's voice startled Heath from a reverie one afternoon. He was sitting in a window seat, trying to soak up as much of the weak winter sunshine as possible. He'd planned to practice his archery in the manor's small training yard, but the cold had sent him back inside immediately. Since becoming so used to Vazula's humid warmth, he found the snowy mid-winter of Valoria harder to endure.

Heath handed over the parchment, saying nothing.

The duke studied it with furrowed brow, his gaze passing slowly up to Heath's. "This is a list of all the power-wielders in Kyona and Valoria."

Heath nodded.

"And it's in my mother's handwriting."

Again, Heath just gave a silent nod.

"Are the two of you planning some kind of coup I should know about?" the duke asked mildly.

Heath laughed, the sound seeming to warm the corridor slightly. "That's right. We're going to overthrow the crowns of both kingdoms, with Grandmother claiming her place as Empress."

The duke chuckled as well, joining Heath on the wide window seat and leaning with his back against the far side of the sill.

"Have I ever told you how unpleasant it feels for me to be lied to?" he said conversationally. "I'll forgive that one, though, since I started it."

Heath inclined his head curiously. "What does it feel like for you?"

The duke looked out the window, considering. "It's difficult to describe," he said. "But I'd put the sensation somewhere between taste and smell. Deception is...bitter. Almost acrid."

"Huh," Heath mused. "That's different from...from what I was expecting," he finished lamely, only just catching himself.

The duke just looked at him with the direct gaze that had always made all three of his children squirm.

"What?" Heath said defensively. "I was telling the truth."

"I know," the duke informed him unnecessarily. "But I don't need magic to tell when you're hiding something, Heath. You're my son." The hint of a rueful smile flickered across his face. "Plus, you're not very good at it."

"It's difficult to cultivate the skill when you grow up with a father who can sense the least hint of deception," Heath reminded him.

He made no comment about his omission, and after a moment, his father released him from that piercing look, directing his eyes out the window with a sigh.

"Loyalty is a complicated thing," the duke said, so quietly Heath got the sense he was talking to himself as much as to his son.

"Do you really think we should go to the Winter Solstice Festival?" Heath asked, changing topic with no attempt at tact. "Given everything that's happening?"

His father nodded. "Definitely. It's more important than ever, especially after the fiasco that was last year's Festival."

"Percival won't be happy," Heath commented. "Aren't you worried he'll get up to mischief, stuck here on house arrest all alone?"

The duke sighed. "Worrying doesn't achieve much," he said wryly. He handed the parchment back to Heath. "What is this actually for?"

Heath took it, his eyes on the names of Laura's twins. "I thought I sensed magic when Percival was attacked," he said bluntly, making a snap decision. "I don't want to believe it was any of the Kyonan branch. But the idea of it being a Valorian is even worse. And even less logical," he added as an afterthought.

"Does the crown know about this?" The duke sounded alarmed.

"I told Prince Lachlan," Heath said, glad of his father's wording. If he'd asked whether the king knew, he would likely have sensed deception in Heath's evasive answers, even without actual untruth.

"He will have told his father," the duke mused, his expression hard to read.

Heath kept quiet, not responding to the incorrect assumption.

"You two look cozy." Percival's resentful voice brought an instant change to the mood of the corridor.

Both men looked around to see him approaching up the polished floorboards. The duke glanced from Heath to Percival, the hint of a question on his face.

"Yes, Percival knows," Heath said, leaning his head back against the wooden frame of the window. "He didn't sense the magic himself, and you know how extremely gracious he is in accepting anyone else's opinion on anything."

The look his father gave him was faintly exasperated, but Heath just shrugged. Why should he be the mature one all the time?

"Don't tell me you're still going on about that blasted theory of yours!" Percival protested. "For the last time, there was no magic there other than mine! And Rekavidur's, when he showed up. That's probably what you felt."

Heath gave him a disbelieving look. "You think I could ever fail to recognize Reka's magic? I know it as well as I know yours. And incidentally, Reka agrees with me that there was magic there. He said he didn't notice it at the time, but in memory he thinks there was some kind of weak—"

"In memory?" Percival interrupted. "Do you realize how ridiculous you sound?"

"Rekavidur said that?" their father asked, his eyes narrowed in thought. "Then there must have been something there...but surely Kyona wouldn't—"

"Of *course* you listen to his madness!" Percival said, outraged. "I'm no longer surprised Heath would find a way to blame the whole thing on magic—it makes sense he's scared of it, given he barely has any himself. But I wouldn't have thought it of you, Father!"

The duke stood slowly, his stiff and austere posture showing no hint of the hurt Heath's power sensed beneath. His father, wise and respected as he was, remained vulnerable to the opinion of his sons. It was an unsettling revelation.

"Perhaps it will do you good, Percival," the older man said calmly. "To experience the sensation of being deeply disappointed in the conduct and attitude of a family member whom you had thought knew better."

Percival swelled, angry words clearly growing inside him. But the duke was already walking away. Left with no other audience, Percival turned his glower on Heath.

Heath raised his hands. "Don't start," he said coldly.

He rose, and had taken half a step when his magic—still active from reading his father—latched unexpectedly on to his brother. Heath faltered slightly. He'd been surprised to discover hurt underneath his father's calm. He was even more surprised to realize that Percival's anger hid not only hurt, but uncertainty, fear...even shame.

If only you'd show any of that on the outside, even a little, Heath thought. The rest of the family might have a little more patience with their overly-proud brother and son.

"Do you know what Father had to do to convince King Matlock to release you?" he asked quietly.

Percival rolled his eyes. "I'm not interested in a lecture on the powers of diplomacy," he said, his voice giving no hint of any of the emotions Heath had sensed beneath.

"He put himself as pledge for you," Heath continued, ignoring his brother's words. "The king knew you might prove difficult to capture and subdue if you broke the house arrest rules. But Father gave a personal assurance of your cooperation. Which means he agreed to face the consequences himself if you commit any further breach and can't be detained to answer for it."

Percival frowned. "So if I run away, he'll get some slap on the wrist. I don't see how—"

"No." Heath cut him off in frustration. "You don't under-stand, Percival. He would *take your place*. King Matlock is still deciding what to do about your actions. If he deemed that you should face punishment for past or future conduct, and you couldn't be found, or you evaded capture somehow, Father would face that punishment. If the king decided you should be flogged, or thrown back in the dungeons, or *executed*, it would happen to Father, not you."

Percival stared back at him, the restless shifting of his hands the only outward sign of his agitation. "I didn't ask him to do that," he growled.

Heath shrugged. "He did it anyway. Which means—"

Heath.

The familiar voice in his thoughts made Heath pause mid-sentence, instantly dismissing the conversation with Percival from his mind.

Yes, Merletta, I can hear you! he wanted to call back, but of course she couldn't hear him. Her image filled his vision, and he was pleased to see not just her face, but all of her. She was floating in shallow water, her hand above her head, just breaking the surface. But it didn't look like the island.

Heath, I...I don't really know how to say this. Her mouth was moving now, as she spoke the words aloud. *I probably should have told you earlier, but there was no way to hear a reply, and...*

She gave a self-conscious laugh. *Tides above, I don't even know if you can hear me now. This feels ridiculous.*

"Heath, did you hear me? What in dragon's flame are you doing?"

Heath heard his brother's voice as if from far away. He ignored it completely, all his focus on Merletta.

But I really hope you can, otherwise I've got no idea what we'll do next. Heath, I'm...I'm here. I'm off the coast of Valoria now.

CHAPTER TWENTY-FOUR

Heath gave an audible gasp, his mind spinning wildly with the information that Merletta was actually there.

There's no way for me to hear you, of course, Merletta continued, her voice as clear in his mind as if she was standing next to him. *So I thought I'd just have to try to tell you where I am, and hope you'll come and find me. I remembered you saying that your manor is near the southernmost point of land, and I think I can see the peninsula you mean.*

Heath could hear the pride in her voice as she stumbled over the word *peninsula*—it was one he'd taught her.

Merletta kept talking, trying to describe her surroundings. But it wasn't enough to go on. Heath considered calling Reka—the dragon would be able to find Merletta within minutes. But without understanding the source of his friend's disapproval regarding Merletta, he was reluctant to bring Reka into the situation before Merletta was safely on land.

Safely on land! With him! He could hardly take it in. Was she really coming to his world, like he'd tried to coax her to do? He'd never thought she'd actually agree.

He told himself firmly that he didn't need the dragon for this. Reka assured him his magic was strong—he would have to trust that it was strong enough for the task. And if he succeeded...his mind filled with visions of Merletta in his world, visiting his home, surrounded by his family.

It filled him with jittery nerves, but it wasn't an unpleasant sensation.

Pushing aside all other considerations, and still tuning out Percival's continued attempts to get his attention, Heath reached inside himself and took firm hold of his magic. It came more easily than it ever had before, and he gasped again as his vision zoomed, giving the impression that he was flying backward in Reka's talons. He found himself looking down at the blurry shape of Merletta, just submerged beneath choppy water. He cast his sight around, and got a good look at the shoreline.

He let out a triumphant cry. He knew that place! She'd over-shot to the west, but not by too far. It wasn't more than an hour's ride.

A sudden painful pressure on his shoulder brought his attention back to his immediate surroundings. Percival was grip-ping him with uncomfortable strength, and although his face showed nothing but irritation, Heath's magic was in full swing, and it brought him a strong sense of alarm from his brother's direction. It wasn't entirely uncalled for. Heath must have looked like he was in some kind of strange trance.

"I have to go," Heath said abruptly. "I'm going for a ride."

"What?" Percival was more alarmed than ever. "What are you talking about? It's freezing out there."

"Good point," Heath said earnestly. He pictured Merletta's usual attire and let out a choking laugh before he could stop himself. "Better grab as many cloaks as I can carry," he muttered.

Without another word to Percival, he took off down the

corridor. He made straight for Laura's old room, shamelessly rifling through those of his sister's belongings which had been left behind when she'd married. He didn't know what would fit Merletta, but he found a few winter dresses, which he shoved into a large rucksack.

Within fifteen minutes, he was on his favorite mare, urging her west along the coastline. The air was freezing, but there hadn't been a fresh fall for days, and the road was clear. Heath barely felt the chill, his mind separated from what was actually around him, focused instead on Merletta's surroundings. She'd retreated underwater to wait, but regularly surfaced to scan the shoreline.

When the landmarks on the road ahead aligned with what he could see in his visions of Merletta, Heath's heart lurched in excitement. He slowed his horse to a walk, searching for a way down to the shore below. There was a path, uneven but not too treacherous. He dismounted, leading his horse by the halter. In finer weather, he would have left her to graze on the grassy hilltop, but he wouldn't do that to her in the snow.

Heath stumbled more than once, his eyes riveted on the choppy surface of the ocean. With a cry, he saw what he was seeking—a head of dark tangled hair emerging.

"Heath!" Merletta's cry carried clearly across the windy shoreline.

Letting go of his horse's halter, Heath stumbled toward the water's edge. Merletta had disappeared under the surface again, but he knew she was just swimming to the shallows more quickly. When her head once again appeared, she was smiling tentatively. Just the sight of her wet hair and bare shoulders made Heath shiver.

"Aren't you freezing?" he asked.

She looked surprised. "The water is definitely cold for how

close I am to the surface," she agreed. She gave an incredulous laugh. "But is that really your first question?"

Heath laughed as well, leaping from one rock to another to get a little distance out into the water.

"Sorry. What I meant was, what are you doing here?"

Merletta bit her lip. "I know I'm imposing shamefully—"

"Don't be ridiculous," Heath cut her off impatiently. "You know I've been trying to get you to come here for months. I just wasn't expecting you to swim all the way here!"

"I know." Merletta grimaced. "Help me up, would you?"

She reached up a hand, and Heath gripped her arm, noting how cold her skin felt. With him tugging and Merletta propelling herself upward with her tail, she flew up out of the water more quickly than they anticipated. Heath caught her against him as she struggled for balance, and the next moment he looked down to see two bare feet on the rock beside his booted ones.

His eyes traveled back up more slowly, suddenly intensely aware of the fact that Merletta was pressed close against him. Unlike her, he was bundled up against the weather, but he could still feel the warmth of her human form, so different from the cool skin he'd grasped a moment before.

"Heath," she whispered, as his gaze reached her face.

He didn't even try to use his magic to see what was happening below the surface—her emotions were in her eyes. She seemed too overwhelmed to articulate it all, and he understood perfectly.

Keeping her locked in place on the rock with one arm, Heath lifted his other hand slowly and brushed a tangled lock of dark hair from her face. She shivered, whether from the cold or his touch, he couldn't tell.

Merletta extricated one hand, placing it against his chest, the gesture more tentative than usual for her. Then she laid her head on his shoulder, something she'd never done before. The way she relaxed against him spoke volumes about her exhaustion. Just how long had she been swimming hard to reach him?

Heath shuddered a little himself. He'd held her before, but this was different. On Vazula, they were in their own world, straddling the line of land and sea, belonging to neither as they existed in a strange and surreal bubble. Having her not only in human form, but actually in his world, was a hundred times more potent. He felt intoxicated by the limitless possibilities stretching out before him.

"I can hardly believe you're here," he breathed.

Merletta lifted her head, giving him a weak smile. "Neither can I. But things got...bad. Very suddenly."

A tangled mixture of alarm and guilt rushed over Heath. He'd been so focused on his euphoria at her unexpected arrival, he hadn't even stopped to consider what horrors might have driven her to such a desperate flight from her home.

"What happened?" he demanded.

Merletta shook her head. "There'll be time for that later. Suffice it to say, we needed somewhere safe to go. Somewhere far away from the triple kingdoms."

"We?" Heath repeated.

As if on cue, another head broke the surface, this one wearing a disapproving scowl.

"Of course it's him," Heath muttered. "I should have known."

"She knows how to stand by herself," Griffin said curtly.

Merletta rolled her eyes, although—to Heath's disappointment—she did maneuver herself out of his arms so that she stood on the rock beside him.

"Where's August?"

"He's here as well?" Heath asked, relieved Merletta hadn't swum all the way from Vazula with just the overly possessive young guard.

Merletta nodded. "All three of them had to come. We weren't sure if Vazula would be safe anymore. Plus, I don't think Tish and I could have made the journey safely without their help. And Eloise's, of course."

Heath blinked. "There are six of you?" He should've brought more horses.

Merletta let out a sigh as she nodded, leaning slightly against him once more. Automatically, he slipped an arm around her, drawing her against his side. Griffin glowered at them, and Heath met his eyes unblinkingly, his own expression deadpan.

"I'll get August," Griffin said, sounding disgruntled. With a splash, he disappeared into the water.

"It really is cold, isn't it?" Merletta said, sounding surprised.

A shiver ran over her lean frame, and Heath rubbed her arm with his hand. When another shiver wracked her body, he slipped his traveling cloak from his shoulders and draped it around her.

Merletta started, looking fascinated by the sensation of the fabric encasing her. "What's this?" she asked.

Heath couldn't help laughing at her amazement. "A simple traveling cloak," he informed her. "It's not as good as being properly dressed for winter, but it is thick."

"Thank you," said Merletta, pulling it close. She looked snug in the overlarge garment, and utterly adorable. "I've never seen you wear anything like this before."

"I don't need it on Vazula," Heath reminded her.

She shook her head in amazement. "You said it got cold here, but I'm not sure I quite believed it. It's amazing—I didn't really feel the cold before I changed from tail to legs. I guess my underwater form is built for the depths, and it's probably colder down there than up here."

Heath nodded absently. "Did you say Tish before? Your friend from the charity home?" He scanned the water.

"She's out deeper," Merletta told him, something in her voice communicating discomfort. "She's not coping very well with...all this." She sighed. "She flatly refuses to even consider coming out of the water. And she was very much against making the journey at all. She was convinced we would all die. But in actual fact, it was mainly uneventful. August led the way, and he knows how to navigate the open ocean better than anyone."

She'd barely spoken the words when Griffin reappeared, this time with August beside him.

"I can bring up the rear, if you like," Griffin was saying.

"No," Merletta responded, her voice flat.

"We've talked about this, Griffin," August agreed. "You're staying with the others. Merletta assures me she and I will be safe with the hu—" He seemed to catch Merletta's eye, and changed course mid-word. "Heath. They'll need the extra protection more than we will."

"Of course you'll be safe," said Heath, perhaps a touch too eagerly.

But he didn't really feel the need to hide his reluctance to host Griffin. He would prefer just Merletta, of course, but he'd take August over Griffin any day. The youngest of the guards had always been hostile toward him, and surely Heath couldn't be the only one to grasp why.

"Well, then." August hoisted himself onto the rock with surprising grace, his muscled tail turning rapidly into two equally muscled legs. He pushed himself to his feet, hands planted on his hips as water dripped off his scaly shorts. "Brisk, isn't it? How far to where you live?"

"I, uh...this way." Heath gestured helplessly toward the shore, and the three of them picked their way over the rocks.

"I'm afraid it's quite a distance," he said apologetically. "I didn't think to bring more than one—"

"What in the depths is *that*?!"

Heath looked up quickly, wondering what horror August had seen. But the merman was staring at nothing more intimidating than Heath's horse.

"That's what I was talking about," Heath explained patiently. "I only brought one horse, thinking Merletta would ride with me, since it's something you have to learn how to do. But the horse won't be able to carry all three of us."

"That is not a horse," August said firmly. "Horses are much smaller."

Heath hid a smile with an effort. "Well, horses are different from seahorses. An entirely different species, actually."

"Clearly," said Merletta, also staring at the mare with unusually wide eyes. "Did you say you want me to ride on that thing, Heath?"

"I won't let you fall," he promised with a smile.

She smiled back, another shiver rocking her body as she did so.

"I brought clothes for you," Heath said quickly, moving to the horse's saddlebags, where he'd stashed his rucksack. "You can take your pick."

He pulled out three dresses of different colors and styles, although all were thick and long sleeved.

"Ah, that's sensible," said August approvingly. "We'll need some kind of cover in this cold. I'll take the purple one."

He reached out a confident hand and swiped one of the gowns from Heath's grip. Before Heath could think of how to respond, the guard had started wrapping it around his shoulders, much as Merletta was wearing Heath's cloak.

"Uh, it's not really...I mean, you don't..." Heath rubbed the back of his neck awkwardly, torn between humor and embarrassment. "That's not how you wear them."

"How do you?" Merletta asked, taking a crimson gown and examining it in fascination.

"Well, like...can I show you?" Heath took the garment from her, bunching it up in his hands and holding it gingerly.

Merletta showed no hesitation as she stepped forward, allowing him to guide her arms through the sleeves and slip the fabric over her head. When he pulled it down and her face emerged, she was laughing. Her utter lack of self-consciousness helped Heath to banish the rush of heat that overcame him. However unusual it felt to him to help her dress, Merletta clearly didn't find the activity particularly intimate.

"This is absurd," Merletta laughed, as Heath knelt in the snow to tug the gown down around her ankles.

"Why?" He reached into the saddlebags again, coming out with boots.

"There's just...so much of it!" Merletta declared.

But in spite of her words, when Heath turned around, he saw that Merletta was twisting her hips back and forth, watching with satisfaction as the skirts swished one way and then the other.

"It's kind of fun," she acknowledged, when she looked up and saw him grinning at her.

"I can't get mine over my head," August said, his voice as unruffled and dignified as ever.

Heath turned to see the broad-shouldered man trying to tug one of Laura's gowns over his close-cropped hair.

"Um, actually..." Heath paused for a moment to master the laugher threatening to burst from him. "Actually, they're designed for ladies. Men don't really wear...these."

"Oh." August pulled the garment off, frowning at Heath's own attire. "That is something of a relief."

Heath allowed himself a small laugh. "I'm afraid I didn't bring extra men's clothes for you," he said apologetically.

"I'll manage," said August, although Heath noticed he was eyeing the horse with misgiving.

"My home is some distance along the coast," Heath told him. "Could you swim alongside the shoreline? I could meet you down at the water's edge with something more suitable." He sized the guard up with his eyes. Percival's clothes would probably fit.

The plan was quickly agreed upon, and with some fairly clumsy assistance from August, Heath managed to get himself and Merletta mounted on his mare at the top of the slope. They watched as August moved back to the water, disappearing without a splash below the waves.

"I hope it's all right for him to come as well," Merletta said, looking back over her shoulder at Heath. "He was quite insistent."

"Of course it is," Heath assured her easily.

She smiled at him, settling back against him contentedly. Satisfaction roared through Heath as he urged his horse to a walk, relishing the feel of her nestled between his arms, heading toward his family home with complete trust in his ability to keep her safe.

As they rode, she told him the story of her flight, a tale which sobered him quickly.

"That's diabolical," he said quietly, in reference to the targeting of Tish. "It shows what kind of people you're dealing with."

Merletta nodded gravely. "I don't know what we're going to do, Heath," she said. "I really don't."

Heath remained silent. For the moment, he had no answers for her. It was enough that she was alive, and safe from the Center, and here with him. More than enough.

CHAPTER TWENTY-FIVE

Heath rode much more slowly on the way back to the manor, both for Merletta's sake and the horse's. Merletta seemed to enjoy the novelty of riding a horse, but Heath could tell she was sore and weary by the time the manor came into sight. He left her with the mare in a small grove of trees, slipping in through a side door and returning with an armful of clothing for August. He'd been fortunate enough not to run into any of his family.

They climbed down the cliff path together, meeting August at the water's edge. The older merman seemed much happier with the new selection of clothes, and by the time he was dressed, Heath reflected with satisfaction that both he and Merletta really did look human. Who would suspect anything else?

"What will your family think when we arrive, uninvited?" August asked bluntly.

"Let me worry about what they'll think," Heath said. "They won't turn you away or anything, don't be alarmed."

August's brow was creased as he looked at Merletta. "I was thinking I should identify myself as Merletta's father."

Merletta looked at him, clearly surprised. But Heath shook his head.

"That won't work. I should perhaps warn you that my father was born with a magic that can detect deception. Any lies will make him instantly suspicious of you. I think you'd better leave the explanations to me."

August's frown deepened, but he said no more. The three of them made their way up to the manor on foot, Heath leading his horse.

It took only minutes to reach the gates, and Heath could feel Merletta's nerves growing beside him. He took hold of her hand with his free one, squeezing reassuringly. She sent a fleeting glance up at him, but her smile was a little strained. Heath led them across the courtyard, calling to a groom as he went. The boy who ran up stared at the visitors with open astonishment, until Heath prompted him to take the mare's halter.

"Was that a servant?" Merletta asked, her eyes not on Heath but on the manor's elaborate front rising above them.

"Uh...yes. He's an under groom," Heath said. Seeing her confusion, he added quickly, "He works for the head groom, who takes care of the horses."

"Even your animals have servants?" Merletta asked, sounding dazed.

Heath gave an uncomfortable laugh. "Well, they work for my father, not for the horses."

He squeezed her hand again, wishing he had the words to wipe the unease from her face. He hadn't even considered this aspect of Merletta's introduction to his family and home. Their worlds and cultures might be different, but wealth and privilege had a universal language of their own. And no one would know that better than a nameless orphan who'd grown up with neither.

No servants appeared to assist Heath upon entry to the

manor, because of course he didn't knock or ring the large brass bell suspended above the door. He personally showed Merletta and August into the smallest sitting room, then hailed a passing maid.

"Can you please request refreshments from the kitchens?" he asked. "And notify my mother that we have visitors. Friends of mine," he added, seeing the maid peer curiously behind him.

He closed the door, turning to his guests with a smile. "Please make yourselves at home," he said, gesturing to the comfortable chairs ranged by the fire.

"It's much warmer in here," said August approvingly. "I was starting to wonder how you all live in these conditions." He lowered himself experimentally into a chair, seeming encouraged when it held his weight.

"I suppose in the water, you can't keep the cold out in the same way," Heath said thoughtfully. "But here we can warm our buildings considerably. It's summer that's the real problem. It's not so easy to cool the place down when the heat is blistering."

"Is this how you warm it?" Merletta asked, approaching the fireplace, in which flames leaped merrily. "It's very beautiful, isn't it?" She reached out a hand toward it. "Ooh yes, I can feel it getting warmer."

"Whoa!" Heath leaped up, grabbing Merletta's hand as it neared the fire. "Don't touch it. You'll be burned."

"Oops." Merletta gave him a sheepish look. "I should know better, shouldn't I? I guess it's just like a thermal vent, and I know from experience that those—"

She broke off as her eyes shifted over Heath's shoulder, and her body went still. Heath spun around, feeling absurdly like a guilty child caught in a misdemeanor as he caught sight of his mother framed in the doorway. She was looking blankly at Heath's hand, which still gripped Merletta's, and he dropped it quickly.

"Mother," he said, moving forward, and hoping she hadn't seen Merletta's illogical behavior. "Let me introduce some friends of mine. This is—"

Before he could continue, the duke appeared behind his wife. He gently prodded her into the room and began to close the door, but before he could do so, it was pushed fully open again to reveal Percival.

Great. Heath sighed slightly. It looked like the whole family had come to see the spectacle.

"Mother, Father...Percival," Heath said, unable to keep a hint of irritation from his voice on the last name. "These are friends of mine. This is August," he gestured to the guard, who'd sprung to his feet the moment the duchess entered the room, "and this is Merletta."

All three pairs of eyes flew instantly to Merletta, and Heath winced slightly. Clearly Laura had shared with the family the way he'd rambled Merletta's name while in his fever dreams the day he was almost killed by August's patrol.

"This is my father and mother," he continued the introduction. "The Duke and Duchess of Bexley. And my brother, Percival."

"We're delighted to meet you," the duchess said, her eyes searching as they studied Merletta's face. She glanced at Heath. "Were we expecting visitors?"

"I invited them some time ago," Heath said. "But they didn't think they were at liberty to accept the invitation at that time. Happily, a change in their circumstances made it possible after all."

Percival was looking from Heath to the guests impatiently, clearly sick of the polite dance. "But who are you?" he asked Merletta bluntly. "Where are you from?"

Merletta cleared her throat, but Heath jumped in before she could speak. "She's not from Valoria," he said. "Truth be told, I met her on a particularly long exploratory flight with Reka."

He could sense his mother's surprise, and saw her cast another look at Merletta's warm skin. "Just how long was this exploratory flight? Are you from the South Lands?" she asked, naming the continent three weeks' voyage south of Valoria.

Merletta swallowed. "My home is further south," she said. Her tone made it sound like she was acknowledging the duchess's words, but Heath could tell she was speaking very carefully, trying not to activate his father's abilities. "I hope we don't impose."

"Of course not," Heath's mother said, her hostess instincts kicking in. "You're welcome to stay as long as you wish." She turned to the maid, who was hovering near the doorway. "Have two rooms prepared for our guests."

"And did you also meet Heath on this exploratory trip?" The duke's quiet question was directed at August.

"No, Sir," said the guard staunchly, his posture straight as he met the other man's eyes.

Only Percival outwardly showed his surprise that August didn't know the appropriate way to address the duke.

"But I was determined to accompany Merletta, for her own safety," August went on. "Although I am not related to her by blood, I feel the responsibility of a father toward her, for reasons I would prefer not to go into."

Heath could tell that his father recognized the truth in all of August's words. Merletta looked at the older merman, her face showing that she was both surprised and touched by his words. She must realize they were true, since Heath's father hadn't called August out.

"Well, shall we have someone bring your things to your rooms?" the duchess asked, after a moment of silence in which the duke considered the guard thoughtfully.

"They don't have any things," Heath said frankly. "The truth is, they were forced to flee from danger. A personal matter," he added hastily. "Nothing to do with us, or Valoria."

The duke studied him, and Heath could feel his father's magic reaching out, testing the words coming from Heath's mouth.

"I'm very sorry to hear of your troubles," the older man said gravely. "We are glad to be able to offer you a sanctuary. Although I'm afraid we are departing for the capital in only a couple of days."

"They'll come, naturally," Heath said eagerly. "I'd love to show Merletta Bryford. And August, of course."

"Are you sure?" Merletta's soft voice brought his attention to her. "We don't want to impose."

"I'm sure," he told her, smiling into her upturned face. "There's so much to see and discover."

For the briefest of moments their gazes held, until Percival's obnoxious throat clearing forced Heath to look away. He glowered at his brother, who raised his eyebrow in what was definitely a smirk. Percival clearly wasn't going to make this easy on him.

"You must be tired from your journey," Heath's mother interjected. "All of these discussions can wait. Allow me to show you to your rooms."

"I'll come," Heath volunteered eagerly.

He led Merletta from the room, August following close behind. At least they were both experienced enough with their legs now that their gaits were steady. It would have been hard to explain if they'd been staggering like drunkards.

When they reached the assigned rooms, Heath's mother moved toward the kitchens, to instruct them to send the requested refreshments straight to the rooms. Ignoring the slightly scandalized look the housekeeper was giving him,

Heath walked Merletta right into her room. He was still euphoric over her presence, hardly able to focus on anything else.

August followed them, looking around him in wonder.

"Is your father related to the regent?" he asked. "I didn't expect such lavish accommodations."

Heath nodded, realizing how much of it must feel strange to them. "King Matlock is my father's cousin," he explained.

"We should really be calling him Lord Heath," Merletta added. "But he's never let me."

"And I don't intend to start now," said Heath forcefully.

He cast a glance at the open doorway. Mercifully, the house-keeper had ceased to hover when August entered the room, evidently considering him chaperone enough.

"All right," Heath said briskly. "We're alone. What do you need to know?" He gestured to the bed. "That's where you sleep, in case it's not obvious. You pull back the blankets and slide under them. You'll need them for the warmth." He looked around. "That bowl of water is for washing your face, and hands if desired. And that pot under the bed…" He hesitated, embarrassed. He'd never had to explain a chamber pot before.

Merletta chuckled. "It's all right, Heath. We've both lived on land for extended periods. We can figure it out."

Heath nodded, relieved. Before he could think of anything else to explain, a maid backed into the room with a heavily-laden tray in her arms. She set it down on a side table and retreated with a curious glance at the newcomers.

"Do we eat that?" August asked, looking doubtfully at the sandwiches and pastries.

"Only if you want to," Heath laughed. "But you're going to have to accustom yourself to human fare if you plan to stay up here. It'll be a little conspicuous if you keep ducking back into the water every time you need to eat."

"I for one am sick to death of cod," Merletta said brightly. She picked up a sandwich and took a large bite. Her eyes narrowed as she chewed it, trying to decide on her reaction. "It's so...dry," she commented. "But the flavor isn't bad."

Heath grinned. "Don't let the cook hear you calling her sandwiches dry."

His mother appeared in the doorway at that moment, her gaze fixing on her son. "Heath."

It was clearly a command, and Heath excused himself, surprised by the strength of his reluctance to leave Merletta's side. She'd been so hesitant when he introduced her to his family, so unsure of herself. It wasn't like her normal bold fearlessness, and he wanted to reassure her.

His determination to reassure her didn't just come from the knowledge that she was in an entirely new environment and might need support, though. It was that he desperately wanted her to like his world. Now that—against all expectation—he actually had her here, he was almost overwhelmed by the intensity of his desire. He wanted her to stay.

It was no surprise to find his parents and brother waiting for him in his father's study. He'd known that the answers he'd given during the introductions would not be adequate for his family. He could only be grateful they'd waited for privacy to interrogate him.

"Who are they, Heath?" The duke wasted no time on pleasantries.

"They're friends," Heath told him. "Like I said."

All three family members fixed him with expectant stares.

With a sigh, Heath dropped into a chair. "Like I said, I met Merletta when Reka took me on an exploratory flight, a couple years ago. August is a more recent acquaintance, but I trust him completely."

"Is this related to King Matlock's accusation that you've been hiding some threat from him?"

For a moment Heath was silent, unsettled. He hadn't known his father was aware of that accusation.

"I don't know for certain," he said uncomfortably. "But I suspect so. He's mistaken, though," he added quickly. "There's no threat to Valoria involved." His eyes passed to his mother, their expression pleading. "I would explain their story in more detail if it was mine to tell. But I promised to respect their privacy, and I'm not sure I can tell everything without endangering Merletta." His jaw set in uncompromising lines. "Which I won't do, no matter what anyone asks of me."

His parents exchanged a look, and a quick prod at his magic revealed a general sense of surprise, with an intention for private speech regarding—

He cut off his explorations as his father cast him a sharp look. Tucking his magic back inside, he showed them his most earnest expression.

"Surely you won't turn them away."

"Of course not," the duchess said quickly. "Friends of yours are always welcome in our home. But are you sure it's a good idea to take them to Bryford for the Winter Solstice Festival?"

"Of course," Heath said enthusiastically. "It will be such an interesting cultural experience for them."

His parents exchanged another glance, but dismissed him without further comment. Percival sent them a look of disgust— clearly he'd been hoping to see his usually biddable brother chastised more strongly for his secrecy—and left the room in Heath's wake.

"A girl, Heath," he said, apparently not troubled by the curiosity of a passing servant. "You've been holding out on me, little brother."

Heath just grunted, in no mood to be baited by Percival.

"She's very pretty," Percival mused. "Maybe I should see if

she prefers an older, stronger man."

Heath looked up sharply, hot words on his lips. But his brother was laughing at him. As he looked into Heath's eyes, Percival's humor slid away, his face becoming more earnest than usual.

"You know I'd never do that to you, don't you?" he asked quietly. The briefest flash of pain registered on his face at Heath's silence. "We are still brothers, aren't we?"

"Of course we are," Heath said, moved in spite of himself. "Much as I want to tip you out that window," he couldn't help adding.

Percival's laughter was back. "If only you could, little brother," he said, already sauntering away. "Well, well, Heath with a girl. What will Laura say about this? Merletta, hey?"

He was around the corner as he spoke, and there was nothing for Heath to do but walk the other way, rolling his eyes. It was a relief that Percival wasn't planning mischief where Merletta was concerned, at least. Griffin and Andre and whatever other mermen might be chasing her were quite enough to contend with.

Heath barely slept that night, his thoughts too full of Merletta's nearness, and the unpredictable but suddenly much more exciting future. He kept chuckling to himself at the memory of her fascination with the food at dinner, and her determination to try every single dish. It had gained her some strange looks from the servants, but he'd heard them whispering that she was from the South Lands, and probably unused to their food. It was a rumor he intended to encourage wherever possible, as the simplest explanation for Merletta and August's undeniably foreign ways.

After breakfast the following morning—during which Merletta caused a bit of a sensation by trying to bite into a boiled egg with the shell still intact—Heath lost no time in dragging Merletta outside with him, away from prying eyes and listening ears.

"Your home is amazing," she told him, with a hint of wistfulness. Her voice dropped to a mutter. "It would make an excellent mind palace."

"What?" Heath asked, bemused.

"Never mind," Merletta said quickly. She gave him a rueful smile. "Vazula must feel so primitive to you."

"Vazula," Heath said simply, "is my favorite place in the world." He stepped closer. "Mainly because it's where you are."

"Ah, there you are." August strode out into the training yard, his eyes appraising the equipment with professional interest. "Is this where your guards train?"

Heath nodded, stepping away from Merletta regretfully to give August a tour of the area. Merletta followed, clearly equally interested.

"You never did teach me to use a bow," she commented, running her hand along one of the general weapons.

"Let me show you now," Heath responded enthusiastically.

August watched with an analytical eye as Heath positioned Merletta correctly and showed her how to hold the weapon. It could have been quite a romantic moment if not for the middle-aged guard's hovering. Heath didn't know him well enough to tell if it was intentional.

It took Merletta some time to get the hang of the bow, but she was a quick learner. Heath took great satisfaction from witnessing Percival's reaction when he strolled into the training yard to see Merletta hit the target with such force that the arrow was half buried into the wood.

"Whoa! Strong arms," Percival commented, his sulkiness temporarily forgotten in his appreciation of a well-handled weapon. "Are you an archer like Heath, then?"

Heath shook his head. "This is her first time using a bow."

Percival looked incredulous, but Merletta nodded her agreement.

"It's incredible how quickly the arrow flies!" she enthused.

Heath had to chuckle at Percival's bewildered expression. He knew what Merletta meant, of course. She'd described the way merpeople used slings as weapons, but naturally the speed of those trajectories would be enormously lessened by the water. No wonder her arms were strong from training in that environment, and her arrows flew so forcefully without the impediment she was used to.

"Archery is the least exciting of all forms of combat," Percival informed her. "Maybe you'd better stay here with me instead of going to the boring ceremony in Bryford. I could teach you more about fighting in a week than Heath could in a year."

The flicker of a grin he sent toward his brother robbed the words of venom.

"Thanks, but I think I'll stick with Heath," Merletta responded, with a hint of amusement. "Truthfully, I've been pretty well trained in combat already, so that's not really something I ask for Heath's help with."

Heath watched Merletta's face as she and Percival dove into a discussion about combat, albeit quite a censored one on her side. There was nothing in her posture to suggest discomfort, but Heath still felt that faint unease that had made him reluctant to leave her side the day before. She wasn't quite herself, and he didn't fully understand why. Somehow it felt like more than just the natural uncertainty of being thrown into such an unfamiliar situation.

With a sigh, Heath picked up another bow, figuring he may as well get some practice in. He could tell from the animated way in which Percival was warming to his topic that his brother was unlikely to give them any peace until they left for Bryford the following day.

CHAPTER TWENTY-SIX

Usually Heath preferred to ride to the capital rather than go in a carriage. But it was well worth the confinement to ride with Merletta, and witness her wonder as she took in the vast expanses of land that formed Valoria's southern region.

Even better, Heath's parents occupied a separate carriage, meaning that he, Merletta and August could speak freely. August updated them on the rest of the group—he'd taken an evening stroll the day before, and slipped into the water to discuss plans with Eloise and the others, who'd set themselves up in a cave a short distance out from the shore near Bexley Manor.

"She said they swam past something that almost looked like ruins," August frowned. "As if there had been buildings down there a long time ago."

"I'd forgotten about that," Heath said, amazed. "Those ruins —if that's what they are—sent me to the records room in the castle. And instead of anything relevant, I found the account that directed me to Vazula!"

Merletta's forehead was creased. "But there can't be

merperson ruins here. It's much too far from the triple kingdoms."

"I remember being told that merpeople had once settled near land, but had abandoned their settlement because dragons nearly wiped them out," August offered.

Merletta made a motion as if flicking her braid over her shoulder, then seemed to remember that it was confined in a complicated mound on her head. One of Heath's mother's maids had done her hair that morning. Heath thought she looked stunning, although she didn't seem entirely comfortable in the new style.

"We know that's more of the Center's lies, though," Merletta told August impatiently. "Dragons aren't vicious and aggressive like they claim. I know that from personal experience. These ruins must be from human buildings."

"That's what I concluded in the end, as well," Heath agreed.

August still looked unconvinced, but he said no more.

"Are you worried to be returning to the capital?" Merletta asked Heath. Her brow was furrowed. "Didn't someone try to kill you last time you were there?"

Heath shrugged. In all that had happened since, he'd almost forgotten about the attack. "I don't think anyone would try anything at the Winter Solstice. Too many witnesses, too many royal guards."

Merletta didn't seem satisfied, but Heath had the impression her mind was on other things. When they passed under the city wall, she looked so nervous that he leaned forward, giving her his most encouraging smile.

"You have nothing to worry about," he assured her. "There's no way anyone would guess you weren't as human as everyone else. If you do things differently, they'll just assume it's South Lands customs."

His words didn't have the desired effect. If anything,

Merletta looked more troubled, and the thoughtful look on August's face made Heath wonder if the older man was seeing something Heath was missing.

There was no time to explore the question, however. They reached Heath's family's city manor in no time, and were soon surrounded by the bustle of servants. A message had been sent ahead, and rooms were ready for Merletta and August. The housekeeper swept them away, and Heath's father bore him inexorably off to the castle, where they were expected.

The formal reception was tedious, and if there was any purpose to it other than to promote the total falsehood that the king and the duke were still on easy terms in spite of Percival's arrest, Heath couldn't identify it.

The king gave a gracious and unruffled welcome speech at the royal reception, with no mention of tensions or concerns. All the whispered discussion, however, was around the ceremony the following day. Given the fact that the dragons had warned they would not come this year if their magic was unwelcome, there was a great deal of speculation about whether the imposed restrictions would be enough to keep them away. No one doubted that they were aware of it.

A few of Heath's cousins asked him if the dragons were coming, but he just told them vaguely—and truthfully—that he hadn't spoken to Reka recently, and had no idea.

He was barely paying attention to any of it. He didn't much care whether the dragons came or not. He had faith that his friendship with Reka would be unaffected by the attitude of the colony at large, so what did it really matter? Whatever the fear-mongers whispered, it wasn't as though the dragons were going to attack. If they disapproved, they'd just withdraw, return to their former reclusive ways.

Somehow, he couldn't seem to muster up any concern over the issue. His thoughts were all with Merletta, eager to be back at home. He was therefore disappointed to be told, upon finally arriving back at the manor, that she'd already retired for the night.

He shook off his unease. She was tired, and understandably so. A stray thought occurred to him, and for a moment he found himself imagining how he would feel if he was somehow—impossibly—thrust into her underwater world.

The thought made him uncomfortable, and he didn't pursue it.

He was up early the next morning, more excited for the day's festivities than he could remember being in years. The Winter Solstice Festival was supposed to be one of the year's biggest celebrations, but even before the tension of the previous two festivals, Heath had found it a little tedious to be dragged from Bexley Manor in the coldest part of winter.

This year was different, however. Merletta would be beside him, and he could hardly wait to show her the city, and watch her amazement at the ceremony. Hopefully even dance with her at the ball to be held after the feast.

A memory flitted through his mind from the previous year's Winter Solstice. Not the dragons' threatening words, but the stranger Heath had seen in the crowd—the one emanating a whiff of power. Heath frowned to himself. He'd been convinced at the time that the stranger was the same man Heath had seen in the markets as a child, the first time he'd sensed magic.

But now a different connection formed in his mind. He'd assumed the man must be a Kyonan power-wielder, visiting without fanfare for reasons unknown. Was it possible it was the same person responsible both for the attack on Percival and the one on Heath? He would have to consult his family tree...but that couldn't be right. The only older middle-aged Kyonan man with magic was Crown Prince Rory, and Heath had met him. He wasn't the stranger in the crowd.

For a moment he strained his memory, wishing he could recreate past events like Reka could. He wasn't at all confident that the magic he'd felt at the festival was the same as the magic present at the two attacks. They'd both come later.

With a shake of the head, he abandoned the attempt. How could he possibly be expected to remember with such detail after so long? It didn't matter, anyway. It wasn't important now. Not when he had a whole city of human wonders to show Merletta.

The family ate breakfast together, Merletta and August eating little. Both seemed on edge, enough so that Heath asked Merletta about it as they began the walk to the castle courtyard for the ceremony.

"I told August that the ceremony involves dragons," Merletta said quietly. "He's...concerned."

"He doesn't need to be," Heath said confidently. "They never stay for long, and there's some uncertainty as to whether they'll even come this year." He dropped his voice as they passed a group of chattering locals. "They don't approve of the restrictions on magic."

Merletta considered this in silence. "If they don't show up, August will be more relaxed," she said. "But wouldn't that be deeply distressing for your kingdom, to have a colony of dragons publicly reject them?"

Heath shrugged. "Deeply distressing is a bit of an overstatement," he said.

Merletta gave him a strange look, but they'd reached the courtyard, and she said no more. Her eyes grew wide as she took in the castle's imposing facade, stone walls rising high above them, and pennants snapping in the brisk breeze.

"Is this where your king lives?" she asked.

Heath nodded. "It's beautiful, isn't it?" He pointed at the enormous stone basin suspended above them, fire flickering faintly from within it. "And that's the Flame of Friendship I told you about, the symbol of peace and cooperation between Valoria and the dragons. It's actually Reka's fire in there, but it's almost out because it's been a year."

Tension radiated off August, walking just behind them, but Merletta seemed more fascinated than afraid as she stared up at the faint orange flame, flickering occasionally purple.

"It is beautiful," she acknowledged, with a touch of wistfulness.

Moving surreptitiously, Heath found her hand and squeezed it. "I'm so happy you're here with me," he whispered. "I can hardly believe it."

"It's certainly surreal," she agreed, smiling faintly at him.

"Time to take our places, Heath."

His mother's voice called Heath's attention back to the courtyard, and he pulled Merletta forward, August still trailing behind them. The duchess looked at the three of them hesitantly, but said nothing as Heath brought the two guests into the section where the royals all stood in their ranked order.

"Are you sure we should be standing with you here?" Merletta whispered, the uncertainty back in her voice.

"Of course," said Heath staunchly. "This is where I stand, and you belong with me."

Merletta's hand was warm in his, but the wave that flowed out from her was definitely not contentment. Heath frowned down at her, wanting to understand her uncertainty, but King Matlock had begun speaking, and there was no opportunity to ask.

He saw several nearby relatives casting curious glances at Merletta and August, and members of the crowd were also looking their way, whispering through the king's speech. Well, at least it was a distraction from the tension. Heath knew that all the power-wielders of his own generation were there under protest at the insistence of their parents, and all the power-wielders of any age were holding themselves with tension. Percival's absence was glaring, and things had never been more fraught between the two branches of his family.

And yet, Heath felt wonderfully divorced from it all, for the first time in a long time able to convince himself that it wasn't his problem to solve. His world felt right with Merletta in it, and all the things that were wrong with it paled in comparison.

Still, even Heath found himself holding his breath when the king spoke the time-honored words that normally heralded the dragons' approach.

"We are honored to mark the passing of another year of peace with our allies."

For a heart-stopping moment there was stillness, then a rush of wind passed around the packed courtyard, and several dark shapes filled the sky.

Merletta's noise of recognition told Heath that she'd spotted Reka's bright yellow, landing amongst the larger, darker-scaled dragons. Heath could see Reka's father, Elddreki, and his mother, Raqisa, landing beside him. All told, there were six dragons present. It was certainly an impressive sight. Snow had begun to fall softly, and it sizzled as it landed on their scales.

A glance down showed him Merletta's awe written all over her face. August was tensed, looking ready to fight for his life at any moment. Heath felt a flash of regret for his guest. Perhaps it was cruel to put August through this. However exaggerated the danger was in his mind, his fears were very real to him. It was how he'd been raised.

"Greetings, King of Men," said the large burgundy dragon who usually spoke for the colony at these events.

"Greetings, Mighty Beasts," King Matlock said, in accordance with tradition. "You are welcome here."

Reka's gaze moved across the royals, clearly seeking Heath.

Heath smiled as the dragon's eyes landed on him, but the expression faltered as he saw Reka freeze in place. Clearly he'd seen Merletta.

The enormous reptile's face gave nothing away, and Heath sent a probing strand of his magic toward his friend. It wasn't like trying to see what was happening inside a human. He could feel his magic encountering Reka's, and getting subsumed into it. Likely with another dragon, it would have overwhelmed his magic, and rendered it useless. But Reka was his closest friend —they'd always had a special connection, and Heath sensed his magic interacting with Reka's, connecting and drawing from it, somehow.

And there was only one word for the writhing, twisting mass of emotion revealed under Reka's impassive face.

Horror.

Truly rattled for the first time by the dragon's disapproval of Merletta, Heath began to question the wisdom of bringing her there. As he cast around for a way out of the situation, he caught catches of the burgundy dragon's words. The beast appeared to be expressing disapproval of the restrictions on magic, something which was sure to get King Matlock's ire up. And sure to make relations between the crown and the power-wielders even more challenging, but the dragons didn't care about that. They were interested only in their own offense over the way magic was being persecuted.

Heath saw Lachlan beside his father, his frame as tense as August's, and his focus fully on the dragon who was speaking. Another face was turned toward Heath, however. His grandmother—the elderly Princess Jocelyn—was looking from Heath to Merletta, growing astonishment on her face.

Just as the king began to respond to the dragon's words, Elddreki turned his head as well, apparently following the trajectory of Princess Jocelyn's gaze. His eyes latched on to

Heath, then—the movement painfully slow and visible—shifted to Merletta beside him. He also went unnaturally still, and although Heath had no insight into his thoughts or emotions, a horrible sense of foreboding washed over him.

The next moment, all six of the dragons were staring at Heath and his guests, and in a way he couldn't possibly describe, Heath felt it building inside them. Fire. Deadly and fierce and unforgiving.

His eyes flew to Reka, and for a moment it really was as though he could read his friend's mind.

Flee, Reka's eyes told him. *Flee now*.

It was all Heath could do to stop himself from grabbing Merletta's hand and literally sprinting from the courtyard. But a quick glance around showed him that everyone else's attention remained on the still-speaking king. Even the burgundy dragon was once again looking at King Matlock, waiting in growing displeasure for him to stop speaking. No one else could sense what he could inside the dragons, and the proud beasts showed nothing on their faces. As far as most onlookers were concerned, the only drama happening was that arising between the king and the dragons over the restrictions. It wouldn't benefit anyone for Heath to cause a scene and in so doing reveal the true source of their anger.

"You know what," he whispered to Merletta, as inconspicuously as he could, "I forgot how intimidating a group of dragons can be when you see them all at once like this. It was thoughtless of me to put you and August through this."

Merletta shook her head slightly, as if to say it was fine. Her eyes were on the burgundy dragon, and she still looked more intrigued than afraid. But Heath didn't give her the option of refusing.

"We can rejoin the festivities once the dragons are gone," he said, gripping her hand more firmly and edging backward through the crowd. "They never stay long."

Merletta looked like she wanted to protest, but they were already halfway back through the group of gathered royals. August followed without a sound, relief evident on his features. A few people grumbled as Heath pushed past them, but everyone's attention was still mainly riveted on the scene before them.

When they cleared the crowd, Heath ducked into the castle, deeming it the most protected place from dragon attack. He led the two merpeople into an empty audience hall, and waved them into seats along one wall.

"Stay here," he said. "I'll check what's happening, and let you know when the coast is clear."

"But—" Merletta started, clearly bewildered, but Heath was already slipping out the door.

He hurried back through the castle, his heart hammering. He hardly knew what he feared, but something inside him sensed that the danger was greater than he'd ever imagined.

He'd just emerged from the castle's entrance when he ran into Bianca, hurrying up the broad staircase.

"Heath!" She pulled up. "Where did you go just now? What's going on?"

"Are the dragons gone?" Heath asked her, grabbing her arm urgently. "What happened?"

"Yes, they're gone," she said grimly. "As for what's happened, no one seems to have any clue! King Matlock said his piece about the restrictions, then the burgundy dragon accused him of hypocrisy."

"He...what?" Heath hadn't expected that.

She nodded, looking anxious. "He said that the dragons wanted nothing to do with a kingdom which reviled natural magic, while at the same time harboring the vilest type of magic."

"What?" Heath could only stare. It made no sense. "He thinks the king is harboring magic?"

Bianca shrugged. "Don't ask me to explain. I was hoping you could."

Heath raised his hands helplessly, his thoughts spiraling. The dragons had definitely been looking at him and Merletta when they got angry. Could they sense her mermaid form hiding inside her—was that what they considered the vilest type of magic? And if so, why? What about her could possibly be so offensive?

He was fervently grateful no one else had his unnatural sight—he didn't see how anyone would connect the dragons' offense to Merletta and August, and he had no intention of sharing the information.

"There's more," Bianca said grimly, and Heath's eyes flew to hers in alarm. "The dragon said there would be a reckoning. And then they all took off together, without re-lighting the flame."

"A reckoning?" Heath repeated, his lips numb.

What did that mean? He reached out with his farsight, searching for Reka. The dragon was in flight, his surroundings a nearly invisible blur. It was hard to tell with dragons, but Heath thought he saw a hint of panic in his friend's eyes.

Terror gripped Heath. He had no idea what any of it meant, but it couldn't be good. He'd been foolish to take Reka's disapproval of Merletta as lightly as he had. He'd let Reka's tolerance for Merletta—however stiff—make him complacent. He should never have exposed Merletta to other dragons without knowing what was behind Reka's change in attitude.

"But they're gone?" he asked Bianca abruptly. "They're definitely all gone?"

"For now," she said doubtfully. "Heath, why did you leave? And who was that with you?"

Heath hesitated, and a new voice interrupted them.

"Heath?"

He turned to see Merletta in the doorway to the castle. She looked determined, her face more like its usual self even while her gown-clad form still looked so unfamiliar.

"Heath, I don't want to hide away like a—"

Heath shifted to the side, and Merletta broke off as Bianca came into view.

"Oh, I'm sorry," she said. She hesitated, but Heath waved her forward.

"Merletta, this is Bianca, my cousin," he said. "Bianca, Merletta is a good friend of mine. She's a guest of my family."

Bianca greeted Merletta politely, surreptitiously taking in her coloring. Heath assumed that she would decide, as most others had, that Merletta must be from one of the South Lands kingdoms.

But he should have given his cousin more credit. As Heath, still rattled by the day's events, put a protective arm around Merletta's shoulders, Bianca's eyes passed suddenly to him. Understanding lit her face, and she drew in a breath.

"You're Heath's mystery girl," she breathed. "From the island."

CHAPTER TWENTY-SEVEN

Merletta

Merletta swallowed, not sure what it was safe to say. She glanced at Heath, and was encouraged that he didn't look alarmed.

"Yes, this is her," he said. There was even a hint of excitement to his voice. "I'm glad you two can meet, actually." He turned to Merletta with a smile. "Remember when I came to the island by ship, and I told you my cousins were on board? Well, Bianca was one of them."

Merletta looked at the other young woman with increasing interest, encouraged to see Bianca smiling at her. She returned the gesture.

"How long are you staying with Heath's family?" Bianca asked.

"I'm not entirely sure," Merletta admitted.

"It's good timing, isn't it?" Heath said, his cheerful tone a little forced. "She's arrived in time for the only celebration until summer."

Bianca looked doubtful. "Do you think the ball will still go ahead? Everyone's in a bit of a state over the dragons."

"What? Why?" Merletta looked sharply between Bianca and Heath, noting that the latter looked uncomfortable.

"Nothing you need to worry about, Merletta," he said firmly. "You have enough to contend with without adding Valorian politics to the mix. Bianca's just told me that the dragons refused to light the flame, that's all."

"So they've all left?" Merletta asked.

Bianca nodded, her eyes passing thoughtfully between Heath and Merletta.

"It might be for the best if the ball you mentioned is canceled," Merletta said. "I suspect I'd make a fool of myself. I've got no idea how these events work, and I don't know what I would need to wear, or—"

"That doesn't matter," Heath assured her. "You can wear the gown you've got on."

"No, she can't," Bianca said flatly. "That's a riding habit, not a ballgown." She cast her cousin a pitying look. "You're officially dismissed from any part in helping Merletta prepare for the ball."

And before Merletta knew what was happening, she found herself being swept away by the other girl, back into the castle, with barely a chance to glance back at Heath. When she passed August, hovering just inside the doorway, she gestured helplessly at Heath, and the guard hurried down the steps, clearly seeking answers.

The afternoon was spent in Bianca's rooms, in a whirl of preparation. Apparently the ball was to proceed as planned, although the dragons' refusal to light the flame had rattled most people much more than it seemed to trouble Heath. At least, so Merletta concluded from the nervous whispers of every servant she encountered.

And there were servants everywhere. It was strange to Merletta to be in a castle, but Bianca was so friendly, Merletta found herself relaxing more than she would have believed possible. The other girl was similar enough in size that Merletta was able to borrow one of her gowns, and she had to agree with Bianca that it was nothing like the dress she'd been wearing that morning.

Bianca couldn't quite hide her shock when Merletta took off her gown, revealing her scaled skirt and shells—the only things she was wearing underneath. The Valorian quickly mastered her reaction, explaining to Merletta with great patience about the undergarments usually worn by women in their culture.

"It's so much," Merletta commented, once she was all dressed. She felt weighed down, like she was doing one of her training exercises where she had to carry a rock up through the water. "And hard to move in."

Bianca laughed. "Not once you're used to it," she assured her.

Merletta nodded. "I suppose it's necessary to have the layers in this cold. Heath said it's warm here sometimes, though. What do you wear then?"

"Much the same," said Bianca with a smile. "It gets very hot, to be honest." She led Merletta to a tall piece of furniture, its surface as reflective as still water. "Look at yourself in the looking glass. What do you think?"

Merletta stared at her own reflection, taking in the simple knot Bianca's maid had created from her braid, and the small white flower tucked into her dark hair. In spite of the cold, her arms were mostly bare. The bands of fabric that formed the sleeves of the gown were set off her shoulders slightly, so that she didn't have the choked feeling she'd gotten from the other dresses. The dress was tight around her waist, but flared out to an improbable size by the time it reached her feet, thanks to the layer upon layer of fabric hidden underneath it.

She turned this way and that to get the full effect of the

gown. She'd been offered options, and she'd chosen a light purple dress, the color similar to that of her scales, although without the shimmer. It swished as she moved, like her hair flowing through water. She could almost picture the full skirts as a tail.

A smile spread slowly across her features, and she turned to Bianca. "I like it," she said. "It feels…graceful."

"It looks graceful," Bianca told her kindly. A sly grin crossed her face. "And Heath will love it."

Merletta felt herself coloring, and turned quickly back to the looking glass. Was it this simple? Could she shed her scales, don the coverings of Heath's world, and take her place at his side? It was clearly what he wanted, and a part of her wanted it, too.

So why did the thought make her stomach clench with unease?

When she followed Bianca into the large room where the ball was to be held, however, she felt no unease. Only wonder. The space was enormous, the darkness lit by thousands of tiny flames of fire somehow suspended over thin pillars. Large swathes of fabric were draped from ceiling to wall in silver and purple—colors of the ocean—then trailed to the ground like seaweed. Long tables lined one side of the room, with many unfamiliar and fascinating delicacies piled upon them.

Merletta had barely made it into the room, however, when Heath appeared, and all thought of decorations or food fled.

"Merletta," he breathed, his eyes seeming to drink her in.

She felt herself flushing again, but not with embarrassment. The warmth in Heath's eyes was comfortingly familiar. She'd never had any need to be embarrassed with him. He held out his arm, and she stared at it.

"That's a very nice jacket," she said, trying to guess what he was after. "Is that the right word?"

"Yes, it is," Heath laughed. "But I wasn't showing you my clothes. I was offering you my arm."

He tilted his head toward a nearby woman who had been approached in just such a way by another guest at the ball. Copying her, Merletta laid her hand on Heath's arm, sending him a grin as she did so.

"This feels silly. Is this some sort of tradition for nobles?"

A stifled laugh behind her brought her attention to Bianca.

"Where exactly did you say you were from?" the other girl asked.

"Thanks, Bianca," said Heath firmly. "I've got it from here."

He led Merletta along the edge of the room, until they were out of earshot of his cousin.

"You look beautiful," he told her, his eyes traveling slowly over her gown. "It suits you."

"Does it?" Merletta asked helplessly. "I can hardly move in this thing. I can't imagine how your women train for combat."

Heath laughed. "No one trains for combat in a ballgown."

"What do they do in a ballgown?" she asked doubtfully.

"Dance," he answered promptly. He glanced at a nearby table. "And eat."

That part of the plan Merletta had no trouble getting behind. She allowed Heath to fill a plate for her, waiting for him to identify each item before eating it. She saw many curious looks cast at them, but no one seemed overly interested in Heath's movements. The general mood of the room was a little distracted, and almost every conversation she overheard seemed to be focused on the dragons' display earlier that day.

Heath, however, made no mention of it. She felt that same unease again, some sense telling her that it was strange how unconcerned Heath seemed to be about the dragons' offense. Everyone else was acting like it was the end of the world. But then, she reasoned with herself, from what she understood,

Heath's friendship with Rekavidur was unusual. He probably knew what to expect of dragons better than anyone else. Perhaps, like the merpeople, the rest of the humans were unreasonably intimidated by the creatures, due to their size and power and general inscrutability.

She didn't ask Heath about it, however. When she tried to bring it up, she had the impression he was dodging the topic. Perhaps he was sick of it. Whatever the cause, Heath kept chatting cheerfully with her about other matters until a strange melodic sound started up on the far end of the room.

"Dancing," he announced.

"Heath, I have no idea how to do that," Merletta said, alarmed. "Not like a human, anyway."

"I'll show you," he smiled. "To tell the truth, I'm not much of a dancer myself. I usually avoid it—I usually avoid these events altogether wherever possible, and spend most of them stuck in diplomatic small talk where I can't avoid it. Tonight is the first time I've ever been excited for a ball." His eyes shone as he looked down at her. "Just one dance?"

"All right," Merletta said, unable to deny that hopeful face. "For you, I'll try."

Beaming, Heath took one of her hands in his, and slid his other hand around her waist. There was so much fabric between them, but it still felt intimate, somehow. He pulled her into the center of the room, where other couples were doing the same. Merletta tried not to look at them, or think about how silly she must look. She did catch sight of August, standing awkwardly against one wall, and sent him what she hoped was a reassuring smile.

And then Heath started to move, and she lost all sense of her surroundings. It was amazingly personal, this dance in a room crowded with strangers. Heath held her firmly against him, so firmly that his straight posture covered her stumbles. His eyes never left hers, and the glow of satisfaction in their depths was so warming, Merletta let her earlier concerns drift away, at least for the moment.

How often had she dreamed of being in Heath's arms, no longer separated by the waterline, no longer plagued by the fears and burdens of her world? And now here she was, swaying to unfamiliar music, certainly, but caught in the most familiar gaze she knew.

And he thought she was beautiful, and that she belonged there. Surely it wasn't wrong to let herself enjoy the sensation, even if only for one night?

When the music ended, Heath pulled her hand gently back through his arm.

"Would you like a drink?" he asked.

"I'll give it a try," Merletta agreed. "It's still the strangest thing about your human ways, you know. Swallowing water even though you're in the air."

Heath laughed. "I'll find you something more interesting than water," he promised. "You'll love it."

A few minutes later, drinks in hand, they walked through an open doorway leading onto a stone terrace. The gardens below were dark, and lightly dusted with snow, but Merletta made a note in her mind to come back and see them in daylight.

"It's cold out here," she commented.

"Do you want to go in?" Heath asked.

She shook her head. "No, I don't mind it." She removed her hand from Heath's arm, strolling up to the stone balustrade in front of her. Her balance was a little off thanks to the voluminous coverings she was wearing, but she managed to avoid visibly stumbling.

She leaned on the stone, reaching a hand out into the darkness. Snow had just begun to fall, soft and silent. The light of the flames inside caught the odd flake, making it glint.

"It's magical," she said, as a small flake of snow fell into her outstretched hand.

A disapproving huff from behind her made her turn. There weren't many others out in the cold, and she hadn't realized anyone was standing so close. The middle-aged woman, resplendently dressed, was looking between Heath and Merletta with a scandalized expression. When Merletta looked at her, she turned a shoulder, striding back into the warmth on the arm of a man her own age.

"What was that about?" Merletta asked anxiously. She cast a quick glance around—for the moment, they were alone on the terrace. "Did I do something not human enough?"

"Not at all," Heath assured her. "She's just one of the more pompous ladies in the court, eager to find offense." Merletta must have still looked confused, because Heath added wryly, "The word *magical* is a little controversial around here."

"Oh," said Merletta, finally catching up.

She turned back to the railing, dismissing the incident from her mind. If the woman was so foolish as to be offended so easily, she wasn't someone whose respect Merletta wanted.

"I'm sorry August was so nervous about the dragons," she commented. "I would have liked to have seen the rest of the ceremony. And I was hoping to greet Reka, as well. He won't warm to me again if he thinks I have no manners."

There was silence for a moment, then Heath spoke, his voice coming from some distance behind her. "He won't think that. It's probably for the best—he's casual with just us, but it's a bit different for him when he's with others from his colony."

Merletta nodded absently, accepting this.

"Actually..." Heath hesitated. "It's worth being cautious of the other dragons, Merletta. They're not all like Reka, you know. They're not as safe."

Merletta frowned, glancing over her shoulder. "Are you

worried about their offense? Everyone else seems to be. Do you think they might attack the city?"

"No," said Heath quickly. "I don't think they'll do that. I just meant that they're...well, more complicated than Reka."

Merletta let out a scoff as she turned back to face the snowy gardens. "He seems plenty complicated to me."

The sudden warmth beside her told her that Heath had approached. He placed one hand on the railing, standing just behind her. Merletta waited for him to speak again, but he remained silent. When she turned to look at him, she found herself suddenly all but pressed against him. She stilled, their gazes locking, and Heath slowly leaned his other hand on the balustrade on her other side.

She was inside the circle of his arms, now, her heart racing at double time. Had she been saying it was cold a moment before? It was hard to remember the sensation—heat was now rushing up her bare arms, everywhere Heath's arms brushed against them.

"What do you think of my world?" he asked, his voice soft and low.

Merletta was finding it hard to marshal her thoughts. "I think it's beautiful," she whispered. "And like nothing I could have imagined."

Heath raised one hand to reclaim a tendril of hair which had come loose from Merletta's knot.

"I am fond of it," he said, his voice warm against her ear as he tucked the hair into place. "But it was always missing something for me. Now it's the most beautiful place in existence, no doubt about it."

Merletta swallowed. Her emotions felt tangled up, but her desire to be near Heath was unwavering. She tilted her head up, her eyes searching his face.

"Do you really like having me here?"

"Of course I do!" he breathed, the sincerity in his eyes undeniable.

"Better than being on Vazula together?" Merletta pressed.

Heath hesitated. "I loved our haven there," he said. "I loved feeling like we had our own world, existing outside either of the worlds we came from." His expression turned a little rueful. "But I'm honest enough to admit my selfishness."

Merletta frowned, confused. "Selfishness?" Heath was the least selfish person she knew.

Heath's hand once again left the stone, this time rising to touch one finger lightly to her cheek.

"I like having you all to myself," he explained.

Merletta tried to laugh, but she was still a little breathless. "That room is full of people," she reminded him.

His smile was a little wry. "Yes, but none of them are unduly interested in either one of us. Which can no longer be said for Vazula."

Merletta sighed, grasping his meaning. "It has changed since the guards came," she acknowledged. "I knew it would affect things, but to be honest I didn't expect them to take such a dislike to you. Well," she amended, "not all of them. I don't think August dislikes you."

"Or Paul," Heath agreed. "We may as well name names. We're speaking of Griffin, and his dislike has nothing to do with me, and everything to do with you."

"What do you mean?" Merletta asked, frowning. "I know you've seen him at his most unpleasant, but he's friendly enough to me most of the time."

Heath laughed, leaning slightly back. Cold air rushed in to take his place, and Merletta felt a definite sense of disappointment. How had they ended up talking about Griffin at such a moment?

"I don't mean he dislikes you," Heath clarified. "Very much

the opposite. Which is why he dislikes me." His eyes were suddenly intense as they rested on her. "It was probably inevitable, really."

Merletta caught her breath as she understood what he was saying. "I'm sure you're wrong," she said quickly, turning around so that she again faced the dark gardens. "Why would he...I mean, I'm not the kind of...before I met you, no one had ever taken an interest in me that way."

"That was when you were a nameless no one, though," Heath said. She stiffened slightly, and he hastened to add, "To borrow a phrase I've heard you use. You know you're not no one to me." He laid a hand tentatively on her shoulder, his words simple but sincere. "You're everything to me."

Merletta turned back around, warmed in spite of herself. "That's because you're an addled human," she teased. "Others in my own world don't see me that way."

"They didn't," Heath corrected. "It's different now. Even I can tell that, and I'm not actually down there."

Merletta frowned. "What do you mean?"

"I mean you're a hero," Heath said simply. "You've said it yourself—you've become visible. You're famous, not for a stupid reason like who your parents are, but for real reasons, like how smart you are, how determined, how much you're defying expectations and shaking things up. Add in that you're young," he shifted slightly closer again, "incredibly beautiful, and as far as anyone knows, unattached...well, it was inevitable that others would start falling for you. I'm just surprised it's not more than just Andre and Griffin."

"Andre's not in love with me," Merletta said, hoping her small scoff hid the way Heath's words had made her heart race.

"So you claim," Heath said doubtfully. "But maybe you wouldn't know. I bet he is. Emil probably is, too."

"Emil definitely hasn't fallen for me," Merletta said confidently.

She lowered her gaze, her eyes fixed on a button on Heath's jacket. "I...I do sort of know what you mean," she admitted. The truth was, his words were touching on one of her deepest discomforts. "I've noticed something in the way Griffin and the others talk about me."

She looked suddenly back up at him, her eyes a little desperate. "But I'm not who they think I am, Heath. I'm not some untouchable hero, with a plan to save everyone. If Griffin admires me the way you say, it's based on a fantasy. I'm not her."

"I know," Heath said, his tone earnest but calm. "Just as you were never a worthless slum-dweller. You don't have to be anyone you're not, Merletta. Just because people expect things of you doesn't mean you owe them something. And just because someone admires you for something that is or isn't there, doesn't mean that's where your worth lies."

Smoothly, easily, as if it was altogether natural, he slipped one hand up the back of her neck, cradling her head.

"I know who you are, Merletta," he said softly. "And I never had any hope of not falling in love with you."

Merletta didn't give herself time to think—thinking was the last thing she wanted to do. She seized Heath's jacket with both hands, lifting onto her toes to be nearer him as she tilted her face up toward his.

He responded immediately, wrapping his free arm around her, and tugging her flush against him as he lowered his lips to hers.

This kiss wasn't like the others they'd shared, always brief, always tasting of goodbye. Whatever Merletta's uncertainties about her place in the human world, Heath clearly felt she belonged. She could feel his joy and triumph in the way he held her, as if he truly believed they were together for good now, and nothing could pull them apart again.

Merletta didn't let herself consider whether she agreed. She just abandoned herself to the feel of his lips on hers. His breath was warm and eager, and she responded no less enthusiastically. She slipped her arms around his neck, deepening the kiss as the snow fell softly around them. She was pressed between Heath and the stone balustrade, but she could feel no chill either from the stone or from the wintry air. All she could feel was Heath's warmth as he kissed her so soundly that stars burst before her eyes, for once no aloof dragon or resentful guard appearing to interrupt them.

When Heath at last pulled back, Merletta felt dazed, although she still retained enough awareness to cling on to his jacket as she made a wordless protest at the sudden distance between them.

Heath gave a low, throaty chuckle. "I agree." His voice was a little breathless. "But I'm worried that if August catches me kissing you like that, he might start acting like a real chaperone."

Merletta acknowledged it regretfully, although she couldn't resist pressing her face against Heath's shoulder for one more second.

"I love you, Merletta," Heath whispered into her hair. "I won't let anything come between us now. A whole colony of dragons couldn't stop me."

Merletta's heart thrilled at the declaration. And if his choice of words sent the tiniest trickle of unease snaking through her mind, it wasn't hard to banish it, not with the warmth of his arms around her.

CHAPTER TWENTY-EIGHT

Merletta

Merletta had expected Heath to want to linger in Bryford after the ball, given how much he'd talked about all the things he wanted to show her. But the very next morning, she heard him speaking with his father about plans to return to their seaside manor.

It was several days before the family actually left, however, and Heath was certainly eager to show Merletta around during that time. He took her to the nearby waterfall that graced the river which formed the border between Valoria and Kyona. He showed her through some of Bryford's markets, and they spent a delightful afternoon losing themselves in the castle's records room.

But with the exception of Bianca, and her twin Brody, he made no effort to introduce Merletta to his extended family. The twins were friendly, considerately keeping their obvious curiosity unspoken. And it wasn't as though Merletta was sorry not to be introduced to the royal family—the thought of rubbing shoulders with a regent was intimidating, to say the least. She still felt a little uncomfortable at every reminder that the carefree, often barefoot Heath of her island memories was actually the titled son of a wealthy duke.

It did strike her, however, that Heath's avoidance of the royal family was at times pointed. He even dodged introducing her to his grandmother, which surprised her. From the way he'd spoken of the elderly princess, Merletta had formed the impression that they were close, and had expected him to want Merletta to meet her.

As it happened, that opportunity arose just as the family was preparing to depart—in spite of Heath's efforts rather than because of them, Merletta thought.

Merletta was carrying a case to the waiting carriage, unwilling to let a servant do it for her. The case was packed with a number of lovely gowns, some of which were gifts from Bianca, and some of which had been generously ordered for her by Heath's mother. She spotted Princess Jocelyn in the courtyard in conversation with Heath's father, and slowed her steps, eager to get a closer look at Valoria's first power-wielder.

"Yes, I was hoping to speak to Heath before—oh, there he is!"

Merletta followed the elderly woman's gaze to see Heath approaching from the stables.

"Heath," called the princess. "You're leaving already, I gather?"

"Yes, Grandmother, I'm afraid so," Heath said, embracing her. His eyes darted around the courtyard, and he smiled as he saw Merletta. She thought the expression looked slightly strained, but she told herself she was being overly sensitive.

Not wanting anyone to think she'd been spying, Merletta sped up, joining the group at the carriage.

"You haven't met Merletta yet, have you, Grandmother?" Heath's voice wasn't entirely natural, although Merletta couldn't pick what had him on edge.

"No, I haven't had that pleasure." The older woman's eyes lingered on Merletta, their expression searching.

"I'm glad to meet you, Your Highness," Merletta said politely.

"Oh, none of that," she responded, flapping a wrinkled hand. "I'm very glad to meet the girl who's had such an effect on my grandson. Are you...are you visiting for long?"

"I, uh..." Merletta hesitated, and Heath jumped in.

"As long as I can convince her to stay."

The duke had been called away by a servant, and Heath's grandmother's tone changed abruptly.

"Heath, I'm not sure that's wise. Surely someone has told you what the dragons said about a reckoning."

"Yes, I know the dragons are upset about the restrictions," Heath said, his voice a little too loud. "But I don't see any immediate danger. You know how dragons are, Grandmother. Their idea of time is different from ours. They might take a decade deciding how best to respond to King Matlock's new laws."

"Heath."

The word was an admonition, the princess's eyes fixed sternly on her grandson. Merletta's suspicion that she was missing something grew to certainty.

"Heath, be careful," the older woman said. "There are things you don't know...things which..." She glanced at Merletta and changed tack. "They won't just let this go."

"Well, we're heading back to Bexley Manor," said Heath, his face unusually stubborn. "So if they descend in wrath on Bryford, we'll be safely out of the way."

"Heath," the princess tried again, but Heath's mother was approaching across the courtyard, a smile of greeting on her face, and the topic was dropped.

Merletta saw Heath's grandmother studying August

shrewdly when he appeared at Merletta's side, but she said no more.

"What was that about?" Merletta asked when they were settled in the carriage. "She seemed very worried about the dragons. Are the king's restrictions so offensive?"

"Apparently," Heath said lightly. His eyes grew a little more serious as they met Merletta's. "Remember what I told you—the other dragons aren't as predictable as Reka. It's wise to be cautious of them. But," he added hastily, "I don't want you to be alarmed. Others can worry about the dragons."

"You don't seem to be worried," August commented. "Even though from all I've observed, everyone else is."

Heath shrugged, his tone evasive. "Today has enough to worry about without borrowing troubles from tomorrow."

Merletta could see that August was as unsatisfied as she was, but neither of them pressed. Merletta could only guess that, like her, August was thinking of the rest of their group, toward whom they were now moving. The guard was probably eager to check in with his wife, and the thought sent a flash of guilt through Merletta. It had been shamefully easy to forget all the rest of them, losing herself in the delight of exploring Heath's world with him.

But when she thought of Tish, cowering in a cave somewhere off the coast, afraid both to return home and to stay where she was—and much too terrified to join Merletta on land —she felt ashamed of herself. She hadn't come to Heath to escape. She'd come for help, for her friends more than for herself. A safe haven was no use if it wasn't a haven for Tish. And it was clear that, delighted though he was that she'd come to him for sanctuary, Heath had no solutions to offer in terms of the bigger problems that had driven her from the triple kingdoms.

She needed more substantial help than he could offer.

The thought rolled around in her mind as weeks turned into months. Life at Bexley Manor was pleasant, even the taciturn Percival seeming to have taken a liking to her. She regularly checked in with Tish and the others—Heath deftly covering for these prolonged absences—but she never had anything new to offer them. Eloise had taken Tish under her fins, and was gracious in her determination to remain in the water with the younger mermaid for as long as Tish was unwilling to brave the land. Since August needed to stay primarily with Merletta—for appearances as much as for her safety—he ordered Paul and Griffin to remain underwater to protect the others.

They'd set up a permanent base in a handy grotto, not too far from the shore. It was a pleasant spot, with good fishing and a very defensible position in case of predators. It didn't have the conveniences of life in the triple kingdoms, but Eloise's careful touches soon made the space feel homelike. The guards seemed to be fine—they chafed at times against being restricted to the water after living so long between two worlds, but they'd had close to two years to adjust to living as fugitives. And the grotto was a more permanent—and more comfortable—home than any they'd lived in during the months they'd been constantly on the move.

As for Eloise, it was clear to Merletta that the older mermaid preferred a more primitive lifestyle where she was near August, and could see him regularly without fear of being followed, to a life back in the comfort of her home but separated from her husband. There was no real reason they couldn't live there forever, if they chose. They were certainly well out of the reach of anyone in the Center who wanted them dead. And there was no port near enough to threaten exposure to the humans.

But still, Merletta's guilt ate at her. And all the more because sometimes she forgot about her friends' situation for days at a time, lost in enjoyment of Heath's company, and the novelty of the human world. Bexley Manor seemed almost as isolated as Vazula, and she could see why Heath felt so relaxed there. It was far from the politics of the capital and the tensions over magic.

Reka never visited, which surprised Merletta. But when she asked Heath about it, he told her that most of his times with Reka involved visiting Vazula, and since the dragon must know he had no interest in doing so right now, it wasn't surprising that Reka was occupying himself with his own affairs.

When they'd first arrived home, Heath's family had seemed concerned about the dragons' behavior at the Winter Solstice Festival. When Merletta raised the matter with Heath, he usually shrugged it off, repeating only his general warning about the wisdom of caution around dragons. And, as time passed without incident, everyone else relaxed as well. Clearly no one really believed an attack by the dragons on the city of Bryford was imminent.

It was certainly an idyllic lifestyle. The duke was often busy with his affairs, but Heath apparently had very little to occupy him, and yet could enjoy every comfort of wealth. Merletta couldn't deny to herself that she enjoyed the luxury, too, but she felt guilty for that enjoyment.

Plus, she felt frustrated by the formality of the life. She saw Heath everyday—a privilege she once could only have dreamed of—but almost never alone. August stuck to her pretty closely, and Heath's mother seemed to feel some need to chaperone her son. Even without their presence, servants hovered constantly, bustling around with plenty to do, but ears no doubt very much open. Thanks to all the secrets Heath and Merletta harbored, their conversation was consequently often stilted, far from the free exchanges they'd been used to on Vazula. Merletta liked being with Heath, but she felt frozen in time. It was as though they were in a constant state of waiting, the passing days changing nothing in their relationship, because they never brought the opportunity for them to truly communicate.

She also couldn't help thinking wistfully of her friends in the program, and her regret over the fact that she would never be able to progress to fourth year now. That future was lost to her, and although she knew it, she still found it hard to accept. Becoming a record holder had been her dream since she was a small child. In a token attempt not to lose everything she'd learned throughout her years as a trainee, she spent some of each day in personal study, traveling her memory journey regularly, going over the information she'd already stored there, and adding to it with things she learned in Heath's world.

She also spent some of each day hard at work in the manor's training yard. Percival usually joined her there, eager to teach her to fight like a human. Not that he phrased it that way. These pastimes helped, fending off the feeling of laziness and failure that constantly plagued her. But when she lay in bed at night, it all came rushing back, the unease that she'd felt in Bryford growing with each passing week of pointless leisure.

After far too many such nights, Merletta's inner wrestle reached breaking point. The weather had warmed considerably, the snow now melted. She and Heath were out on a grassy hilltop, where wildflowers once again dotted the grass—he was teaching her to ride a horse.

Slowly and painfully.

When the manor was out of sight, Merletta pulled her horse to a stop, knowing she needed to seize this opportunity for private speech. Percival usually joined them, but he'd still been in bed when they left the manor that morning. Merletta suspected Heath had been so eager to leave straight from breakfast for that very reason. Even August was absent, having expressed no interest whatsoever in learning to ride the beasts.

"Heath," Merletta said, "Tish is still unhappy. And it breaks my heart to see her so afraid. When I brought the others here, I never intended to doom them to life in an isolated new home in a random place in the sea. But she just won't believe me that it's safe to come on land."

Heath turned to her, his expression full of sympathy. "Is there anything I can do?"

"Actually, I think there might be," Merletta said.

"Anything," Heath promised recklessly.

Merletta decided to let this foolishness pass. "Remember how you told me that you're working on seeing places with your farsight?"

He nodded.

"Do you think you could try to see Vazula? I want to know if it's been overrun by the Center. Or if the waters nearby are being watched."

Heath frowned. "I can try," he said slowly. "What are you thinking?"

"I'm thinking that if it's clear, I should send them back," Merletta responded. "Tish, the guards, Eloise, all of them. There's nothing for them here if they have to stay in the water. The waters near Vazula are just as good for hunting—better, probably. And Paul and Griffin still have family in the triple kingdoms. They won't want to be so far away forever."

Heath was silent for a moment, and she could read his hesitation. "And you?" he asked softly, seeming to hold his breath.

Merletta couldn't quite meet his eyes as she answered. "I'm not going anywhere just yet."

She heard Heath's indrawn breath, and she could actually feel the delight radiating out from him.

"I'll do my very best," he promised. "I'll study it every day, if I can get a clear view. I'll look for any sign of activity in the water or on the shore."

Merletta nodded her thanks, still not looking at him.

"Merletta." His soft voice forced her to bring her eyes around to him. He pulled his horse close to hers, taking her cheek in one warm hand. Clearly he was also determined not to waste their unsupervised moment. "I can't tell you what it means to me that you want to stay."

She smiled at him, and he leaned in, pressing his lips softly to hers. Even though her conscience was squirming, she couldn't help leaning forward to respond in kind to the quick, chaste kiss. She didn't think they'd been this genuinely alone since their private moment at the ball. Intoxicated by Heath's nearness, Merletta would have deepened the kiss if she'd been a little more steady in her saddle. But her attempt to lean further toward Heath had her wobbling dangerously, and he helped right her with a laugh that broke the moment.

She couldn't bring herself to correct Heath's assumption—that she planned to stay indefinitely. The truth was that she'd grappled with her situation, and reached a conclusion. She had to return, and face whatever consequences arose. She owed that much not just to Sage and the others, but to Tilssted. To the whole triple kingdoms.

But if she went back now, she'd probably just get killed on arrival. Nothing would have changed, and the Center's lies wouldn't be exposed. She needed a way to convince everyone that they'd been deceived. And Heath couldn't do that. Not safely, at least. He was too vulnerable.

But there was someone else who might help. Someone whose life wouldn't be in danger no matter what the Center threw at them. And Merletta was staying only until she could pursue her idea.

True to his word, over the next few weeks, Heath scrutinized Vazula from afar with his incredible gift. When he told her that he'd seen no sign of anyone on or near the island, Merletta was satisfied. If the Center had sent someone to investigate Vazula, they were long gone by now.

That evening, Merletta asked Heath to join her down at the water for the first time. The sun had been shining weakly all day, but it had grown cool as sunset approached. Heath remained bundled up as Merletta pulled off her heavy dress, leaving it by the water's edge.

"I don't really understand why you feel the need to turn your back," she informed him. "This shift, as the maids call it, covers as much of me as the dress. Much more than my shells ever did."

"I just do," Heath said firmly. "It's a human thing."

Merletta shrugged, flicking water at the exposed back of his neck in a teasing gesture. "If you say so."

Checking that no one else was in sight, she slipped into the water, breathing a sigh as she felt her tail shift. It felt good to be back in her natural form. She liked her legs, but she didn't like going so long out of the water all at once.

Once fully submerged, she pulled off the shift. It was impractical for swimming. She broke the surface again and threw the wet bundle at the back of Heath's head.

"Wring that out for me, would you?" she said cheerfully.

She could see his cheeks reddening, and she let out a chuckle as she dove below again. Even after all the weeks she'd spent in his world, Heath was delightfully easy to bait.

Her laugh was long gone by the time she coaxed Tish out of the cave where the rest of the group were living. Her friend finally gave in to her entreaties, but her reluctance was clear as she followed Merletta up to the surface.

"But what if someone else sees us?" she insisted, hovering just below the waterline. "We could get speared."

"There's no one else around but Heath," Merletta assured

her patiently. "And he would never spear anyone." She broke the surface as she spoke, tugging Tish's arm gently but firmly.

When her friend's pale hair emerged into the brisk evening air, Merletta beckoned Heath over. Abandoning her wet garment on the shore, he picked his way over half-submerged rocks until he was out far enough to speak with them.

"Letitia, is it?" he said politely. "I'm Heath. I'm delighted to finally meet you."

Tish eyed him warily, her gaze flying to Merletta then back to the human. "Yes, I'm Letitia," she said at last. Her tail flicked nervously in the water.

Merletta smiled encouragingly at her. "Do you remember I told you that Heath is gifted with magic? He can see things from far away. He's been watching the island for me. Right, Heath?"

He nodded earnestly. "I'm confident it's safe. No one's been near there in weeks, if not longer."

"You think we should go back to the island?" Tish asked slowly. "The one near the triple kingdoms?"

She seemed pleased with the idea, so Merletta nodded. "I won't be coming just yet, but the rest of the group will." She met her friend's eyes seriously. "I know it scares you, Tish, but you'll be much more comfortable—and safer—if you can spend time *on* the island as well as near it."

Tish shook her head frantically. "No, thanks."

"It's quite simple, once you get over the shock of it all," Merletta assured her. "Let me show you."

She swam to Heath's rock and hoisted herself up onto her arms. Tish let out a warning cry—apparently involuntary—as Merletta flipped her tail up and around her. With a last heave, Merletta completed the change. Heath offered her a hand up, and next moment she was standing beside him, water dripping from her scaled skirt. Tish stared with wide eyes at Merletta's feet, her gaze traveling up her friend's legs and back down again.

"It's perfectly safe, Tish," Merletta assured her.

Tish gave no response, clearly unconvinced.

With a sigh, Merletta let it go. She would have to trust Eloise to help Tish work through this. If Tish was still confining herself to the water when Merletta joined them, she would try a tougher approach.

As Merletta walked back up to the manor with Heath, her dress over the top of her scaled skirt and shells, and her wet shift bundled in her arms, she was struck by his somber expression.

"What is it?" she asked.

"I don't know." Heath glanced at her. "You said she's your oldest friend?"

Merletta nodded. "I know she didn't exactly put her best fin forward, but you have to remember her circumstances. She's lovely when you get to know her."

"I don't doubt it," Heath said quickly. "I just...I don't know. I could see something under the surface that was...murky."

"Under the surface?" Merletta repeated, bewildered. "What do you mean?"

"It's hard to explain," Heath said. "It's part of my magic. But maybe I'm just imagining things on this occasion."

"Maybe," Merletta agreed. Her thoughts were already on the task that stood between her and her unappealing duty of saying goodbye to Heath, perhaps forever, to join the others on the island.

She debated telling Heath her whole plan, but she couldn't bring herself to do it. He would try to talk her out of it—try to talk her into staying. And she didn't know if she had the strength to withstand his entreaties. Not without a more concrete means of achieving her goals. She would end with putting it off, telling herself it was only for a little while. But more months would pass, while Tish cowered in fear in Vazula's shallows, and the triple kingdoms suffered under the Center's lies. Not to mention whatever dangers were being faced by her friends in the program all this time.

No, she needed to act now, while she had the nerve. She just needed an opportunity to do it without Heath realizing what she was up to.

CHAPTER TWENTY-NINE

"This is ridiculous." Heath scowled down at the parchment in his hand, his breakfast forgotten.

"What's wrong?" Merletta looked up from her egg—shelled, this time—her brows puckered.

"I've been summoned to the capital," Heath said darkly. "It seems the king feels I've been neglecting my duties as liaison."

"It's not such an outrageous observation," the duke pointed out mildly.

Heath frowned at his father. "We all know that role is just for show," he said. "King Matlock doesn't listen to a word I say. He's restricted the power-wielders to the point of offending the dragons. What benefit is going to come from my intervention at this point, when nothing I said before made any difference?"

"That didn't seem to prevent you from working with Prince Lachlan only a few months ago," Heath's father reminded him.

His eyes traveled to Merletta, and Heath felt a flicker of guilt stir. He pushed it down. His father might be right that he'd been so distracted by Merletta's presence he'd ignored everything else. But should he really feel guilty for being happy? It hadn't done anyone any good for him to carry the burdens of his kingdom before Merletta's arrival. Now she was here, he no longer felt weighed down and frustrated. Even his relationship with Percival had begun to improve. His brother had warmed quickly to Merletta, and Heath seemed to be benefiting by association.

"I have no new information to offer Lachlan," Heath said. "It really doesn't seem worth me riding all the way to Bryford to tell him that."

"Maybe he has information to tell you," Heath's mother chimed in.

"Whatever the reason," the duke said calmly, "the outcome is the same. It's a royal summons. You must and will respond."

Heath fell silent, but inside rebellion raged. He didn't want to go to the capital, not when life at Bexley Manor was so pleasant. But at the same time, he knew his father was right. He had no valid reason to disobey a summons from the king.

"I suppose a trip to Bryford won't be so bad now the roads are clear," he said. He looked at Merletta. "What do you think?"

"What?" Merletta looked startled. "I think I'd better stay here to see August off."

August nodded from his place beside her. "I would appreciate it," he said gruffly.

Of course. The guard was leaving that evening, the rest of the group along with him. It had taken some doing for Merletta to convince August to leave her, and it came as no surprise to Heath that August was more comfortable to leave Merletta in the care of Heath's parents than off on an unexpected journey with Heath.

"I can delay my departure until after August leaves," Heath suggested.

"No, you can't." There was no compromise in the duke's voice. "A royal summons is a royal summons. You will leave this morning."

It was with a bad grace that Heath took his leave of the family two hours later. He swallowed his irritation to say a proper goodbye to August, realizing he may not see the merman again.

Last of all he turned to Merletta, pulling her in for a quick embrace. He was aware of his family watching with interest, so he lowered his voice.

"I'm sorry to leave you on your own like this. I'll come back as quickly as I can."

"I'll be fine, Heath," Merletta assured him. She lowered her voice. "I think I might swim a little way with the others, get them started. I don't know when I'll next see them."

Heath frowned. There was something behind her words, some extra layer. He sent his magic out tentatively, wanting to understand, but not wanting to pry.

"You're not leaving with them after all, without telling me, are you?" he asked.

"Of course not!" Merletta's protest was genuine. "I wouldn't sneak off like that."

Heath nodded, not entirely satisfied, but trying to respect that whatever else she was thinking, she didn't want to tell him about it.

"Be careful, all right?"

"I will," she told him. "I'll see you soon."

Within minutes, Heath was on the road, the manor disappearing behind him as he turned his horse's head toward Bryford. He couldn't shake his unease over the farewell with Merletta, not liking the feeling there was something he was missing. His thoughts flew to the dragons, and their alarming reaction to her and August at the Winter Solstice Festival.

His conscience squirmed as he tried to deny what he knew deep down—that he should have told Merletta all about that reaction, and his guess as to its reasons. But after all, he'd warned her that dragons weren't all as safe as Reka, hadn't he? He'd told her of the need for caution with the beasts, more than once. And it wasn't as though he actually knew what they were upset about. They'd seemed to be offended by Merletta and August's presence, but he didn't know why that would be. And it was all just conjecture, after all. It was possible he was wrong.

Besides, he argued with himself, there was no reason to think Merletta was in danger from them right now. What he'd said to his grandmother was true—time worked differently for the immortal beasts. If they hadn't responded immediately— and there had been no sign from them for months—then they would probably take a long time to act, at least in human terms. He would only be gone for a few days. Surely Merletta would be safe enough at Bexley Manor for that short span of time.

When he reached Bryford, he and his horse were both exhausted from many hours on the road, and he went to his family's city manor to freshen up before proceeding to the castle. By the time he walked around, dusk had fallen. He was received by the king's steward, and told that he would need to return the following day.

Grumbling to himself about the waste of his time, Heath retraced his steps. He sobered when he passed the place where the chimney had collapsed, however. The debris had long since been cleaned up, but the mystery remained unsolved. In spite of himself, Heath found his mind emerging a little from his self-imposed bubble, engaging once again with the matters that had consumed his focus before Merletta arrived so unexpectedly.

Who stood to gain from killing him? Or—a slightly different but perhaps more telling question—who was at risk from him remaining alive? He couldn't see how he was that great a threat to anyone. Certainly not to the same someone who might see Percival as a threat. Unless someone just wanted to wipe out all the power-wielding line. But no one else had come under attack.

For once, his dreams that night were not about Merletta. He dreamed that Lachlan and Percival were locked in combat. Lachlan held a shield above his head, emblazoned with the Valorian royal crest, while Percival pummeled it mercilessly, with the full force of his legendary strength. Heath hovered on the sidelines, terrified that one would hurt the other, not knowing whom to help, or how. Then, abruptly, Lachlan turned his shield sideways, and Heath saw that its edge was sharper than any blade. So sharp that as Percival brought another blow to bear, it sliced his arm clean off.

Heath awoke with a cry on his lips, tangled in his bedsheets, and wet with sweat.

He was chastened as he once again made his way to the castle, and when he was shown to Lachlan's study, he was in a more receptive frame of mind than he had been the night before.

"Heath."

Lachlan stood to greet him, looking worn. Heath felt a flash of guilt. While he'd intentionally put his head in the sand, Lachlan had continued to carry the burden of the kingdom's tensions.

"I'm glad to speak with you before you see my father," Lachlan continued. "Thank you for returning to the capital at short notice. I hope it wasn't too inconvenient."

Heath stared at his cousin. It was unusual for the crown prince to offer anything akin to an apology, especially as related to what he would certainly have seen as Heath's duty. Why was Lachlan concerned about keeping Heath in an amiable frame of mind?

"It was overdue," Heath said simply. "Why did you wish to

speak to me first? Have you found anything further regarding the attacks?"

Lachlan shook his head. "Not really. I discovered one more death which could have been poison. From a village to the south. It can't be confirmed, though, so it doesn't especially help us."

"That would make seven in total," Heath mused. "There were around ten attackers. And it's quite possible the mastermind was present, in which case we have to assume that he at least wasn't poisoned."

Lachlan nodded, but his mind was clearly elsewhere. "Listen, Heath," he said. "I'm sure you remember that Lord Percival's loyalty ceremony wasn't entirely a success, and I know you were as grieved by that situation as I was. I realize things have become even more complicated since then. But I hope you will still wish to make your own ceremony—"

"My ceremony?" Heath interrupted. "I'm turning twenty-one in two weeks, aren't I?"

He'd completely forgotten what that meant—that he would be the next member of the power-wielding branch of the family to face the requirement of a public declaration of his loyalty to King Matlock upon reaching twenty-one years of age.

"Is that what the king wants to speak with me about?" he demanded.

Lachlan nodded, watching his face carefully. "Primarily. It's a little bit...uncertain, given no one is entirely sure of the extent of your magic."

Heath gave a grim laugh. "You mean whether I have magic. Does that get me out of the ceremony, by any chance?" he added hopefully.

"I don't believe that's my father's view," Lachlan said dryly.

Heath sighed. "I'm not sure what to say, to be honest. Like you said, I was sorry for how Percival's ceremony went. I thought he was over-reacting to everything, and should have been more supportive of the crown. But now...I don't think it *would* be over-reacting to publicly object to the whole situation. The king has placed absurd restrictions on my family, most of whom have done nothing to incur anything of the kind."

Lachlan looked extremely troubled by Heath's words, but before he could respond, the door swung open rather forcefully, revealing King Matlock himself.

"Lord Heath," he said crisply.

"Your Majesty." Heath rose to his feet, as did Lachlan.

"Father. Is all well?"

"I was told that Lord Heath had arrived," the king said calmly, his eyes on Heath. "And was therefore surprised when he did not present himself as requested."

"I asked him to come here first, Father," said Lachlan unemotionally.

"Indeed." The king's face gave little away. "Perhaps it's simplest if I join you here, then."

Lachlan moved aside, offering his father his seat. "By all means."

King Matlock lowered himself into the chair, his eyes steely as they rested on Heath. Prince Lachlan took another seat—after closing the door on the king's guards, who now stood in the corridor with his own—and Heath sat slowly also.

"My son has perhaps told you that I wished to speak with you about your upcoming loyalty ceremony, Lord Heath," said the king.

"Yes, Your Majesty," Heath said carefully.

"I trust that you will be especially eager for the opportunity to demonstrate your loyalty given the accusations leveled against you."

"Father."

Lachlan's interjection was quiet, but it spoke volumes about the arguments that lay behind it. Heath had never heard the prince challenge his father before, however mildly. It gave Heath the courage to speak his mind.

"I am loyal to you, Your Majesty," he said, sitting up straight. "But I don't feel any burning need to demonstrate it. The accusations you mentioned were too vague for me to even respond to, except to give you the assurance I've already given."

The king's expression hardened. "Your friends who joined you at the Winter Solstice Festival," he said abruptly. "Where are they from?"

Heath froze, too startled by the abrupt change in conversation to hide his surprise. What could he say that would be both true and safe?

"No answer, Lord Heath?" the king asked bitingly. "The rumor I heard is that they're from the South Lands. Are they, by any chance, from an island off the coast of the South Lands kingdom of Thorania? An island where a previously unknown offshoot of the Dragonfriend line has been living in secrecy, aided by you, who have knowingly concealed potentially hostile power-wielders from your king?"

"What?" Heath didn't even try to hide his astonishment this time. "Of course not!" He was recoiling as much from the suggestion that Merletta was some kind of cousin of his as from the absurdity of the king's claim. "They're no relatives of my father's line. Every descendant of King Calinnae and Queen Elnora is accounted for in either Kyona or Valoria. Surely there are no other power-wielders."

The king stared at him out of narrowed eyes. "Your friends will present themselves for examination," he said coldly. "Then we will know for certain."

"What do you mean present themselves for examination?" Heath demanded. "They are guests of my father's, and we will not offer them any such insult."

"Do you refuse your king?" King Matlock remained seating, but he seemed to swell, his presence suddenly suffocating in the confined space of Lachlan's study.

"I have no desire to refuse my king anything," Heath said, trying to remain calm and defuse the situation. "But there are boundaries I am unwilling to cross. And I won't blindly subject my guests to interrogation without understanding what will be expected of them."

The king narrowed his eyes, but didn't immediately retort. "You need not think that because magic is relatively new, there are none with knowledge of it," he said at last. "There are those in Valoria who have made a study of it since it first appeared. They assure me there are signs to watch for, and ways to determine how great a threat a power-wielder might be. They will examine your friends, whether you wish to permit it or not."

He paused, taking a breath in through his nose. "I am not unreasonable. I will give you time to notify your guests of this requirement, and to prepare themselves for the week of observation."

"A week of observation?" Heath demanded.

"Under tightly controlled conditions," the king went on. "The first such period is about to commence, and after it's complete, the scholars will contact you."

"Who's being examined first?" Heath demanded, an ominous feeling building inside him.

"Father, please," Lachlan cut in. "This is not the time to—"

"Who else but the only thus-far untested members of the power-wielding line?" said King Matlock, ignoring his son's words completely. "The infants must be assessed so their powers can be properly monitored and, if necessary, contained."

Heath found himself suddenly on his feet.

"The infants?" he repeated, his voice deathly quiet. "You're talking about Jacqueline and Germain? But Laura and Edmund will come with them, surely?"

"The parents cannot remain during the observation." King Matlock sounded irritated, as if he'd already had this argument and was sick of reiterating himself. Glancing at Lachlan's face, Heath was pretty sure who had been on the other side of that argument. "As you are very well aware, your sister has a type of magic which could substantially affect the accuracy of any assessment."

Heath stared at the older man in growing horror. "You're going to remove them from their parents for a week to observe them and assess their *threat*?"

He thought of his sister's pride as she held her babies. To have them ripped away like this, for such a purpose, would be torture for her.

"The children will not be harmed," the king said dismissively. "My physicians assure me they are old enough to safely spend a week apart from their mother."

"And you called yourself reasonable, Your Majesty."

Heath's vision was spinning with his fury, but he tried to rein it in. It wasn't that he cared about placating the king—King Matlock had crossed a line Heath had once thought him far too sensible to come anywhere near, and he found he didn't care what the king thought of him. But he would get no answers by losing his temper.

He actually closed his eyes for a moment, studying the king instead with his magic. Vision flared inside his mind, not shapes and colors like his eyes saw, but sensations...certainties. He could see the man King Matlock was—wise, measured, responsible. But he was glimpsing that form through something else. There was something dark beneath the surface of the king's thoughts, something that was twisted around everything else. It was a malignant influence, drawing out the king's fears and uncertainties, choking his good sense.

It wasn't magic. There was no hint of that type of power about the king. But its influence was pervasive, nonetheless. Heath's mind flew to Lachlan's admission that he didn't know who or what was influencing his father in recent months.

"Who fed you that bizarre story about another line of the Dragonfriends living on an island near Thorania?" Heath asked the king abruptly. "You didn't make that up, or hear it in castle gossip. Someone planted the tale, though for what purpose I can't imagine. Who is in your ear, Your Majesty, leading you astray?"

For the briefest moment, he thought he sensed uncertainty flickering inside the king, then King Matlock stood. He towered over Heath, and there was anger in his eyes.

"You will not speak to your sovereign that way," he said, his voice no less intimidating for being calm. "I have tolerated a great deal from you and your family, but there is a limit. I am your king, and I will have your loyalty."

"I once gave that loyalty without hesitation," Heath said coldly. "I wish I could give it still. But I cannot publicly support a king who would separate a mother from her children simply because they were born with a power he can neither attain for himself nor control. My family has given you no reason to fear them, and yet you're determined to paint us as dangerous. I never wanted to take sides, but since you force me to do so, there can be no doubt where I land."

"Do you refuse, then, to pledge your loyalty as required?" the king demanded.

"I do," Heath said. "At least while you hold to your intentions regarding Laura's children."

"There will be a consequence for this defiance," the king said, anger sparking in his eyes.

"So be it," Heath told him, his own fury just below the surface.

He fully understood the weight of what he was doing, but he felt no uncertainty. For Percival's mule-headedness, he hadn't been willing to take such a stand. But for sweet, cheerful, non-combative Laura—for innocent little Germain and Jacqueline—he was more than willing.

King Matlock strode to the door, pulling it open with more force than necessary. "Guards," he snapped. "Arrest Lord Heath. Take him to the flogging post."

Two guards surged into the room and seized Heath's arms. He made no attempt to resist, too stunned at the turn of events.

"Father, you cannot be serious!" Lachlan was on his feet as well, his face ashen. "Heath is part of our family. He's a titled lord. Flogging is for criminals. I can't even remember the last time you ordered a flogging, even for a common thief!"

"If you truly cannot see his open defiance as a crime, Lachlan, then you have been blinded," said the king, clearly still in the grip of his anger. "He has been guilty of more than you know. I have my own sources regarding his conduct. The power-wielding relatives he has been concealing have been working against us for some time. They were behind the attack for which my own guards were framed."

He threw a furious look at Heath. "No doubt the treasonous suggestion that the Kyonans were behind the attack came from Lord Heath himself."

Lachlan gaped at his father, as Heath's mind spun. Who had been telling the king these clever lies? Just enough truth mixed in to make them credible, and to give the appearance that they solved all the unanswered riddles.

"I should not have let your father talk me down from punishing your brother's crimes as they deserved," King Matlock said, turning back to Heath. "And he is not here now to protect you from the consequences of your defiance." He nodded at a guard. "Take him to the post."

Heath made no protest as he was marched from the room. It was all too surreal, too absurd. Could he—the only power-wielder of his generation who had truly tried to heal the breach —really be under arrest, about to be publicly flogged like a criminal? Whatever lies King Matlock had been fed, they had been powerful enough to send him past the point of reason.

Heath was aware of muttering servants on every side as he was dragged through the castle, and by the time his arms were tied to the post, a sizable crowd had gathered. A herald stepped forward immediately, reading the charge. Clearly King Matlock didn't intend to give anyone time to intervene.

"Lord Heath, as a member of the power-wielding line approaching his twenty-first birthday, has refused to pledge his loyalty to king and country as the law requires. His disloyalty incurs his king's deepest sanction. He will receive five lashes."

"Heath."

Heath had been watching the crowd in a daze, but the frantic voice brought his attention around. Lachlan stood as close as the guards would allow, his face twisted in distress.

"Heath, I'm so sorry."

"Your father will be angry if you're seen to be supporting me," Heath told him.

"I don't care about that," Lachlan said, more upset than Heath had ever seen him. "I tried to convince him this is madness, but he won't listen."

Heath met his cousin's eyes unflinchingly. "I will tell the truth about why I'm here," he warned him. "I won't make a secret of why I refused the pledge. If this saves Jacqueline and Germain from being treated like criminals from birth, it will be worth it."

Whatever Lachlan might have responded, Heath would

never know. The whip came down against his back at that moment, and his world exploded in pain. He'd thought he was braced for it, but it was so much more agonizing than he'd expected.

A second time it came down, and his vision darkened, fire exploding behind his eyes. He was back nearly two years ago, on a rain-drenched beach, watching his lifeblood drain from him as agony erupted in his side and his leg.

A third time he felt the lash, and this time he couldn't stop himself from crying out. His clothing was ripped now, his bleeding back exposed to the cold air. He was too caught up in the pain to even know if the crowd was jeering at him. His magic flailed, out of his control, and he saw a sudden image of Merletta swimming. Was she underwater right now? He struggled to hold on to his surroundings, but his magic continued to roil.

A fourth lash. Again he cried out. Reka flashed before his sight, flame spurting from the dragon's mouth. Strange, Heath thought, in a detached way. That was a rare sight from Reka. As pain lanced through him, Heath acknowledged to himself that he was partly to blame for all of this. He had allowed himself to discard his responsibilities like a used garment, to pretend none of it was his problem. He'd gotten so caught up in Merletta's presence, he'd missed any chance to use his position to influence a decision which would be devastating for Laura and her family.

The fifth and final lash slashed across Heath's already burning back. This time he made no sound, his back arching in before he let himself collapse. It was over. Pain still radiated across every part of his consciousness, but his defiance was undimmed. There was a time for diplomacy. But there was also a time to take a stand—Merletta knew that. How many times had he tried to rein in her quest for justice, out of fear for her safety? And she'd never allowed his caution to dissuade her from doing what was right. He would be ashamed to do less in the face of such obvious injustice.

Heath remained slumped on his knees for only a moment, before gentle hands helped him to his feet.

"Call the physician to the Duke of Bexley's residence." The familiar voice was sharp and furious.

"Great-Aunt Jocelyn." Lachlan's voice had a quaver that Heath had never heard there before. "I couldn't talk him out of it...I didn't know how to—"

"We can discuss all that later." Heath's grandmother's voice was still as hard as steel. "Help me support him. He might do himself an injury if he tries to walk unaided."

"I'm all right," Heath mumbled, as he felt Lachlan grip his other arm.

"You're not," said his grandmother. "You're a mess. This whole situation is a mess. How Matlock could possibly think that—"

Her words were cut off by a roar of pure fury. Heath's vision had been blurry since the flogging, but he forced his eyes properly open in time to see a familiar yellow shape descending into the middle of the scattering, screaming crowd.

Reka took one look at Heath's bleeding, sagging form, and let out another roar.

"Who did this?"

"Reka, it's all right!" Heath shouted.

His mind sharpened, the pain momentarily forgotten in genuine fear. He'd never seen Reka riled up like this before. And while he might be done trying to prevent conflict between the crown and the power-wielders, he retained enough sense to know that war with the dragons was to be avoided at all costs.

"It is *not* all right!" Reka roared. "I saw your punishment, and

I came at once to hold the perpetrator responsible. You are the best of these sniveling worms, and they think they can—"

The rest of the dragon's outrage was lost to Heath. As magic surged out from the beast, Heath's own magic responded. His awareness of Merletta, always present in his mind, burst suddenly into full image. She was swimming hard, not out toward open water, and not along the familiar shoreline near Heath's home. He zoomed out with his farsight, and gasped in horror at the rocky islands emerging from the water up ahead of the mermaid. Surely it could only be one place. But why in dragon's flame would she go there?

"Reka!" he cried, panic forcing every other consideration from his mind.

"I will not be silenced!" the dragon fumed. "You will not convince me this is a small matter of—"

"No, Reka, it's Merletta!" Heath shouted over the top of him. "I have no idea why, but she's going to Wyvern Islands! She's almost there!"

He heard his grandmother gasp in horror beside him, and saw his own terror reflected in Reka's eyes. At least the dragon had stopped roaring.

"If she is almost there," he said solemnly, "then it is already too late. They will kill her."

"No!" Heath shouted, fury rising up in him. He asked Reka no questions about the dragons' dislike of Merletta. There was no time for that. "No, I refuse to accept that! Take me there now! We have to stop her!"

Reka hesitated, and Heath pulled free from his cousin and grandmother, stumbling toward the dragon. He caught a glimpse of Bianca and Brody through the crowd, running toward the commotion. But he had no time for any consideration but Merletta.

"Reka, if my friendship means anything to you at all, then

please, I'm begging you. Nothing matters more to me than this. Than her."

The uncertainty in the dragon's eyes suddenly gave way to determination.

"Heath," Lachlan protested. "You're in no condition to—"

If he finished the sentence, Heath didn't hear it. Reka's talons had closed around his shoulders, and he was already high in the air. His back was agony, and his eyes were streaming against the wind as they streaked eastward, hoping desperately that it wasn't too late.

CHAPTER THIRTY

Merletta

Merletta broke the surface, both glad and nervous to see the rocky islands up ahead. It seemed she'd been right about how simple it would be to find Wyvern Islands. It had looked on the map in Heath's father's study like they couldn't be missed. She knew the Valorians avoided these waters, because the magical barrier around the dragons' home made the area impassable for regular humans. But she also knew from her experience at Vazula that mermaids could pass through those barriers, so she had expected no trouble.

She'd swum right through the night, and was now exhausted. The timing wasn't ideal, but they'd all decided that it would be least suspicious if the group left under cover of darkness, so as to have the first leg of their journey less scrutinized by the humans. And Merletta had thought the most logical course was for her to swim a little way with them, then branch off and continue on when they thought she was heading back. She didn't want to tell August and the others her plan, given how much—and how unjustly—they all disapproved of dragons.

Merletta ducked mostly below the water, so that only her eyes were above, fixed on the islands ahead. As soon as she felt her throat close over, she drew in a calming mouthful of water.

She could do this.

Heath's half-hearted warnings flashed through her mind, about the need for caution with other dragons. But she'd thought it over carefully, and she couldn't see any way in which her mission could inflame the dragons' resentment over King Matlock's restrictions. Even if they didn't welcome her arrival, it surely wouldn't lead to the attack on Bryford that some of the humans seemed to fear. The matter had nothing to do with the Valorian crown, after all, or even the Valorian power-wielders. Besides, she wasn't going to ask anything of any dragon except Reka.

And while Reka might be aloof, he wasn't unreasonable. She'd once considered him a friend. Surely he would want to correct the outrageously slanderous image the Center had created regarding dragons.

Merletta felt the ripple when she passed through the barrier. It was just like the one around Vazula—and in fact the one around the triple kingdoms. She had no idea how many dragons there were, or how hard it would be to find Reka.

She was still swimming toward the nearest outcrop when she saw the first dragon wheel overhead. It was a deep green color, so clearly not Reka. But she still paused to watch in fascination as it dove down, disappearing into the rocky center of one of the larger islands.

Perhaps that was where they all gathered. Merletta redirected her strokes, but she was only partway to the island when another dragon swooped overhead, this one seeming to spot her. It let out a shrieking cry, so piercing that Merletta covered her ears with her hands.

The creature wheeled away, but fear flashed through

Merletta in an instinctive response. She hesitated, wondering if her whole idea was foolish beyond forgiveness. Should she just have asked Heath to call Reka? But he wouldn't have done it, not once he understood her intentions. Surely Reka would speak for her among the dragons if they were inclined to be suspicious of her.

Merletta was still deciding whether to retreat or proceed when the dragon returned, this time with two others. They sped toward her with purpose and, acting on impulse, Merletta dove beneath the waves. She swam downward as rapidly as she could, ready to abandon the whole venture.

The splash of the dragons' bodies entering the water above sent adrenaline racing through her. Her fatigue was forgotten as she sped down, down toward the distant ocean floor. Her tail propelled her powerfully, but it wasn't enough. A glance behind showed the dragons gaining on her, streaking through the water as if it was their natural environment.

Merletta was deep enough now that the pressure was painful on her ears, but the dragons showed no sign of discomfort. Just as the water before her grew too dark for her eyes to see, Merletta felt talons close around her middle. She let out a scream, but the sound was lost in the thrashing water as she was dragged backward. Within minutes, she emerged into air, the dragons taking off from the water as effortlessly as they would from land.

Panic clouded Merletta's mind as her tail transformed into legs, which dangled below her. All she could think was that the dragons' reaction to her—so different from any behavior she'd seen from Reka—was completely in line with the story the Center told about dragons. A story she'd always dismissed as another lie.

Not completely in line, she tried to tell herself, as the one carrying her swung toward the largest island. The dragons hadn't eaten her yet. And if that was their sole intention, they surely would have done it without delay. Although the creature's grip was strong, its talons hadn't even pierced her, which must have required care to achieve.

They were moving so quickly, Merletta could hardly make sense of her surroundings until she was dropped painfully onto a circle of grass right near a cliff's edge. Her landing dislodged a few small rocks, which fell noisily into the water far below. A nearby dragon reared up in apparent horror, looking to her abductor, who landed silently beside her.

"Gather the elders," the dragon who'd carried her said grimly. "We found the creature in our waters. Inside the barrier."

Without a sound, the other dragon took off, disappearing out of Merletta's range of vision.

"Please," Merletta said shakily. "I don't mean any harm. I came looking for Rekavidur."

The dragon's eyes narrowed, and smoke curled from his nostrils. Merletta fell silent, clutching her knees against her chest. A horrible fear overtook her, that this had been her greatest—and last—mistake. Perhaps the Center had been right about dragons all along. Heath had always seemed so confident of Reka, so comfortable in his company. But maybe Reka was the anomaly.

The other dragon had barely left when the green one Merletta had seen before landed nearby.

"What is this?" it demanded, its voice a reverberating growl. "What magic do I sense? It is not the power of the human line of Dragonfriend."

"I do not know for certain," the other dragon responded gravely. "But I sensed it from above, and when I investigated, I discovered this creature in the water. It had the tail of a giant fish, and emanated power. Even worse, its magic enabled it to enter our realm unaided. I very much fear it is the power that was sensed at the human ceremony. I have called the elders. They will wish to examine it."

"Examine it?" The other dragon's tail flicked angrily, scoring a deep groove in the grassy ground. "You know the law. They will wish to destroy it."

"I expect so," the first dragon agreed unemotionally.

"Wait." Merletta struggled to her feet, fear lancing through her. "Please, don't kill me. I don't mean anyone any harm. I came to speak with Rekavidur, that's all. But if it was wrong of me to come, I'm sorry. I'll gladly leave."

"What is this?" The angrier of the dragons ignored her words completely, seeming to actually look at her for the first time. "I thought you said the creature had the tail of a giant fish. I assumed you referred to one of the abominations from the deep, escaped from the elders' purge."

"That is what I assumed also," agreed the first dragon.

Merletta could feel her body shaking, her mind grappling with the terrible truth she was hearing. Purge? Was it true, then? Had the dragons really tried to annihilate merpeople, as the Center had always claimed? But why? When they had co-existed so peacefully with humans for so long?

"By what devilry has such a creature now acquired legs like a human's?" the newly arrived dragon demanded.

"That I cannot answer," said the first dragon. "I thought perhaps an exception should be made to the law, to allow the opportunity for it to be examined, and answers to be found."

"There are no exceptions to the law," growled the other dragon. "Abominations must be destroyed. I know it seems human, but you can feel the strange power that clings to it. It is no mercy to prolong its suffering when its death is assured. If you do not have the resolution to do what you must, then I will."

The dragon turned toward Merletta, opening its jaws. She

could see a red glow in its throat, and heat washed over her, heralding something much worse to come.

"Please!" she cried. "Give me a chance to—"

Her words were lost, not in dragon flame, but in a crunching crash as an enormous body hurtled out of the sky and collided with the attacking dragon. Merletta fell back onto the grass, her eyes wide as she took in the newcomer.

It was larger than the other two dragons present, and much larger than Rekavidur. Its scales were not as bright as his yellow ones, but they still glimmered with clear purple, blue, and green. Flames poured from his mouth, but they were not directed at Merletta. They engulfed the other dragon, who emerged from them unscathed, but clearly irked. Apparently their only purpose had been to express the larger dragon's displeasure.

"What are you doing?" he demanded.

"Do not interfere, Elddreki," said his companion in irritation. "Your love for the humans has made you soft, but this is no human. You must sense the magic that hangs around her. Were you not at the ceremony yourself? This is one of the creatures who was present!"

"So I've heard," the dragon called Elddreki barked. "I also heard she claims she is here in search of my son!"

"Rekavidur has enough to answer for already," interjected the dragon who had carried Merletta. "Bringing an abomination into our very realm only makes his conduct worse."

"He didn't bring me here," Merletta cut in. She had to almost shout to be heard. "I came looking for him. He didn't know I was coming."

Elddreki turned his yellow eyes on her, the expression on his reptilian face impossible to read. For a long moment he stared at her, then he glanced at the other two dragons.

"If she is, as the elders suspect, an abomination from the deep, how is it that she has legs?"

Neither of them answered him, and his eyes narrowed as they returned to Merletta. Whatever their belief about Merletta's origins, something about her appearance clearly didn't add up with their expectations.

"How do you know my son?" the dragon asked her, his voice quieter now.

"Heath," she managed, through dry lips. "Heath brought us together."

"What are you?" Elddreki demanded.

"I'm..." Merletta hesitated, unsure what answer would make them less likely to kill her. "I'm Merletta."

"I don't want to know its name," said the angry dragon impatiently. "Do not attempt to make a pet of it, Elddreki. You see what harm has already come of your fondness for the humans."

"Conflict and change are not harm," said Elddreki shortly. "They are necessary, and only as good or as evil as the manner in which they are handled." He glared at the other dragon. "I have seen things you have not. It would not be the first time a dragon offered violence to an innocent human on the mistaken belief it was an abomination."

He turned back to Merletta. "Where do you come from, Merletta?"

"Yes," agreed the dragon who had plucked Merletta from the water. He sounded pleased. "That is information worth discovering before she is destroyed."

Merletta shook her head, backing away instinctively. Her heel suddenly hit air, and she realized she was on the edge of the cliff. She stopped, her heart racing but her mind quite clear.

"I can't tell you that," she said. "Not if your intention is to kill anyone like me simply for existing."

"So be it," said the irate dragon. "There is then no reason to delay."

A rushing sound filled Merletta's ears as he once again opened his mouth. For a moment she thought it was death speeding toward her, then her eyes caught a rapidly growing shape in the sky at the dragon's back. Before she could do more than gasp, Reka had landed behind his father, Heath tumbling from his talons.

"No!" Heath shouted, fury and fear evident in his voice. "Don't touch her! You have no right to mete out death!"

The dragon pulled up, letting out a roar as he turned to face the new arrivals.

"Rekavidur!" he bellowed. "You bring a human into our realm without leave, and allow him to tell us what rights we have in our own home! Is it not enough that you have already shown yourself a traitor?"

"You are quick to judge," snarled Elddreki. "But Rekavidur is a member of this colony, and he has the same right to be heard as any of us. The elders have made no ruling on his decisions."

Reka lashed his tail angrily, rocks splintering under the impact. "Your unprovoked violence toward Merletta confirms my doubts as to the wisdom of the colony's position," he said angrily. "I do not regret my decision."

Merletta stared at him, amazed that he'd not only referred to her by name, but actually defended her. But the other dragon was clearly not impressed.

"Enough!" he cried. His glare encompassed Elddreki as well as Rekavidur. "Do you think you can come here from Vasilisa and change our ways so casually? Humans we tolerate. But abominations are beyond what can be accepted. The law is the law."

His movement as he turned back to Merletta was so rapid, she realized his intention a second too late. She hadn't even moved as his jaws opened, but someone else did. A lithe form came flying out of nowhere, pushing her out of the way as flame erupted from the dragon's mouth. She felt a flicker of heat sear her foot, but the next moment her mind knew nothing but falling, her stomach left behind on the cliff above.

For a heartbeat, time was suspended, the descent seeming endless. Then Merletta hit the water with enough force to knock the air from her lungs. Mercifully she'd dodged any rocks, but her whole body still ached from the impact. She twisted wildly in the water as she felt her tail return, turning so that she could look up toward the surface, half expecting to be followed into the ocean by wrathful dragons. She was winded, but several steadying mouthfuls of water helped restore her balance.

When the imminent shock of her near miss passed, her mind caught up, and panic flared once again. Heath had pushed her out of the way, sending her over the cliff in the process. Where was he? Had he been engulfed in the flame in her place? Had he fallen as well?

She spun back around, her eyes searching the water on all sides, terror rising in her. With a choking cry, she spotted him, his unmoving form sinking slowly into the gloom.

With a mighty flick of her tail, Merletta dove down toward him, her hands outstretched. One of his arms trailed behind him, and she grasped his wrist, pulling him toward her. As she tightened her hold, he suddenly burst into motion, his legs kicking wildly and his eyes wide as he instinctively tried to take in air. His body convulsed horribly as water poured into his mouth.

"Stop!" she cried, her voice cutting clearly through the water. "I've got you, Heath, don't try to breathe. I'll get you to the surface."

His eyes fixed on her, silently communicating his understanding, even as his body continued to spasm. A trickle of red crossed Merletta's vision, and horror washed over her. Heath was bleeding into the water. Had he hit the rocks on the way down?

There was no time for answers now. As gingerly as speed would allow, she wrapped her tail around his torso, holding him securely in place as she moved toward the surface with desperate strokes. A moment before, their depth had seemed a good thing—extra protection from the dragons. Now every inch of water was another agonizing stab of fear that Heath wouldn't make it. But she could feel Heath gripping her tail, his arm wrapped around it and his skin as hot against her scales as a thermal vent. He was conscious, then.

When they finally broke the surface, Merletta grabbed Heath with her arms, pulling him up to float beside her. With a horrible choking cough, he expelled water from his mouth. Merletta kept her arm under his shoulder, finding no great challenge in keeping their heads above water with the motion of her tail.

"Heath, how badly are you hurt?" she cried.

He shook his head. "I'm...all right," he said, his voice faint and unconvincing. Even as he spoke, his eyes drifted closed for a moment.

"Heath!" Merletta cried, anguished.

Her eyes scanned his form, and she drew in a sharp breath at the sight of the mangled flesh across his back, his clothes in tatters, and his blood seeping into the water. The fall hadn't caused that.

"What happened to you?" she demanded.

Heath's form was limp, but he opened his eyes. "Worth it," he said thickly. "Laura's babies...gone too far..."

His words trailed off, and Merletta floated, in an agony of uncertainty. Was he in danger? What should she do?

"I'm so sorry, Heath," she choked. "I was such a fool to come here. I didn't know...I never dreamed the Center was right."

"Not your fault," Heath grunted. "I didn't know...how bad it was." His voice was labored. "I knew the dragons were angry about you...that's what they...got upset about...at the ceremony. I hid it from everyone." He winced in pain, and his eyes slid shut again. "I'm sorry, Merletta. I should have told you. But I wanted you...to stay."

Merletta pulled him more securely into her arms, struggling for words. So that was what had been behind his vague words of caution. She'd never dreamed the danger was to her rather than the humans. What fools they'd both been!

A sudden movement above made her freeze in fear. Her first instinct was to dive below the waves, but she remembered just in time that Heath couldn't flee to safety that way. With a gasp of relief, she realized that the dragon swooping toward them was Reka. He and his father must have delayed the others somehow because no other forms followed him.

"Heath!" Reka cried, pulling up just above the water line. "Is he alive?"

Merletta nodded. "He's conscious, but he's hurt."

"I will take him to safety," Reka said, the water rippling under the beat of his powerful wings. "It's not him they wish to destroy. Flee, Merletta, while you still can. If you remain in Valoria, they will come for you."

"No, wait." Heath struggled in Merletta's grip, but Reka's talons were already closing around him. "Merletta—"

Merletta didn't let him finish. "Take him," she told Reka, relinquishing her hold. She didn't even stay to see the dragon take off. Turning away from Heath's helplessly outstretched hand, she dove below the surface and swam as hard as she could toward home.

CHAPTER THIRTY-ONE

Heath moaned as he rolled over, awareness returning in patches. He was lying on his side on a hard surface. Stinging pain still lanced across his back, and the wind whipped against his face. He could taste salt in the air.

He'd just flown from somewhere with Reka. His memory wasn't total blackness, but everything was a little hazy.

A burst of flames, the rushing terror of a fall, sudden suffocation, a flash of scales.

"Reka," he groaned. "Where have you brought me? Where's Merletta?"

"I've brought you to a secluded spot of coastline," responded his friend's gravelly voice. "And as far as I am aware, Merletta is fleeing through the water toward her home."

Heath pushed himself into a sitting position, cradling his pounding head in his hands. "But the triple kingdoms aren't safe for her," he protested. "She can't go back there."

"Are they more dangerous than the home of my colony?" Reka asked dryly. "Where half the inhabitants feel a compulsion to reduce her to ash on sight?"

Heath peered up at the dragon. "Why? Why do they hate mermaids so much?"

Reka let out a gusty, smoky sigh. "It is a long tale. One I had not even heard when first I laid eyes on Merletta."

Heath didn't push for more answers straight away. His head was throbbing viciously, but he forced himself to focus. The awareness of Merletta that always sat at the back of his mind expanded outward to fill his vision. She was, as Reka had said, swimming hard. She looked exhausted and terrified. But at least she was alive.

"How long since we left Wyvern Islands?" he asked groggily.

"An hour, perhaps two," Reka said carelessly. "Once I was sure we were not being pursued, I flew slowly, out of concern for your injuries. The bleeding seems to have slowed, but your back is in a sad state."

"Never mind my back," Heath said shortly.

But the dragon's words did remind him of the disastrous circumstances he'd fled in order to pursue Merletta to Wyvern Islands. For a moment he hovered, uncertain. If Reka flew straight over the water, they would easily catch up to Merletta. He had to bring her back. She would get herself killed if she went to the triple kingdoms. If she even made it there, that was—it was a treacherous journey across the open ocean for a solitary mermaid. She wasn't even armed.

On the other hand...his family tugged at his mind, igniting his guilt over the way he'd ignored everything these past few months. Did Laura even know her children were about to be taken away from her? What would be the consequences of his defiance of King Matlock, and his humiliating public punishment?

"I need to go home," he said reluctantly. "Back to Bexley Manor."

"Very well."

In his usual delightful way, Reka asked no questions. He just lifted Heath gently in his talons, taking to the sky much more slowly than usual. Even so, agony ripped across Heath's wounds as they sped through the air.

Relief washed over him when Bexley Manor finally came into view. Within minutes, Reka set him down in the courtyard, and Heath let himself drop to his knees. The dragon's approach had sparked a flurry of activity from passing servants, and soon Heath found himself engulfed not only by his mother, but his grandmother.

"Grandmother?" he said, confused, as they helped him inside out of the brisk air. "Aren't you in Bryford?"

He stumbled as he spoke. Now that the flight was over, and his destination reached, he hardly had the strength to keep moving. The open wounds on his back felt like they were on fire, and every inch of him throbbed from his painful fall from the cliff into the water. His head was spinning, and it was with relief that he felt stronger arms go around him, and let himself slump.

"You're in a state." It wasn't his father's voice, as Heath had expected, but his grandfather's, vibrating with an anger he'd never heard from the older man.

"We came straight here when you disappeared with that dragon of yours," Heath's grandmother explained, her voice tight. "We didn't know where else to look for you, and we thought your family needed to be told what had happened."

"Oh, Heath, your back," his mother said tearfully. "I didn't want to believe it was true. How could the king do this?"

"He's let his fears drive him past reason," growled Heath's grandfather. "And it's going to push us all into disaster."

"Heath!"

The new voice caused Heath to look up, confusion once again cutting through his foggy mind.

"Laura?"

"How many times do we have to see you carried in half dead by that dragon?" she demanded, sounding as close to tears as her mother.

"I'm not half dead," Heath said wearily, hardly aware of his surroundings as someone lowered him onto a long settee. He heard his mother sending a servant to fetch the local physician. "It hurts like dragon's flame, but I'll be all right. How are you here so quickly?"

"We didn't come for you, although we would have if we'd known," Laura told him. "We were already here when Grandmother and Grandfather came. We arrived last night, a few hours after you left for Bryford. We didn't know where else to go for protection. Heath, King Matlock is going to...is going to..."

"So you know." Heath nodded wearily as he stretched out on his side, laying his pounding head down with relief.

"How do *you* know?" Laura demanded. Then he heard her sharp intake of breath as the pieces connected. "Heath! Is that why...was that what you said to—"

"Being frustrated with Percival I can understand," Heath said, his eyes sliding shut. "I want to smack him upside the head often enough myself. But targeting little Jacqueline and Germain?" He shook his head, subsiding quickly as the movement sent pain shooting through his body.

"Oh, Heath," Laura whispered.

He heard her drawing closer, and the next thing he knew, something warm was bundled next to him on the settee.

"If he understood what was happening, Germain would want to thank his Uncle Heath," said Laura, her voice firmer now.

"Laura." Heath's mother spoke admonishingly. "We're all extremely fond of Germain, but Heath's in no state to hold a baby."

Laura shook her head stubbornly. "It will make him feel better, Mother, trust me. Germain has a way about him. I can't explain it."

Heath put his arm instinctively around the infant. He'd been too out of it to even realize Laura was holding one of her babies, and he was inclined to agree with his mother that he was much too likely to drop the child off the settee in his current condition.

But as his nephew snuggled into him, he found to his surprise that Laura was right. There was something incredibly comforting about the child nestling there. Was this why Laura seemed to love motherhood so much?

A picture flashed before his mind, not farsight, just imagination. A child with Merletta's brown skin and dark eyes, sitting in Heath's lap in the shallows, splashing gleefully. Belonging to both sea and land.

He shook his head slightly to clear the image. When Merletta had been here with him, he'd allowed himself to imagine that kind of a future. But it was painful to think of it now, when everything had fallen apart so spectacularly.

To his relief, the movement of his head didn't cause it to throb nearly as much as before. In fact, as he lay quietly, waiting for the physician to arrive, and letting his mother and grandmother fuss over him, he found that the aches in his body lessened rapidly. Much more rapidly than he would have expected. His back still stung viciously, but his bruised muscles were inexplicably soothed.

And with the gradual lessening of the pain, his mind began to clear as well.

"Where's Percival?" he asked suddenly. It was an hour since Reka had brought him home, and the physician had finally arrived. Heath glanced around the room. "And Father?"

His mother and sister exchanged tense looks, but before

they could respond, the physician clucked his tongue disapprovingly.

"You need to hold still, My Lord," he scolded Heath. "These wounds are in serious danger of infection. They should have been treated immediately. I have no idea what you've been doing since receiving them to make them look like this."

"Just some cliff diving," Heath said flippantly. His eyes sought his grandmother, deciding she would be most likely to tell him the straight truth. "Where are Percival and Father?"

She drew in a slow breath, glancing at her husband. "They rode for the capital not long after we arrived."

Heath sat up straight, eliciting another protest from the physician. "But Percival's under house arrest! Surely Father would have stopped him from leaving."

His grandfather shook his head, his expression somber. "Norik didn't blame Percival for wanting to challenge the king, and neither do I."

"I've never seen Father so angry," Laura agreed. "He was already worked up over Edmund's and my predicament, and then when Grandmother and Grandfather arrived with news of what the king had done to you..."

Alarm flared through Heath, and he remembered his father's words after the accident with the chimney.

If someone is going after my family, I'm not going to stand idly by.

Things had reached breaking point indeed. Just as the growing tension had eroded King Matlock's moderation, events had broken even the duke's habitual calm.

"This is all largely my fault," Heath muttered, putting his head in his hands.

"No, it isn't." His grandmother's voice was so sharp, Heath looked up in surprise. "I spent my own youth blaming myself for things that weren't my doing," she said, "and I'll be hanged if I sit on my hands while my grandchildren do the same."

Heath met her look seriously. "I appreciate the sentiment, Grandmother, but even you cautioned me. You knew Merletta's presence was likely to cause an explosion, and I refused to listen to you."

"What does Merletta have to do with all this?" Heath's mother asked, bewildered.

Heath didn't answer, his eyes still locked on his grandmother's. Their silent communication lasted so long that Laura began to fidget impatiently.

"Can I please have a moment alone with my grandson?" the princess asked quietly. "We won't be long."

After a faint protest from the physician, and a bewildered moment of hesitation from Heath's mother, his grandfather herded everyone from the room. As soon as they were alone, Heath's grandmother spoke.

"Where did Reka take you after you were flogged?"

"Wyvern Islands," Heath said wearily.

"What happened there?" she pressed. "Tell me exactly."

Heath did so, noting that while she grew visibly distressed, she showed no sign of surprise.

"You were expecting something like this," he said quietly.

"I was afraid of it," she acknowledged, her voice heavy. She shot him a quick look. "And you knew there was a risk as well. Everyone else may have been oblivious to it, but I know you realized the dragons were looking at Merletta and her guardian when they took offense."

"Believe me," Heath assured her, "I don't deny I was being willfully blind." His voice turned wistful. "I just wanted her to stay."

His own heart condemned his selfishness. His insufficient warnings to Merletta about caution looked unforgivably weak in the hindsight created by the incident at Wyvern Islands. If only he'd been fully honest with her, as his conscience had told him, deep down, that he should be.

His grandmother was silent for a moment, her eyes full of sympathy rather than the judgment Heath knew he deserved.

"Did you know that there is a way for a dragon to die?" she asked, the soft question so unexpected Heath could only blink at her. "Even ones who've chosen immortality, I mean."

He shook his head slowly. "I thought they were invulnerable."

"Almost," she said. "Nothing you or I could do would ever be able to kill them. But there is a way—they just don't speak of it."

"I can understand why," Heath said, intrigued. "How does it happen?"

"By the dragon's own choice," his grandmother went on. "Their magic is their lifeblood. Without it they simply...wither away. And although it's not exactly something they teach their dragonlings, it is possible for a dragon to choose to forfeit its magic, and so end its life."

Heath stared, transfixed.

"But the magic can't go into nothing," his grandmother added. "It has to be received by a living thing. And that creature gets warped by the power it should never have had. Its effects are unpredictable, and the whole process is deeply offensive to the dragons. There was a dark time in their history—many centuries ago—when there was war between them, and many dragons forfeited their magic, for reasons I won't go into. The dragons who remained called the resulting creatures abominations, and sought to wipe them all out."

She drew a shaky breath. "They thought I was an abomination when they learned of my magic. They didn't know of any other way a human could carry it as I do. Now, of course, they understand that our magic is part of us, something we are naturally born with, not something we have received from a dying dragon."

"The angry dragon called Merletta an abomination," Heath whispered.

The princess nodded. "When Elddreki told your grandfather and me the history I've just told you, he spoke of various types of creatures who received forfeited magic. Wolves who grew overlarge and supernaturally savage. Horses which sprouted horns and gained other strange abilities. They were wiped out by the dragons with relative ease. But they also spoke of enormous fish from the ocean who were warped into something unnatural, and who escaped into the deep. They were harder to catch, but the dragons believed they'd tracked them all down."

Heath's mouth had fallen open. "You're saying Merletta, and all her kind, are descended from these abominations? That their ancestors were fish which were warped by this dragon magic?"

She shook her head. "I'm saying that's what the dragons likely think. I'm certain now that it was this discovery that changed Rekavidur's attitude toward Merletta. You must remember that many of the dragons—perhaps most—were not yet born when all this occurred. Their understanding of the nature of these abominations is imperfect. But from what you've told me—from what I've seen—I don't see how Merletta and her kind could be the result of forfeited magic. The creatures who received that magic were, at their core, fish. Perhaps they could have gained some non-fish features—some capacities fish don't normally have. But Merletta isn't a fish with a hint of other abilities. She's human."

She chuckled uneasily. "Obviously she's more than a regular human—there's a part of her that is sea creature, that belongs in the ocean. But when she wears her legs..."

"She's just like us," Heath agreed. "Which seems far beyond

the power of this warped magic you're talking about." He looked up at her eagerly. "I remember Reka's surprise when I told him about Merletta's legs. He was amazed that instead of becoming completely sea creature, she lost the part of her that was fish and became completely land creature. He must have realized that such a capacity didn't fit with the idea that she was descended from these abominations. Do you think it's possible to convince the other dragons that they're wrong about her origins?"

His grandmother hesitated. "I don't know. They're not practiced at listening to humans, or taking our perspectives seriously. They think us fleeting and foolish. Rekavidur is an exception—he takes after his father. For the moment, Merletta is safer far away from them."

"But she's not safer," Heath said, anguished. "You don't understand, Grandmother. Her world has turned against her. She has no refuge in the ocean."

As he spoke of Merletta, her image flooded his mind. She was curled in the dark, sleeping uneasily. He was glad to see she was resting—presumably in some hidden cave or fissure—but he knew the respite was temporary. She was surrounded by danger behind and ahead, and he couldn't see a clear path for her.

He shuddered at the memory of the dragon's rage as the beast had turned its flame on her.

"Poor Reka," Heath murmured. "No wonder he's been so strange about it all. I know dragons don't lie to each other—it must have been eating away at him to be hiding something like this. But he knew it would destroy me if he told the others and they wiped Merletta out. I had no idea of the sacrifice he was making for me."

"I'm sure he would appreciate hearing that from you," his

grandmother said. "He'll be eager to know that your injuries aren't as severe as they first seemed."

"Is he still here?" Heath asked, surprised.

She nodded. "Last I saw, he was waiting in the courtyard, making all the servants nervous."

Heath struggled to his feet. "I'll speak with him now."

She made no attempt to stop him, but he still paused in the doorway.

"What do you think Father and Percival are going to do? How big a mess are we in?"

"A very big one," she responded gravely. "Your father even said something about the whole family leaving forever, moving to Kyona. He was already extremely distressed over Laura's situation. The news of your sufferings on top of that…"

She broke off, a hitch in her voice. Heath could feel her grief over the splintering of her family—it was a potent force, pervading the room.

"We'll fix this," he told her softly. "I don't know how, but we'll find a way."

He made his way outside, shaking off the protests of the physician. As his grandmother said, Reka was still there, a motionless statue crouched in the courtyard.

"Reka," Heath greeted him. "Thank you for saving me yet again."

The dragon studied him out of unblinking eyes. "You seem better."

Heath nodded. "The injuries weren't as severe as they appeared. My back is still in a bad way, but it will heal. The physician has no lasting concerns." He hesitated, then laid a hand on his friend's scaled side. The warmth of Reka's flame radiated through the yellow scales, spreading into Heath's hand.

"Reka, my grandmother just told me about the history of your colony with…with the abominations."

Reka gave no visible response.

"I don't think Merletta can be one of them, though," Heath said. "I think her people must be something else. I think they came from Vazula, not from this land."

"I have begun to wonder the same thing," Reka acknowledged heavily. "It is why I could not countenance her destruction today."

"Thank you," Heath said fervently. "But none of that is what I actually wanted to say." He leaned his head forward against the dragon's hide, struggling for a moment for words. "I understand now the balance you've been walking all this time. I was angry with you when I should have been sympathetic. I'm sorry."

Reka let out a faint exhale of surprise.

"You are a true friend, Heath," he said in his gravelly rumble. "I do not have another to match you, even among my own kind."

Heath lifted his head, the dragon's warmth still lingering on his forehead.

"What do you wish to do now?" Reka asked. "Do you plan to go after Merletta? To try to protect her from those in her world who wish to destroy her?"

Heath bit his lip. He could see her, without really trying, still sleeping in the cave. She couldn't be too far. They would still easily be able to intercept her. But as his magic flared to life inside him, other images rose. Other people important to him, who deserved his attention as well.

His father's face flashed before his mind. The duke had reached the capital. He was arguing with Prince Lachlan, towering above the younger man with cold anger on his face. Lachlan's features were no less vivid. He was pale, both apology and resistance showing on his features. He was clearly torn between his duty to his crown, and his horror over his father's actions. He didn't deserve the duke's wrath, and he was as powerless as Heath was to fix the tangled mess in which they were all caught.

But someone was missing from this picture. As Heath's concern touched on another person, so did his sight. Percival was stalking away from the argument, unnoticed by his father. Heath saw him demand the king's whereabouts from one servant after another. No one answered, everyone scurrying away from the rage in the eyes of the powerful young lord. Uneasy, Heath watched as his brother connected with a city guard, a particular friend of his. The young man told Percival that the king was outside the city, inspecting a royal grain house that had been damaged by a violent spring storm.

Percival hesitated, his eyes darting back toward the anteroom where his father still argued with the crown prince. But as Heath watched, Percival seemed to decide not to involve his father. With his usual recklessness, he plunged out of the castle's entrance, toward the stable where their father always kept fresh horses.

"We need to head toward the capital," Heath said, shutting off his internal vision abruptly. "As sick as I am of saying this, I think Percival's in trouble. Or he's about to cause trouble. Either way..." His thoughts flew regretfully to Merletta, hiding somewhere in the open ocean. "I think I'm needed more there."

"Very well," said Reka.

With a spring, he took to the sky, his talons clutched around Heath's shoulders.

CHAPTER THIRTY-TWO

Merletta

"Merletta, I don't think this is a good idea."

The concern in Eloise's voice almost brought Merletta to tears, but her resolution remained firm.

"I appreciate you looking out for me," she told the older mermaid seriously. "But I have to do this. I can't hide here forever."

"Forever?" Griffin said, his voice gruff with worry. "You arrived on the island yesterday, Merletta. Surely you can at least give yourself a few days."

Merletta shook her head. "If I put it off, it will just get harder. I've had a good night's sleep, and plenty to eat. That's as much as I need."

"I'm amazed you made it back here, traveling alone," said August regretfully. "I wish you'd caught up to us."

"So do I," Merletta assured him. "But there's a lot of ocean. I wasn't sure how to find you."

"Merletta, you don't have anything to prove," Eloise said softly. "You've done what you could to expose the Center's lies. It's all right for you to choose to live."

Merletta looked at her helplessly. How could she explain it? They seemed to think she had a death wish, but that wasn't it at all.

"My friends are still in the triple kingdoms," she said. "I can't just swim away and never look back. And I need answers."

Her thoughts flew to the investigations she'd asked Emil to undertake on Founders' Day. It felt like a lifetime ago.

"Especially now I know that some of what the Center says is true," she went on. "I need to understand. I don't want to spend the rest of my life as a fugitive, trying to survive in the open ocean. And none of you should have to do that, either."

A shudder ran over Tish's frame. She was sitting in the shallows, where the water could lap comfortingly over her feet, but at least she was in human form now.

"I don't want to live here forever," she said softly. "I want to go back."

"Have you forgotten that they tried to murder you?" Griffin demanded. He had little patience for the timid mermaid.

But Merletta knew Tish, and she understood. "It's your home," she told her friend. "You have every right to be there. You did nothing wrong, and I'm going to make sure everyone knows that."

"It doesn't matter how much we know the truth," Paul burst out, weighing in for the first time. "Those in power will never let the real story come out. You'll be cast as a traitor and a criminal, and they'll kill you. And I don't see how that helps Letitia, or anyone else."

Merletta shook her head stubbornly. "Things are only as bad as they are because anyone who knows the truth is too afraid to speak up. Well, I'm not afraid. I'd rather die in the Center than spend my life hiding."

"We can't talk you out of it, can we?" Eloise asked softly.

Merletta stayed silent. They knew her answer.

"Then we should all go," Griffin said.

August shook his head sharply. "I'll go with her. And Eloise, if she wishes to come. But Letitia isn't a trained guard. You and Paul need to stay with her, for her protection. We don't know what might come this way, if our re-entry goes badly."

It took a considerable amount of arguing before Paul and Griffin gave in, but in spite of all that had passed since they'd left the triple kingdoms, they were still a patrol squad, and August was still their leader. He overruled their objections just as firmly as he rejected Merletta's attempts to convince him and Eloise to stay on the relative safety of the island. And in truth, she was so relieved to have the support, she didn't try too hard to dissuade the couple.

A few hours after her declaration, Merletta found herself swimming away from the island, August and Eloise on either side of her.

"Should we go the long way?" Eloise asked.

Merletta shook her head. "I'm not trying to hide anymore, and we all know this might be my last time doing this. I'm going to enter the triple kingdoms through my home waters."

"Tilssted it is," August agreed gravely.

As soon as they approached the barrier, it was immediately clear that things were not well with the triple kingdoms. Instead of the regularly rotating patrols Merletta had expected, the boundary was lined with guards in apparently permanent positions, spaced far enough apart to just be within hailing distance of one another. Most telling of all was that their scanning eyes turned inward as often as outward.

Clearly the border was now officially closed.

Merletta gripped Griffin's spear in her hand. She'd lost her own weapon in her hasty flight from Wyvern Islands, but the guard hadn't hesitated to give her his in preparation for her treacherous journey. It looked like she'd need it sooner than she'd thought.

Luck was with them, however. A guard had spotted the trio, and Merletta was just sizing him and his nearest companions up—deciding whether she, August, and Eloise could break through their defense before back-up was summoned—when August called a bold greeting.

The guard's eyes widened, and he almost dropped his weapon. "August? I thought you were dead!"

"Skulssted guards," said Eloise, sounding as relieved as Merletta felt.

"I'm not so easy to kill," August said, his voice grim.

The guard's eyes had passed on to Merletta, and he drew in a sharp intake of water. Clearly he recognized her.

"Is there a problem?" August asked mildly.

"She's a wanted criminal," the guard said, swimming forward a stroke. "We thought she'd perished in the ocean—I'll need to take her straight to—"

"Just like I perished in the ocean?" August's voice was dry. "Merletta is no more a criminal than I am. Her only offense is attempting to expose corruption."

The guard stared between them, his hand tightening and loosening on the shaft of his spear as he clearly debated what to do. The nearest of his fellows swam toward them, his eyes narrowed in suspicion.

"Afternoon," August greeted the newcomer pleasantly.

"August?" The second guard was clearly just as rattled by August's appearance as the first had been.

"Of course," August said calmly. "I'd love to stay and catch up, but we have somewhere to be. We'll just be on our way."

"No one comes in or out," said the first guard, exchanging an uncertain look with his companion."

"I trained both of you myself," August said, lifting his spear.

"I'd hate to accidentally kill either one of you in a pointless and unnecessary fight." When they still hesitated, he scowled. "Have I been given a demotion I'm not aware of? I was under the impression that I'd been hailed as something of a hero. So unless either of you has risen drastically in rank since we last spoke…"

With a final shared look, the guards shifted aside, allowing the trio entry. Merletta and her companions swam quickly through the kelp farms, emerging much too soon into open water. Merletta let out a strangled cry at the sight before her.

The once idly waving fronds of kelp were gone. So much of the farms had been cleared for habitation, and she could see the signs of building work everywhere. But that wasn't what horrified her. The sounds of conflict assailed her from all sides. The builders were being protected by armed guards, their work hampered by crowds of angry merpeople. Even as she watched, one merman darted past a distracted guard and seized a builder from behind, raising a stone to strike.

The merman was swarmed by guards, and after a quick tussle, he was dragged away southward, to what destination, Merletta didn't know. This action did nothing to calm the rest of the crowd, who continued to hurl both insults and stones toward the builders. As she watched, the guards started beating the more intrepid protesters with the blunt ends of their spears, forcing them back further from the building work.

"Stop!" Merletta cried, propelling herself forward. 'What's going on?"

One of the guards turned to her, angry words on his lips. But he paused, clearly confused at her escort.

"We're not going to let them take our homes and our livelihoods without a fight, that's what's going on!" roared an onlooker. An answering shout passed through the crowd, and chaos broke out again.

"Merletta?"

The astonished voice brought a lull to those nearest to them. Merletta's eyes sought the speaker, settling on a familiar form.

"Felix!"

"They said you were dead," the young guard said wonderingly. "How did you survive in the open ocean all this time?"

"I had help." Merletta looked meaningfully at August and Eloise, and Felix's eyes widened in shock.

"Merletta?" the first guard repeated sharply. "You're the fugitive?"

The conversation had caught the attention of others, as well. Slowly, word spread through the crowd like ink in the water, stilling the fighting.

"It's our trainee!" someone shouted. "She's alive!"

"She's a criminal," one of the guards said, steel in his eyes as he swam forward with purpose.

A roar of fury greeted his words, and he was immediately swamped by a dozen of the onlookers. As other guards rushed to his aid, panic rose quickly in Merletta. This would be a bloodbath if she didn't calm the frenzy.

"Stop!" she cried. There was a pause, as many pairs of eyes darted to her. "Yes, I'm Merletta. I'm very much alive, and I'm not guilty of the crime I was accused of. I'm not hiding. I'm here to respond to the allegations made against me. Please, don't anyone kill anyone else over me."

"It's just like those shellsmiths said," someone told their neighbor excitedly. "It was all a set up, and she escaped."

The guard who had been going to seize Merletta made no immediate move to grab her again, although she noticed the subtle nod he sent toward a fellow guard at the back of the crowd. The mermaid detached herself from the group, swimming rapidly away toward the Center.

Merletta wasn't perturbed. She'd never expected to be able to sneak in, not this time.

"You have nothing to answer for, we all know you were framed!" someone called from the back.

"Don't speak nonsense," snapped one of the guards. "She's been convicted of stealing records from the Center."

"Convicted without any chance to give an answer to the allegations?" August chimed in. All eyes flew to him.

"Who are you?" the guard asked rudely.

Felix made a tsking noise, and the two guards from the barrier shifted uncomfortably.

"My name is August," August said calmly. "I'm a squad leader from Skulssted. I haven't been inside the triple kingdoms for some time, but I understand that my patrol and I are reported to have died of land sickness. That's not quite how I remember events, however."

Shocked exclamations sounded throughout the crowd—which had doubled in size by now, everyone in the vicinity sensing a commotion. No one could fail to remember the furore over the supposedly dead guard patrol.

"Enough of this," said another guard uneasily. "I don't know what's going on, but I think we'd best escort you all back to the Center."

"By all means," August said coolly.

"You're not taking our trainee off to the Center!" shouted an onlooker. "We're not giving you another chance to kill her somewhere out of sight."

"Thanks for the support," said Merletta, sending the speaker a grin. "Why don't you come along?"

The crowd roared its approval, everyone surging forward to swim alongside the group. Merletta saw merpeople darting off on all sides, no doubt telling their friends of the imminent showdown.

Perfect. The more public the coming scene, the better.

"I hope you know what you're doing," muttered Felix, coming up alongside her.

"Just barely," Merletta informed him lightly. She frowned, taking in the new stress lines on his face. "Where are Freja and the others?"

"Freja was demoted for standing up for you," Felix said shortly. "We were all reassigned."

Merletta winced, gratitude and guilt shooting through her. But she was too distracted by her surroundings to say more. As they progressed through Tilssted, she was horrified to see how far things had deteriorated in her absence. The city was swarming with guards, and fights like the one she'd witnessed near the farms were happening everywhere. More than once she caught the cloying taste of blood in the water, and her heart broke a little more for the city of her childhood.

Not that the fighting continued in her path, of course. As the cavalcade continued southward, everyone stopped to gape. The whispered rumor was traveling more quickly than the group, and everyone seemed to already know that their supposed champion had returned from the dead, full of accusations and ready for a reckoning. By the time they crossed into Skulssted's cleaner waters, there were hundreds of merpeople swimming in their wake. The onlookers now considerably outnumbered the guards, who were growing visibly nervous.

No one knew what to expect from the coming confrontation, Merletta least of all.

As they passed through Skulssted's tidy streets, Merletta felt a flicker of outrage at how normal everything seemed. No sign of the conflict that had turned Tilssted into a battle zone.

"Seems like Tilssted was the right choice for an entry point," Eloise said in an undertone.

Merletta nodded fervently, watching as the crowd poured

through the Center's receiving hall, observed in terrified confusion by the mermaid behind the desk. She didn't even try to stop them—she must have recognized how readily the scene could turn violent.

When they entered the drop off, those in front pulled up abruptly, and Merletta couldn't see what had made them stop.

"Maybe you'd better stay here," Felix told her nervously.

She ignored him, pushing upward with sure strokes and emerging above the crowd. The drop off was lined with guards, a scowling Ibsen right in front.

"Merletta," he said sourly, his eyes finding her where she floated over the angry crowd. "Was it not enough to steal valuable records for your own gain? Must you also raise a violent mob?"

Angry murmurs passed through the crowd, but Merletta ignored them.

"I never stole anything," she said, her calm voice carrying clearly. "I was accused, but given no opportunity to respond."

"You can't wriggle out of it now," Ibsen retorted dismissively.

"Where are these stolen records?" Merletta pressed. "I want to see them."

Ibsen glared at her. "They've been destroyed, of course," he said curtly. "They were dangerous—"

"If you've destroyed the evidence of my supposed crime, Instructor, I'm not sure how you plan to demonstrate my guilt," Merletta said mildly.

"You are no longer a trainee," Ibsen hissed. "You will not refer to me as your instructor."

"You can't kick her out!" someone from the crowd yelled. "You have no proof she's done anything wrong!"

"On the contrary," Ibsen seethed, his eyes searching the crowd angrily for the source of the shout. "She ceased to be a trainee months ago, when she fled the triple kingdoms and failed to meet her obligations in the program."

Merletta raised an eyebrow, ignoring these details. "So, I take it you have no answer regarding the records I supposedly stole?" She raised a hand, waggling her finger condescendingly at him. "You're not used to actually having to show evidence for your claims, are you? No one holds the Center accountable." Her voice and expression hardened. "Well, I will. Even if it costs me my life."

"Well said," Ibsen growled.

As he spoke the words, a senior guard swam up. Merletta realized with a jolt that he was the very one who'd accused her on Founders' Day.

"Guards." He gestured to the squad at his back. "Seize her."

The guards began to swim forward, but they hadn't come far when Merletta found herself engulfed by a squad of her own. The crowd below her rose up through the water, surrounding her, many of them carrying crude weapons.

"Stay away from her!" one shouted.

"If you kill her, we'll kill you!" another agreed.

"Anyone who attempts to interfere in the course of justice will be executed as well," barked the guard.

There was an outcry at his words, and Ibsen darted forward, whispering in the guard's ear. A look of consternation crossed the merman's face. Merletta had the impression that he wasn't supposed to acknowledge Merletta's impending execution. After all, she'd only ever known the Center to execute in secrecy.

"Enough of this spectacle!" The cold new voice belonged to Instructor Wivell, who swam over the head of the guards with cold outrage. "What is the meaning of this?"

"This needn't concern you, Instructor Wivell," the head guard told him stiffly. "Instructor Ibsen has informed us that this mermaid is no longer a trainee in the program."

"Has he?" Wivell sent Ibsen a hard look. "That is not his declaration to make."

"This is no time for your obsession with following the program's rules," Ibsen growled at his fellow instructor. "We cannot allow this scum to—"

"The integrity of the program is paramount," Wivell interrupted coldly. "Merletta has passed the second year test, and is therefore a third year trainee until such time as she sits the third year test, or is formally disqualified from the program."

"Oh, good," said Merletta flippantly, her voice raised in a provocative lilt. "So if I were to pass the test, I could go on to fourth year?"

Wivell glared at her. "Of course," he said coldly. "But it is irrelevant, given you cannot sit the—"

"With all due respect, Instructor," the head guard interrupted impatiently, "I can't see that the program has anything to do with this. This young mermaid has been accused of a crime which—"

"A crime for which there appears to be absolutely no evidence." August's commanding voice rang over the drop off as he swam up to Merletta's side.

His appearance caused something of a sensation among the gathered guards, many of whom clearly recognized him as the supposedly deceased leader of the ill-fated patrol.

Wivell showed no hint of either surprise or dismay. He studied August dispassionately, then turned to the head guard next to whom he floated. "Is it true that there is no objective evidence of the crime?"

The guard shifted in the water, looking irritated. "That's not my area," he said gruffly. "My orders are to apprehend her and—"

"Apprehend me and kill me quietly, where no one can see," Merletta called out over his words, making sure the crowd could hear her. "I remember from last time. And it's not like I didn't know that was what I was coming back to. But I want to make sure that this time, everyone knows it."

"That's nonsense," the guard growled, although he looked distinctly uneasy now.

The crowd's mutterings were growing in volume, and several burly mermen floated up alongside Merletta again, cracking their knuckles menacingly.

"Your allegation is absurd," said Wivell, also sounding irritated. "If there is no evidence of a crime, then I have no doubt this matter can be peaceably resolved."

"Wivell," protested Ibsen. "You cannot seriously be considering allowing her to re-enter the program. Your rules be seared, I will not allow—"

"You are becoming excited unnecessarily," Wivell cut him off, and Merletta sensed a warning in his words. "There is absolutely no need to step outside the rules of the program in order to appropriately respond to this situation. This former trainee has surrendered her place in the program due to her prolonged and unsanctioned absence from her studies."

Ibsen scowled. Merletta could tell that he thought her exclusion from the program was a tame response compared to the summary execution he'd been hoping for.

"I didn't want to surrender my place in the program," she said, her eyes on Ibsen. "But you didn't give me much choice, did you? You made it impossible for me to succeed, openly refusing to teach me the material, blocking me from doing my own study at every turn. You even changed the watchword that's stood for generations, just to keep me out of the records I needed to access in order to pass." She pointed back toward the receiving hall. "You've hated me from the moment I swam through those doors, and it's just about killed you to see me make it as far as I have, hasn't it?"

Ibsen ground his teeth, his eyes angry as they rested on her. But he wasn't really the one Merletta had been trying to get a reaction from. The group behind and around her had grown even in the time they'd been in the drop off—a glance behind showed more merpeople pouring through the receiving hall even now. And as she'd hoped, her crowd of champions were taking offense on her behalf, angry cries greeting her words.

"We knew you'd never give our trainee a real chance!"

"And the Center claims that anyone can apply!"

"Corruption!"

"You can't kick her out!"

Movement from behind the line of guards caught Merletta's eye, and she started forward in the water. Two forms were streaking across the drop off, green and coral scales glinting through the gloom.

Merletta was taken aback by the strength of the emotion that rose up in her at the sight of her friends. Emil looked as serious as ever, but Sage's face showed joy alongside her evident fear. She must have wondered if Merletta was dead.

Ibsen followed Merletta's gaze, his scowl becoming more pronounced at the sight of the approaching pair.

"Stay back, record holders," he barked out. "This is a matter for the guards."

For a moment Merletta was confused by his words, then understanding bloomed. Of course! Sage's test had been weeks ago. She must have passed. She was a junior record holder now, like Emil. Merletta felt a surge of pride for her friend's achievement, even as her mind reeled from the bizarre realization that life had gone on as normal in the program after her desperate flight.

Looking behind the pair, Merletta saw another group approaching. Agner soon came into clear view, a disordered mess of swimmers behind him. With another lift of the heart,

Merletta spotted Andre's crimson scales. It must be a combat day for the trainees—she'd lost track of days of the week.

"Trainee Merletta!" Agner gave an amazed laugh, his expression suggesting that for him, at least, the surprise was a pleasant one. Merletta actually thought he looked a little impressed.

"Not a trainee any longer, Agner," Ibsen growled.

"Well, I don't know about that," said the combat instructor jovially. "Until she's formally ousted from the program, I suppose we should continue to address her as a trainee."

"How much more formal would you like it to be, Agner?" Wivell asked. Although his tone was more measured than Ibsen's, annoyance glinted in his eyes.

"You might be the chief instructor, Wivell, but you're not the only one," Agner said mildly. He dropped his voice, holding a whispered conversation with a nearby guard. The instructor nodded rapidly, presumably getting an update on all that passed before his arrival.

"Well," he said at last, his volume once again raised. "At the very least, this matter requires proper discussion. We have been operating under some misapprehensions, it seems, not least the mistaken belief that Merletta was dead."

He met Merletta's eyes, a glint of something almost like humor in his own. Whatever else was in his mind, he at least was glad that Merletta had returned to make life at the Center more interesting once again.

"If you come with us, I'm sure we can sort this whole situation out," he told her.

Angry muttering rose up again, Merletta's self-appointed bodyguards unimpressed with the suggestion. Agner ignored them, his eyes on her.

"Do you trust me, Trainee?"

"Not entirely," Merletta told him frankly. She gave a faint smile. "But I trust you most out of my options." She glanced at the crowd around her, a slight frown marring her face. "And I don't want anyone to get themselves killed on my behalf."

"Very honorable," Agner said approvingly. "Come on."

After only a moment's hesitation, Merletta swam forward, August and Eloise rising up to flank her, and Felix not far behind. Agner started at the sight of August—it seemed his informant had left that part out—but made no comment.

A stiffly disapproving Wivell and an incensed Ibsen followed them, as did the senior guard and his squad. The rest of the guards stayed to contain the angry crowd. Merletta could hear their noise growing as she swam the rest of the way across the drop off, into the Center itself.

She could see Sage and Emil—now joined by Andre—trying to get to her, but the guards around her weren't letting anyone else into the center of the knot. She sent them what she hoped was a reassuring smile, but the truth was she had no more idea than they did whether she would emerge from this debacle alive.

Even if she didn't, she was inclined to think she'd made enough of a stir to ignite a real rebellion now. Hopefully it achieved something other than getting everyone from Tilssted killed.

They were moving toward the Center's central spire, but before they'd reached it, they were intercepted by a guard whom Merletta recognized. He was thickly muscled, with a deep blue tail.

One of the Record Master's personal guards.

"What's the meaning of this commotion?" he asked coldly.

For a moment there was silence, as everyone waited for someone else to explain.

"I've returned inconveniently alive and ready to share my experiences," Merletta said flippantly, watching the merman's face for a reaction. "I believe I'm being hauled before the Record Master to be held to account for my fanciful crimes."

The guard's eyes—as blue as his tail—held about as much warmth as the bottom of an unplumbed drop off.

"I cannot imagine that there is any need to disturb the Record Master over a dispute within the program. With all three instructors present, it is surely possible to resolve the matter satisfactorily." His gaze seemed to hold both message and warning as it rested on Wivell.

The meaning was clear. Evidently the Record Master didn't want to be dragged into a situation that had become so public. He no doubt wanted—and fully expected—the instructors to get rid of Merletta through their own rules, without involving him.

"Very well," Wivell responded, with an inclination of the head. The blue-tailed guard drifted away, back toward the central spire.

"You little sea snail," Ibsen spat, as soon as he was gone. He seized Merletta's arm and gripped it painfully. "You think you've made yourself untouchable, but you were never going to become a record holder."

"Contain yourself," Wivell said to his colleague, a snap of impatience in his voice. "As Agner has said, we have been remiss in not formalizing Merletta's expulsion from the program. Until we do so—which we shall imminently—we are bound to treat her with the deference owed a trainee."

"That's not quite what I said," Agner pointed out, his good humor unruffled.

Ibsen had released Merletta's arm, but he was glaring at her with poison in his eyes. "How dare you accuse me of corruption? As if it's my fault you never had a hope of passing the program."

"Was I wrong?" Merletta challenged. "Can you really deny that you blocked me from learning at every turn this year?"

He sniffed. "A truly gifted scholar would be able to succeed without preferential treatment from her instructors."

Merletta couldn't help snorting. "I wasn't asking for preferential treatment. But how I could learn when even the records were barred—"

"I had nothing to do with that," Ibsen spat.

Merletta stared at him in bemusement. What was the point of lying, given everything that had just happened?

"You want access to the restricted records?" Wivell interjected smoothly. "Very well. Since you are *apparently*," he cast a disapproving look at Agner, "still a third year trainee for the moment, you are of course entitled to that access."

He looked at Ibsen and tilted his head meaningfully. The two mermen swam a short distance away, where they held a rapid whispered conference. Ibsen's tail flicked compulsively throughout the conversation, and he sent Merletta a venomous look as he nodded. Then he turned abruptly, swimming away toward the central spire.

"Merletta."

It was almost eerie how emotionless Wivell's voice was, given the circumstances. Merletta swam up to him cautiously.

"The new watchword is *fidelity*," Wivell told her, his voice so quiet she could barely make out the words. "You may spend as long in the records room as you wish. When you are finished, we will discuss your future in light of the allegations against you."

Merletta considered him thoughtfully.

"Do I have your word, Instructor?" she asked gravely. "That I can spend as long in there as I want, and I won't be disturbed?"

"Certainly," Wivell said. "Take all the time you wish. But when you emerge, we will finalize the matter of your status in the program once and for all."

Merletta thought it over. Clearly the instructors wanted an

opportunity to plot their course, and perhaps fabricate evidence against her. But she still considered the offer a boon. She'd been itching to get back into that records room since her one look inside, and had despaired of ever getting another chance.

With an uncertain glance toward her friends, who were still hovering just behind the wall of guards, she swam toward the central spire.

CHAPTER THIRTY-THREE

Merletta

August and Eloise followed Merletta toward the spire, over the guards' protests. No one actually stopped them though—no one seemed to know quite what to do with the couple.

It was surreal, swimming up to the records room once again, and writing the watchword on the leaf she was offered, as if she was back to being a regular trainee. The guard waved her in, and she passed through the doorway. Just inside, Ibsen hovered. He loomed over her, anger radiating from him.

"Enjoy your stolen time," he ground out. "Because I promise you that when you come out, your expulsion from the program will already be finalized. Although I imagine that will be the least of your problems."

He showed no vicious glee at the thought of her downfall. He was clearly still too consumed with anger for any positive emotion.

Merletta ignored him, swimming further into the room as he exited. The space was deserted, no educators or trainees in sight. Merletta's eyes were drawn at once to a slab in the center of the room, on which a record was conspicuously waiting. She moved toward it cautiously, realizing that its preparation must have been Ibsen's purpose in coming here before her.

She picked it up with hands that weren't entirely steady, curiosity battling with foreboding. It was some kind of report, although it appeared to be an excerpt—there had clearly been more pages that came before, which were not on display.

In short, the cull dealt primarily with the problem. However, a handful of dissenters remained, mostly from Hemssted.

They held a series of public meetings, alleging deception and corruption within the Center. Standard approach undertaken—known dissenters convicted on charges ranging from assault to fraud.

Merletta swallowed. So far, this account was uncomfortably familiar. Except her fabricated charges had been stealing restricted records. The standard approach, was it? That came as no surprise. Her eyes flew back to the top of the page, dwelling on the word *cull*. Ominous. Flicking her tail tensely, she read on.

Error discovered some weeks later. One dissenter had evaded notice. When pursued, fled outside the barrier. Escalation approach number twelve utilized against family members and close friends. Three perished in unrelated accidents before contact with dissenter established. Approach successful—dissenter turned himself in and was eliminated.

Merletta felt a chill pass over her as she read the final words—a date some fifty years previously. None of it should surprise her, but she was a little stunned by the revelation of just how organized and formalized the Center's more brutal tactics really were. And how long they'd been doing this kind of thing. It was shocking to read those admissions, stated so plainly and unemotionally, like she was reading harvest records rather than an account of cold-blooded murder.

She dropped the record as though it had seared her, watching as it drifted to the floor. The message was clear: we've done this before, we'll do it again. They obviously believed they were past the point of being able to hide their true intentions from Merletta. Instead they were telling her plainly—desist, or we go after those you care about.

Merletta's thoughts flew to Sage and the others. To Tish, who'd already been the target of an attack such as that described in the record. To Heath, although she knew that was foolish. How could anyone from the triple kingdoms touch him, far away and safe on land?

She couldn't bear to see any of them killed because of her rebellion. She'd accepted that she may well die upon re-entering the triple kingdoms. Perhaps it was best to embrace that fate before anyone else had to join her.

But even as the thought passed through her mind, defiance rose up in her. It was the same defiance that had caused her to fight with every ounce of energy she possessed against the restrictive future the charity home had dictated to her. It was the same defiance that had led her—against all advice and discouragement—to pursue a position as a record holder, instead of letting herself be sent to labor on some outlying farm. It was this defiance that had sent her exploring outside the barrier, above the surface.

She needed that defiance. It had been her lifeblood for so long. Without it, she would never have discovered the wonders outside the triple kingdoms. She would never have met Heath, never have found her legs, never have made it into the program and met Sage and Emil and Andre.

And the triple kingdoms needed that defiance right now. If she let herself be cowed by the Center's threats, she might save her friends' lives today. But what about tomorrow? What about when the Center next decided to murder guards because they'd seen too much, or frame an innocent apprentice for knowing the wrong mermaid? If someone didn't stand up to them, it would never end. This record was proof of that.

Merletta floated for a moment, perfectly still except for the gentle movement of the current. She knew her heart, but she still didn't know her course. How could she best defy? Should she flee to Tilssted, try to rally an army of apprentices and farm laborers? So many would die, and would it change anything? She'd hoped to change things from the inside, but that path was closed to her now.

Wasn't it?

She frowned as she remembered Agner's defense of her. He'd clearly wanted her to stay in the program, little as even he believed it possible. But what if it was possible? Even Ibsen acknowledged that she wasn't yet expelled. The thought of Wivell's words—spoken in front of an angry crowd—were what finally decided her.

Merletta jerked into motion, swimming around the perimeter of the room, searching the labels. She found a section marked *Trainee Program*, and began to hunt feverishly through the records.

It took an hour and a half, but eventually she uncovered a pearl. She almost let out a triumphant cry, but held it in. She didn't want to draw the attention of the guards at the door. Not now she had a plan. She didn't have her satchel—another item left behind in the frantic flight from Wyvern Islands—so she tucked the record into one of her shells, after one last fond glance at the most pertinent two sentences.

Trainees are not permitted to miss more than five days of classes during the study year. Exceptions can be made only with approval from one of the instructors.

"I'm trusting you to come through for me, Agner," Merletta whispered to the water.

Her stomach grumbled, reminding her that she'd skipped lunch on her arrival at the triple kingdoms, but she ignored it. She stared around at the enormous room, trying not to let the scale of her task overwhelm her. There were so many records in here, and she had only a limited understanding of which ones she needed to focus on.

She set her jaw in determination as she closed her eyes, summoning up an image of her memory journey—her version of the mind palace where she'd been taught to store information. It might be time to come up with some new mnemonics as well.

She could only hope Wivell would honor his word when he said she could stay as long as she chose.

It was two days later that Merletta finally surrendered to the hunger. The exhaustion she could manage—she'd slept for several two hour stretches in that time. But she was growing so faint from lack of food that her mind was starting to be affected. She could no longer concentrate enough to take in information, which meant there was no point in staying longer.

She'd utilized every trick she'd ever gleaned—both in her own training prior to entering the program, and in the extensive memory training she'd received since—and her mind was bursting with information. She knew it was all stored in her short term memory, with no opportunity to lock it into place through interval repetition, as she'd been taught to do. The information would be nowhere to be found in a few months. Perhaps even a few weeks. But that would be long enough.

No one had troubled her in all that time, no one else even entering the records room. She wasn't surprised. The scene at the drop off had given her a valuable insight into her instructors' minds, one that tallied with what she'd experienced from them in the past.

Ibsen hated her, there was no doubt. And much of what he did and said seemed to be motivated by that hatred. But Wivell was different. While his motivations might not be acceptable to her, he had an unshakably high value for both his word and the integrity of the program. He had believed from the start that she was bad for the program, and would threaten its sanctity. Whether that was because of her background, or because of her determination to question the status quo, she didn't know. But it had been that desire to protect the program that had driven him to discriminate against her, not a personal dislike.

None of which made him a friend or ally, of course. But it did cause him to honor the word he'd given.

Two guards were at attention outside the door, but Merletta was surprised to see August alongside them.

"Still alive, August?" she asked him. She intended to speak teasingly, but her words came out slurred.

"Merletta!" Surging forward, he gripped her elbow bracingly. He searched her eyes, apparently satisfied enough by what he saw to smile wryly at her words. "I would say I'm alive thanks to you. You succeeded in making us both...complicated to kill."

"That is one of my few genuine talents," she agreed.

"What's going on, Merletta?" August pressed. "Why did you stay in there so long? I assume you have a plan?"

Merletta glanced toward the guards, realizing that one of them had slipped away. She didn't have long, then.

"What's in your shell?" the other guard demanded suddenly.

"I beg your pardon?" August's voice was as forbidding as a real father's.

Merletta gave a drunken chuckle, pulling out the record. "Oh, I forgot about this."

The guard made an angry noise and lurched forward. "You dare to—"

"Relax." Merletta dodged out of his way. "I'm not trying to steal it. I just need to show it to the instructors. It's my secret weapon."

"Merletta, I'm not sure you know what you're saying," August said, sounding exasperated. "Or else you don't understand the concept of a secret weapon."

Before Merletta could respond, an angry cry reached her ears. She looked up to see Ibsen streaking toward her, Wivell and Agner not far behind.

"So, the sea snake emerges from its lair," Ibsen hissed. He came to a stop a couple of feet from her. "Did you think you could escape justice by hiding in there forever?"

Merletta studied his face curiously. Maybe it was the gnawing hunger and the sleep deprivation confusing her senses, but he didn't look right. He should be triumphant to have her in his grasp at last, but instead he looked like he was about to explode from frustration.

"Of course not," she told him, blinking rapidly. "I just needed the study time. But I'm done now. I'm ready for my test."

"Your—?" Wivell's voice was sharp. "What are you talking about?"

"My third year test," Merletta explained groggily. "I'm ready."

"You can't take your test," Ibsen raged. "You've been absent from your classes for months. That precludes you from—"

"Ah ah ah," Merletta interrupted him, waving her record through the water hazily. "My secret weapon."

All three instructors stared at her in bewilderment. Merletta turned to Agner, holding out the leaf.

"I distrust you least, Instructor," she told him with a bleary smile. "What do you think?"

Agner took the record and scanned it quickly. He obviously had no difficulty grasping the relevant part, because he threw back his head and let out a booming laugh.

"Tides above, you're a quick one," he told her. "Yes, all right, I'll play. I'm positively bursting to see how this ends." He handed the leaf on to Wivell. "Is there something I need to sign, Wivell?"

The other instructor snatched the leaf from Agner's hand, his face paling as he read it over. Ibsen, on the other hand, was growing redder by the second.

"This is an outrage!" he shouted. "Agner, you cannot seriously consider—"

"I know you don't agree, but I think she's great for the program," Agner cut him off. "She just needs the chance to show what an asset she can be."

The two mermen stared each other down, fury meeting cool amusement. Finally, Ibsen turned to Wivell.

"Surely you won't allow this."

Merletta cleared her throat. "If I understand these regulations correctly, Instructor Agner's support entitles me to sit the test, provided it hasn't been more than a year since I sat my previous test. Which means I'm eligible now." Her eyes found

Wivell's. "Let me remind you, Instructor Wivell, that you announced publicly, just a couple days ago, that if I passed the test, I could go on to fourth year."

Wivell looked as though his next words cost him physical pain. "These are the regulations under which the program operates." His eyes were serious as he turned to Agner. "I also caution you to think carefully before taking a course which will have consequences for you as well as the trainee you intend to sponsor."

"No doubt it will have consequences for us all," Agner said lightly. "Where do I sign?"

"It makes no difference," Ibsen growled maliciously. "I administer the third year test. And I have *total* confidence that Merletta will fail."

"No." Wivell's voice was colder than ever. "Your inability to swallow your personal prejudices has already brought the program under public criticism for discrimination. I will not allow it to be robbed of all credibility by your conduct. The program *must* be protected, whatever the outcome of the current conflict. Due to the accusations Merletta has made against you, I will administer the test."

Ibsen swelled with rage, but Merletta felt a sweet trickle of relief. Wivell wouldn't fail her unless she actually failed.

Which, she reflected, as she drooped in the water, was still a very real possibility.

"She needs food first," August barked. "And sleep."

Merletta shook her head. "I won't say no to food," she said. "But I don't need sleep."

Wivell regarded her with narrowed eyes. Did he suspect that some of the memory choreography she'd used would be wiped out by sleep? She tried to look innocent.

"There have been more than enough irregularities in this process already," Wivell said shortly. "If Instructor Agner is determined to sanction the trainee's absences, she is entitled to sit the test. But only if we commence now, before any other external circumstances have the opportunity to sully the integrity of the process."

Fair enough, Merletta thought. *If I won't sleep, I can't eat either.* She'd be taking the test on an empty stomach, then. She nodded her agreement, and in less than fifteen minutes, she found herself in a small room, across from Wivell.

"As you know, this test is designed to assess your capacity for the role of an educator," he said, his words clipped. "Ordinarily, part of the test would take place out in the community. But given the circumstances, I will take the part of the various individuals you will be asked to educate."

Merletta nodded wisely, her voice still a little slurred. "I am a little too hot to handle out there in the public eye," she acknowledged.

Wivell's tail flicked in irritation, but he made no further comment, instead diving into the first question.

By the time the test was complete, five hours had passed. The questions had been more complex and nuanced than she'd expected, and Wivell's role-playing of community members in need of education had been surprisingly convincing. Merletta's head pounded with the agony both of her need for sleep and her hunger. But judging by Wivell's increasing agitation, she was performing satisfactorily. The thought bolstered her.

There had been some entire slabs of information she'd memorized unnecessarily, and one section of the test she couldn't answer very comprehensively, even after pausing for several minutes to complete an entire mental swim through of her memory journey. But most of what she'd learned, she'd needed. Already she could feel some of the rote learning slipping away from her exhausted mind. She let it go strategically, gambling that Wivell was unlikely to return to topics already covered successfully.

When Wivell fell silent, no new question forthcoming, Merletta looked at him hopefully.

"Is the test finished?"

He was still for a long moment, then he nodded. "It is."

Merletta waited, but he didn't continue. "Well?" she asked quietly. "What will it be, Instructor? Will you sacrifice your principles, or will you put up with my presence in your program?"

Wivell's fins twitched convulsively, although his face remained impassive. His gaze scanned her face, settling on her eyes.

"Yours is one of the most promising minds I have seen in a generation," he said quietly. "To succeed in this test, under the conditions you currently face..." He shook his head, looking resigned. "Had you been more teachable in all other ways, you could have been Record Master one day. I truly believe that. As it is..." He gave a fatalistic shrug. "I hate to see such potential wasted. Congratulations. You have passed third year."

Merletta stared at him, struggling to process all his seemingly contradictory words.

"I passed?" she asked stupidly, needing a simple answer.

"You did," Wivell confirmed gravely.

Merletta nodded, rising into the water. She felt none of the elation she'd felt the previous two years. This wasn't a lasting victory. And it certainly wasn't an achievement that would allow her to rest. All it meant was that she could proceed to the next challenge, the next impossible, life-threatening struggle.

But that was something. She'd chosen her course. She wasn't going to back down now.

"Thank you," she said sincerely. "For having a code of honor, even if it doesn't match mine."

Wivell let out a stream of water, looking neither gratified nor offended by her words. "Do not expect your code of honor to get you far down your chosen trail," he said disinterestedly.

"So..." Merletta hovered uncertainly. "So what happens now?"

"That," said Wivell, rising from his seat as well, "is out of my hands. I will, of course, make the standard public announcement regarding your results."

And with that he swam from the room, not even glancing back.

Merletta followed slowly, her mind reeling, no particular emotion able to hold sway for long. She had only a very hazy idea of where she was, and was relieved to be charged by a wonderfully familiar figure as soon as she emerged into open water.

"Merletta!" Sage cried, enveloping her in a hug. "Merletta, you're alive! Wivell just said you passed...don't tell me they let you take your test?"

"That's right," Merletta said groggily. "Speaking of which, congratulations on passing yours."

"Never mind that," Sage said impatiently. "Merletta, we thought you were dead! Not for all these months," she added, by way of clarification. "These last two days. I mean, we thought you were dead all these months, as well, but—oh, Merletta, I just can't believe you're here!"

"I can't believe no one's tried to kill you yet." Andre's voice chipped in, causing Merletta to disentangle herself from Sage and beam at him.

"I can," Emil said dryly, appearing alongside Sage. "If they did that now, they'd have to be ready for war, I think."

"But they are ready for war," Andre said skeptically. "I mean, surely the Center guards would wipe out Tilssted without any great trouble."

"Yes, but Merletta's entrance was too public," Emil said.

"Everyone would know the fighting was over her, and the Center doesn't want to turn her into a martyr, with itself as the persecutor."

"Why are we talking about war?" Merletta asked faintly. Her stomach chose that moment to give a painfully audible gurgle.

"When's the last time you ate?" Sage asked, her forehead creased in concern.

"Two and a half days ago?" Merletta guessed.

Sage's expression merged into one of utter horror. "If we hurry, we can still catch the end of dinner!" she declared, tugging Merletta through the water by one arm. "You're almost dead in the water, look at you!"

Minutes later, Merletta was stuffing her face blissfully with salted cod, only half aware of the ongoing debate between Emil and Andre.

"I'm so sorry, Merletta." Sage's quiet voice caught Merletta's attention much more completely than the boys' heated discussion. "About my mother. I...I never dreamed she was spying on you on someone's orders."

Merletta laid a hand over her friend's. "I don't blame you," she assured her. "I don't really even blame her that much. She was following orders from someone she had more reason to trust than she did me." She grimaced. "I thought her kindness and hospitality were astonishingly generous."

Sage shuddered. "I haven't spoken to her since," she said quietly. "Not even when I passed my test. I didn't go home for my break. I..." She looked down quickly, her face coloring a little. "I stayed with Emil's family."

"Did you, now?" Merletta felt a flicker of glee, but Sage's next words drowned it out.

"And Andre barely speaks to Indigo now."

"I never wanted to destroy your relationships with your families," Merletta protested, distressed.

Sage shook her head. "You're not the one who destroyed anything," she said. "Remember, we thought you were most likely dead. It wasn't easy to forgive their part in that."

Merletta bit her lip, troubled. She could only hope that her return might create an opportunity for her friends to be reconciled with their families. Probably not if Center guards executed her before the week was out, though.

"I'm telling you," Emil's deep, steady voice broke into their conversation. "The last thing they want is for Merletta to die now. They have to find a way to discredit her first, at the very least. Even if she genuinely did die of an accident, that army out there would storm the place."

"Army?" Merletta repeated, startled. "What are you talking about?"

"He doesn't mean an actual, trained army," Andre clarified helpfully. "Just the hundreds of merpeople who are currently besieging the Center."

"What?!" Merletta dropped her octopus tentacles, which drifted down into the basin before her.

"Yes, the crowd has only grown since you disappeared," Sage said matter-of-factly. "They think the instructors took you off somewhere to kill you, and they're ripe for murder. Come to think of it, someone will probably insist you show yourself to the crowd soon, so they know you haven't been knocked off."

Merletta just stared at her, still trying to wrap her head around the rapid escalation of...well, everything.

"But maybe you should sleep first," Andre said, scanning her. "You sort of look like someone's tried to murder you."

Merletta gave a hollow laugh. "I feel a bit that way," she acknowledged.

"You can come and sleep in my room," Sage said firmly. "I have my own room now that I'm a record holder. We'll all stand guard outside."

The others nodded, and Merletta followed Sage blindly from the dining hall. She felt significantly better for the food in her system, but her mind still felt like it was caught in a maelstrom.

They'd barely made it three streets over when Sage came to a sudden stop, hissing.

"Get out of here, Ileana," she said sharply. "You're not getting near her."

"Ileana?" Merletta looked up blearily, her eyes fixing on the other mermaid in bewilderment. "They sent *you* to kill me? That's a surprise."

"I'm not here to kill you," Ileana snapped. Her tail was swishing back and forth in evident tension, and her jaw worked furiously. "I want in," she said abruptly.

They all just stared at her.

She let out a grunt of frustration. "I know you all hate me, and I won't pretend to have any love for any of you." Her eyes narrowed on Merletta. "But to be perfectly honest, the fact that you've survived this long astounds me. I thought for sure you'd be shark bait after the first time you came back here. But that was almost two years ago, and not only are you still alive, but you've somehow mobilized an entire city to your defense. You're obviously the best chance there is of succeeding in what I would have said was an impossible goal."

Merletta blinked stupidly. "You want protection?"

"No, you blithering—" Ileana stopped herself, drawing in a long pull of water as she gathered her patience.

Merletta could practically see the other mermaid's mind working, questioning her own sanity in expressing faith in such an imbecile.

"I want to help you bring the Center down," Ileana said. "I don't care about whatever your noble reasons are. If I was on the inside," her voice turned to a growl, "like I *should* have been, I'd be fighting to protect the Center's lies. I won't deny it. But they turned their backs on me, even after I showed my loyalty. I want to see them pay."

"That's not what this is about," Merletta said, still struggling to comprehend what Ileana was offering or asking.

"Just think about it," the other mermaid snapped. With a swish of green fins, she turned, disappearing into the gloom.

"Well, that was...strange," Sage said, casting an uncertain look at Merletta.

Merletta just groaned, far too tired to grapple with such developments. "When Ileana wants to join our team, you know the world is really upside down."

"Well," Sage said, searching her face with her usual kind concern, "I doubt it will get any worse in the next few hours. So you can afford to sleep."

"Sleep," Merletta repeated, her eyes already drifting closed at the blissful thought, although she was still swimming. She felt steadying arms grab her, and didn't even try to fight as they bore her through the water.

She could let go and let someone else carry her. She had no idea what the morning would bring, or whether she would survive the week. But tonight, she was with friends.

CHAPTER THIRTY-FOUR

Heath's back throbbed as Reka streaked through the air, but the pain was much more manageable now the wound had been treated and bandaged. And the aches from his fall from the cliff into the water were entirely gone. Remarkable.

There was no leisure to ponder this reprieve. Based on Heath's description, Reka wheeled north once the capital came into view, heading for an enormous grain house several leagues outside the city.

Heath knew well before they reached it that his instinct of impending disaster had been sound. The grain house was impossible to miss given the column of smoke rising from it. The smell assailed them as they began to descend, Heath's heart in his throat. He could see the orange of the flames licking at the structure, and an ominous groaning suggested that the grain house wouldn't last long.

"Do you want me to alight?" Reka's rumbling voice reached Heath from above. "Or do you wish to change course given the grain house appears to be on fire?"

"Set me down!" Heath shouted above the roar of the flames. "I need to make sure no one's in there!"

"That seems foolhardy," Reka commented conversationally, but he angled downward as requested.

Heath stumbled forward as soon as his feet touched the grass. He had no idea if people usually worked inside this grain house during the day, or whether it was full, and only guarded from the outside. As he sprinted toward a door set in the center of the wooden wall, his breath caught in horror at the two figures slumped on the ground outside it.

These weren't the guards who would usually protect a grain house. They wore a familiar livery in purple and silver—they were the king's own guards. A quick examination showed that they were alive, but unconscious. Heath wondered uneasily whether they were in danger from the smoke, but he didn't even consider trying to haul them out of the way. If the king's guards were here, the king must be as well. And Heath had a horrible feeling he knew exactly where King Matlock was.

He tugged at the door, but it wouldn't budge. On closer inspection, he saw brackets alongside it like a barn door, designed for a wooden beam which wouldn't prevent a human entering, but would stop animals from escaping. Heath saw with horror that this door wasn't secured with a normal wooden beam, but with an enormous iron rod across the brackets. He tried to pull it up, but it was much too heavy for him. Perhaps with another person it would be possible. Certainly with three. But on his own, Heath had no hope.

If only Percival was there, he thought fleetingly. The thought sent a jolt of fresh fear through him. The unexpected discovery of the fire had temporarily driven his initial purpose from his mind. Percival had been heading this way, in search of the king. Surely he wasn't trapped in there as well!

"Hello?!" Heath shouted, his lungs burning from the smoke. "Hello? Is anyone in there?"

He heard a muffled shouting, but couldn't make anything out clearly. Forcing himself to focus, he drew his magic out of him and cast his extra sight over the store house. He caught a flicker of an image—the king crouched on a dusty floor, coughing desperately. But where was Percival? At the thought, his sight showed him his brother's face. In his panic, he couldn't channel his farsight with enough finesse to see Percival's surroundings. But the golden afternoon light on his face told Heath that wherever he was, he wasn't trapped in the grain house. He looked like he was sleeping peacefully, which made no sense whatsoever.

Heath dismissed the thought. There would be time enough to look for Percival when the king was safely out of the fire. He gave the iron bar another fruitless tug before turning to his companion.

"Reka!" he cried desperately. "Can you help me lift this?"

The dragon was sitting on his haunches not far away, studying the blaze in a detached kind of way.

"I can, of course," he informed Heath. "For what purpose?"

"I think the king is trapped in there!" Heath shouted, barely able to contain his impatience. "Please, Reka, it's too heavy for me to lift alone! I need your help."

Reka sighed, smoke curling from his nostrils to join that already choking the air. "Very well," he said. "Although I would be more inclined to help if it was some other individual. I do not relish becoming involved in human politics."

He leaned forward, placing his vast head underneath the iron bar and nudging it upward. With a scraping groan, it cleared the brackets, falling heavily to the ground. Heath only just leaped out of the way in time.

"Thank you!" he called, racing forward to throw the door wide.

Smoke poured out of it, and the shouting became more distinct.

"Your Majesty?" Heath yelled, stepping through the portal.

Immediately unbearable heat washed over him, and he dropped to his knees, spluttering on a mouthful of smoke.

Someone seized his arm roughly and hauled him back into the daylight. He heard a cry of anger as whoever it was saw the unconscious guards, but he was more focused on the richly dressed figure being led out of the grain house immediately behind him. Heath let out a sigh of relief as King Matlock emerged, coughing and sooty, but clearly in one piece.

"Was there anyone else in there, Your Majesty?" he demanded, his voice coming out raspy from all the smoke.

The king's eyes focused on him, suspicion in their depths. "Just my guide," he said. "A beam fell on him."

Heath looked behind him, to see three more guards emerge, two of them carrying an unconscious figure. Even as he watched, the man began to stir. Heath caught his breath at the sight of the man's mangled leg, and looked away quickly.

The two unburdened guards escorted the king further from the blazing building, while the ones carrying the guide deposited him on the grass some distance away before returning for their unconscious fellows. The guards on the grass were beginning to wake, moaning and clutching their heads.

"What happened?" Heath demanded. "How were you trapped in there?" He gestured at the abandoned bar of iron. "That was no accident."

"That much is clear," the king agreed grimly. "Is that what was over the door?"

Heath nodded, and one of the guards went to investigate it.

After a brief attempt to lift it, he gave up, retreating back to safety.

"Much too heavy for a normal man to lift, Your Majesty," he said, his face hard.

His words sent unease curling through Heath's stomach. A normal man?

"Go to the nearest village," King Matlock commanded the guard curtly. "Sound the alert. We cannot allow this fire to spread."

The guard jogged off toward where a group of horses was tethered—mercifully well clear of the smoke—and the king turned to Heath.

"What's the meaning of this, Lord Heath?" King Matlock's voice was also hoarser than usual. "What are you doing here? How did you lift that beam off the door?"

"Reka and I saw the smoke from the air," Heath said, gesturing to the dragon, who was sniffing at a spot further along the burning building, utterly unconcerned either by the smoke billowing around him or the flames licking at his scales. "He lifted the beam off. I couldn't budge it."

The king started visibly at the sight of the dragon, whom he clearly hadn't noticed. With resolution, he marched up to Reka, bowing slightly as soon as he caught Reka's attention.

"I thank you for your intervention," he said, his eyes watering from the increased proximity to the flames.

Reka sat back on his haunches, considering the king. "You have no call to thank me, as I did not act on your behalf, King of Men," he said coolly. "I merely did as Heath asked me to, for the sake of our friendship."

King Matlock took this rebuff in surprisingly good part, turning a thoughtful countenance on Heath. One of the guards approached him and murmured something quickly into his ear. The king nodded slowly, his expression growing graver. When he strode back toward Heath, however, his face showed no anger.

"Evidently it is you whom I must thank, Lord Heath," he said solemnly. His eyes flew to the bandages showing below Heath's tunic. "Particularly in light of recent events."

"If you mean the flogging," Heath said flatly, "that's hardly enough to prompt me to regicide. And as far as I'm concerned, Your Majesty, finding you in a burning building and failing to assist you out of it would have been no better than assassinating you myself. Which I have never had the smallest desire to do."

"I do not doubt it," the king said quietly. "It is clear I misjudged you. You were undoubtedly hasty and disrespectful regarding the matter of your loyalty ceremony. But perhaps I was also hasty in my response. You have demonstrated your loyalty in a more substantial manner."

Heath bowed stiffly, not quite as ready to forgive and forget as the king seemed to be. The exertion with the iron bar had caused his back to throb more viciously, and although the wounds would heal, the humiliation of his public flogging would be harder to erase. But King Matlock's next words softened him further.

"And if your objections do not arise from lack of loyalty, as I at first assumed, perhaps I should more fully consider your concerns about the proposal affecting Lady Laura's children."

Heath unbent slightly, but before he could speak, one of the remaining guards gave a cry.

"Your Majesty!"

Both Heath and the king turned quickly, and Heath gasped at the sight of Percival stumbling out from behind an enormous boulder nearby.

"Percival!" Heath cried, berating himself as he hurried toward his brother. If he was more adept with his farsight, he would have realized Percival was so close by when he checked on him. "Are you all right?"

"Heath?" Percival blinked groggily. "What's going on? What's that smell?" He cleared the boulder, and his eyes widened as they settled on the grain house. "What happened?"

"That is a question for you, I take it, Lord Percival." King Matlock appeared at Heath's shoulder, rage simmering in his eyes.

Percival's face showed anger as well, and he drew himself up. "I don't know what's going on, Your Majesty, but it will take more than a fire to stop me from giving you a piece of my mind. You'll answer for what you did to my brother."

"Percival, stop talking." Heath said sharply, a sudden fear lancing through him. "You don't understand the situation."

"He understands." King Matlock's lip curled. "Guards, seize him."

Three guards surged forward, and Percival raised his fists furiously.

"I know you can evade them if you choose," King Matlock said coldly. "But there will be consequences if you do."

Percival's eyes flew to Heath's, and Heath knew that, like him, his brother was remembering their conversation all those months ago. If Percival fled, their father would pay whatever penalty the king determined. Heath read a brief struggle in Percival's eyes, but then he deflated. Heath's mind spun with terror as the guards led Percival away, toward the horses.

"Your Majesty." Heath spoke through numb lips. "I know what you're thinking, but you've got it all wrong. Percival didn't do this. He would never—"

"Enough, Lord Heath." The king's voice wasn't as angry as Heath expected. He studied Heath's face. "I believe you truly didn't realize, in light of which, I am grieved for you. Perhaps the most brutal disillusionment of all is finally seeing a fallen loved one for who they truly are."

"No, there's no way—"

"It is no news to me that your brother was enraged by the punishment I carried out against you," the king interrupted calmly. "My own guards reported to me on the approach of your brother and father before I left Bryford. I expected to be met with bitter conflict upon my return, but I acknowledge even I did not expect this."

He gestured to the ruined building. The departed guard had returned with a group of men, and a bucket line was being established.

"It is understandable that you would wish to find another explanation," the king went on. "But no one without your bias could doubt the evidence. The two guards at the back of our group were attacked from behind, each felled with a single blow. The door was barred with a rod too heavy for a normal man to lift. Discounting the arrival of yourself and your dragon friend, your brother was the only one present at the scene of the blaze." His face hardened. "You named the crime yourself earlier. And there is only one possible penalty for attempted regicide."

Heath stared back at the king, unable to master a single word amidst the horror that gripped his mind.

"He will be executed in the morning," King Matlock said, his face still as hard as stone. Without another word, he swung into the saddle of his waiting mount, spurring the horse toward the capital with his guards around him.

"Percival," Heath whispered.

He stood rooted to the spot, paralyzing fear shooting through him, a thousand times more potent than any pain he'd experienced that day. Grief slashed across his mind as his own words came rushing back to him from that day in the markets.

When your unguarded tongue lands you in real *trouble, don't expect me to come to your rescue.*

He hadn't meant it. Not for a moment. As infuriating as Percival might be, he was Heath's brother. Even at his angriest, Percival had been frantic when he thought Heath was in danger. And it was no different for Heath—he would do anything to save his brother.

"Reka." There was no volume to Heath's voice, but the dragon appeared alongside him anyway. "Reka, I need your help."

Reka inclined his head expectantly.

Heath swallowed, grasping desperately at the only hope he could think of. "We need Grandmother."

CHAPTER THIRTY-FIVE

Reka said nothing, still watching Heath patiently.

"Can you take me to Bryford?" Heath asked, pulling himself together. "Then go to Bexley Manor and tell my grandmother what's happened? Tell her she's needed in the capital urgently."

Reka asked no questions. Soon they'd left the effort to put out the fire far behind them, streaking toward Bryford well ahead of the king's party. As soon as Reka set him down in the castle courtyard, Heath was running, desperate to find his father. Maybe the king would listen to him. The duke had steered him well all these years, hadn't he?

Heath had expected to feel relief when he handed the crisis to his father, but he found himself more afraid than ever. The duke tried to keep his countenance, but Heath's magic flared out of his control, and with its help he could see the abject terror beneath his father's curt words.

Heath had always assumed that the duke's frustration with Percival's inflammatory behavior came primarily from a desire to protect the crown from the resultant conflict. But the instant and potent onset of the duke's fear now told Heath that this outcome was exactly what his father had most feared all along. The duke's primary concern had always been for his family. Somewhere underneath everything, Heath felt chastened for doubting his father's loyalty, and withholding his own secrets on that basis. But there was no time to reflect on such matters now.

When the king and his escort clattered into the courtyard, Heath and his father were waiting, a pale faced Prince Lachlan beside them.

"Percival!" The duke's cry on sight of his son—who was positioned, hands bound, in front of one of the guards—was agonizing.

"Norik." The king's use of the duke's name shocked Heath, but there was no disrespect on King Matlock's face. He looked weary. "It cannot serve anyone to make a scene."

"Not make a scene?" the duke demanded. "Your Majesty, do you expect me to say nothing when I'm told that my son has been sentenced to death?"

"I take no pleasure from it," the king said, a bite of frustration in his voice. "But there is no other course open now."

"Father!" Percival cried, his eyes intense as they bored into the duke. "Father, I know he won't believe me, but I need to be sure you know. I didn't do this, Father! I was angry, but I had no hand in it. Someone must have knocked me out. I woke up on the grass, with my horse gone, and—"

"Enough." The king cut Percival's words off coldly. "You have been given more chances than you deserved, Lord Percival. Your actions today have shown that my lenience was a mistake."

"But he's telling the truth." The duke's face was light with relief. "Every word he just spoke was true. You know I can tell."

"Norik." Again the king sounded weary. "Do not perjure yourself as well. I understand your feelings—I am a father, too." His eyes flicked to Prince Lachlan. "But the evidence is overwhelming."

"No!" Heath cried. "The evidence wasn't clear at all. It could all have been staged, like the other attacks."

The king's brow darkened, and Heath could tell he'd done their cause no favors by bringing up Percival's other allegation.

"Execute me instead." The duke's voice was clear and calm, but Heath could sense the desperation beneath. "That was the bargain we made, was it not? When you released Percival from the dungeons?"

"Father, no!" True terror crossed Percival's face for the first time. Heath could see his thoughts as clearly as if they were written on his face. He'd rather die than live with that weight, and Heath didn't blame him.

A pained look crossed the king's face, as if he couldn't bear to witness his cousin's anguish. "Norik, you know I cannot do that. We made that bargain in the event that your son evaded the consequences of his actions through use of his magic. But he has come quietly. There is no cause to shed innocent blood."

"But he is innocent of this!" Heath cried. "He didn't—"

"The matter is decided." The king's voice was final. He swept into the castle, leaving his guards to deal with the ashen-faced Percival.

The duke fell to his knees, his head gripped in his hands. Heath and Percival exchanged a look of agony as Percival was led away. They'd never seen their father lose control, and it was the most horrible sight imaginable. Heath forced his mind to operate, pushing aside the fear and despair.

"Father." He knelt beside the duke, lowering his voice to a whisper. "I sent Reka to the manor with a message for Grandmother."

His father looked up, his eyes searching Heath's eagerly. "Yes," he whispered. "She's our best hope now."

"Heath." Lachlan's voice was strangled. "Your Grace. I'm

sorry. I didn't...I don't..." His eyes flicked between them. "Was he really telling the truth?"

"He was." The duke stood at last, pulling himself together. "I know you have reason to doubt my honesty on this, but I swear to you. There was no deception in his words."

Lachlan swallowed, a shudder running over him. "Father will never believe that," he told them. "Not based only on your word."

Neither of them answered. Heath shrugged hopelessly in his cousin's direction, unwilling to share this particular plan even with Lachlan. He took his father's arm, steering him firmly toward their city manor.

Heath had already told his father what had passed at the grain house. They waited in near silence for over an hour before the duke bestirred himself, asking Heath about the incident earlier in the day, when Heath had been publicly punished. That crisis seemed distant and unimportant now, and Heath struggled even to remember the details.

"Merletta's gone," he said dully, remembering that fact as he spoke it. "She went to Wyvern Islands, and the dragons tried to kill her. Reka and I followed her there, and we made it just in time. She fled, back to her home. I don't know what will happen to her there, or if I'll see her again."

His father stared at him, clearly at a loss for words. Heath shrugged again, unable to articulate the maelstrom of emotions swirling somewhere deep inside him, underneath the frozen horror of Percival's predicament.

The duke leaned forward, gripping Heath's shoulder. His hold was so tight as to be painful, but Heath found it strangely reassuring. Neither spoke again as the hours trickled past. It was well after midnight when carriage wheels sounded in the courtyard, and both men sprang to their feet.

Not only Heath's grandparents, but his mother and brother-in-law poured into the house, panic on all their faces. Laura must have stayed with the children, desperate as she would have been to help.

"Norik!" Heath's mother burst into tears at the sight of her husband, throwing herself into his waiting arms.

Heath strode straight to his grandmother, seizing her hand in entreaty.

"Can you help him, Grandmother?" he asked desperately. "And will you? I know you said the conflict between the crown and the power-wielders needs to be resolved naturally, but—"

"Of course she can," his grandfather said grimly. "If you'd seen what she can really do, you wouldn't need to ask that."

"And this is different," his grandmother assured him, her expression grieved but not despairing like her daughter-in-law's. "Of course I won't let Matlock kill Percival based on such flimsy evidence."

"In the king's defense," Heath said faintly, "it was all perfectly orchestrated to make it seem like Percival's guilty. But he's not," he added fiercely. "I knew even before Father sensed the truth of his words! Percival would never do this."

"Of course he wouldn't," Heath's grandfather growled. "If Percival ever tipped over the edge like that—which I'm not saying he would," he added hastily, "he'd come at the king head on, to his face. Not sneak around knocking guards out from behind and lighting fires."

"Should we go to the castle now?" Heath pressed.

His grandmother shook her head, sinking into a chair. "We need to be careful how we go about it. It will be best to wait for the morning."

Heath could hardly bear to wait another minute, but he knew there was nothing to be done but follow the elderly princess's lead. None of them slept that night. Heath's sight flickered occasionally to Merletta from force of habit, his magic connecting with her even while his mind remained too preoccupied to engage with her surroundings. It would be days before she would reach the triple kingdoms, anyway. There was nothing he could do for her now.

The whole family was at the castle at dawn. King Matlock had said Percival would be executed in the morning, and Heath knew they were all terrified of leaving their plea too late. But Princess Jocelyn seemed confident that she didn't need a great deal of time.

When they reached the king's public audience hall, Heath could only hope she was right. They burst in just in time to hear King Matlock give the order for Percival to be fetched from the dungeons for sentencing. No onlookers were present yet, but the place would soon be full, Heath knew. Word of such dramatic happenings would spread like wildfire through the castle, and the capital.

He winced at the mental choice of words. He hadn't washed during the interminable night, and he could still smell the ash on his clothes.

"Matlock." Heath had expected his grandmother to appeal to the king, but it was his grandfather who spoke. "Matlock, this hastiness isn't like you."

"You know I have the deepest respect for you, Uncle Kincaid," the king said stonily. "But it is not your place to interfere in the exercise of my authority."

The elderly prince stepped forward, and Heath's eyes flicked to his grandmother. Still she didn't move, didn't open her mouth. The door to the throne room clattered open, footsteps slapping against the stone floor. Heath spared only a brief glance to see that Brody and Bianca had arrived along with their parents, all looking pale and horrified.

"I'm not trying to tell you what you can or can't do." Prince Kincaid said placatingly.

Heath felt frustrated at his grandfather's slow, calm words. But he had to trust that his grandparents knew what they were doing.

"I don't dispute for a moment your right to execute someone who attempted to assassinate you. No one would dispute that right. I just want to make sure that's what really happened. As you surely must, as well."

Suddenly, Heath felt it. At first it was subtle, cast out like an intricate, fragile web. But it wasn't fragile. It was powerful. As he followed it in fascination, he felt its potency. The magic coming from his grandmother was strong. And it wasn't like the magic of his generation, targeted and specific, formed to some tangible task. It was all-pervasive, reaching for every corner of the king's mind.

A quiet gasp from Bianca told him that she'd felt it, too. Every power-wielder present must have. Heath threw her a warning look, and she schooled her expression.

He understood now. His grandmother was willing to use her magic—an incredibly strong power of change, which she'd honed over decades to the point where it was as easy for her to change someone's mind on just about anything as it was for Percival to throw an overpowered punch. But she was still wise enough to understand the need for caution. She wasn't gambling everything on Percival's rescue—she still wanted to preserve the precarious balance between the crown and the power-wielders. And that couldn't be achieved if it was widely suspected that she'd used magic to supernaturally persuade the king to pardon Percival.

No wonder she'd always been so meticulous about not abusing her power. Sensing its strength and effectiveness, Heath appreciated for the first time the extent of her restraint. She could have controlled them all if she'd chosen. But that had never been her path.

So she hung back now, seeming to anyone without the ability to sense magic like a passive onlooker, while her husband apparently persuaded his nephew. But it was her magic changing the king's mind.

And it was quickly clear that King Matlock's mind was being changed. As soon as his aunt had sent her power toward him, he'd begun to visibly waver. The arguments his uncle was making were rational, sensible, measured. To anyone watching—and anyone hearing about it afterward—it would be perfectly credible that he'd been swayed by these words. Of course he should be sure, absolutely sure of Percival's guilt before executing him.

"I accept the wisdom of your words," the king said, when Heath's grandfather stopped speaking. "I will publicly announce the charges this morning, but I will not pronounce the sentence. A more thorough investigation will occur first, so that justice may not only be done, but be seen to be done."

"Now, as always, Your Majesty, your wisdom makes you a strong king." Prince Kincaid dipped his head, stepping back to join the rest of the family.

Heath let out a long breath of relief, as his mother wept silently beside him. Percival was spared, at least for now. The following scene was painful, as a chained Percival was led before the gathering crowd and publicly accused of attempting to kill his king. But it was endurable, because there was still a chance to prove that it was all a terrible mistake.

As soon as it was over, Heath struggled through the crowd, making for the crown prince.

"Heath," his cousin said, looking almost as relieved as Heath felt. "Stars above, that was a near miss. But I knew Father wouldn't really act without proper investigation. It wouldn't be just, or wise."

Heath's thoughts were a little more sour than the prince's,

but he didn't blame Lachlan for wanting to believe the best of his father.

"Our investigation just became a lot more urgent," he said curtly.

Lachlan cast a sharp glance over him. "You're inclined to think this incident was orchestrated by the same party who attacked Percival and tried to kill you? Did you sense power at the grain house?"

Heath shook his head, frustrated. "No, they must have been gone by the time I arrived," he said. "But it's the only logical conclusion."

"Is it?" Lachlan frowned. "Why would someone who wanted to kill Percival now want to kill my father?"

"Killing your father wasn't the central aim," Heath said. "It was framing Percival. It has to be."

Lachlan ran a hand over his face. "I was going to speak to you about our investigation," he said. "Before," he gestured vaguely, "all this."

"Did you find something out?" Heath asked eagerly.

"Nothing very useful," Lachlan sighed. "Just a description that caught my attention, because I heard it more than once. I arranged for questioning of various acquaintances of the men who died suspiciously. A few of them claimed that the dead men had met with a stranger some time before their death. A thickset man with striking blue eyes."

"That's it?" Heath asked, disappointed.

Lachlan frowned. "They also said he had a slight accent, but he didn't look like he was from the South Lands."

Heath's heart lurched uncomfortably. Did this support the Kyona theory? Some of Kyona's mountain dwellers spoke with a bit of an accent. He frowned. But only the royal family would have power, and they surely wouldn't have an accent.

"It's a start," he said abruptly. "We can speak more later. I need to be with my family right now."

The prince nodded, releasing him. Heath rejoined the rest of his family, but there was nothing much to be done or said. Everyone was relieved by Percival's reprieve, of course, but they all knew it was temporary, unless someone could prove to the king's satisfaction that the most obvious answer for the attack wasn't the true one. The knowledge hung over all of them.

It wasn't until hours later, back at the city manor, that Heath thought to ask his grandmother about Rekavidur.

"He returned to Wyvern Islands after passing on your message," she told him. "Although he seemed saddened by your distress, I didn't get the sense that he was overly invested in Percival's fate."

Heath nodded, unsurprised. "Dragons," he sighed.

She gave him the flicker of a smile. "Yes. Quite."

As she moved off to speak with her husband, Heath let his mind turn to Reka. His magic followed his thoughts, his farsight flickering to life. He could see his dragon friend. Perhaps it was the presence of his father and grandmother, and therefore the extra magic in the room, but he could even see Reka's surroundings with relative clarity. The dragon was on Wyvern Islands, deep in conversation with others of his kind.

Heath frowned, leaning forward into his seat as he pressed into the vision. Conversation? Or argument? Not only Reka's form, but that of his father Elddreki, and his mother Raqisa, came into focus. The three of them seemed to be ranged against at least half a dozen others, literal sparks flying between them as they spoke rapidly.

It would be a slaughter! The words burst from Reka, his tail flicking angrily. *Would you truly wipe out an entire civilization over a story from century upon century ago?*

Spoken like the youngling you are, another dragon responded coldly. *None of us take pleasure from killing, Rekavidur. But sometimes it is the appropriate response.*

Not this time, Reka said in a hard voice. *I don't accept that.*

We do not need your acceptance. The words came from a third dragon, and even across the connection, Heath could read the determination on the creature's face.

He pulled out of the vision with a gasp, a fresh wave of fear washing over him. Would the onslaught of disaster never slow? He grasped the back of the chair next to him, drawing shaky breaths as he tried to clear his mind enough to think.

In his folly and his selfishness, he'd dragged Merletta into his world. He hadn't even had the sense to show restraint—instead he'd paraded her before everyone, dragons included, just as if she was nothing more than an ordinary, uninteresting human, instead of the incredible, wondrous being she was. And in doing so, he'd brought death to her doorstep.

What was he going to do? How was he going to warn Merletta? Because warn her he must. There could be no doubt as to the meaning of what he'd just witnessed.

The dragons were coming for the triple kingdoms.

CHAPTER THIRTY-SIX

Merletta

erletta angled up toward the surface as the water became shallower. She was almost at the island.

She glanced behind her compulsively, although the triple kingdoms were now far back. Careful as she'd been, it was hard to shake the fear of being followed. But if someone had seen her leave the barrier, they hadn't followed her out, of that she was certain.

Her fear wasn't unfounded. It had been a week since she'd taken her unconventional test, and she'd been aware of being watched almost every time she left Sage's room, where she was still sleeping at night.

Things had calmed down considerably once the crowds had dispersed from the drop off—everyone apparently satisfied that Merletta was neither dead nor thrown from the program. But it had still been a week before Merletta managed to slip away from the Center inconspicuously. And she'd only made it through the barrier because she'd picked a time when Felix was on patrol at the boundary, and willing to let her through. She pushed down the twinge of guilt over involving him in illicit activities. She was past that point now.

It was no longer about her desire to explore the open ocean—it was about all of them. If she, and everyone else who believed her, didn't stand up to the Center, nothing would ever change.

When she flipped her tail up onto the sand, Paul immediately appeared by her side, hand outstretched. She took it gladly, letting him pull her to her feet.

"Merletta!" he said, relief clear in his voice. "You're alive! A few more days and we were going to come after you all. Not knowing what happened is worse than the risk. It's been all I could do to keep Griffin from racing off for this long."

"Where is he?" Merletta asked, looking around. "He hasn't done anything rash, has he?"

Paul shook his head. "No, he's fine. He's hunting, that's all."

She nodded. "And Tish?"

A sigh escaped Paul. "She's at the lagoon. That's where she lives now. She's not adjusting well."

Merletta was silent, her heart aching for the trouble she'd brought on her friend. It made it worse that she'd managed to re-enter her own life, albeit in a strange, precarious way. It felt wrong, when Tish was still trapped at the island.

Eager to go and talk to Tish, she rushed Paul through a quick summary of what had passed in the triple kingdoms.

"August and Eloise aren't with you?" he asked, scanning the water behind her.

She shook her head. "It would have been too conspicuous if we traveled together. They're staying with friends—basically avoiding going anywhere without witnesses. For the moment, no one has moved against them."

Leaving Paul with his thoughts, she struck off toward the lagoon. Just as Paul had said, Tish was floating in the water, amongst the mangroves. She brightened at the sight of Merletta, swimming quickly toward shore.

Merletta slipped into the water, the two of them sinking below the surface to speak.

"You're back," Tish said. "What happened?"

Merletta told her, stumbling over the information that she'd passed her test. She half expected Tish to look angry, but she should have known her friend better.

"You're amazing, Merletta," Tish said, with a soft smile. "I could never have managed half of that."

"Tish..." Merletta swallowed, fiddling with a strand of her own hair as it floated by her face. "I'm so terribly sorry for all of this."

Tish shook her head. "None of this is your fault, Merletta," she said. "I won't deny that I wish I hadn't gotten tangled up in it. But I know you didn't cause the problems. You just...found them."

"I was always good at that, wasn't I?" Merletta said ruefully.

Before Tish could reply, rushing wind caught their ears, audible even beneath the surface.

"Heath is here?" Excitement shot through Merletta, and she started swimming toward the surface. He must have been watching her with his magic sight, and seen that she was headed for the island.

"Will the dragon be with him?" Tish asked, sounding frightened.

Merletta hesitated, then nodded.

"I'll stay here," said Tish. "I don't want the dragon to see me."

Merletta nodded again, sobered by her friend's fear. She'd once been so impatient of that attitude toward dragons. The memory of her own foolish overconfidence was painful. If she'd taken the Center's warnings about dragons more seriously...

But there was nothing to be gained from what ifs.

Merletta clambered quickly onto the rocks at the lagoon's

edge, her scaled skirt settling into place around her hips as she hurried toward the beach. That was where Heath usually landed.

Sure enough, the dragon was alighting just as she arrived, Heath clutched in his talons. Merletta noted that Reka didn't take off this time, instead sitting back on his haunches on the sand, as if he meant to stay. It was the first time in a very long time.

Merletta saw Paul melting into the brush, although she suspected he was motivated less by fear and more by the desire to give her and Heath the opportunity to talk. He'd always been a little more tactful than Griffin.

"Merletta!" Heath cried at the sight of her.

She ran straight to him, throwing herself against him as his arms closed around her. She could feel the tension in his muscles, and she pulled back slightly, looking up at his face in concern.

"What's wrong?"

"You first," he insisted. "I saw you back in the triple kingdoms. What happened? Are you safe there?"

Merletta sighed, laying her head back against his shoulder. "This is the only place I feel genuinely safe," she whispered.

"If only that was true." Heath's voice was bitter, and Merletta stepped back.

"What's happened?"

He shook his head. "You haven't answered my question."

"I don't know how to," she admitted. "I think it would be a stretch to say I'm safe, but no one's openly trying to kill me at present." She gave a wry smile. "I even passed my test. My fourth year classes will start in a few weeks, at least theoretically. But everyone of relevance knows the position is a facade. I have about as much chance of becoming a record holder as you have of sprouting a merman's tail."

Heath smiled at her joke, but it didn't reach his eyes.

"Merletta," he said, his voice strained. "I can't tell you how sorry I am. I knew the dragons were worked up over you. I should have told you that, instead of giving you useless veiled hints. Then you would never have gone to Wyvern Islands. But I was too selfish to be honest with you. I wanted you to stay, and I kept lying to myself, telling myself it was possible, that there was no barrier to you just joining my world."

Merletta looked down quickly. "I don't think I could ever do that, Heath," she said. "Even though there's a part of me that wants to so badly. I wish..."

"You have nothing to explain," Heath said, when she trailed off. He lifted a hand, running the pad of his thumb down her cheek. "I'm the one at fault. I could tell you weren't entirely comfortable there, and I understand why now."

Merletta peered up at him. "You do?"

He nodded. "When you fled Wyvern Islands, Reka carried me to safety. I wasn't unconscious like the time you were drying out, and Reka wasn't determined to avoid you anymore. I had the opportunity to choose where to go. I knew we could catch up with you, help you on your journey. But I didn't. I knew I was needed at home, and I couldn't turn my back on that responsibility. I chose my family." He swallowed, seeming ashamed at the admission. "I chose Valoria."

"I don't blame you," Merletta told him quickly. "I understand better than anyone. For all the triple kingdoms' faults and dysfunction, I can't just turn my back on it. I don't want to."

"I know." Heath gave a twisted smile. "Neither of us want to abandon our homes. We want to save them. And it will probably get us both killed."

With a sigh, Merletta pitched back against him, closing her eyes and feeling the warmth of his skin through his tunic as she listened to his heartbeat.

"At least we've had exciting lives so far."

Heath gave a hollow laugh, pulling her against him.

"I am grieved, Merletta." Reka's gravelly voice startled Merletta. She hadn't expected him to initiate speech with her. "Grieved by my colony's aggression toward you. It is not what I would have you—or any intelligent being—experience from my kind."

Merletta blinked at him, amazed to hear him...well, not quite apologizing, but almost.

"Why do they hate me?" she whispered. "What have I done?"

"You haven't done anything," Heath said fiercely. "You're not in the wrong. They're prejudiced against your kind because of an old tale from their history, about sea creatures warped by tainted dragon magic. It's complicated, but I'm convinced they're wrong. I don't think that's your origin."

"Then why do they think it is?" Merletta asked.

"I suppose when they saw your tail—" Heath started, but Reka cut him off.

"It is not just that. They sensed your magic."

"But I don't have magic," Merletta objected.

"Not the way Heath and his family do," Reka agreed. "But you are a creature of magic. Whatever the origin of your kind, it was certainly a process influenced by magic. Your ability to transform is not a naturally occurring phenomenon. It has been gifted to your kind at some point in the past. Gifted through magic. I can sense it lingering still."

She frowned at him. "Are you saying you can feel magic around me? Like Heath can feel the magic of other power-wielders?"

For some reason, Heath was staring at her, some realization growing behind his eyes.

"I can feel it, too," he whispered. "I sensed it the first time we met, although I didn't identify that until later. It's much fainter than the magic of the power-wielders. I...I've grown so used to your...your signature, I suppose, that I've stopped thinking of it as power. It's so different from my family's."

"All right." Merletta searched his eyes, confused. "Why do you look like that realization is upending your world?"

"Because." Heath swallowed. "Because like a fool, I'd forgotten that there might be another source of magic, other than the dragons and the power-wielders."

Merletta waited for him to elaborate, but he didn't. With a little shake of the head, he brought his attention back to her.

"That's not what I came to talk about," he said. "Merletta, it's bad. I didn't know how to warn you...I've been waiting for an opportunity, and when I saw you swimming here this morning..."

He swallowed, and Merletta felt anxiety swell inside her. What could be so terrible Heath struggled to even say it?

"It's all right, Heath," she told him softly. "Whatever it is, we'll tackle it together."

"That's the worst part." The words burst from Heath. "This is all my fault, and there's nothing I can do to stop it! I can't even enter your world, let alone save it."

"Save it from what?" Merletta asked sharply.

Heath reached out for her, as if needing the reassurance of touch. She took his hand readily, still searching his eyes.

"The dragons aren't letting it go, Merletta," he said. "Reka and his parents have tried to talk them down, to convince them that they must be wrong about what you are. But their law regarding these abominations is absolute. They feel compelled to destroy you."

"They're coming to kill me?" Merletta's voice sounded unfamiliar in her own ears.

"Not just you," Heath whispered. "Merletta, I'm so sorry."

"What are you saying?" she demanded. "The dragons can't possibly want to kill everyone from my world."

Heath and Reka were both silent, their expressions grave.

"But..." Merletta struggled for words. "But they don't know where to find me, or the triple kingdoms. Unless..." She looked fearfully at Rekavidur.

He shook his vast head slowly. "I will not betray your location," he said, his voice a deep rumble. "But they will search. And the magic which surrounds this place will draw them like a beacon. You will not be hard to find."

"When?" Merletta whispered. "How long do we have?"

Heath shrugged hopelessly. "Impossible to say. They're determined, but time moves differently for dragons. If they say they'll deal with it soon, they might mean this very moment. But it's equally possible they mean in a decade."

Merletta was silent, wrestling with the terrible truth of what she'd brought on her kingdoms. Her eyes sought Heath's, and she could see her own fear reflected back at her.

"What have I done, Heath?" she whispered.

"This isn't your fault," he said fiercely. "None of it is."

"But if I hadn't gone to Wyvern Islands—"

"Or if I'd told you more clearly to be wary of dragons, I know," Heath cut her off. "We were both foolish there. But those mistakes aren't deserving of slaughter."

Merletta raised a shaky hand to her face. "I was so sure that the stories about dragons' aggression were just more lies. August and the others tried to warn me, and even you told me to be cautious, but I wouldn't listen. Like an arrogant fool, I assumed that I knew better."

"You are not entirely to blame," Reka said slowly. "Dragons are not aggressive by nature, as you have been taught. But there is much that none of us knew when first we met on this shore. We could not have predicted what we would unleash."

Merletta stayed silent. She could take no comfort from the dragon's words. She was touched that Reka had expressed grief over her predicament, and she knew that Heath felt the impending disaster keenly. But it wasn't the same for either of them—their kinds were not at risk of total annihilation.

"Reka." Heath looked up at the dragon. "Can you please give us a minute?"

"Give you a minute?" the dragon repeated blankly. "I cannot create time."

"I meant give us a minute of privacy," said Heath patiently. "Although what I actually meant was several minutes."

The dragon shook his head in bemusement, clearly baffled by the imprecision of human speech. But he took to the air without protest.

"Heath," Merletta whispered in anguish, as soon as they were alone.

"I know, Merletta," Heath told her, gripping her shoulders bracingly. "But we can't let it crush us. Otherwise we won't have the strength to fight."

"But can we fight?" Merletta cried. "What hope is there against a colony of dragons?"

"There's always hope," Heath told her firmly. "We'll find a way."

Merletta shook her head, a lump rising in her throat. "They don't want to kill you, Heath. You should return to Valoria, and never look back. There's no reason for you to die with us."

"There's every reason," Heath said fiercely.

His grip on her shoulders tightened for a moment, then suddenly went slack. He slid his hands down her arms, cupping them under her elbows.

"You said it yourself," he told her softly. "We'll tackle it together."

"I don't want you to get yourself killed," Merletta told him earnestly, tears pricking her eyes. "Even without this threat, there's no future for us. The gulf between us is too big to bridge —not when neither of us can abandon the world we come from. You know it's true. You'd be mad to die for a future that could never even happen."

"No gulf is too big, Merletta," Heath told her. "Not when you're on the other side. I'd swim across the entire ocean if that's what it took."

Merletta couldn't help giving a shaky laugh. "You're not a good enough swimmer."

Heath smiled briefly. "I'd count on you to rescue me when I started to sink, then."

"Heath." She was whispering again, tears welling up in spite of her best efforts. "If I'm going to lose everything else, I can't bear to lose you, too."

"We started this, Merletta," Heath told her. "And we'll see it through together." He cupped her head with one hand, his fingers tangling through her wet hair, and his voice clear and certain. "Nothing you can say will convince me to abandon you now."

Merletta searched his eyes, his words at the Winter Solstice Ball running through her mind. She'd never reciprocated— expressing those things wasn't her greatest strength. But with death by dragon flame speeding toward her and her entire civilization, it seemed like the time to be bold.

"I love you, Heath," she said. She laid a palm against his chest. "And if it was only me affected, I'd say it was all worth it."

Heath's eyes burned into hers for a moment, before he pulled her suddenly against him. The breath left her body in an involuntary exhale, then his lips were on hers. She pressed into him, her arms threading around his neck, and her heart on fire.

In spite of the worlds between them, in spite of the disaster hanging over them, she would choose Heath, every time. The knowledge that he chose her as well was enough to make her feel like she should have wings as well as legs and a tail.

As Heath kissed her with the reckless abandon of an uncertain tomorrow, there on the sand of Vazula's beach, Merletta felt hope—foolish, illogical, defiantly persistent hope—sprout inside her. In spite of the dragons' aggression, the Center's deception, and the incredible odds stacked against them.

Impossible as it seemed, with Heath's arms around her, she couldn't help but have faith, even just for this moment.

Perhaps they could find a way through it after all. As long as they were in it together, there was surely hope.

The story concludes in *A Kingdom Restored*—the fourth and final book in *The Vazula Chronicles*.

NOTE FROM THE AUTHOR

Thank you for reading *A Kingdom Threatened*. I hope you enjoyed this third adventure in the world of Vazula! I would be so grateful if you would consider leaving a review on Amazon—it would really make a difference!

If you want to find out what happens next for Merletta, Heath, and Reka, check out *A Kingdom Restored*, the fourth and final installment of the series. As well as more adventure, fantasy, mystery, and romance, you'll find answers to all your questions!

Join up to my mailing list at deborah-gracewhite.com to be kept up to date on new releases, specials, and giveaways, such as bonus chapters. You'll receive some great freebies, too, including *An Expectation of Magic*, a novella which serves as a prequel to *The Vazula Chronicles*, telling the tale of Heath's parents.

You'll also receive *Dragon's Sight*, an 8,000 word prequel to *The Kyona Chronicles* (a series set before *The Vazula Chroni-*

cles, in the same world), told from the perspective of the dragon Elddreki (Rekavidur's father).

Again, thanks for entering the world of *The Vazula Chronicles*! I hope to see you back again.

ALSO BY DEBORAH GRACE WHITE

The Kyona Chronicles: YA Fantasy

The Kyona Legacy: YA Fantasy

The Vazula Chronicles: YA Fantasy

The Kingdom Tales: Fairy Tale Retellings

The Singer Tales: Fairy Tale Retellings
(releasing throughout 2023)

ACKNOWLEDGMENTS

Thanks so much to all my usual accomplices. Firstly to my husband Ray, for once again listening through the unedited version of this book like the champion you are. You always help make it better.

To my wonderful betas: Andrew, Steph, Tamara, Adrian, Mel W, Berri, Dad, and Mum. And extra thanks to Dad for developmental editing.

Thanks again to my fabulous proofreader, Shae, for a fantastic job! Any remaining errors are all my own.

Karri, thanks for the dramatic cover—this one was tricky!—and Becca, for the gorgeous map.

To you, the reader, thank you for giving me the privilege of being an author.

And most importantly, to God, who is stronger than any threat we will ever face, and has already won the victory.

ABOUT THE AUTHOR

I've been a reader since I can remember, growing up on a wide range of books, from classic litera- ture to light-hearted romps. The love of reading has traveled with me unchanged across multiple  continents, and carried me from my own childhood all the way to having children of my own.

But if reading is like looking through a window into a magical and beautiful world, beginning to write my own stories was like discovering that I could open that window and climb right out into fantasyland.

I cannot believe how privileged I am to actually be living that childhood dream and publishing my own novels. I do so from my hometown of Adelaide, Australia, where I live with my husband and our three little ones.

I've never outgrown my love of young adult stories, so the genre of young adult fantasy was always going to be my niche. Feel free to email me at deborah@deborahgracewhite.com and introduce yourself! Or subscribe to my mailing list at deborah gracewhite.com for free giveaways, sales, and updates.